FRANCIS

ITTY

CORA

TD RAMAKRISHNAN

FRANCIS

ITTY

CORA

Translated from the Malayalam by
Priya K Nair

Published in India by Harper Fiction 2024
An imprint of HarperCollins *Publishers*
4th Floor, Tower A, Building No. 10, DLF Cyber City,
DLF Phase II, Gurugram, Haryana – 122002
www.harpercollins.co.in

2 4 6 8 10 9 7 5 3 1

Originally published in Malayalam by
DC Books, Kottayam, Kerala, India 2009

Malayalam edition copyright © TD Ramakrishnan 2009

English translation copyright © DC Books 2024

P-ISBN: 978-93-6213-335-9
E-ISBN: 978-93-6213-445-5

Typeset in 11.5/15 Adobe Garamond at
Manipal Technologies Limited, Manipal

Printed and bound at
Replika Press Pvt. Ltd.

MIX
Paper | Supporting
responsible forestry
FSC™ C016779

This book is produced from independently certified FSC® paper
to ensure responsible forest management.

This is not history. It's just a tale spiced with lies and anecdotes.

Contents

1

www.cannibals.com

As Francis Itty Cora googled 'the art of lovemaking' the
search engine spewed out 6,73,423 results. When he narrowed the
search to 'the art of lovemaking in Kerala', the list shrunk to 377.
Cora exclaimed, 'So many!' and started browsing. Most of the sites
were clearly put up by swindlers asking for credit card payments of
five or ten dollars.

After browsing through eight to ten such sites he reached a page
that struck him as different:

The School

*We teach you the art of lovemaking at an exotic location in Kerala.
Rejuvenate your mind and body in excitingly novel ways.*

Cora double-clicked the mouse. He reached a website that quite
startled him with an image of a hibiscus flower over a bunch of
grapes.

'Would you like to chat with our Customer Service Officer?' Cora typed, 'Yes.'

Hi! I am Rekha. Welcome to the School.

Hi! How can I join your school?

ASL Plz.

24, Male, New York.

GR8, u might already be an expert in this art. A professor! What do u want to learn from us?

Professor?! Surely not ... am only a learner ... ur ASL?

20, Female, Kochi.

Amidst laughter, fun and jokes, the chat continued.

R U a teacher in the school?

Yeah, I'm the Principal.

How will u teach me?

Only thru practical sessions. U've to pay $5,000 for a week.

Thts ok. But I've a prob. I CAN'T

Can't Wat?

I can't ... do it.

Y?

18 months ago ... I was in Fallujah, ... Iraq. Itty Cora began to narrate his tale.

I joined the US military three years ago with a single aim: to go to Iraq and rape a full-blooded, beautiful, young Iraqi girl. To pin her down and bite her lips, cheeks, and breasts till they bled even as she lay struggling beneath me.

r u a beast?

I don't know. I grew up in a poor neighbourhood in Brooklyn, where Palestinians, Costa Ricans, and Mexicans brawled their way through life: there was gambling, thievery, and murder all around. I don't know who my father was. My mother was an Italian from Florence. She came to the States with a drug smugglers' gang. She was thrown to the streets when she lost her looks and health.

She slept around to earn a few dollars. A real bitch, she blew up all her money on booze and drugs. She is the one who taught me to smoke a cigar, to steal, and to use a gun.

I was sent to a local school but was thrown out for trying to rape a classmate. Later I became my mom's pimp. She was sadistic; she beat up and cursed me at whim. I hated her. One night, dead drunk, she came to me naked. I shot her dead. A gamester helped me escape and on the seventh day we reached another city. From then on his casino became my home. I always scored with women. But soon I got bored. Then the Iraq war began. On TV I saw tears glistening on the ruddy cheeks of Iraqi girls. The sight excited me. I wanted to point my gun at the beautiful helpless girls, strip them and force myself on them.

R U mad?

Maybe ... I was longing to rape a girl but I had to wait three years for an opportunity. Last year in Fallujah our battalion moved at the crack of dawn into the city that had been destroyed the previous night by shells. By then the rebel army had retreated. After making sure no one was left to resist, we searched the houses. We got hold of the first Iraqi girl we saw and presented her to Commander Wilson. After that we were free to do whatever we liked. Most of the houses were empty. In a few houses we found old men and women; not a girl in sight. As we marauders pillaged our way ruthlessly through the streets, we heard loud wheezing from a house. We entered and saw an old man and a girl who was probably his daughter, rubbing his back. When they saw us, uniformed soldiers, they folded their hands in respect.

She was a full-blooded girl with red cheeks. She pleaded for her father's life. We tied the old man to a pillar. Shiang, a fellow soldier, and I had chosen her as our prey for the day, the others moved on searching for theirs. From experience I knew that in these circumstances the victim usually freezes, becoming cold and unresponsive like a cadaver. A few women cooperate readily and then demand money. But, surprising us, the girl did neither; she tried to flee. My greatest desire was fulfilled. By the time I had overpowered her, I had bitten off half of her left breast. I didn't realize that she was bleeding to death in my hands. I was still growling like a tiger.

Sorry plz stop. U better get medical help.

Yes, that's what happened. They sent me back home. I spent the next year in an institution. I became normal. By the time I came out, I lost it. Can u help me?

Rekha hesitated a moment before typing.

Plz come, we'll try ... but y did u choose Kerala, India?

Oh, because of my whore mother. Francis Itty Cora who is supposed to have been my great-grandfather went from Kerala to Florence in the 15th century. There he established the Itty Cora family. He excelled in the art of lovemaking and was famous all over Europe.

A male prostitute?

I can't say ... maybe.

The next day when Rekha checked her inbox there was, as expected, a mail from Itty Cora.

Hi Rekha

I don't remember most of the conversation I had with you yesterday. My memories are clouded; yet I vividly remember incidents that are irrelevant. It may be because I occasionally eat human flesh. I can see the surprise in your eyes. Yes. I am a cannibal; there are many like me. Not in deep Africa, but in the US, France, UK, Italy, even in your India. cannibals.com has seven hundred and ninety-seven members. There may be many more who are closet cannibals.

It is said that consumption of human flesh causes many changes in the mind and body. It was that hope that spurred me to start eating human flesh. Some friends told me it would help me regain my vigour. It hasn't yet though. But I can feel some changes in myself. My mind plays tricks sometimes ... mixing memories with dreams, making me doubt whether I am dead or alive ... a feeling that my body is being digested in the guts of another.

Human flesh is the tastiest, but it's very expensive. In New York it costs $1,000 a pound, and is available only in very few places. cannibals.com has thirty-one members in New York. We have an efficient system for distributing human flesh among members. The flesh of African girls tastes best. Whites aren't very tasty. Asian flesh is middling. No matter how well cooked, you can always make out if the flesh is that of a male ... It is tougher. The flesh of girls between fifteen and twenty-five is the best but extremely difficult to get. We don't usually eat corpses but an exception is made for the bodies of accident victims. The only requisite is that they should have been healthy. Usually we locate a healthy prey, kill it, and then eat. There is no risk then. We have a doctor in our midst. He examines the prey. The rituals are held on Saturdays. The killing happens at twilight. If the prey is healthy, it will weigh about fifty-five pounds after removing the skin and bones. Refrigerating human flesh changes its taste so it has to be consumed quickly. By midnight the cooking is over. Then we party till daybreak. Half of our members are women. Our members pursue different professions. We even have soldiers who have returned from Iraq. Don't worry. I am not coming to Kerala in search of prey.

Cora with love.

Rekha was shocked. She hadn't in her wildest imagination thought that the client was a cannibal. Not losing her composure she replied in a single sentence:

Then Y R U coming? Rekha.

When Rashmi returned, Rekha said in a disappointed voice, 'Our plans have gone kaput. He is a cannibal.'

Rashmi was startled when Rekha showed her the messages on the laptop.

'God! A cannibal! I thought we could tame him—a half-cracked warmonger. But he seems insane. Just forget the $5,000.'

'I haven't lost all hope. If he spends $1,000 per week on parties, he must be rich.'

'I've told you before, canvassing customers through the net will land us in trouble. If he comes here, what do we have to show him?'

'We don't need to show him anything. It's just a bait to lure him to Kerala. We receive him at the Kochi airport and bring him to the flat. Then you use your expertise. By the time he reaches me after having tasted Bindu and you he should be putty in our hands. We'll use history, psychology, literature, music, and cinema as the situation demands. The syllabus should be moulded to the responses of the client. "The School" is an intellectual hub. It is not a mere brothel. We have a history and tradition.'

'But for all that he is a cannibal. I'm spooked.'

'Oh, we have tricks enough to tame him.'

Though she said this to comfort Rashmi, Rekha was troubled. The reply arrived three days later.

Hi Rekha,

I was a bit lazy in checking my mail. Yesterday was Saturday and I was tired after the party. The prey was an Indian girl. It was the first time I tasted Indian flesh. Not bad. It was soft as she was very young. But there was very little flesh. No one was satisfied. Your question requires a detailed answer.

I'm a cannibal. The lion hunts to eat. But for humans hunting is not an end in itself. Even when in a state of ecstasy at the sight of the trembling prey, the mind is searching for something else. Constantly trying to untie the knots of memories tangled with thoughts.

I am not coming to Kerala just because you promised to help me regain my virility. My history begins in Kerala. My great grandfather Itty Cora lived in Kunnamkulam. He died in Florence in 1517. When I went to my mother's old house in Florence, I discovered palm-leaf manuscripts and copper tablets. I want to know more about these. See if you can help me.

Cora with love.

'So history it is ... That is the client's area of interest. We have to begin with collecting information about the Itty Cora family.'

'To go back five hundred years in history won't be easy.'

'It may not be that difficult. Susannah's father had an areca nut shop in Kunnamkulam market. Now her husband George has a jewellery shop there. Let's go and meet her.'

'But if she comes to know of our business ...?'

'She is never going to guess. In the eyes of the public, I am a college teacher, you are into banking, and Bindu is a designer. We share a rented flat in Kochi.'

'All right, we'll meet Susannah next Saturday.'

'Our cannibal will be feasting on a new prey on that day.'

'Oh my God!'

'I was a bit comforted when he praised the taste of African flesh, but I am worried now that he has tasted Indian.'

'Well, you and Bindu needn't worry. Both of you are scrawny. I am the one who'll get into trouble.'

2
Body Lab

Inflicting pain on captives will not be considered torture unless it causes death, organ failure, or permanent damage.
— From a memo sent by the US Justice Department to the Pentagon, March 2003

Hi Rekha,

After John Negroponte took charge as the Ambassador in Iraq, it was decided to launch the 'Salvador Option'. In the 1980s Negroponte as ambassador to the Honduras had masterminded the mass killing by the CIA in the notorious operation called 'Salvador Option'. In the effort to suppress a left uprising in El Salvador, 1,40,000 people were killed. Teenaged boys were given alcohol and drugs and then let loose in the rebel villages to kill the Salvadorians. He called it draining the sea, the society being the sea and leftist insurgents the fish in that sea who needed to be flushed out. The sea was drained to catch the fish. The US wasn't willing to settle for anything less than complete victory in Iraq and so the Pentagon issued orders to launch the Salvador Option. There was no other way of annihilating Saddam sympathizers.

I joined the Salvador Option after I was secretly recruited by the US military. They were recruiting layabouts, junkies, and alcoholics to put together a murderous gang. After training for a month, we were given arms and uniforms and sent to Iraq.

You might have seen photos showing the torture inflicted on Iraqis. Do you remember one of a US soldier prodding a prisoner in a cage with a bayonet? I was that soldier. In Abu Gharib they kept dangerous prisoners in kennel-like cells. Soldiers were on duty twenty-four hours a day. Each prisoner was assigned a guard. During my early days in Iraq, I was given guard duty.

In spite of an official directive that prisoners shouldn't be tortured, the prison in Abu Gharib was a university that specialized in experimenting new methods of torture. I learnt valuable lessons there. Colonel Abdul Rashid, a Moroccan immigrant, taught me that torture isn't merely mindless battering. The prey should be crushed in both body and mind. Don't kill. You are free to do anything but make sure that nothing happens to the internal organs.

On the first day Colonel Rashid took us to the torture chamber called the 'Body Lab'. New prisoners were brought there first, as were the new recruits to learn methods of torture. Captain Victoria was in charge of the Body Lab. Everyone called her Victory. A thirty-five-year-old blue-eyed beauty from Boston with a bewitching smile, she looked more like a supermodel than a military officer.

'Cora, don't be taken in by the captain's beauty. She is a tough woman,' Jons, who had been there a while, told me, adding that she was the cruellest soldier in the camp.

Victoria welcomed the prisoners, 'Blessed are the persecuted for they inherit heaven.' She had a Bible in her hand and a mesmerizing smile on her lips. I wanted to kiss her full lips. I saluted her.

But she slapped me on the shoulder and said, 'Smart boy. Are you twenty yet?' When I nodded she gave me a hundred page handbook titled *Salvador Option*.

'This is just a guideline. All the techniques of the Salvador operations are described in graphic detail. But we don't intend to follow this in entirety in Baghdad. Our aim is to annihilate Saddam loyalists. You are free to use any method of your choosing. But remember that this is the twenty-first century. Everything you do should have a facade of decorum. Our goal is not to make the prisoners speak the truth or persuade them to change their beliefs but to obliterate them. Remember, we can never hope to change Saddam's dogs.'

A new prisoner was brought to the Body Lab, a handsome young Iraqi. He was naked, bound in chains, and made to walk on all fours like a dog. Two women soldiers held the chains; one of them carried a whip.

'You dog! Are you done with barking for Saddam?' Victoria asked him as she kicked him on his buttocks. The wretched prisoner, fatigued with torture, fell on his side. One of the women prodded him, 'You bastard! We didn't bring you here to fall asleep in front of our captain. Get up.'

When the wretch tried to get up, staggering with the effort, Victoria kicked him, roaring, 'You idiot, use your four legs like a dog.' The Iraqi, moaning loudly, fell on all fours like a dog.

'Private Cora, this is your first prey. Begin. Show us what you know, then I'll teach you.' Victoria pushed him towards me. As he fell at my feet, I looked at him closely—my first officially sanctioned prey. The helplessness in his eyes was tinged with hatred. I pushed two of my fingers into his nostrils and thought about the next step.

'Are you going to kiss your Pomeranian?' Victoria called out mockingly. The rest of them burst into derisive laughter. I pushed my sharp nails up his nostrils and pulled till his face was splattered with blood. He howled with pain. I tugged at one of the chains that bound him, forcing him to fall at my feet.

I cupped my hands and the blood from his nose streamed into my palms. I poured the blood into his mouth. Let Saddam's cur drink his own blood. He started whining like a street dog.

I kicked his head and more blood poured out; when I raised my foot again, Victoria shouted 'Fool! Don't kill him.' I brought my foot down on his right hand and crushed his fingers. 'Fantastic. We have umpteen innovative machines of torture but to inflict torture without using any of them as you've done is really an art.'

Victoria brought the whip down on the Iraqi. Seeing him cringe with pain everybody burst into laughter. His body was lacerated and bleeding. Each time he tried to rise, the women guards would whip him with greater force. Unexpectedly, the whip caught my face. Eyes dazed, I stood stupefied as Victoria cried out, 'Bastard! Don't stand and stare, crush his balls. He shouldn't use his tool again.' His balls were crushed in my hand. By this time Victoria's whip had landed on my back a couple of times. When the prisoner was led away, I had my reward—a long kiss from Victoria.

When a sweating Victoria languorously murmured, 'Go and powder the prey,' I did not know what she meant. She explained, 'Sprinkle sulphur on his wounds. They should never heal.' The unconscious Iraqi did not move. When I emerged from my first lesson in the Body Lab, Jons was waiting for me with a shot of whisky.

I'm not trying to scare you. It's just that when you wrote of the Body Lab in 'The School' I was reminded of Abu Gharib. The Body Lab in Abu Gharib experimented in torturing the body. What does your lab do?

Itty Cora with love.

Dear Cora,

Don't imagine you can frighten me with your horror stories. Tell me when you'll be arriving in Kerala.

Our Body Lab, unlike the one in Iraq, is not a torture chamber. We experiment in pleasuring the body. Don't worry, we don't use modern technology. We merely guide the client into discovering the marvellous possibilities of his own body. Welcome to our Body Lab.

We are trying to get information about your great-grandfather, Francis Itty Cora. We hope to have some details by the time you get here.

From
Rekha with love.

By the time she sent the message, Rashmi arrived. 'What's up with the cannibal?'

'He was trying to scare me with his gory tales about Iraq. I think he is crazy.' Rekha said.

'I've no doubt he is, but that's not important. We have to find out whether he is rich.'

'I think he is loaded. After all, he is a US citizen. I can't figure him out. He doesn't reply to our questions but he is very eager for details about his great-grandfather. I feel we have prospects there.'

'What do you mean?'

'Rashmi, Francis Itty Cora arrived in Italy as a pepper merchant from Kerala. In the fifteenth century pepper was one of the most valuable commodities: black gold. Kerala met most of the international demand for pepper. Cora more or less monopolized the trade. It gave him the freedom to enter the noblest homes in Europe. The rulers gave him a red-carpet welcome, the kind now given to people like Bill Gates. Lorenzo Medici who ruled the Florentine Republic was one of Cora's closest friends.'

'What do these old tales have to do with us?'

'There lies the mystery. Some new information has surfaced about the death of Lorenzo de' Medici who was known as Lorenzo the Magnificent. He died on the night of 9 April 1492. One of the guests who stayed at the palace that night was Cora. Though he was one of Medici's closest friends, he did not stay for the funeral but returned to India the very next day. Lorenzo was only forty-three years old when he died. Not unnaturally, suspicion fell on those who were involved in the power struggle to control Florence.'

'Are you saying that Cora had a hand in Medici's death?'

'It's a possibility.'

'So, things are more serious than we imagined,' said Rashmi and went for her bath. She was a happy-go-lucky person quite uninterested in the more serious things in life. As Rekha started cooking dinner, Bindu reached home. She was also eager for the latest update on Cora. 'Hey, Madam Principal! When does our guest arrive?'

'Are you in a hurry to meet him?'

'Of course. His lessons begin with me. From Bindu to Rekha through Rashmi. Isn't that our curriculum?'

'There's more to it this time. Itty Cora isn't merely a sex tourist. He has other intentions.'

'I don't care. We should get our money and a few thrills.'

'Thrills! Don't forget he is a cannibal.'

'I'm not bothered even if he is a Narasimha. I'll pull out his nails and teeth.'

'All right be ready. We've to meet Susannah tomorrow.'

'Sorry Rekha, you and Rashmi go. I'm leaving for Chennai by the morning flight. I'm designing costumes for a movie. I'll be back in a couple of days. Besides, you know I'm not interested in history and geography.'

'You can't just slip away, Bindu. You will be the first of us to meet the cannibal. We are professionals who study our clients' interests

so as to be able to converse intelligently with them: to discuss the
ups and downs of the share market with a businessman, cricket with
a cricketer, literature with a writer, and with a smuggler we have
to talk about his line of work. Not just small talk; it should be an
intellectual discourse. Itty Cora is interested in his ancestry. So, we
have to do some research on that.'

'So, ask Scripter. He reads a lot. He would know.'

'Do you think we should tell people about this?'

'It's better we keep it to ourselves. I even told Susannah that we
were just doing some research for the university. But we must tell
Scripter. I don't think he is merely a client. He has a more intimate
relationship with us, especially with you, Rekha.'

'Why do you say that? He is close to all of us.'

'He is but I don't understand a lot of what he says. They're the
kind of high-flown things you talk about sometimes.'

'Bindu is right,' Rashmi said. 'Sometimes he starts reading out
his stories. I lie beside him pretending to be interested. But he asks
for my opinion and tells me what you said then. Then I too say
something nice. That makes him happy, and he kisses my hand.'

'I use the same tactics ... but he is a pervert. There isn't an inch of
my body that he hasn't kissed. Rekha, tell him about Itty Cora. I'll
feel safer with a man involved.'

'Okay! I'll drop a hint. If his response is positive, we'll go ahead.'

3
The Holy Book of the 18th Clan

Why write novels? Rewrite history. The history that then comes true.

— Umberto Eco

WHEN REKHA TOLD ME ABOUT ITTY CORA, I FOUND IT INCREDIBLE. I felt that someone had lied to her during a net chat. When I googled cannibals.com, I reached the site of a New York-based rock group. Growing suspicious, I called my friend Benny to clarify my doubts.

'You planning to write a new novel?'

'Not at the moment, but it is a possibility I can't rule out. For now I'm looking for details to help a teacher who is involved in a research project.'

'Well, in that case, come over. Let's go meet Tharu master. He is about eighty-five years old. He was a physical education teacher in a boys' school. His memory is still sharp; you just need to jog it with a little alcohol.'

When I got down from the bus in Kunnamkulam, Benny was waiting for me in his car.

'Let's have a drink before we meet Tharu. We can buy him a bottle as well.' Benny was a tobacco merchant. He was carrying on the family business. In the darkness of the bar, I asked him, 'How's business?'

'Bad. Not like it was in the old days. The number of tobacco chewers is falling. Twenty years ago, there were nearly four hundred households that would buy at least one stack of tobacco leaves a week. Now no one buys a bunch at a time; it's come down to a leaf or two. The sale of flavoured tobacco has all but stopped. The number of smokers is also decreasing. Now even young boys start with liquor. I survive thanks to a few old timers who still smoke and chew tobacco.'

'People are afraid of cancer.'

'Cancer? Didn't cancer exist before? It hasn't suddenly sprung up. Dying is just fate. You don't get cancer just because you chew tobacco; you may get it even if you don't.'

I didn't agree but refrained from saying so. If I started an argument about tobacco, I wouldn't be able to carry out my inquiries. I paid the bill and we got into the car and on to the Vadakkanchery road towards Chovvanoor.

'I heard you are writing a novel about us, the people of Kunnamkulam.'

'I am thinking about it, but haven't started yet.'

'You must write about us. People think we deal in duplicate goods. But we are tradesmen. In trade, adjustments are necessary. We don't cheat. We always put a price on everything. We buy stuff we can afford and when we get a higher price, we sell.'

We stopped in front of a typical Kunnamkulam Christian house with a shop in the front veranda. Business was dull. On the shelves there were a few glass containers of gooseberries, mangoes, and white chillies pickled in brine. Soda, syrup, sweets, cigarettes, and betel leaves made up the rest of the merchandise. The old woman in the shop recognized Benny.

'Benny, how are you?'

'I'm okay. Is he at home?'

'Grandpa? He is inside. Lost in thought as usual. Who is this man with you?'

'A friend. We want to meet Grandpa.'

'Go in. He is alone.'

The room was dark. The light wasn't switched on. Tharu master was sitting by the window reading. Despite the open windows, the walls of the neighbouring house effectively blocked sunlight from entering the room. Immersed in reading, Tharu master seemed unaware of our presence. There was a yellow bulb burning beneath a picture of Christ. After a while, he looked up.

'It's me, Benny, the tobacco merchant.'

'Benny! You hardly ever come now,' Tharu master said as we sat down on the old couch. The old man's eyes glinted as Benny took out a bottle. He got up and switched on the light, saying, 'As I can't go out anywhere, I've to wait for visitors like you for a drink.' The woman brought glasses and snacks. She warned us not to get the old man drunk and left the room. The old man's hand trembled as he lifted the glass to his lips.

'I've never heard of an Itty Cora. I know that there is a ritual called Corakku kodukkal where offerings are made to Cora in the homes of the people who belong to the 18th Clan. Are you talking about the same Cora?'

'Do they belong to the schoolteacher Thandamma's family?'

'Yes. The Syrians. They have some secrets in the family that they don't divulge to outsiders. In other respects, their church, priests, and rituals are similar to ours.'

'I've heard my father say that nobody would marry their girls into the 18th Clan.'

'Yes, we don't encourage marriages into that clan.'

'Why?'

'Well, that's how it is. They have a secret text: *The Holy Book of the 18th Clan*. It's written on palm leaves. Outsiders are not allowed to see it. The public does not know the identity of the members of this clan. I know only two or three such families; Thandamma's is one of them.'

'Will we get information from her?' I asked eagerly.

'It's difficult. They'll just deny belonging to the clan.'

'How did you get to know about them?'

'It's a sixty-year-old story. I was working as a physical education trainer in a school in Calicut. I was twenty-four, an age when blood courses passionately through your veins. This was before India became independent. There was no bus service here. So, I used to come home only once a month. My father was in the areca nut business. Each time he saw me he would harp on me to get married. But I was in love with a neighbour—a beauty named Anna. The villagers would ogle at her as she walked through the streets. She was the daughter of one of the richest men in the village. My father and I were good friends. We used to share a drink occasionally. I told him about my infatuation. He was against the alliance. When I asked him why, he told me to speak to Anna herself. I asked her and she revealed the secret.

'They belonged to the 18th Clan. They had *The Holy Book of the 18th Clan* written on palm leaves in the house. They observed a ritual called Corakku kodukkal, offering Cora food and liquor before they allowed it to touch their lips. Cora was entitled to a share of the profits in business and a measure of the harvest. I didn't see anything wrong in that. Then she told me that when a girl belonging to the clan came of age, she was given to Cora. I asked her whether it had happened to her, and she admitted it had.

'My love evaporated. I didn't want to marry a girl who had been given to Cora. I think my father understood. I married Mary next year. She died four years ago.' Tharu fell silent.

'Is Anna still alive?'

'She married a man from Goa who belonged to the 18th Clan. I heard she was quite happy with her brood of children. I didn't bother to find out more as I felt that it was safer to stay clear of the 18th Clan.'

'What is wrong with them?'

'They believe in powers other than God. They practice things that are taboo for a Christian.'

Tharu crossed himself in front of Christ's portrait. Suddenly his eyes reddened in anger. He threw his glass against the wall smashing it to smithereens and shouted, 'That's all I know about the 18th Clan.' Hearing the noise, the lady came running and took him away.

Seeing my surprise, Benny took me outside. 'He turns violent at times; Let's go.'

Benny started his car.

'How can we get more information about the 18th Clan?' I asked.

'There is a priest who was defrocked by the church—Father Porinju. He practises black magic, which is why the church threw him out. He is bound to know more.'

'Can we meet him now?'

'Let us try.'

Father Porinju was in the garden watering the plants. He was wearing his cassock though he was no longer part of the established church. He greeted us with a smile thinking he had got some new prey. 'Where are you from? What do you want?'

'From Kochi. We need some information,' Benny replied.

He led us into his house, which was done up fashionably. Crucifixes carved out of sandalwood and ivory adorned the table. When Benny told him the reason for our visit his face fell, but he pretended to be amiable. He said, 'I too have heard of the Holy Book of the 18th Clan. They do not show it to outsiders. The people of the 18th Clan are said to consist of eighteen families spread all over the world. Three or four families have settled in Kunnamkulam.'

'Which families are these?'

'I can only guess. By the way, why are you interested?'

'My friend is doing research in history.'

'I know some stories that are spoken of in private. I don't know whether they are true or not. Please don't ask for evidence. The first is about Pathrose, a man who belonged to the 18th Clan. He lived about one hundred and fifty years ago. His house was the First House of the 18th Clan. It is in the cellar of this house that the stone and cloth of Cora are preserved. The young girls of the Clan are offered to Cora in this cellar.

'The first Christmas after a girl has attained maturity, she is offered to Cora. She is made to drink, and is disrobed and shut in the cellar. The cellar is opened only the next day. No one is supposed to talk about the happenings in the cellar. Pathrose's second daughter was shut up in the cellar one night. There was no electricity then, so an oil lamp would be lit. The next day when the door was opened, they saw her dead body. Pathrose went mad seeing this, but they did not dare to stop the ritual.

'There are many such stories. The 18th Clan won't celebrate Christmas without offering gold and women to Cora. A new bride is given to Cora before she enters her bridal chamber. Some twenty years back, a boy married a girl from Kottayam without telling her of these rituals. Kottayam also has a couple of families that belong to the 18th Clan. The marriage was on the seventeenth of November. The boy somehow put off the nuptial night till Christmas Eve. At night they got the bride drunk and pushed her into the cellar. Unfortunately, she regained consciousness before dawn. She wailed and howled till daybreak. Though her in-laws tried to explain the situation to her she left and filed for divorce.

'The clan sets apart one-tenth of their profits for Cora. Earlier, they used to put gold coins in brass pots and throw them in the cellar. Now, they have opened a Christian bank in Thrissur. They are all extremely wealthy. If you have faith in Cora wealth flows in, but Cora keeps strict account of his share. The same goes for women. If anyone tries to cheat him, he will retaliate. The entire clan are believers, not only in Cora but also in black magic. Some of them come to me.'

'Why?' Benny asked.

'They are human, after all. Sometimes mistakes happen when they make offerings to Cora or when girls like the one from Kottayam start creating a fuss. Then, they came running to me. But even then, they don't reveal the truth about Cora. They just say that there are some problems at home or that their business is showing a loss and ask if I can do anything to help. I recognize them instantly from the scars on their necks—men have it on the right side and women on the left. I don't know how they get it. After I make sure that they belong to the 18th Clan, I ask them whether it is money they have lost. I advise them to pay the capital and interest in three days. If it is a woman who has caused trouble, she has to be locked up in the cellar for three days.'

'There are certain rituals to be observed when they do these things. When the problems are resolved they come back and pay me well. But none has ever told me where the First House or the cellar is located.'

'Who was Cora?'

'He lived four or five centuries ago. He was the great-grandfather of the present-day clan. Francis Itty Cora was his full name, a trader who travelled across the seas. He was a man of tremendous abilities. He wrote the Holy Book of the 18th Clan.'

'Can we see the book?'

'Impossible. I've been trying for twenty years without luck. It's engraved on palm leaves with a nail. There are eighteen books in all—a copy for each of the families of the 18th Clan. They keep the book wrapped in silk and enveloped in fragrance. It is not exhibited to outsiders.

'Even among them very few have read it. The reading follows certain rituals. On a Sunday that comes ten Sundays after Christmas, all the family members gather in the living room at midnight. They close the doors and put out all the lights, except an oil lamp. They drink liquor brewed from sweet cumin seeds and eat fried mutton. After that they close their eyes and chant. Then, the head of the household opens the book and reads from it. The reading takes nearly an hour. By this time one of the women unties her hair and writhes as if possessed. Only women are possessed by Cora. The possessed woman gives certain commands that family members must obey. The woman has to sleep alone till the next reading.'

A car roared up the drive. Porinju said, 'There is a prayer meeting tonight. Those people have arrived. We will meet later.'

We thanked him and left. Benny exclaimed, 'Never thought I was living among such blasphemers.'

4

Tupac Amaru

They claim that I'm violent just 'cause I refuse to be silent
These hypocrites are havin' fits 'cause I'm not buyin' it
— *2Pacalypse Now,* Tupac Amaru Shakur

Hi Rekha,

Sorry I haven't mailed you in the last couple of days, but I was busy. Last week I had to leave New York unexpectedly. I am now in Estraap, a small village near Lima in Peru, with Katrina, a friend. I met her too through the internet. Like you she too is beautiful, though a bit overweight. Katrina is trying to help me solve my problems in an unusual way, with the help of some occult rites practised by the Inca tribes in Peru.

Her instructions, unlike yours, were not logical or scientific. But my belief in science and logic has come to an end and that realization took me to Peru—by air from New York to Lima. Estraap is eighty miles from Lima. Katrina's friend Leo came to the airport in his jeep to pick me up. After driving a while, when the jeep turned from the highway on to a mud track, he spoke to me in Aymaran-accented English, 'We are going to Tupac Amaru's palace.'

'Tupac Amaru's palace?'

'Tupac Amaru's actual palace is somewhere in Cuzco. He was the last of the Inca kings. In 1572, the Spaniards killed Amaru.'

Katrina works magic with Amaru's jawbone. This is our hideout. The laws are very strict about black magic practitioners and punishment is severe, so we can only work in secret. During Alberto Fujimori's time, there were no such problems.'

Dust filled the open jeep. Tupac Amaru reminded me of the American rap singer Tupac Amaru Shakur who was shot down on 13 September 1996. Like me, he too had grown up in the streets of New York. We grew up listening to his songs.

Tupac Amaru means the shining serpent. His mother Afeni Shakur belonged to the Black Panther Party. When she was pregnant with Tupac, whose father was unknown, she was accused of being involved in a bomb blast and put in jail. A childhood spent on the streets, steeped in poverty and violence, turned Tupac wild. When he was ten years old, Afeni moved to Baltimore. Tupac started his education in the Baltimore School of Arts. But life didn't flow smoothly. When Afeni slowly became a slave to drugs, her son left school and became part of the rough and savage streets: looting, stealing, and peddling drugs.

It was his deep interest in music that made Amaru, a wild kid on the streets, into one of America's great rappers. But he couldn't escape from the darker side of his nature. Tupac, who was never far removed from the violence that erupted from time to time on the streets of his rough neighbourhood, had been arrested many times by the time he started singing for *Digital Underground* in 1990.

His first solo album *2Pacalypse Now* was an instant sellout and, in the 1990s, Amaru became an icon of rap music. His subsequent albums continued to set sales records. By the time he left Digital Underground to join Death Row Records, he had become the hero of street kids like me.

In the ghettos we sang his songs and danced to them and even tried to ape his style in clothes. In between the rat race and infighting in the music world, Tupac was in and out of jails and hospitals. There were several attempts on his life.

During this period Tupac acted in two movies, *Juice* and *Poetic Justice*. On account of Tupac's wayward life, his costar in Poetic Justice Janet Jackson refused to do kissing scenes with him until he underwent a test for AIDS. Five eventful years later, on 7 September 1996, as Tupac was returning after watching a boxing match between Mike Tyson and Bruce Seldon in Las Vegas, an unidentified person fired four shots at him. When a severely wounded Tupac died on the sixth day, he was only twenty-five. This is the Tupac I was familiar with. His mother, who was involved in the Black uprising had named him after the last Inca king.

The jeep reached 'Tupac Amaru's palace'. Katrina was waiting outside to greet me. She was as beautiful as she had seemed on the video chat. She had a smouldering cigarette between her lips and was wearing dark clothes.

She hugged me, saying, 'Welcome to the Castle of Tupac Amaru,' and led me inside. Though it was called a palace, it was just an old house with small rooms that lacked even basic amenities. Thankfully, it had power supply. Tupac Amaru's jawbone was wrapped in silk and kept in a box that was placed on a throne-like chair.

Katrina led me to it and asked me to pray and beg pardon for my sins. As I stood hesitating, she started chanting in Aymara. Several voices echoed her prayer. I closed my eyes and stood in silence. When the loud prayer ended, Katrina placed a small crucifix on my forehead. Forcing down the repugnance that arose in me, I kissed the crucifix carved out of the bones of some animal.

'Weep and seek pardon for your sins,' commanded Katrina. I couldn't shed tears. I stared at her as if I didn't understand her. A bestial look flashed across her face. My dead mother's face appeared on the crucifix. I started to tremble.

I swept the cross from her hand, shouting, 'You bloody bitch.' Katrina left the room as if nothing had happened. I was panting and sweating profusely. Leo took me to the next room and poured me a whisky.

'Don't worry. This happens to all the visitors who come here. They see their enemies in Katrina's eyes. She is a powerful sorceress. All your problems will be resolved after the "Ritual of the Skull" at night.' I remained silent, wiping the sweat from my brow. 'You needn't get upset thinking about the ritual. It's an occult rite where the blood of a lamb is poured into a skull. The jawbone will not be removed from the throne. All the rites are done with the skull.'

'Is it Tupac Amaru's skull?'

'No. It belongs to Katrina's grandfather Cora Gonzalvos, who was Viceroy Toledo's chief executioner. In those days the victim's skull was the property of the executioner. The jawbone and skull are part of Katrina's inheritance. They pass from one generation to the next. People in Estraap call Katrina 'The Princess'. They had called her mother by the same title.'

I saw certain possibilities in the name Cora Gonzalves. I had decided to go to Estraap the moment Katrina mentioned that name during our video chat. If Cora Gonzalves was the chief executioner in 1572, he might belong to the third generation of Grandfather Cora. Katrina had told me that her ancestors were Italian.

I can't remember when I fell asleep or when I finally woke up. When I opened my eyes, Katrina was sitting beside me on the bed. She had changed her clothes. She was in a pink gown with a fur cap on her head. The long nails on her right hand were caressing my chest. After a long time, I felt a tightening of my nerves. I looked at her body expectantly. 'Cora, how do you feel now? Has the whisky washed away your fears?' she asked me with an enticing smile. I lay still, just looking at her.

'Okay, get up. Steaming hot pork is waiting for you.' She lovingly tried to pull me up from the bed.

'It's not pork that I want now, it's you.' I pulled her into bed. She lay unresisting, tempting me like a sumptuous feast. But I couldn't give her what she expected from me. The fire that had entered my veins ran cold. In Katrina's place I saw my mother and the young Iraqi girl I had raped and killed. As I started to howl, pounding the bed with my fists, Katrina held me close to her stomach and planted a kiss on my forehead.

'Don't worry, calm down.' She ran her fingers through my hair. I opened my eyes to the softness of her belly. I gave a start when through her transparent pink gown, I saw her navel that was tattooed with two mating serpents, one small and the other big. My mother had had a similar tattoo.

'Katrina, are you Satan's virgin?' I fell back in bed.

'Yes. I am Satan's virgin. He restores my virginity each time I have sex. I make use of that gift to please people like you.' She went out of the room.

Leo brought me my dinner—a glass of the local brew and pork. But he didn't speak to me. I drifted in and out of sleep. As the clock struck midnight a loud song accompanied by music, resounded through the palace. Leo came to me and said, 'Hurry up, Satan's dinner held in your honour is about to begin.' He took me to the room where Tupac Amaru's throne was placed.

The dark room I had seen in the morning was bright with electric lamps. Yellow lights, not fluorescent lamps. Katrina was sitting on a big chair that looked like the throne of a princess. Twelve tribal women surrounded her. They all wore clothes in shades of red, yellow, and green and sported stone-studded jewellery. They carried

an assortment of musical instruments, many of which I was seeing
for the first time. A black sheep was tied in the centre of the room.
There was another group with musical instruments behind the first
row. The troupe led by Leo consisted of both women and men.
Though the women carried musical instruments, they were just
pretending to play. The music came from the back of the room.

As Leo pushed me forward, the noise died away. Katrina
announced, 'Let us begin Satan's dinner.' She pulled apart her
clothes to reveal the entwined serpents. It was only then that
I realized that all of them were wearing robes that could fall open in
the middle.

The women came forward one by one, kissed the tattooed
serpents, went around Katrina once, and returned to their respective
places. Meanwhile, the rest of them were singing and dancing.
When the last of the women had kissed Katrina, everyone turned to
me and said, 'Now let's partake of Satan's dinner.' I moved forward
as if in a trance.

Suddenly, the twelve women who stood around me lifted me up
in the air, three taking hold of each limb. Even before I realized
what was happening, I felt that I was flying upwards bound by four
chains. The women rocked me back and forth as if I were in a cradle.
The singers who had till then been singing songs in Aymara, which
was incomprehensible to me, started singing a song in English,
'The Satan of Today is Born'. When the song ended, I found myself
looking at Katrina's navel.

Everyone shouted, 'Hey Devil ... Kiss your serpents.' I wasn't
scared any more. I vigorously kissed the serpents. As I lifted my face
to get some air, someone poured alcohol down my throat. While I
was greedily gulping it down, Katrina took her place in the group of
twelve women and the woman at the extreme right whom she had
replaced came to me. Her navel too bore the snake tattoo. I greedily
kissed her serpents as well.

Though I was exhausted, I continued kissing the serpents tattooed on the navels of the women with vigour till I reached the thirteenth woman. My limbs were racked with pain. They laid my exhausted body in front of Tupac Amaru's throne. The thirteen beauties danced around me. Then they made the sheep stand over me, its legs on either side of my body. The twelve women who had lifted me up earlier lifted up the sheep, two on each side sharing the burden. The sheep was bleating in terror. Katrina placed my head on her lap and asked me to repeat after her: *'Ccollanan Pachacamac ricuy auccacunac yahuarniy hichascancuta.'*[1]

I repeated the words without knowing what they meant. By the time I had repeated them thrice, the women had pulled the sheep apart in four pieces. Its blood splattered all over my face and body. The women put the legs of the animal into the skull placed in front of Katrina. She chanted a few words and poured the blood into my mouth. I thirstily drank the hot blood. At a sign from Katrina all the electric lights were switched off. Leo lit two torches, one on either side of me, Katrina placed the skull on my abdomen and then the music and dancing stopped. A heavy silence fell. The twelve women sat around me. Each one of them took the skull filled with blood and poured it into my mouth. After that Katrina took off my clothes as if it were part of the ritual. The music and signing began once more. The women, one by one, kissed the entire length of my body starting with my toes till they reached my brow. As each woman finished her turn, Katrina looked at me expectantly. I lay as still as a desert frozen in winter. When the twelve women failed, Katrina herself came forward, only to meet the same fate.

---

1   Mother Earth, witness how my enemies shed my blood. Tupac Amaru's last words.

She shouted, 'Your body is filled with poison, the poison of sin.' I waited for her return anxiously, not knowing what was going to happen next. I felt fear creeping in.

She came back with a snake basket. Leo switched on the lights. She opened the basket and took out a serpent that was nearly a foot long. Tupac Amaru; a shining serpent. It wound itself around her hand like an obedient child and raised its hood occasionally to glance around the room.

'Poison can be combated with poison. I'm going to make this good-looking fellow strike the venom out of you.' Saying this, she placed the snake at my feet. I trembled in fear. The snake slowly slithered over my foot and reached my thigh. I too slowly lifted my head and saw that it was calmly moving forward. As it reached my groin it stopped as if it had met a friend and raised its hood and spat. I felt I was in danger and jumped up, thrusting the snake away.

Satan's dinner party came to an end.

Itty Cora with love.

5
Sora

Agar firdous bar rooy-e-Zameen ast
Hamin ast-o Hamin ast-o
Hamin ast-o

If there be paradise on earth
It is here, It is here, It is here.

THE SCHOOL WAS A POSH THREE-BEDROOM FLAT ON THE SEVENTH
floor of a building on the banks of the backwaters. Rekha and her
friends had bought it three years earlier for twenty-one lakhs. Now
it was worth thrice the amount.

The large living room was beautifully done up. On the walls
the words 'If there is paradise on earth, it is here, it is here it is
here' were inscribed in letters of gold in three languages: Farsi,
English, and Malayalam. The three sofas bore large sunflowers
embroidered in cream on black velvet. An Egyptian carpet of

the same design covered the centre of the room. This living room was the Discourse Centre of the school. To the west of this L-shaped hall was the dining area with the kitchen close by. The three bedrooms were on three sides, and they were done up in different styles.

The first bedroom was the Body Lab. This room that had mirrors on the walls and ceiling had only one piece of furniture in it, a cot made of rosewood. Each leg of the cot was carved in the shape of a woman. The half-hidden openings in the ceiling would fill the room with light and music. The cot could be moved up, down, and sideways with a mechanical contraption. All this could be operated by remote control. There was an attached bathroom with a transparent glass wall where an artificial garden with flowers, sunlight, and breeze could be created. Only guests who paid very high fees were allowed into the Body Lab.

The second bedroom was the Liberation Centre. Instead of a cot, there was a table with a granite top. The guest was made to lie down on this for a massage and sprayed with steam, hot air, warm water, and perfume. The table could be converted into a hanging cot by attaching it to copper chains. The walls were decorated with paintings in the Khajurao style.

Masochistic visitors had a choice of whips, canes, and knives. Though the entrance fee was high, it was still lower than that for the Body Lab. It was not just because it was less exotic but also because while three people served guests in the Body Lab, there were only two in the Liberation Centre. Rekha and her friends used the third bedroom. Guests were not allowed to enter this room.

The Discourse Centre was the only area where guests did not have to pay to enter, but they needed high recommendations to be invited and had to come bearing expensive gifts. Only trusted people who were allowed entry into the Discourse Centre could pay their way into the Body Lab and Liberation Centre. But there were several regular guests at the Discourse Centre who were unaware of the existence of the Body Lab and the Liberation Centre. To guide the discussions at the Discourse Centre, experts would be called in. They would actively participate in the discussion, have a couple of drinks, and leave.

Once a week, on a Saturday or Sunday, guests were invited to the Discourse Centre. These sessions were called sora. In accordance with the taste of the guests, the conversation would revolve around literature, music, cinema, or art. Rekha would decide upon and introduce the topic. Rashmi and Bindu would join in. Food and drinks would be offered to the guests.

On Saturday Rekha had gone to Kunnamkulam so the sora was fixed for Sunday. The visitors arrived before evening. Rekha received the guests in an ethnic Kerala sari with a green border. Everyone looked at her in surprise. They had only seen her in western clothes. She wore Indian garments only to work. As the topic chosen for that day was literature, I the Scripter, Nirupakshan the critic, Femi the feminist, and an intellectual from the city known as Brain were the guests. Femi, Brain, and Rekha's friends often came together for the sora. I had brought Nirupakshan as the expert for the evening. The three beautiful women and the presence of alcohol in the luxurious flat troubled my habitually cynical friend. Rekha shook hands with him, kissed him on both cheeks, and led him to a seat. When she kissed him, he looked like a middle-aged housewife terrified of losing her chastity. Everyone sat down—I beside Rekha, Brain next to Femi, and Nirupakshan with Rashmi.

'Friends let's begin with cocktails.'

Rekha handed everyone glasses. 'Cheers.' Another round of kisses. This time, it was Rashmi who attacked Nirupakshan's chastity. But as he was gulping down his drink greedily, he didn't notice. He must have found solace in the fact that Femi, who led ideological attacks on him in public debates, hadn't kissed him.

Rekha sipped her drink before she began. 'I'm sure you've heard of Nabaneeta Deb Sen. She is the first wife of Amartya Sen, the Nobel Laureate for Economics. Today, we will discuss her short story "Stand Back, Please, it's The Nobel!".'

Though there was enough space on the sofa, Rekha moved closer to Nirupakshan, as if deeply engrossed in the conversation. Femi stared into space, waiting for someone to begin the discussion. Nirupakshan, under the misconception that everybody was waiting to listen to him, cleared his throat and began.

'When my friend invited me to a group discussing literature, I expected a small audience, not this sort of group. I don't think this group will be discussing literature in depth. I read Nabaneeta's story before coming for this meeting. So, I will say a few things about it. Nabaneeta's narrative cannot be classified as a story. The element of fiction in it is very minimal. In fact, there are no characters. Nabaneeta, who is the narrator, is the central character. The story revolves around the problems her family and society posed for Nabaneeta when Amartya Sen was invited to Calcutta by the West Bengal government after receiving the Nobel Prize. I feel she has tried to magnify her problems in an effort to secure a share of Amartya Sen's fame. I don't think this short story deserves a place in modern fiction.'

By this time Femi had lost her temper and she intervened. 'Excuse me for interrupting. This skewed interpretation is the result of a male-centred reading of the text. Look at it from Nabaneeta's point of view. She is a famous Bengali author and I don't think she is desperate to bask in her husband's reflected glory. She has problematized the way society treated her at a particular juncture in her life. Conservative society cannot digest the fact that Amartya Sen, his children, and his present wife share a friendly relationship with Nabaneeta. This story demolishes the conventional and deeply entrenched notions of wife, ex-wife, ex-husband, and children of the ex-wife.'

'I felt the same about the story and that's why I decided that we should discuss it today. What do you say, Brain?' asked Rekha.

'Rekha, I agree with Femi up to a point. But Nabaneeta only focuses on the outlook of middle-class Bengalis. I don't think she addresses the power politics which create this attitude.'

'No, no, Brain. Power politics is part of the identity politics of women. The politics of identity has no relevance if divorced from power politics. The fame that Amartya Sen gains by accepting the Nobel Prize makes him part of the established authority or the centres of power that are trying to draw him in. It is the splendour of power that draws people to it.'

Nirupakshan looked at me as if I were a traitor who had deserted him and crossed over to the opposition, but he continued arguing with renewed vigour. Glasses emptied and were refilled. Rashmi refilled Nirupakshan's glass, put her palm on his lap, and left it there. She moved closer to him. Surprising me, he put his arm around her shoulder. Rekha threw me a covert glance and smiled. Femi quickly grasped the situation. She sipped her drink sparingly. The fiery feminist unfortunately did not have a good head for liquor.

Rekha announced, 'Now let's change places.' Rashmi moved next to Brain, Femi was next to me, and Rekha sat with Nirupakshan. Rekha said, 'Why don't we situate this story in Kerala?'

'Impossible. It couldn't have happened in Kerala. No matter how progressive, the Malayali male will never tolerate his former wife being friendly with his present wife. For a Keralite, a phase of life ends with divorce. They completely forget or pretend to forget the spouse with whom they had lived together for decades. They make sure that they don't meet, and if they do happen to meet accidentally, they avoid each other. There is no question of dignified friendship. You must remember they once slept together.'

'This attitude is not peculiar to Kerala. It is the average Indian mindset. A postmodern writer who belongs to Tamil Nadu and his author ex-wife would kill each other if they happened to meet.

We have any number of examples around us. Amartya Sen and Nabaneeta have attained intellectual maturity and they are broad-minded. This makes things different in their case.'

While I supported Brain's argument, Rashmi, pretending not to understand, leaned on his shoulder. As Brain finished his drink and lit a cigarette, Rashmi took the cigarette from him, took a puff, and put it back between his lips. I felt that the conversation was getting a bit dull and created a diversion by asking Rekha why she was in ethnic clothes.

'I was wondering why no one had asked. For my research in Kerala history both of us had gone to Kunnamkulam. This outfit is an outcome of the trip. In the fifteenth century the liberated women of Kerala had platforms to discuss politics and culture. These women were called Deva Achi, which means wife of God. This later became corrupted to thevidichi, which means whore in Malayalam. "Achi" means an independent woman well versed in art, music, and literature like the women who frequented salons in eighteenth-century Europe.'

Nirupakshan, who had finished his fifth drink, slurred, 'So this is a recreation of the great tradition of Kerala.'

Brain disagreed, 'I don't agree that this is the traditional attire of Kerala. Women those days never wore stitched blouses, they merely tied a cloth around their breasts.'

'This is just a temporary improvisation. Next time my attire will be more authentic.'

'The innerwear should also be authentic,' I said.

'That's just how your mind works, Scripter!'

Rashmi spoke for the first time, 'The dress code is applicable for men as well.'

'Agreed. Let us all wear traditional clothes for the next meeting. But now to go back to Nabaneeta. Let us take a position against Nabaneeta but not in the way Nirupakshan wants us to.

Don't you feel the story shows how much she admires Amartya? Don't you think that this is a sort of male worship rooted in the subconscious?'

'The admiration you feel for a Nobel Laureate isn't simply male worship. It is hero worship. It is not gender specific. Even at the level of the unconscious, it doesn't have a sexual connotation. It is what you feel for a cricketer or a movie star. Nabaneeta admires Amartya's intellect,' Femi said.

'Femi's stand is right up to a point, though it shouldn't be mistaken for the whole truth. A woman's admiration for a man has undeniable sexual impulses. We cannot be sure that Nabaneeta's consciousness is devoid of this.'

'We are wandering from the topic, Rekha. Nabaneeta Deb Sen is one of Bengal's most prominent writers. She was professor of Comparative Literature in the University of Jadavpur. She has doctorates from several universities in India and abroad and is the recipient of several awards including the Padmashree. She has two daughters who are older than I am: Antara Dev Sen, a prominent journalist who is the editor of *The Little Magazine*, and Nandana Dev Sen, who is a film star.'

'Femi, we have to get rid of all such considerations when we approach a story. This is a complex situation. What Nabaneeta presents to her readers and what she actually thinks may be two quite different things,' Brain said.

'Brain, I don't think we should go so deeply into it. We are discussing the relevance of this work as a piece of creative writing and whether it is appropriate to present personal experiences and problems as fiction.' As I diverted the discussion, Rashmi refilled the glasses and served us fried mutton with chopped pineapple. Nirupakshan, tired out, had withdrawn from the debate.

'The twenty-first-century reader typically likes to peek into the lives of others. People have lost interest in ideologies. Given this,

I don't think that it's wrong to fictionalize one's personal life,' said Rekha.

'But this story is not a mere narration of incidents in someone's personal life. Nabaneeta feels that the identity of Amartya Sen's ex-wife is too big a burden to bear and she tells a fellow traveller in a tram that she is not Nabaneeta,' I said.

'There lies the twist in the tale. Denying her identity, she loses an opportunity to forge a friendship with an admiring reader. This is a story that has appealed to me in recent times.'

Brain got an urgent call. He and Femi made their excuses and prepared to leave. Nirupakshan cadged a lift from them. Rekha, Rashmi, and I were left to continue the conversation.

'In a way it's a blessing they left early. We met Susannah in Kunnamkulam today. She gave us some shocking information. Did you manage to get anything?' asked Rashmi.

'I got a lot of interesting information too. But let's first listen to what Susannah had to say,' I said.

6
Susannah

I can resist everything except the temptation of a beautiful woman.

— A text message from Itty Cora to Rekha

As we had told Susannah that I intended to do research on the Christian culture in Kerala, she took us straight to Arthhattu Melevalappil Kunjipalu's house. An old house in the Christian style built in the middle of a one-acre plot. Kunjipalu was Susannah's maternal grandfather. He was well over eighty. In his youth, he suddenly gave up his undergraduate studies in St. Aloysius College in Mangalore and came back to Kunnamkulam and went into the areca nut business. When he grew old, he entrusted the business to his children. At present, he is engaged in fashioning crosses in wood, stone, iron, and gold. All the churches and cupolas in the vicinity sport Kunjipalu's crucifixes. He also makes holy crosses out of gold. Some call him 'the cross'. When he saw us, he thought that we had

come to commission him to make crucifixes. When Susannah tried
to introduce us, he interrupted saying, 'I've still to complete crosses
for three churches. I can't take up fresh work for at least a month.
I'm growing old. I've to make thirty-three crosses, three in gold, six
in silver, and the rest in wood and concrete. They decide the date
of the consecration first and then come to me, asking me to carve
crosses for them. Making crosses is not a joke.'

'But they have not come to ask you to make crosses. They are my
friends.'

'When strangers show up, they usually come for a purpose.
Christians come for crucifixes, Hindus go to Kanippayur Mana to
order idols. Then they go to Kurukkan Para for pillars and lamp
towers for temples. Islam is against idolatry. Yet some rich Hajis go
to Kurukkan Para for beautiful meezan stones. Well, my children,
what have you come for?'

'Grandpa, this is Rekha,' Susannah introduced us. 'She teaches
in a college in Kochi. She is doing research on the Christians in
Kunnamkulam. She feels that you can give her some valuable
information. This is her friend, Rashmi. She works in a bank.'

Grandpa eyed us with growing suspicion. Then he asked Susannah
in an audible aside, 'Will I get something out of it?' Susannah looked
at us, embarrassed. I gestured, indicating I would be willing to pay
1,000 rupees per day. His face cleared.

'Susannah, take them in and give them something to eat. I've to
complete some urgent work on a crucifix which I've to hand over by
afternoon. We'll talk after lunch.'

Grandpa's daughter-in-law, who was Susannah's aunt, greeted us
warmly. She gave us achappams to eat, but she looked glum. She
started talking about her husband, 'Thambi chettan's business is
not doing at all well. That is to be expected because the rituals are
not conducted properly nowadays. The money Grandpa's crucifixes
bring in is not sufficient.' Susannah quickly changed the topic. After

drinking tea, we walked around the land surrounding the house. It was thickly planted with coconut, areca nut, banana, and nutmeg bushes. If we looked southwards, we could see Arthattu Church. The land slanted from the south to the west. Behind the house were paddy fields and next to it a pond. 'We started the work of making crucifies after St. Thomas came here. We did it in memory of his mounting the first cross here. After Grandpa, my husband will take it up. That's the pond where St. Thomas used to bathe.'

'Isn't the Church of Palayoor established by St. Thomas?' I asked.

'That is still debated. St. Thomas came to Kerala in A.D. 52. During that time the sea stretched up to Arthattu. It was called Arthattu beach. St. Thomas came here straight from Muzaris, the old Kodungalloor. The seven churches he established in India were dedicated to St. Mary. Guruvayoor and Chavakkad emerged later when the sea receded. We don't believe that the church in Palayoor was established by St. Thomas.'

'Rashmi, Sussanah is only voicing the opinion of the Orthodox Syrian church. The people of Palayoor do not subscribe to this view. Such differences are common among the different denominations of Christianity.'

'Our belief is right.'

'Let's not argue. Your aunt spoke of some rituals that are no longer conducted. What are they?'

'Oh, we have certain rituals on Christmas Eve. They haven't been observed for six to seven years.'

'What are they?'

'We are not supposed to speak of them to outsiders.'

Aunt invited us inside for lunch. As we finished eating, Grandpa called us. He sat on a reclining chair, and we sat around him on the floor.

'The history of the Christian community in Kunnamkulam began with the arrival of St. Thomas. Till then this was a Jewish colony.

St. Thomas disembarked from his ship in a sailboat. It was the Jews that St. Thomas converted when he came here. That the Namboodiris were converted by St. Thomas is a false story. The Namboodiris came to Kerala nearly six hundred years later. What aspect of Christian history are you working on?'

'I'm doing research on Itty Cora, an international pepper trader who lived in Kerala in the fifteenth century.'

'Good! It's time someone wrote about Corappappan, Cora, our illustrious forefather. I've read several histories written about us Keralites. Corappappan is never mentioned. Cora was second only to the king in Kochi. He was richer than the king. He owned four hundred acres of paddy fields, four farmhouses, more than forty head of cattle, twenty-four ox carts, seven horses, a hansom carriage, a mansion on the north side of Adupputty hill, granaries near the fields, and huge farmhouses near the granaries. He had eighteen ships and catamarans out at sea, and employed nearly a thousand people. Itty Cora had an empire of his own in Kunnamkulam.

'He would enter the market on his white horse, it was a sight to behold! He was as regal as an emperor—6 foot 3 inches tall, big built, clean-shaven, as fair as a white man. After he came back from his travels, he wore only trousers. Unlike other rich men of his time, he sported a hat instead of a turban. His word was law in the market. He was not a mere merchant; he had a say in everything: from matters of the state and wars to the affairs of the church.'

'What did he trade in?' asked Rashmi.

'Pepper! Pepper was as valuable then as gold is now. He also traded in ginger and herbal oils. He would trade in any commodity—buy anything that could be sold for a profit and sell anything to make a profit. That's how the people of Kunnamkulam are. He traded in everything from pepper to diamonds.

'Out of his eighteen ships, if four were anchored in Ponnani, four would be in Italy, four would be sailing towards Italy, and another four would be on the way back. One of the two big ships would be with any one of these groups. Cora would travel only once a year, returning after six to eight months.

'If he was in Kunnamkulam his mansion would be surrounded by people. Even the king would visit him. He was the one who negotiated for peace when the King of Kochi entered into a war with the Zamorin of Kozhikode.'

'Then why isn't he mentioned in any history book?'

'What do our history books contain? They're written by the high-caste Nairs and Namboodiris. We do not have accurate details even of events which happened two hundred years back. Europeans have documented in detail events that happened as far back as five hundred years. Anyway, who told you about Itty Cora?'

I was at a loss for words at this unexpected question. I escaped by saying that I'd read about an Itty Cora who was mentioned in the history of the Renaissance in Italy.

'That's what I said. Europeans record historical details accurately. They are not influenced by caste, religion, or region. Our history is inseparably tangled with religion. It is difficult to separate fact from fiction. Cora lived during the latter half of the fifteenth century. Vasco da Gama reached Kerala in 1498. The decade before that was the best phase in Cora's life. Gold, riches, and women from all over the world flowed to Kunnamkulam. Cora was a bit of a womanizer. He would try his luck with each and every good-looking woman he met, and no woman ever refused him. Each time he came home from his travels, three or four beauties, black or white, would alight from the ship.'

'Didn't he have a wife and children?' I asked.

'Yes. Kattakambil Thottungal Mary was his lawfully wedded wife. But she did not receive any preferential treatment in comparison to the other women in his life. It was said that Cora had seventy-nine children inside and outside India.'

Disregarding my exclamation, 'Seventy-nine!', he continued. 'Cora was a good artist. He painted and sculpted. When Michelangelo was creating the Pieta, Cora stood close by watching. He was an excellent singer. He used to write lyrics for songs too. In those days our songs were our literature. Those songs are still sung at our homes on special occasions.'

Grandpa stopped suddenly as if he had said something he shouldn't have. I looked at Susannah, but she looked away. Eagerly, I inquired, 'I heard that certain rituals connected with Cora are still observed. What are they?'

Grandpa's face reddened with anger. He looked searchingly at me.

'Cora is the Karanavar, the most respected patriarch of our family. He is God to us. We have a lot of secrets in connection with him that are not supposed to be divulged to outsiders. Susannah, you know this. Then why have you brought them here?' Grandpa got up abruptly and went inside.

'There are certain problems regarding Cora's rituals. Let's go to my house,' said Susannah, guiding us to her car.

Susannah lived in a house in Presidency Colony, on the left side of Unity Hospital on Trichur Road. It was a mansion with all the modern amenities. Georgekutty had gone to his jewellery shop, and the house was empty. As we entered, I whispered in Susannah's ear, 'I've brought you a treat.' We had encouraged her to sin by making her drink beer and gin while we were in hostel together. Susannah had changed since then; she had put on weight, lost the vivacity of youth, and settled into respectable matrimony. I knew that I wouldn't get any more information from her till I got her drunk. When Susannah came back from the bathroom, we greeted her with a glass of whisky. She looked at me questioningly. I announced, 'Rashmi is getting married next month, so we are celebrating.' We clinked our glasses, saying, 'Congratulations and a hundred cheers for Rashmi,' and raised them to our lips. Knowing her weakness,

I refilled her glass several times. After a while, when I felt that the whisky had started to relax her, I asked, 'You spoke about some special rituals. What are they?'

She hesitated but intoxication, added to our friendly compulsion, loosened her tongue.

'We aren't supposed to talk about Cora's rituals to outsiders. I am telling you everything because I consider you family. Please don't talk about this to anyone.'

We nodded in assent. Susannah insisted that we pledge our secrecy. So we touched her palm, swearing to keep her secret. She lowered her voice.

'In our family there is a ritual called Corakku kodukkal. This has no connection with the established church. When a girl in the family attains puberty, she is offered to Cora on the next Christmas night. They get her drunk, and in a semi-conscious state she is locked up in the cellar. No matter what noises are heard from inside, the cellar is opened only in the morning. The girl is not supposed to speak of what happens in the cellar. If a new bride is brought to the family, she is given to Cora before her marriage is consummated. Till a few years back, all these rituals were conducted faithfully. In this generation our family has very few girls. For the past seven years these rituals haven't been observed. No girl has attained puberty and no new brides have come into the family. A girl offered to Cora brings prosperity to her home. I was fourteen when they offered me to Cora. George now owns three jewellery shops, and his assets are worth three to four crores. My aunt is sad because we don't have a girl in the family to offer Cora.'

'Do you remember what happened to you in the cellar?'

'Ten years ago, I thought that what had happened in the cellar was quite enjoyable. My mother had spoken to me about it only that morning. She said, "We have to observe certain rituals tonight. They will begin at the First House at twilight. After dinner, you will be made to drink alcohol and locked up in the cellar. The only source of light in the cellar is an oil lamp. You mustn't be scared. After midnight, Cora will come to you in the form of a handsome young man. Tonight, you are Cora's woman. He will teach you what it means to be a woman. He will take what he wants from you and give you what you need. He will like you only if you behave nicely to him. If he likes you, he will leave his mark on you in the form of a love bite. After that, your life will be filled with prosperity. It is all up to you. But when you come out of the cellar the next morning, you should not speak about it to anyone." I looked forward to the night with anticipation. I had just reached puberty, and boys held great fascination for me. I was longing to experience everything I'd heard my friends talk about. And this was with my parents' consent. Though I pretended to be innocent in front of everyone, I was longing to go inside the cellar.

'The celebrations began at twilight. Children were not allowed to participate. I was a well-built girl, rather big for my age. I was given new clothes. Attar was sprinkled on me, and I was taken to the central room and led to a chair decorated with silk and flowers. Other women who had been offered to Cora earlier crowded around me, making slightly lewd jokes. Unfamiliar songs and music filled the air. After a while, the eldest male member came up to me. He held a plate with burning frankincense in his left hand and a curiously shaped cross in the other hand. He made me stand up and made signs with the cross on my forehead, cheeks, and chest, and started chanting. As if made to order, I saw that the ends of the cross touched my nipples and the length of it fit into my neck and hand. The crucifix was grey in colour and carved out of the bone of some animal. I felt revolted when I looked carefully at it. When the prayer was over, he took the cross away and announced, "Dinner!"

'It was a fabulous meal, eighteen dishes made of seven different types of meat. We all sat on the floor—I was in the centre, with the rest of them in a semicircle around me. My parents sat on either side of me and fed me. Even the feeding was part of the ritual. I just tasted everything. The ladies who stood around me joking warned me not to eat too much as that would ruin the night ahead. At the end of the dinner, my parents raised a goblet of wine to my lips and kissed me on either cheek. I did not realize that wine had been replaced by whisky. When they led me back to the chair I was really drunk. The old patriarch burnt frankincense and started the next phase of the ritual. My mother came with a red gown in her hand. She stood to my left and my father on my right. The music and noise, the smell of frankincense, and the liquor in my belly had a dizzying effect. Karanavar continued the ritual, chanting prayers. I, who had been watching carefully till then, fell back in my chair. Suddenly Karanavar shouted, "Take off her clothes." My father made me stand up and removed my clothes. In my drunken stupor I stood up, forgetting shame. Karanavar pulled both my hands up and started whipping me on my chest, waist, cheeks, and feet. He lashed me with his whip eighteen times, shouting, "You are Cora's woman for tonight. Satan's Virgin!" As I started crying out with pain, everyone knelt down and prayed. "Oh Cora! We offer you this virgin. Celebrate her tonight and return her restoring her virginity. As you blessed the other maidens shower her too with your blessings." There were red weals all over my body, and blood was flowing from my wounds. As I received the eighteenth lash, I fell on the chair. Karanavar said, "It's time to tattoo her." My mother wiped my body and put the red gown on me. I drank the whisky my father poured me in one gulp and held out the glass for more. I don't remember how much I drank or who tattooed me.

'When I opened my eyes, it was pitch dark. The lamp was burning dimly. I didn't know whose arms had enveloped me. The red gown my mother had made me wear was lost. I was lying in the arms of a muscular man with my face pressed against his chest. He lay pressing his chin on my head, but I told myself, "It's Corappappan. Don't be scared."

'The long neck was fair and smooth. My hands pressed into his back. His back was as hairy as his chest. I wrapped my arms tightly around him. I touched his body with mine. Handsome, muscular, he was waiting to play naughty games with me. He moved lower, whispering, "Don't be scared." He extended his hand to move the wick of the lamp for more light and I pulled his hand towards me. He said, "Clever girl" and kissed my hands. It was the first time I tasted lust. I gave back more than I received. Both of us were in a great hurry ... the speed of a hurricane. When pain, pleasure, and happiness had been exhausted, we lay in each other's arms, tired out.

'After a long while he said, "Let me see you properly." He lifted me up and stood me on the floor and turned up the lamp.

'In the scattered beams of light that fell on him, I saw the might of the male hood that I had experienced for the first time. I held him close to cover our naked bodies. I realized that I only reached up to his shoulder. I hadn't felt so tiny in comparison to him when we lay together. As I bent my head on his shoulder, I felt his teeth biting into my cheek just below my left ear. It was a bit more painful than an injection. Blood oozed. As pain spread over my body, he drank my blood greedily. When the blood stopped flowing, he raised my face and kissed the wound and said, "Satan's Virgin! This is a token of my love. You will always be prosperous." For hours he tickled, hurt, and pleasured every pore of my body and guided me to the peak of ecstasy.

'I was woken at dawn by the noise of heavy knocking at the door. I opened my eyes eagerly, wanting to see his handsome face. But I was shocked to see that the body next to me was wrinkled like that of an Egyptian mummy. As I jumped up in horror, it turned into a spider running down my navel. When it reached the big toe of my right foot, it turned into a butterfly and flew away. When they led me out of the cellar, I ran out in search of that butterfly like a child.'

Susannah was tired out by then. She vomited the seventh glass of whisky, and I took her to her bedroom. As we were wondering how much of what she had told us was fact and how much fiction, George came back.

He said, 'Susannah doesn't have a head for liquor. She can't take more than one and a half pegs. Don't forget to invite us for the wedding.'

7

Hashimoto Morigami

Whoever wants to be happy, let him be so: about tomorrow there's no knowing.

— Lorenzo the Magnifico

Dear Rekha,

The day after the unsuccessful Satan's dinner, Katrina took me to meet Hashimoto Morigami, a researcher in the field of mathematics at Catholic University in Lima. Morigami, who is of Japanese origin, was born and brought up in Lima. She was awarded her doctorate by Princeton University in the US for her thesis on 'The History of Non-European Mathematics'. When I first heard her name, I was reminded of the famous tennis player Akiko Morigami, a beauty from Japan. Though Morigami was young and pretty like Akiko, she did not have typical Japanese features. She looked more like a Latin American. She was taller than the average Japanese and had a physique like Gabriela Sabatini's.

She lived in a posh apartment near Larcomar Shopping Center, which was in the middle of the city of Lima, paying a rent of $1,500. When we rang the bell, she opened the door wearing blue jeans and a light yellow top. I entered a beautiful living room that boasted of a deep red Brazilian carpet. A replica of Botticelli's *The Birth of Venus* adorned the wall. My boss, who ran a casino in the US, was a link in a gang that specialized in creating replicas of paintings that in their perfection rivalled the originals.

As I was mentally visualizing the jeans-clad Morigami as a nude Venus emerging from the sea, she welcomed me like an old friend by kissing me on both cheeks. The sun setting in the Pacific Ocean could be seen through the window. It reflected Morigami's alluring beauty.

'Welcome, Mr Itty Cora, I've been waiting a long time for you,' she said.

As I stood puzzled, Katrina explained that Morigami was doing her postdoctoral research on the Italian connection of the Kerala School of Mathematics. She had carefully examined the copper tablets and palm leaf inscriptions that Katrina had. She had been to Florence several times and had visited Kerala two or three times. She had been to our old house in Florence. Morigami knew about my mother who had gone to New York from Italy. But she had got to know about me from Katrina. 'I've been searching for someone with connections with the Itty Cora family,' Morigami said, 'with no luck. It was Katrina who finally told me about you.' She poured red wine for Katrina and me, saying, 'I am really happy to meet you, dear.'

'I've gone to my old house in Florence just once or twice, but I've never been to Kerala. I just have a few stray bits of information about the Itty Cora dynasty and Francis Itty Cora from the stories that my mother told me,' I said.

'It is very difficult to find links to a period that existed five hundred years ago. Where are the palm leaves and copper tablets in your possession? We may be able to find something there. Let me have a look.'

'Sorry. They are in New York, where I know they are safe. I'll bring them with me next time.'

'I don't want to bother you. I'll come with you to New York. I've some work in Princeton'.

Morigami had a naughty smile on her face as she poured wine and said to me, 'I heard your grandpa was an excellent lover.' I couldn't stop my eyes from straying to her waist. It wasn't flaccid like Katrina's. It still held promise.

Katrina, who sensed my mood, said, 'Maybe Morigami can restore your lost empire.' Her phone rang. She said that something urgent had come up in Estraap and left without waiting for dinner.

'Itty Cora, tonight you are my guest in every way,' Morigami said with a mischievous smile. I couldn't believe that she was ten years older than me or that she was teaching in a university. She flirted with me as she refilled my glass and extracted all the information I knew about Francis Itty Cora. She had changed out of her jeans into a transparent white gown. After a delicious dinner, she invited me to her bed.

'Darling, please get ready for an unimaginable experience, but you have to give me your documents in return. Okay?'

I felt there was a catch somewhere but replied 'Okay, but only if you win the game.' By then she had metamorphosed into Botticelli's Venus. Unfortunately for Morigami, she failed miserably with me. Though her Japanese-Peruvian moves created explosions in my mind, they failed to create even a ripple in my body. As she retreated admitting failure, she growled like a tigress, 'Fuck off, you bloody devil! Bringing shame on the great Francis Itty Cora.' I started sobbing, something I hadn't done in ages.

It was past midnight when, unable to bear the failure of her perfect body, Morigami donned her silk gown. 'As a last resort, shall we go down to El Parque del Amor?'

El Parque del Amor is the Love Park on the cliffs of Chorrillos in Lima that juts into the Pacific Ocean. When the famous Peruvian poet Antonio Cilloniz lamented that South America was full of memorials for war veterans and martyrs, the people of Miraflores in Lima responded by throwing open the park on Valentine's Day in 1993. In the middle of the park is Victor Delfin's statue *El Beso,* a pair of lovers locked in an erotic embrace. Below the statue, Antonio Cilloniz's words are engraved. Lovers can enter this park whenever they want. Though copulation in public is not allowed, no one complains about what lovers do there. That is where Morigami took me that night.

It was 1 a.m. on a chilly moonlit night when we reached the gates of the park. She parked the car near the gate. As we were entering, our arms draped around each other's waists, the security guard smiled knowingly at Morigami. He happily accepted the money she put in his palm. 'Madam, the north end of *El Beso* is empty. You'll get a lovely view of the statue in the moonlight. It'll get very cold soon. Hope you've brought whisky.' She nodded and walked into the park, hanging on to my arm. Just as Morigami had told me, we were not the only visitors in the park. Around us were a number of couples in various stages of lovemaking. In the centre was *El Beso* bathed in moonlight and inspiring us all. When we reached the lawn at the north end of the park, Morigami threw off her gown and transformed herself once more into Botticelli's Venus. She took the whisky out of her bag and both of us sipped from the bottle. Then she hugged me and gave me a long kiss. 'Itty Cora ... Look at *El Beso*—a very different posture ... let's try it.'

But she failed to arouse me. The next day, we flew to New York together.

Cora with love.

Rekha shut her inbox and googled Morigami. Amidst the many Morigamis, including tennis player Akiko Morigami, she found Hashimoto Morigami on the Princeton University website. She was Rekha's prime rival in the game with Itty Cora. But Rekha felt that she had no cause to worry as Morigami had failed in the first two rounds.

Morigami had published seven papers in the history of mathematics and abstract mathematics. Rekha was taken aback when she reached Morigami's blog through a hyperlink. She realized that her website on 'The School' of which she was so proud was nothing compared to Morigami's highly sophisticated blog titled *Morigami's World of Plus and Minus*. An image of Botticelli's Venus was on the homepage. Morigami did not write in the opaque language generally favoured by academics. Rekha double clicked the link 'Itty Cora: An Erotic King of Kerala Mathematics'.

Itty Cora, an ardent votary of Bacchus and Venus—no! the right order is Venus and Bacchus—was a fifteenth-century pepper merchant from Kerala. His interests were mathematics, literature, and art, and more than anything else, women. When Vasco da Gama discovered the sea route to Kerala, Itty Cora lost his monopoly in sea trade and settled down in Italy. It was through him that the advances in the field of mathematics that Kerala had achieved reached Europe in the fifteenth and sixteenth centuries. But Itty Cora was not a mathematician. He was an extraordinarily intelligent pepper merchant, a man who knew enough tricks to turn everything to his advantage. What made him popular among the kings and royals in Europe were the spicy Afro-Asian beauties he brought along with his cargo of pepper.

In 1486, he brought the Babylonian beauty Leila to Italy, called her Lousia, and set her up in Florence in a mansion.

He slowly spread his business network all over Europe and established himself as Italy's most important international trader. He became a close friend of Lorenzo de Medici, who was a powerful man in Italy. Cora built a mansion, Palazzo Cora, on the northern banks of River Arno. Though it wasn't as large as other Italian mansions built during the Renaissance, Palazzo Cora had seven bedrooms and could accommodate a hundred people, including the servants. It was said that the fifth bedroom was especially equipped for sexual pleasures and set apart for important guests like Medici and Raphael. The famous painter, who was a good friend of Itty Cora's, drew the nude painting titled *Hypatia Teaching the Art of Lovemaking* for this room. When fanatics obeying the Pope's commands burnt down Palazzo Cora, deeming it a centre of prostitution and black magic, the painting was destroyed.

The beautiful and intelligent Leila soon captured the attention of the artists and intellectuals of Florence. Michelangelo, Botticelli, Raphael, and Filippino Lippi were often Leila's guests at Palazzo Cora during the time when Lorenzo Medici was a force to reckon with.

Medici once wrote, 'Let those who wish to be happy be happy, we know nothing about tomorrow.' Though in public they pretended to lead strictly pious lives, the intellectual elite broke all taboos in private. The thousands of paintings, literary works, and sculptures that emerged from Italy during the Renaissance were part of this hedonistic celebration of life. Up until 1498 when Gama's people sunk Cora's ships in the Mediterranean, Cora used to spend only a few weeks a year in Florence. The rest of the time was spent in travel or in his hometown in Kerala. In Cora's absence, Leila managed his affairs. It was not only the destruction of his fleet of ships by Gama's crew that persuaded Cora to stay permanently in Florence. The Portuguese celebrated their Mediterranean victory by torching Cora's business houses in Kerala and killing his people. They spread a rumour that the atheist Cora after being killed in battle had flown away, assuming the form of a black tiger with wings. That is a story that is still believed in Kerala. But the truth was that after getting knifed in his left shoulder in an altercation, Cora lost the use of his left hand and decided to settle down in Florence with Leila. As he had expanded his business from pepper and fragrant oils to other commodities, he did not find life difficult. Cora, who was attracted to art, literature, and the European way of life, lived in Florence, the nerve centre of the Renaissance, from 1499 till his death in 1517.

Itty Cora, who was born in an old business family, in Kunnamkulam in present-day Kerala in the south-west of India, used to accompany his father on business trips. At the age of fifteen, his father enrolled him for three years in a 'secret school' in Alexandria. The Hypatians, who worked secretly in many parts of the world, ran this school. They were free thinkers who had studied astronomy, mathematics, chemistry, and medicine scientifically, and were interested in art and literature. As their activities were against the beliefs propagated by the Catholic Church, they were forced to work in secrecy. It was his education in the secret Hypatian School in Alexandria that made Cora an expert in mathematics and astronomy, and it was also this school that lit the lamp of eroticism in Cora's mind.

When he turned eighteen, Cora returned to Kerala having completed his education at the Hypatian School. At the age of twenty-one, his father died suddenly, and he had to take over his father's business empire. In the intervening three years, Cora spent his time engaging in debates with learned men in Kerala. He must have shared the knowledge he had acquired from the Hypatian School with them and accepted their formulae and hypotheses and expanded them himself. However, for Cora, who was a pragmatist, this knowledge gathering wasn't merely for knowledge's sake but had practical applications in his nautical journeys and trade.

I now wish to connect Cora to Madhava of Sangamagrama, Nilakantha Somayaji, and Jyeshthadeva, who are commonly referred to as the Kerala School in academic circles. They made immense contributions to mathematics and astronomy.

It has been accepted that the principles of calculus and the infinite series were discovered by mathematicians in Kerala two hundred years before Newton and Leibniz. They were able to determine the value of Pi up to the seventeenth decimal. It is not through the missionaries who came to Kerala following Gama that this knowledge reached Europe, as has been mistakenly represented in *The Crest of the Peacock,* written by George Gheverghese Joseph and published by Princeton University in 1998. I am not trying to trivialize Joseph's research. I have great respect for his finding that the first principles of Calculus came from Kerala, years before Newton and Leibniz. It was this information that led to my quest. But Joseph never took into account the possibility of a global exchange of knowledge through international traders. This is because he doesn't question the accepted framework of history. For this reason, I have turned away from the realm of accepted history in my quest for knowledge.

It is a Eurocentric belief that it was Vasco da Gama who discovered the sea route to India. It is absurd to believe that no one else had travelled that route before. Such notions are a result of the myths created by the whites to establish European supremacy. Actually, even before the European colonization of India, there existed international trade and exchange of knowledge. Unfortunately, evidence proving this was destroyed by the whites owing to their ignorance and intolerance of the indigenous people of the East.

Bloggers who read this may wonder how Hashimoto Morigami got these details about Itty Cora. Owing to certain constraints concerning the field of research, it will be possible to reveal the answer to this question only at the last stage of research.

When Bindu returned from Chennai the next day, Rekha told her about Itty Cora's mathematical connection. She was the most academically oriented person in the group. She had turned to fashion designing after completing her MSc and MPhil in mathematics. Disbelievingly, she took her laptop and checked Itty Cora's mail and Morigami's blog over and over again. 'I've also heard about this Kerala School. But this connection ... anyway, it is a wonderful idea ... Looks very interesting. By the way, one of our most privileged clients, the minister's son, was on the same flight as me. He was wearing a khadar shirt and sat three seats away, pretending not to know me. Mentally, I damned him to hell. But after landing, as I was getting into the car, I got an SMS from him: "Sorry. Will you give me a one-day appointment on Friday?" I replied, "The marks that you left on my breast last time haven't yet faded." I think he was upset. He kept ringing me. I answered his fourth call and agreed to his request.'

'Well, that's good. It's his first visit after becoming a minister. We should arrange a party.'

8

The Wages of Sin Is Death

Reserve your right to think, for even to think wrongly is better than not to think at all.

— **Hypatia**

Ever since the school set up its website, the trio usually spent all their free time on the laptop. Rekha liked to browse after dinner, which she usually had with a drink. She would lie on her stomach and idly browse the net with Rashmi and Bindu on either side of her. When they weren't entertaining guests, they would sleep together. They shared a drink after dinner, booted their laptop, and logged on. After reading Morigami's blog on Itty Cora, Rekha clicked a thread titled:

'The True Story of Hypatia' by Isabella
Swan

I feel that the source of Itty Cora's knowledge in mathematics and astronomy was the secret Hypatian School in Babylon.

If you want to know the background of these Hypatian Schools, it is imperative that you know about Hypatia first. Hypatia was the daughter of mathematician Theon, who was a professor in the famous University of Alexandria. Hypatia, who was born in 370 CE, is considered to be the world's first female mathematician and astronomer. The beautiful and intelligent Hypatia went to Athens for higher education and returned to work as a teacher in the university. Hypatia's thoughts and actions were rational and therefore against the beliefs of the Church. Religious fanatics murdered her in 410 CE at the behest of Cardinal Cyril. With her murder the decline of Alexandria's position as the world's centre of knowledge began, culminating in the burning down of the magnificent library at Alexandria.

There are several books written about Hypatia, but unfortunately none of her own works have survived. Letters written by her students and allusions to her in the texts of other mathematicians of the time remain our only sources for reconstructing her life and work. In the modern age, most of the works written about Hypatia either valorize her in order to decry the Catholic Church or portray her in a negative light so as to support the church. But the short story 'The True Story of Hypatia' written by Spanish author Isabella Swan in a magazine called *Nostalgia* that was published from Istanbul in 2004 is quite different.

The True Story of Hypatia

Isabella Swan

Dear Reader,

Today is Good Friday. We are now away from the crowds in Alexandria in the 'Geometrica', an octagonal building that is home to Hypatia, who is considered to be the first woman astronomer in the world.

The large rooms built for specific needs were located at each one of the eight corners: a living room, a library, a room to welcome guests, a room to exercise in, a dining room, a kitchen, a room for the servants working in the kitchen, a bedroom, and in the centre was the atrium. All the rooms opened on to the marble-paved corridor that circled the atrium. There were 16 granite pillars on either side, carved with the figures of Nefertiti and the Sphinx. Near a triangular pagoda 3 foot 4 by 5 on top of a 48-foot-high pillar was a small swimming pool full of fish and blue lotuses and around it a beautiful garden. The spiral staircase with 144 steps led to a room equipped for viewing and studying the planets and stars. Theon built this house for his daughter Hypatia when at a very young age she became interested in mathematics and astronomy. She had lived here all her life. Every corner of Geometrica, built entirely in polished granite and marble, either exemplified or symbolized some mathematical principle.

In those days Good Friday was not a holiday in Alexandria. Though the Christians had a strong presence in society, they did not form the majority of the population.

Intellectuals like Hypatia and scientists who belonged to the free-thinking community of the university looked upon Christianity with suspicion. They questioned the concepts of the resurrection and miracles with the tools of rational thinking. Cardinal Cyril combated them by portraying these intellectuals as pagans and condemning their scientific experiments as blasphemy and devil worship. But this did not affect the fame of the university nor of Hypatia. Every year foreign students flowed to Alexandria. Hypatia was the most famous teacher in the university. But in Alexandrian society, Hypatia was not just an academic. She was able to wield considerable influence with her dignified and intelligent interventions in politics and social

life. Orestes, the new Prefect of Alexandria, was captivated by her
beauty and intelligence.

Hypatia was busy as usual that day. She woke up before dawn,
exercised, bathed, and sat in the library to prepare notes for lecturing
foreign students on Apollonius's *Conics*. Though she had crossed
40, age had not dimmed her glowing beauty created in the perfect
golden[2] ratio. Theon had schooled Hypatia from a young age to
maintain her divinely proportioned figure with a regime of exercise
and diet.

Wearing a light cream, transparent *Doric chiton*, her curly hair
tied high, as she leaned towards her left studying her papyrus scrolls.
She looked like a Grecian goddess. Her face unwrinkled by age, her
firm breasts, and flat stomach created waves of suspicion among
the Alexandrians. The envious accused her of being a lifeless statue,
totally devoid of human emotions, as she had chosen to remain
unmarried. She chose not to marry because she valued her personal
freedom above everything else. Not taking into account the rigorous
schedule of exercise, horse riding and strict diet that she followed to
maintain her beauty, people accused her of being Satan's woman. In
reality, Hypatia, who believed in celebrating life, invited lovers of her
choice to Geometrica and travelled along different avenues of sexual
pleasure.

When the maid hesitantly entered the room to tell her that she
had a visitor, Hypatia folded her papyrus scrolls and stood for a
moment, unwilling to relinquish the comfort of the Doric chiton.
Reluctantly, she donned a gold-embroidered *himation* that fully hid
her sparkling diamond necklace. She tied a scarf embroidered with
corals and pearls over her hair and looked in the mirror. Maybe
due to sleeplessness, her eyes lined with light green *udgi* were red.
The left side of her lower lip bore the bruise Osrestes's teeth had

---

2   0.6180339887. It is believed that all creations in the world are in this
     ratio. Hypatia's limbs were in this proportion at birth.

made the previous night as he left hurriedly. Well, she had asked for it, hadn't she? She had pulled him back as he bid farewell and this was the result. Her students would definitely notice tomorrow. The students who sat looking greedily at her were not mere children. Many of them had proposed marriage to her. Eager to know the identity of her guest, she tried to mask the bruise with a smile and went to the living room.

Disappointing Hypatia, a low-ranking Roman soldier handed her a message on a papyrus scroll very respectfully, without looking up at her. Though she accepted it quite disinterestedly, when she started reading it, her heart filled with joy.

Dear Hip,

Last night I entered heaven for the first time. When we parted, like you, I too yearned for more. I couldn't sleep when I reached the palace. When I closed my eyes, I saw Geometrica, the paradise you threw open for me, the polished marble on top of the triangular pagoda. I came back. The Roman soldier standing in front of you is none other than me. The Prefect of Alexandria cannot travel without an entourage in daylight.

Incredulous, Hypatia read the letter again: the salutation 'Dear Hip' unlike the usual 'Philosopher', as well as the same handwriting. She felt a pleasurable numbness creeping up her body from the big toe of her right foot. When she had invited Orestes to Geometrica after he had spent days pleading for an invitation, she hadn't expected this. She had captivated him in the space of one night. Within no time, Orestes transformed from a respectful soldier to the ruler of Alexandria. He pulled her close and swiftly moved towards the bedroom.

He impatiently removed her *himatian*. She took off all her jewellery and raised her hands to push her hair to either side of her face.

Orestes exclaimed at the perfect proportion of her body. Unheeding, Hypatia applied fragrant oil on her face and body. By this time, her maid had placed wine goblets and blue lotuses on the table. Hypatia poured wine into small glasses and dropped three blue lotus petals into each glass. Then, realizing that she should not test Orestes's patience any longer, she went up to him and looked at him with a naughty smile, placing her hands on his shoulders.

'Look, Orestes! The gift you gave me when you left hurriedly last night.'

With remorse in his eyes, he looked at the bluish bruise on her lips. Pulling her close, he ran his finger over the bruise.

'Forgive me, I blame my uncontrolled passion. You will receive a procession of gifts to make up for it. Last night, the future king of Alexandria chose the most beautiful Hypatia to be his queen.'

'How lucky I am! But is it something the honorouble emperor can decide by himself? Don't you want my opinion?'

'My darling Hip, what will you feel except untold happiness? I thought you'd jump for joy when I said this.'

'Certainly, I am happy. You are the strongest, most intelligent, and most dignified lover I have had. But I am not a young girl to jump with joy. I am three years older than you. There are things we should deliberate upon before we come to a decision.'

'Emperors only command, subjects obey.'

'All right, this humble subject obeys your command. But I don't want to be one among your many beautiful consorts. I want to be your empress. Don't imagine I'll be content with being a satellite like the other women. I refuse to be your shadow. Even after marriage, you must continue to treat me as you do now.'

'Dear Hip, you are my Cleopatra.'

'Thank you, but you will neither be my Caesar nor Antony, and don't compel me to leave Geometrica.'

'What if I provide a more congenial atmosphere in the palace?'

'That is impossible. You can make Geometrica an annex of your palace. Let us think about these matters later. I've poured you chai brought from Israel that has been preserved for eighteen years. By the time the blue lotus petals and naphthenic dissolve in it, I will divest you of your soldier's uniform.'

He stood silently like an obedient schoolboy. Hypatia removed his armour. Bathed in the morning rays of the sun, the naked Orestes resembled the bronze statue of Hercules in the Theatre of Pompey. She stood gazing in lust at his muscular shoulders, her eyes travelling over his chest and powerful limbs.

'Hip! We don't have much time. I have an assembly to attend at ten and you have a lecture at the university.'

'Oh? What is the decision at the assembly? If Maghreb comes fully under our control, will freedom from Rome be declared?'

'Definitely. The situation in Rome is very bad. Acting on your advice, we are nearing success. If the people agree, Alexandria will declare her independence today. It is Cardinal Cyril's people who are stirring up trouble. Some Christian fanatics are behind him. I am trying my best to negotiate with them.'

By this time, the blue lotus petals had completely dissolved. Both of them sipped chai as they discussed diplomatic matters. Even when the chai burnt through his veins, Orestes continued to pay close attention to Hypatia's advice. When he was completely intoxicated, he twirled her in his arms, exclaiming, 'This is why I say you should be my queen. If your brains and my strength come together, we will be undefeatable.' She was crushed in his embrace.

Hypatia liked being crushed in the arms of strong lovers. Only such people were invited to Geometrica. Even as she stood without any outward display of happiness, Orestes removed her chiton. She repeated what had happened on the flower-strewn bed twice or thrice the night before in a completely novel manner. Her pace, which began slowly, quickened in geometric progression. After about fifteen minutes, like a long-distance runner reaching the final post, she flopped on Orestes's chest, panting and satiated. When she regained her breath, she gulped down chai and asked him, 'This is called a horse race. Did you enjoy it?'

'Very much, but I feel sad when I my horse falls tired and sweating.'

'This method needs a lot of effort from the woman. Sometimes she falls without tasting success. And if she succeeds, it's like winning an Olympic laurel. You are lucky I was able to win the medal today.'

'But Hip, this requires a lot of physical effort. I don't think the diet restrictions you follow to maintain your divine proportion will allow you to take part in such horse races.'

'The divine ratio of my body is an accidental blessing. I have to maintain it, and don't imagine that this horse race is all I have to offer you. I have yet to teach you many more novel methods of making love.'

With a mocking smile playing on her lips, she leaned against his chest. Orestes placed his hands on either side of her chest and lifted her up. Hypatia in his arms stood suspended in the air for a few moments.

'Were you scared? You can't achieve this with your golden ratio. You need my muscular strength for it.' He laid her down on his left side.

'I am experiencing the strength of a Roman warrior through you. Marvellous!'

'Then why do you hesitate to accept my proposal?'

She thought deeply. She had decided that she wouldn't get married if she couldn't find a complete man. She couldn't live submitting herself to a man who was inferior to her. Finally, she had found fulfilment in Orestes. Powerful, intelligent, strong, handsome, and dignified—what was more, he loved her. Above everything, what he had promised her was the position of Empress of Alexandria. If she could reap victories in politics as she had in mathematics and astronomy, in the future she could be the Empress of Egypt like Cleopatra. Her intelligence combined with Orestes's strength ... anything would be possible. But she couldn't leave Geometrica; she couldn't be the silent smiling queen by his side at public functions or an instrument to give birth to his children. Still, she couldn't reject his proposal. If she did, her life might be in danger.

Finally, she came to a decision. She slowly moved upwards, entwined her hands around Orestes's neck, and kissed him on both his cheeks.

'My love, I accept.'

'I can't believe it! My Hypatia has agreed to be my queen?'

'Yes, with great happiness. My search for a complete man ends with you, like the Nile empties itself into the sea. But you must allow me to continue living at Geometrica.'

'You can stay where it pleases you. But I can't say when the fish in me will demand your presence. So, I need you with me all the time. Whenever you feel the urge to open your father's papyrus scrolls, we can come here. The rest of the time, wherever I am—in the palace, in assembly, in the hunting grounds, in the battlefield, in Alexandria or Luxor or Rome or Athens, wherever I am—you must be with me, or else the fish in me will sulk.'

'So, am I needed only to satisfy the fish?'

'No, no, I can't do without your advice in matters of public administration either.'

'I accept all your conditions. My dearest Emperor should shoulder the responsibility of preserving my father's papyrus scrolls.'

'Not only your father's scrolls but also your curves! You can trust me,' said Orestes, crushing her in an embrace.

The bells tolled from the Caesareum, marking the special prayer on Good Friday. The time was 9 a.m. Orestes quickly donned his soldier's armour and left. Not much later, Hypatia set out for the university in her horse carriage.

It was past noon by the time Hypatia finished her lecture analysing Apollonius's principle of the division of a pyramid into infinite parabolas. As she came out of the lecture hall, one student among the many who crowded around her to clear their doubts detected the bluish bruise on her lips and questioned her about it in an oblique manner. When she boldly answered that it was caused by someone like him who got overexcited, they wanted to know who the lucky man was. She replied that she would officially announce it in a couple of days, and got into her horse carriage. An image of riding through the city along with Orestes flashed across her mind. The difficulties she faced now would be resolved with this marriage. The slander campaign unleashed by religious fanatics under the leadership of Cardinal Cyril would end. He was jealous of her influence on the Prefect and the elite and hated her for speaking openly against the irrational beliefs of the Church. With this marriage she would be able to pull the logically inclined Orestes out of the constraints of Christian belief. He had already forsaken God and started to worship the fish. The Roman Empire was disintegrating. If things continued so, the empire would crumble. With that, the seat of power this side of the Mediterranean would be with Orestes. He would become emperor of Alexandria. Then, Cyril with the other Christian fanatics would have to flee the country.

As the carriage moved forward, it met an unexpected crowd—a mob of nearly five hundred people. Their attire revealed that they were not town dwellers. They looked as if they had come from the desert. Most of them wore animal skins. They stood blocking the passage of the vehicle. Cyril's principal ally Peter led the mob. He had converted to Christianity just a few years back. They were shouting in Latin against Hypatia.

When it became impossible for the carriage to move forward, the scared driver stopped the vehicle. He hadn't seen such a sight before. Usually, people waited to pay their respects to Hypatia. Now, for the first time, they were hurling abuses at her. Hypatia, who guessed that they were trying to provoke her, sat silent. The abuse became more vitriolic.

'Whore! Don't hide in the carriage, come out! Let them see the woman who has ensnared the representative of the Roman emperor,' Peter shouted. When he saw that Hypatia was unmoved, he pulled the cart driver down and untied the horse. The shaft of the carriage touched the ground and the rear with Hypatia in it rose up in the air. The mob started to attack the carriage with sticks, spears, and crosses, crying out, 'Whore! Get down.' When the driver tried to protect her, they beat him up and he ran away. Peter poured oil out of a can all over the carriage and shouted, 'Hypatia! You vile sorceress, if you don't come out you will be burnt to ashes.' He set fire to the carriage. When the flames leapt up in the air, Hypatia jumped down and tried to escape. But Peter's men formed a circle around her. They said, 'You sorceress, we are going to subject you to a trial.'

'I am not a sorceress. I am a teacher at the university.'

'We know all that. If you answer our questions, we will end the matter without hurting you too much. Why were you not in the Ceasarium, despite it being Good Friday today?'

'I had a lecture at the university.'

'You should have avoided giving the talk today. By insisting on teaching, you compelled even those students who are believers to stay away from the special prayers. You did not even end the class on time; instead, you deliberately continued teaching till the prayer in the Caesareum ended.'

'I had no such intention.'

'Not just you, but your lover Orestes, the representative of the Roman emperor, failed to attend the prayer.'

'I do not know why he did not attend.'

'Oh? Didn't Orestes sleep in your house last night? After spending the night with a man who is married to a conscientious believer, you don't know why he didn't attend church?'

'Attending church prayers is his personal decision. I don't know anything about that.'

'You corrupted a man who became a Christian after receiving the Holy Communion by enticing him with your breasts and hips. You persuaded him to commit sin. In your university you create atheists by encouraging the students to think against the Holy Book.'

'We only teach scientific subjects.'

'Don't you teach them that the resurrection and miracles are false?'

'No, we don't touch upon such matters.'

'Then what do you do there? Prostitute yourself?'

'You are a priest. Shouldn't you talk in a more dignified manner?'

'Are you, who just prostituted herself this morning, talking to us about dignity? Who has left bite marks on your lips? The lips of an unmarried woman.'

When a shocked Hypatia lowered her head, he lifted her face up. 'Believers, look at the mark of sin on this whore's lips.'

Looking at the blue bruise on her lips they screamed, 'The wages of sin is death.'

'No. Don't kill her over such a small issue. Speak the truth. Didn't you sleep with Orestes last night?'

Hypatia stood helplessly with her head lowered. Someone who knew everything had betrayed her.

'She is a wicked witch. She will not speak the truth. Let us examine her body for further signs of prostitution.' He tore off her himation. Then the rest of them tore off her chiton and other undergarments.

When someone untied her hair and pulled off her ornaments, she tried to cover her nudity with her hands. Peter started to count the bite marks on her body 'One-two-three... . You whore! Raise your hands above your head. Let me count the marks of sin. Only then will I be able to give you fitting punishment.'

Helplessly, she raised her hands. The mob around her looked greedily at her nudity and shouted, 'The wages of sin is death.'

'Your body has eleven unhealed bruises. These are living evidences of your sin. If you admit your guilt, you will escape the death penalty. Speak the truth! Didn't you prostitute yourself with Orestes this morning?'

Realizing that Orestes's future depended on her words, she remained silent. Peter lashed her with a whip several times until blood flowed down her body. Still, she did not utter a word. Peter lost his patience. 'Believers! Let us take her to the Caesareum. They will have brought him there by then. The last trial should be conducted with both of them present.'

He picked up her himatian and threw it at her. 'Cover yourself. Your vile nudity should not arouse lust in the minds of the Alexandrians.'

They led her to the Caesareum screaming and throwing stones at her. Alexandrians gazed horror-struck. As Hypatia ran to the altar of the Caesareum to escape the relentless pelting of stones, someone pulled the himatian off her body.

Seeing this, Orestes, who was bound to a pillar, wept helplessly.

Peter entered the Caesareum.

'Believers! If she admits her guilt, we will set fire to her and banish Orestes. If she refuses to admit guilt, we will burn both of them on the strength of the evidence.'

They pushed a naked, bleeding Hypatia in front of the altar. Peter's deep voice resounded in the Caesareum. 'You witch! I am asking you once more. Do you admit guilt?'

She looked at the captured Orestes and, drawing on the last reserves of strength closed her eyes, raised her hands, and said loudly: 'Holy God, benevolent Christ! Citizens of Alexandria! I am a whore, a sorceress, and a sinner! Pardon my sins and allow me to live.' She said this thrice before fainting. Then, Peter lifted her body up.

'As Orestes, a believer and a Roman, has admitted to his guilt earlier, we take away the honours bestowed on him and banish him. But this blasphemer, who is a sorceress and Satan's child, is guilty of leading Orestes astray. God will not forgive her. The wages of sin is death.'

The crazed mob rushed towards Hypatia. They tore her limbs apart. They used oyster shells to scrape the flesh off her body and then burnt it.

The fanatics then burnt Geometrica. Orestes escaped to Timbuktu in present-day Mali in Africa, salvaging what he could of Hypatia's papyrus scrolls. Hypatia's students, who sought refuge in different parts of the world, set up Hypatian Schools secretly and continued with research in science and mathematics. Though several brilliant scientists and artists were members of these schools, they did not speak of it in public as they lived in fear of the Church.

9

Pain for Pleasure

Pain for pleasure (he's the hunter, you're the game)
Pain for pleasure (Satan is his name)
Watch out

—'Pain for Pleasure'
Sum 41

WITHIN MINUTES OF REKHA SETTING PAPA ROACH'S 'LAST RESORT' as the new ringtone on her mobile, Kuttan called her. 'I'll be there by evening. I've to leave before dawn to take the morning flight back to Delhi. I want Rashmi to sing. You can spare Bindu, I hurt her badly last time. I am really sorry.'

'Okay dear, you are welcome. What are you planning this time? Should I have an ambulance waiting?' Rekha asked teasingly.

'No, no nothing like that will happen this time. I want to have some fun with music. That's why I've specifically asked for Rashmi.

I've a very different reason for this visit. I'll tell you about it when we meet.'

When Kuttan reached the school before twilight dressed in a T-shirt and jeans, Rekha was surprised. She hadn't expected him to arrive so casually dressed after being sworn in as minister of state. Though he was only twenty-eight, he projected a very serious image in the media. Rashmi and Bindu, who had gone shopping to prepare for his visit, were not yet back. As per the rituals of the school, Rekha welcomed 'the most privileged guest' with a kiss. Without releasing her from his embrace Kuttan looked at her breasts. 'Girl, you are putting on weight. Unless you are careful you won't be in demand any more.'

Rekha cringed in embarrassment. He was right; despite rigorous exercise and a strict diet, she had put on two kilos in one year and expanded from 32-28-34 to 34-28-35. She joked, 'I'm young and still growing.' She poured red wine as he sank down on the sofa. His eyes took in her low-slung jeans and the red T-shirt emblazoned with the word 'Temptations' that ended three inches above the jeans.

'God! A navel barbell! These Kochi women are giving their counterparts in Bangalore and Mumbai competition when it comes to fashion.'

Rekha nodded in agreement, sashayed her way to the sofa with the wine glass in her hand, and sat down next to him. Kuttan touched her new ornament curiously.

'I got it on my last Mumbai trip. Ikka's birthday gift ... twelve small diamonds on the upper bead and a big one below. It cost him 27,000 rupees and the piercing was extra. Alian Angel, an American who was camping at the Taj, did the piercing for me. Her "rings of desire" is considered the best in the world of body piercing.'

He gently stroked it and drew a circle around it with his forefinger. 'Really beautiful ... but it must have been painful, like getting anti-rabies shots?'

'It's just like getting your ears pierced. Haven't you seen the small gun they use in jewellery stores to pierce your ears painlessly? It's used for navel piercing. It doesn't go very deep inside the skin. It's quite painful as it's a very sensitive area. They fix a medicated fake one at the time of the piercing. The original jewel is put in only a week later, after the wound has properly healed. No pleasure without pain. Is it Liberation as usual? Or do you want to go into the Body Lab?'

'My choice is always Liberation, but today I want Rashmi and you. Okay?'

She shook hands with him, saying, 'With pleasure.'

'Oh, there is something else—the reason I came here today in spite of being extremely busy. George from Kunnamkulam is my friend. He called me a couple of days ago. He said that two women had got his wife drunk and wormed out details of his family history that shouldn't have been divulged to outsiders. When he said that one of the women was a lecturer in a college in Kochi and the other a bank employee, I guessed it was you guys. What is your game?'

His question was unexpected. She faltered, but feigning nonchalance, replied, 'Oh, that was just for a research project on the history of Christianity in Kerala. George's wife Susannah was our classmate. We just met her for old time's sake. But unfortunately, all of us got drunk. I don't even remember what she told us. Tell him not to worry on that score.'

'He suspects there are other people behind this investigation. It is something involving rituals that have been observed for more than five hundred years, and a great deal of money is also at stake. Leave it alone, understand?'

'Oh, we have forgotten about it.' By this time Rashmi and Bindu were back. They too were dressed like Rekha, making it seem as if it were the School's uniform. Only the navel ring was missing. They had brought dinner from an expensive restaurant. Rekha took their bags and went inside.

'Hello, honourable minister! We were worried that your party conferences and inaugurations would make you late. We have practised some new numbers for you,' said Rashmi, shaking hands with him.

'Very good. My afternoon is free exclusively for the School.'

'Thank you, sir, thank you very much.'

When Bindu bent down to kiss him, he held her hands together and begged forgiveness for his naughtiness. Bindu showed him her wound.

'It's healed beautifully. I was only kidding because I was cut up with you for ignoring me on the flight. Your friend, the surgeon at Lakeshore Hospital, made sure that there will be no scar. I was in hospital for a week though, and as you had paid the bill online, we gave him a free appointment.'

'I didn't come here after that because I felt guilty. I was uncharacteristically violent that day as I was stressed about my political future after my dad passed away.'

'Hope you've shed your violence now and become a good boy.'

'How can that be, honey? I'm violent by nature.'

Rekha came in hurriedly.

'Let us begin quickly. He has to leave early in the morning. Music first then dinner and Liberation, okay?'

Kuttan took a pinch of smack from a secret nook of his purse, mixed it with tobacco, and started to smoke. Rekha played the guitar, and Bindu was on the drums. Rashmi stood ready to sing with the microphone in her hand. Each one of them took a puff of Kuttan's cigarette as they clinked their glasses of martini. Rashmi sang, 'Three cheers for our honourable minister.' The karaoke provided the background score. Everyone danced, and as the music ended Rashmi kissed Kuttan on both his cheeks. For many hours, music, dance, martini, and smack flowed. Rashmi started with Amy Winehouse's Grammy-winning 'Rehab' from the album *Back to*

Back, aping Winehouse's moves. Kuttan gave her another puff of his cigarette. As she said, 'Thank you', and pulled at it eagerly, Kuttan took the microphone from her and started singing 'Gasoline'. Then they sang songs by Sting, Papa Roach, Eminem, and Cheb Mami. Intoxicated with the mixture of smack and martini, they danced. Rashmi threw off her T-shirt, saying, 'Honourable minister, next is your item number.' Taking another puff, she sang 'Pain for Pleasure' by Sum 41.

> The seas have parted, the ending's started
> The sky has turned to black
> A killin' spree through eternity
> The devil stabs you in the back
> It's midnight now, you must escape somehow
> Torture is his leisure
> Don't try to hide, he'll make you subside
> As he exchanges pain for pleasure

Everyone joined Rashmi in the chorus. She sang again:

> Pain for pleasure
> (He's the hunter, you're the game!)
> Pain for pleasure
> (Satan is his name!)
> Watch out!

As the three of them again sang together, the veins on Kuttan's face tightened. Unable to control himself, he slapped Rashmi on both cheeks. When she refused to stop singing, he yelled 'You bitch,' and tried to strangle her. The karaoke continued playing as she gasped for breath. When Rekha and Bindu somehow pulled Kuttan away, Rashmi fell down. The music ended at the same moment. Rekha

and Bindu pulled her to her feet and took her to her room. Kuttan
continued to sip his martini, unperturbed.

When she felt Kuttan had become normal again, Bindu laid out
his favourite dishes—mussels, pork, and parottas—on the dining
table. She mixed four martinis. An exhausted Rashmi wiped her face
with a light green towel and came to sit near Kuttan. He asked her,
'If you are exhausted now. How will you manage the next session?'
and pinched her dimples.

It was Rekha who replied, 'We'll show you when it's time.'
They finished dinner quickly and went to change their clothes in
preparation for Liberation.

At the stroke of midnight, the door to Liberation was opened.
Kuttan entered in a suit and Rekha and Rashmi, dressed in star-
spangled black gowns, eyes lined with mascara, bowed him in. He
said, 'You are my slaves. You will not be free till morning.' He made
them stand on either side. Rekha and Rashmi were wearing dark
brown lipstick and had drawn crosses on either cheek with it.

Their perforated gowns revealed parts of the body that are usually
covered. The backs of their gowns had a picture of a huge spider. A
ray of light from an unspecified source fell on Rekha's navel barbell
and made it glitter. Rashmi had stuck a red rose on her navel. Slowly,
light suffused the entire room.

Rekha and Rashmi smilingly put their arms around Kuttan. 'Pain
for Pleasure' flowed from a hidden speaker. When Kuttan said,
'Today, we will play "butterfly and honeybee",' Rekha was shocked.
Though 'butterfly' was interesting, 'butterfly and honeybee' was a
difficult game to play. Even as Rekha stood hesitating, the whip
landed on her back. She climbed up on the granite table and lay
down, spreading her legs in the shape of the wings of a butterfly.

Rashmi was the honeybee. Kuttan commanded, 'You are not
an ordinary bee, you are a wild bee.' Rashmi got on the table and
sat with her knees crouched like a bee. 'Come on,' said Kuttan,

and Rashmi brought her hands together and started poking Rekha with her sharp pointed nails. When Rekha cried out, Kuttan would get excited and whip Rashmi harder. Bindu, who was carefully watching them from another room, turned up the volume of 'Pain for Pleasure'. The hourlong 'butterfly and honeybee' session ended when an exhausted Kuttan rolled a joint for a smoke. Bindu switched off the music. When Kuttan poured a glass of whisky each for the wounded Rekha and Rashmi, they thought that he had finished for the day. Suddenly, his demeanour changed as if he had remembered something. He swung the whip and commanded Rekha and Rashmi to stand in front of him. He brushed Rekha's cheek with his whip and stood staring at her. She stood looking at him bewildered. This was a new person, not the Kuttan who derived pleasure from their pain. Even when his violence had forced Bindu to go to a surgeon to get herself stitched up, his eyes hadn't been so cruel.

He threw the whip away and clutched Rekha's hair and slapped her across her face. Rekha felt the pain whizzing through her ears. Rashmi stood paralysed with fear.

'Tell me who is behind this?'

While Rekha stood stupefied, Rashmi asked him, 'Behind what?'

'Who is behind your investigations into Itty Cora?'

'We inquired because we got some information from the net,' Rekha tried to explain.

'You whore! Are you lying to me?' he roared, tearing her perforated gown and slapping her. 'I know you are lying to me. You and Scripter have been inquiring about Itty Cora. Tell me, who are you working for?'

Crying with pain and trying to ward off the whip, Rekha said, 'There is no one behind it.' He went on whipping Rekha and turned the lash on Rashmi, who tried to stop him. When he saw that the lashes had no effect, he threw the whip away and pulled at Rekha's navel barbell. She squirmed with pain like a fish on a hook, and pleaded with him to let her go. Rashmi fell at his feet.

Unable to bear the pain any longer, Rekha cried out, 'I'll tell you everything ... let me go,' folding her hands in supplication. Still he didn't let go of the barbell. Her navel was red and the skin about to tear. Her lipstick, mascara, and the crucifix on the cheek had spread over her face, mixing with sweat and tears. She told him all she knew about Itty Cora.

But he was not satisfied. 'The UTC (Ukroo, Tharu and Cora) group has several business enterprises including jewellery stores all over the world under the brand name "Rose"; it's worth crores. Ikka is trying to use you to create trouble for Rose as he is competing with the brand. That's why he gifted you the diamond navel barbell and the platinum waist chain.'

'No, I don't have such connections with Ikka. Like you, he is among the ten most privileged clients of the School. He comes here at times or invites us to Mumbai, just for pleasure.'

'But you must be acting for him, or else, why should you try to unearth Itty Cora's secrets and tarnish Rose's image by exposing it to the world?'

'We have no such intentions. Since Itty Cora is coming from the US, we went to Kunnamkulam to get some information.'

'The American Itty Cora is a fake. I'm sure.'

'Please believe me. I've saved all his mails. I'll show them to you.'

'I don't need any evidence. Why don't you just mind your own business? Why are you meddling in other people's lives? Now you know that it is not just Georgekutty's problem. If you don't give this up now, I'll kill all of you and throw your bodies into the sea.' Kuttan changed his clothes and left without even saying goodbye.

Rekha, Rashmi, and Bindu lay sleepless, crying in one another's arms. As they drifted into sleep in the morning, Rekha's phone woke them up to the sound of 'Cut My Life into Pieces'. It was a message from Kuttan.

'Hello! Madam Principal. Were you scared? Sorry. Forget everything that happened last night. I was only trying out mental torture on you guys, just an experiment. Georgekutty doesn't even know anything about this. Scripter told me about Itty Cora. You go ahead. I've transferred 2,50,000 rupees to your account as "school fees". Oh, and Rashmi sang very well. A navel barbell each for Rashmi and Bindu, a gift from me. Let them choose what they like. Get it pierced by someone who knows the job. I'm leaving by morning flight. Bye.'

The three of them were overcome with joy. Rekha texted her profuse gratitude to him.

Pouring whisky, Rekha said, 'I somehow felt he was tricking us.'

'Shut up! I saw you trembling with fear.' Rashmi switched on the karaoke and played the song,

Pain for pleasure, he is the hunter you're the game, Pain for pleasure, Satan is his name!

10
Itty Cora the Sailor

*Yes, I know, it's not the truth, but in a great history little truths
can be altered so that the greater truth emerges.*
— *Baudolino, Umberto Eco*

I WAS AT THE SCHOOL SHARING A DRINK WITH REKHA WHEN BENNY
rang me. He said, 'I'm in Kochi. I've come to deal with some legal
matters. I'll be free by evening. We must meet. I've got hold of a
book which mentions Itty Cora.'

I told him, 'We must meet. Give me a ring when you are free.'
Incurious, Rekha sipped her drink and leant back on the sofa. 'What
happened? You look depressed,' I said.

'It's nothing.'

'Then why did you take leave from college and ask me to meet
you? Tell me what the matter is.'

'Did you speak about Itty Cora to anyone else?'

'Not here, but I asked some people in Kunnamkulam about him. Why?'

'A problem has cropped up. Like you, our new minister of state, Kuttan, is one of our most "privileged" clients. He had taken an appointment yesterday. He always chooses "Liberation"; Rashmi and I were his hosts. As usual, he unleashed the most bestial torture on us. Once before, we had to admit Bindu to the hospital. Last night, it wasn't that bad. But he tortured us asking repeatedly why we were inquiring about Itty Cora. Georgekutty is his friend. He went back threatening to kill us if we continued to dig for information about Itty Cora. But in the morning, he sent a text from the airport saying that he was just experimenting mental torture on us. He said that it was you who had told him about our interest in Cora and he wished us luck. He has transferred 2,50,000 rupees to the School's account. But I feel there is something more to it. That's why I called you.'

'He lied to you. I don't know Kuttan. I've never spoken to him. But someone has told him of our interest in Itty Cora. The 18th Clan is fiercely secretive. Many of Kerala's prominent business enterprises belong to it. The huge amount of money they collect as tribute to Cora is their capital. They have shares in every sort of business ranging from liquor to gold. With legal and illegal business ventures, the Corappanam (Cora's money) in Kunnamkulam is like a parallel economy. Many of the big banks are dependent on this capital. Naturally, the clan has immense political influence.'

Rashmi walked in sleepily, smiling weakly at us. She sat down near Rekha.

'Hello! Where is the third partner of the triumvirate?'

'Bindu went out as usual in the morning. She has a show next month. Last night, it was Rekha and I who retired hurt. Bindu didn't have to enter the arena.' Rashmi tied up her hair and sipped from Rekha's glass. She asked, 'Are you saying it is serious?'

'Definitely. That is the conclusion I've come to, based on our inquiries. When we research Itty Cora, we don't just arrive at a history but a parallel culture that cannot be explained by science or logic—covert lives with Itty Cora as its icon. A secret icon whose secrets the clan will never allow to be exposed.'

'But we don't intend to expose its secrets.'

'Maybe not. But they are suspicious of our intentions.'

'Will there be more trouble?'

'Not immediately perhaps. Their plan must be to scare you and then watch you carefully. I was threatened when I began my inquiries in Kunnamkulam. When you got Susannah drunk, it rattled the clan. Susannah who is scared of Corappappan went to the First House of the 18th Clan to confess. They are now worried about what she must have revealed in her intoxicated state. It is only wise for us to stop our search for the time being.'

'Isn't that cowardice?'

'No, the 18th Clan is very powerful. We have to deal with them very carefully. In the pre-Independence era, a man called Porinju attempted to uncover the secrets of the 18th Clan. Like us, he too did a lot of research and finally wrote a book about it. Cora, who was an expert in astronomy, was known as "Nakshatra Cora"[3]. The book was titled *Nakshatra Cora alias Cora the Sailor* and was published in 1931 by Akshara Ratna Prakashini Press in Kunnamkulam. Though it was scheduled to be published on a Maundy Thursday, which was also Itty Cora's Memorial Day, it was not to be. Porinju was brutally murdered the previous night. Someone stabbed him at Thazhethepara. They broke open the publishing house and burnt all five hundred copies of the book. It was the first time something like this had happened at the ARP Press.

---

3   Cora of the Stars

'No one undertook to publish the book after this. Porinju had taken a copy home to proofread and his family preserved it secretly. That is the book Benny is bringing us.'

'That's great. Rashmi, shall we make Benny our honorary guest for the day?'

'Certainly, go and bring him, Scripter.'

When I returned with Benny in the evening, Rekha and Rashmi had freshened up for the guest. Rekha greeted Benny with a kiss, as per the School's ritual. Benny stood electrified. Rekha said, 'Welcome to the School', and led him to the sofa and sat down beside him.

'A school ... like this?' Benny looked about him incredulously. Comprehension slowly dawned on him, and he looked at Rekha knowingly. By then Rashmi had arrived with a drink for him. He gulped down the red wine and asked, 'Hadn't you come to Kunhipalu's house?'

Rekha nodded.

'That's created a real commotion. Susannah is under treatment for mental instability. I heard that she went to the First House and confessed her guilt to Corappappan. Well, let's not worry about it now. Hey! I've come with a special mix. Let's drink that... then, I'll give you the book and leave. Don't know whether they will like it. I'm in a bit of a hurry. Have to catch the Guruvayoor Passenger train. Have to open the shop in the morning.'

'First let's drink your special drink.'

Benny took a bottle of vodka, some limes, and a few green chilies out of his bag. Then he asked, 'Molu, do you have soda here? And bring some salt.' Rashmi brought soda, glasses, a knife, and a saltshaker on a tray. Benny poured a peg of vodka into of each of the glasses and topped it up with soda. Then he cut two limes into halves. He took a small bottle from his pocket and took some white paste from it and spread it over the lime. 'It's the essence of tobacco.

It will explode like fireworks inside your body.' He squeezed the lime into the glasses. 'This is nico chilly vodka. It might be a bit strong for women. But it is good, doesn't make you feel tired.'

As he took the glass in his hand, Benny turned serious. Speaking about his secret inquiries regarding Itty Cora he poured two more shots of the vodka.

'I was looking for information very discreetly. But these ladies spoilt it all. It's wiser to retreat for the time being.'

'Why?'

'It's dangerous. The money they have been collecting as Corappanam for the past five hundred years is not a small amount. If you calculate the interest and profit, I hear it'll amount to thousands of crores. We have to be careful in dealing with them. The 18th Clan cannot speak about Itty Cora in public. The Catholic Church is not prepared to admit that Itty Cora ever existed. It's complicated.'

'Why does the Catholic Church have a problem?'

'Well, Itty Cora had good connections in the Vatican too. But it is not a connection that can be spoken of in public. It was during the time of Pope Alexander VI. He was not the ideal candidate for papacy. Porinju described some of his activities in his book. Porinju wasn't killed because he had written about Itty Cora but because he had written about the Pope. But the copy we've got doesn't mention the Pope. It only outlines Itty Cora's life in Kerala. You read it. It's time for me to leave.'

Benny took the book out of the bag and prepared to leave. As I leafed through the book hurriedly, Rashmi went to drop Benny off at the station. Rekha and I started to read the book greedily. White ants had destroyed the first three pages and all the pages after the forty-third one. It was a yellowed book with the paper almost crumbling in our hands. The only part of the book in readable condition was from the second part of the first chapter to the fifth chapter. Yet we started reading joyfully as a door had finally opened up revealing the enigma that was Itty Cora

The flood of 1341 was a deluge. The afternoon sun was shining brightly on the day of the new moon in the month of *Edavam* when suddenly the rain clouds gathered, the sea turned turbulent, and there was continual rain for 18 days. Thunder, lightning, and strong billowing winds; nature was unleashing her turbulence. The water reached the altar of Arthaat Church. The sea entered even the Kunnamkulam market from Cheralyam. Trees were uprooted. Lanes turned into streams along which carcasses of dogs, cows, and buffaloes floated into the sea.

In Kunnamkulam, most of the shops and houses were destroyed. There were no business transactions for three weeks.

People died of fever and starvation. The cross at the junction in the market was covered with mud and stones. Cora's mansion at Aduputtikunnu built entirely of granite remained unscathed. Cora *mapla* sat on the parapet surrounding the atrium wrapped in a blanket, sipping toddy brewed from cumin seed. People who had lost their shops and houses had taken asylum in the nooks and corners of Aduputty mansion. Looking at the lashing rain that continued to pour unabated, they asked desolately, 'Cora mapla, do you think that Kunnamkulam market will be submerged in the sea?' Cora took another gulp of his drink.

'What nonsense! Arthaat Church and Kunnamkulam market under the sea? If that happens, it will be the end of the world.' On the eighteenth day, the rain stopped. The sea retreated as it had entered. The storm had spent itself, and the sun shone brightly. When the sea retreated, new masses of land emerged, Guruvayoor and Vypeen among them.

The harbour in Kodungalloor, Muziris, was the most affected. A new harbour came up in Kochi. The smaller ships and the catamarans disappeared from the Arthaat seashore. Cora mapla shifted his business to Ponnani. It was five generations later, in 1456, that Itty Cora—who later came to be known as *Nakshatra* Cora—was born. It was Nakshatra Cora who later became the Corappappan of Kunnamkulam.

We know very little about Itty Cora's childhood. It was at the age of eighteen when, he, along with his father, alighted from a ship on Ponnani beach with an Arab stallion that people noticed Cora mapla's son. On one of his business trips, his father had paid a hundred gold sovereigns for a Grecian beauty, who later became Itty Cora's mother. Once he got her, Cora wound up his business trip, and on the return journey that took twenty-one days and nights, he did not allow her to sleep at all. The exhausted girl was brought to Adupputty mansion in a palanquin. When she entered the house as the fourteenth woman of the forty-five-year-old Cora, she had not yet turned sixteen. Having conceived on the ship, she gave birth to Itty Cora on a Christmas night seven months after she reached Kunnamkulam. She died before daybreak, owing to excessive bleeding. She was interred according to Grecian rituals in a specially prepared ground behind the mansion.

Itty Cora's father, who recognized the intelligence of his young son, took him along on one of his business trips and had him educated somewhere abroad. It was the *Zamorin* Itty Cora first challenged when he returned after mastering seven languages, mathematics, and astronomy. The third *Kettilamma* of Padinnjare Kovilakam and her daughter, whose hand had been promised in marriage to

the younger thampuran of Nilambur, were on their way
to Guruvayur temple. It was afternoon by the time they
reached Kadavaloor. They were in a hurry to reach the
temple before twilight. The mother and daughter were in
a palanquin. Twenty Nair warriors accompanied them. The
Nair commander Padakuruppu and his assistants made
up the entourage. Itty Cora and his friends were galloping
across the terrain on horseback and saw them. Though he
knew that someone important was approaching, Itty Cora
made no effort to alight from his horse or to move out of
their way. Even as Padakuruppu and his band tried to stall
him with their swords, his horse reached the palanquin.
'Who is the invalid being carried in a palanquin?' he asked

'The *thamburatimaar* are on their way to Guruvayoor.
Do not defile them.'

'Are they going to see God after committing the sin of
making you carry them in the palanquin?'

By this time, more of Itty Cora's friends had arrived
on the scene. Someone whispered in Padakuruppu's ear,
'This is Adupputty mapla's son.' He felt a twinge of fear as
Adupputty controlled the area stretching from Chalisserry to
Arthaat. They were tradesmen who would stop at nothing.
If the Christian touched and defiled the thamburattimaar,
they would be considered dead by their family. They would
be baptized and converted to Christianity. If anything
happened to the thamburatty and her daughter who was
about to be married, Padakuruppu was sure his head would
roll. He sought an escape route.

'We are the Calicut Zamorin's men, your father is close
to us. Don't create trouble.'

The *Kettilamma,* the Zamorin's consort, parted the
curtains of the palanquin and looked out to see who was

making all the noise. The daughter, not knowing what was happening, looked at the handsome youth on horseback and whispered in her mother's ear, 'What a beautiful horse!' Itty Cora heard her voice. He was determined to see her. He would take her if she were beautiful; otherwise, he would let her go.

'This is Kunnamkulam. Cora Country. Our word is law here: even the Zamorin or the King of Kochi will have to obey our commands. Let the princess alight and take a couple of steps. If she finds it impossible to walk, she can go back to her palanquin.'

Left without a choice, the mother and daughter got down from the palanquin. The Kettilamma was around forty years old; the daughter was seventeen or eighteen. Even though she had covered her breasts with a gold-edged cloth and draped a silk shawl over it, the green emeralds glittering in her necklace were visible. The Kettilama was wearing a long chain made of corals and pearls and a thick bangle on her wrist. Jasmine flowers adorned their hair. Though the mother was a bit thin, the daughter was a beautiful, healthy girl. Her heavy derriere caught Itty Cora's attention. As they walked, stumbling on the stones on the road, Itty Cora urged his horse forward. The soldiers, the palanquin bearers, and Itty Cora's friends followed him. After walking a while, the daughter lifted her face to look at Itty Cora.

'You have made us walk, but you are on horseback. Isn't it a sin to trouble that poor animal?'

Itty Cora had not expected such a smart retort. 'Clever! Let her be my first woman in my country,' thought Cora and jumped down from the horse. Though it was the first time he was abducting a woman, he showed no sign of nervousness, and the presence of his followers added to his courage.

'I'm not going to sin alone. I'm taking you with me.' Saying this, he lifted her on to his horse. She started crying loudly. While Itty Cora's followers stopped Kurup and his warriors, who tried to intervene, the Kettilamma stood watching helplessly. 'You get into the palanquin and proceed slowly. By the time you reach Arthaat, I'll return your daughter after making her sin a while,' Itty Cora said and jumped onto his horse. Before riding off he added, 'If you speak of this to anyone, you will not return to Kunnamkulam alive.'

He held the frightened thamburatty tightly with his left hand and loosened the reins. His hands were just below the cloth covering her breasts, a little above her stomach. Forsaking her pride in her royal birth, the thamburatty started pleading with him to let her go. Unheeding, Itty Cora kept riding on. Though she tried to distance her body from Itty Cora's, the moment the horse took a step forward she fell against him. 'It's your first time on a horse. If you aren't careful, you will be thrown off.' Itty Cora raised his left hand a bit more and held her tightly against him. She was almost gasping for breath in his grip. As the horse galloped forward leaving the Kettilamma and their entourage far behind, she knew that she had been truly abducted and sat speechless with fear.

'What is your name?'

'Chi-ru-theyi,' she stuttered. Her silk shawl and jasmine flowers had been lost in the flurry of seating her on the horse. The cloth covering her breasts lay loose on one side. As the horse galloped forward, the cloth meant to cover her breasts and her curly hair billowed in the wind.

When he felt that she would manage to stay on the horse
without falling, Itty Cora loosened his grip. In the relief
she felt, she unconsciously leaned back. Feeling that
her fear had abated a bit, Itty Cora planted a kiss behind
her neck.

'Don't be scared. I won't hurt you. I'll just kiss you like
this whenever I like.' Her heartbeat returned to normal.
A soft kiss, a loving voice; he might not be as cruel as she
had feared. Maybe he was a good man. It was no use crying
now. Once touched by a mapla, she knew that she couldn't
go back to the palace or her old way of life. 'Luckily, he
does not seem a bad person.' Comforting herself with the
thought that even the Zamorin was not as wealthy as the
Aduputtys, she hesitantly placed her right hand on his left.
He responded to her action by pulling her closer. Within
minutes they passed Perumbilavu and Parembedam and
reached a godown in Thazhathepara in Kunnamkulam.
When he got down from the horse with a woman, the
workers realized what was happening. They opened the
room on the left that was used for storing pepper and lit a
lamp. With dishevelled clothes and tousled hair, Chirutheyi
entered the room. She walked towards Cora with her head
bowed low. The room filled with dust and spices glowed
in the dim light of the oil lamp. Cora sat her down upon a
couple of sacks filled with pepper.

'We are pepper merchants. It will be hot.' Chirutheyi
put her head on her knees and sat silently. As if following a
ritual, Itty Cora started to plant light kisses from the big toe
of her right foot upwards, releasing her from the clutches
of fear. After a while, she stretched her legs, raised herself
on her elbows, and leant backwards, a strange intoxication
seeping inside her. Before Itty Cora could complete the first

half of his rituals, unable to bear the pleasure, she pulled him towards her. A storm ensued. Somewhere in between when he asked, 'Shouldn't I take you back?' she replied resting her head against his chest, 'No I will never be able to go back.' As evening came, he rose silently and left. Fatigued, Chirutheyi fell back on the sacks.

She remembered the advice her mother and aunt had given her on the night before her engagement. She had become engaged to the Nilambur Melatoor Elamura thamburan when she had turned thirteen. When her mother had insisted that the marriage be conducted only after she attained puberty, they had agreed half-heartedly. Unfortunately, last year in the month of Chingam, the ruler of Nilambur had attacked Melatoor, beheaded the young thamburan who had surrendered, and annexed Melatoor to Nilambur. This meant that the girl affianced to the dead thamburan now belonged to the Nilambur prince. When he came to her kovilakam and demanded to see the girl, her mother dressed her up and sent her to him. He exclaimed, 'Beautiful! We shall get married on the next auspicious day.' She nodded and went back.

'Tomorrow onwards the young prince, Cheriyambran, is your master,' her aunt had told her. 'The women of this kovilakam are always loyal to the master. To whoever is the master. When local rulers like the Konathiri, Koltathiri, or the Zamorin fight battles, the women always belong to the victor. When the Zamorin captured the Kolathiri I happily left him and went off with the Zamorin, though the Kolathiri had taken good care of me for seven years. You are in the same situation. Don't worry. Always be in the arms of the powerful. Power doesn't mean physical power; it is authority that bestows power. You're lucky that next to the

Zamorin, the Nilambur thamburan, is the most powerful man in the land.

'Whenever the new master asks you to open the inner temple for puja you should oblige. If he understands the power of the deity inside the temple, he will be punctual in conducting puja. It's not enough to have a temple. Daily rituals are a must. These men have many temples to pray at. You must make him aware that the deity in your temple is very powerful. That is up to you. Then it won't be merely the nightly *Athazhapuja* that will be performed but also the morning *Ushapuja* and the *Uchapuja* at noon. Every day will be a celebration. The *Pallivetta* ritual that commences the festival and the *Aarattu* which marks its end will be grand. Wonder how long *cheriya* thamburan will be able to manage all this.'

She smiled at how cleverly her aunt had explained the sexual act that was never openly spoken about. The thamburan, like Padakuruppu and the soldiers he had sent along for security, would only have been able to watch helplessly today. Though he was the younger thamburan, he was already seventy. She thought of what had happened when he tried to break tradition and entered her room after their engagement. To use her aunt's language, even after trying for two hours, he was unable to lift the flagpole and had given up, panting. The festival can begin only after the flag is hoisted. He disappeared, saying that everything would happen only after the wedding as per tradition. To establish his proprietorship over her he had showered her with regular gifts of silk, gold, and money and sent his soldiers to escort them, but he had never made another attempt to break tradition and enter the sanctum sanctorum. He had been delaying the ritualistic opening of the temple for a year and a half, saying that there wasn't an auspicious moment suitable for the marriage. Finally, it was a Christian who was destined to perform the puja. The first puja had been grand.

As she lay thinking, Itty Cora came back. She became aware of his presence when he lit the lamp. She got up obediently. He had brought her food and clothes.

'I spoke to my father. He said to convert you to Christianity if you had no objections and to marry you. If you have a problem with that, he said you could stay in the outhouse of Iyyala. What do you want to do?'

'Do whatever you like ... as long as the daily puja is performed.'

She realized that her aunt's language had betrayed her. She laughed silently at the gaffe and smiled naughtily at Itty Cora. He did not catch the pun and just said, 'It's the outhouse then. There you can have your daily pujas.' She nodded. From next day, Chirutheyi took her place at the Iyyala outhouse as the *Kotha* of Iyyala. Itty Cora's father sent a letter written on a palm leaf to her kovilakam: 'My son has brought a woman from the kovilakam. We will take care of her.'

11
The Kotha of Iyyala

*Which voluptuous damsel has captivated you and entered your
mind? Who is she who refuses to succumb to your lures as she is
chaste? Who is she you wish to lock you in her embrace?*
— *Kumara Sambhavam*, Kalidasan

BY THE TIME REKHA AND I FINISHED READING THE FIRST CHAPTER OF
Nakshatra Cora, Rashmi had returned after dropping Benny off
at the station. The three of us together started the second chapter
entitled 'The Kotha of Iyyala'.

Four miles from Kunnamkulam to the south, beyond the
fields of Chovannur, lay Iyyala. You could see Iyyala from
atop Adupputty mansion. The fields of Iyyala that yielded
three hundred measures of rice were the biggest stretch of
arable land owned by the Coras. The fields of Choondal,
Chavanoor, and Parambedam were not as large. Itty Cora's

forefathers had cleared the forest of Koombuzhakkara and turned it into paddy fields. South of Iyyala were the Kadongode forests.

Iyyala, which had a huge population of deer and panthers, had been so named by Itty Cora's father. Once, when he had gone to Israel for trade, he had seen a fertile stretch of land called Iyyal. In Hebrew the word *iyyal* means deer. Cora mapla liked venison and doe-eyed women. There was always such a woman in the outhouse that was used to store grain. Though he used her occasionally for his pleasure, she had complete freedom. She would receive guests with venison and liquor brewed from bran.

The Iyyala outhouse was lying empty, as Unnooly, Cora's woman, had drowned in Koompuzha while bathing. So, Itty Cora had brought Chirutheyi to Iyyala.

The Iyyala outhouse lay north-south of the fields: a barn big enough for four or five cows and their calves, on the left was a granary that could store bran, coconut, pepper and other produce, and in between was a sixty-four-square-foot house with two floors. This house, known as *Corappera,* had a roof of straw and beams made out of timber from the jackfruit tree. On the ground floor were a large sitting room, bedroom, granary, and kitchen. When you climbed the staircase and reached the upper floor on the west side, there was a fully open verandah 181/2 feet long called the *randha* and a beautifully decorated bedroom next to it. Below, in the room on the west, lived Chakkappayi, who looked after the granary. Chirutheyi used the bedroom downstairs when she was alone and the one upstairs when she entertained guests.

Once he brought Chirutheyi to Iyyala, Itty Cora's life changed completely. People who till then had treated him like a child started addressing him respectfully. His father entrusted him with the responsibility of the Ponnani godown. As he was extremely intelligent and could speak six to seven languages, the Arabs and Chinese came in search of him. He took only a legitimate profit, and so his reputation as an honest and intelligent merchant spread far and wide. Even people in far-off places like Kozhikode and Kochi believed that Cora would never cheat. Very soon, Itty Cora started managing their businesses in Kerala when his father travelled across the seas for trade.

When his father was in town, Itty Cora would first go to the mansion after closing shop to settle the day's accounts with him. After this, he would go to the granary. Sometimes, he would have dinner with his father or at least drink a glass of home-brewed liquor with him. His father would send him to the granary saying, 'She must have cooked dinner for you, go.' But he reminded his son that she was a woman who had to be shared with others and warned him not to grow too attached to her. For the Coras, a woman was a commodity like everything else. They would use her to the full when she was with them, and if they got a good price for her, she would be sold outright or rented out to those who wanted her. Though it was more profitable to sell a woman, they preferred to use her in the wily games that lay behind their business transactions. His father advised Itty Cora to prepare Chirutheyi for all this. But Itty Cora had a soft corner for Chirutheyi and could not bring himself to do so. Finally, when the father realized that his son was incapable of informing Chirutheyi of her position in the Cora household, he took matters into his own hands.

Once, when Itty Cora came to the mansion in the evening, his father was not there. He was told that his father had gone to the Iyyala granary and that he shouldn't go there himself. He spent a sleepless night. He was overcome with mixed emotions of sorrow and anger when he thought about Chirutheyi. Trying to convince himself that he was a merchant by birth and profession and that everything must be bought and sold, he somehow got through the night. Even when he left for Ponnani the next morning, his father had not returned from Iyyala. At the godown, Itty Cora's mind was disturbed. He quickly returned, entrusting everything to the newly appointed accountant Neelakandan Namboodiri. For the first time he went to Iyyala without going to the mansion first.

Though Chakkappayi at the main entrance told him that everything was all right, he was comforted only when he saw Chirutheyi's smiling face. Still, he fumbled for words, not knowing what to ask her. She greeted Itty Cora, 'You rushed home worried, didn't you? Don't be upset. There are no problems here,' and took him upstairs. The minute he sat in the veranda, he asked her.

'Appan?'

'He just left. He came here suddenly last evening. In the morning two women from the mansion had come here to explain the situation to me. As soon as he entered he asked me: "They have told you everything. Do you have any objections?"

'"What is the use of objecting after everything has been decided?" I answered. Then, without speaking any more, he took Chakkappayi and went to the forest. He came back at midnight with venison. "How am I supposed to know how to cook meat?" I asked. Chakkappayi did the cooking.

When I went outside with the venison and liquor brewed
from bran, your father was there. A fire was burning brightly
in the middle of the yard, and people wrapped in black and
red blankets sat around. As soon as they saw me, they got
up and Appan made me stand in front of them. Someone
came and took the food and drink from my hands. Appan
put a piece of meat in my mouth. As I somehow chewed
it down, he mixed the liquor with water and gulped down
most of it, pouring the rest down my throat. You know I
am not used to it. I tasted liquor only after coming here,
it has a sour taste. As I gulped it down and turned my face
away in distaste, Appan pushed me, saying, "They are going
to transform you into Kotha." I fell headlong into the fire
but didn't get burnt. Some people lifted me and swung me
up and down in their arms. The others beat an instrument
like the chenda and loudly chanted, "Iyyala Kotha—Cora's
woman—the country's woman". Then they said, "Cora
mapla! We will transform her into Iyyala Kotha and return
her to you before dawn." They blindfolded me and took me
somewhere deep inside the forest.

'When they took off the blindfold I was lying inside a
cave and was surrounded by people holding torches. Some
people were standing around me, talking. An old man and a
woman sat on either side of me and tattooed me. Look here!
These intertwined serpents around my navel. Then they
made me stand in the centre and sang in chorus:

"'Namboodiri, Nair, Pattar, or Thamburan, we have
made this girl Kotha.

Wiped off the sandalwood and vermillion from her
forehead
Removed gold and corals from her ears, neck, and waist

Removed her breast cloth, waistcloth, and undercloth
Anointed her with gingelly oil
Smeared her face and body with turmeric
Bathed her at midnight in the Koomba river
Dried her hair and adorned it with forest flowers
Decorated her eyes, cheeks, and breasts
with the *kohl* of the Mountain Gods
Poured wild honey in her cleavage
Wafted fumes of burnt herbs to her nostrils
Intoxicated her with liquor brewed at night from bran
Fed her with mutton, beef, and venison
Six lashes on her behind and a hundred kisses to cure her
of fear and shame
Beaten her with a broom to make her part her arms and
legs without shame
Tattooed her with twin serpents on her navel and taught
her the skills to defeat any man with her waist
We have made her the Kotha.

'After doing everything their song described, they brought
me back much before dawn. Appan was waiting outside. I
had lost my fear and shame as soon as I had become the
Kotha. As I entered, Appan placed his hands on my head
and thrice called out: "Iyyala Kotha." After the third call, he
hugged me and took me to the room upstairs. He went back
just a while ago. I am his sixth Kotha.'

'Are you upset?'

'Well, I've to say that I am, a bit. But it's all right. I've
anyway lost my roots and the status my birth gave me. If
we live with each other, both of us will get fed up after a
while. That will not happen to a Kotha. We can be together

whenever we want, but if we like someone else then it won't be a problem. This will reduce our selfishness.'

Itty Cora gained fame in areas other than trade. People who heard of his expertise in mathematics, astronomy, and foreign languages came to see him. If some came to learn new things, others came to test him. Cora scoffed at and mocked those who came to test his knowledge. Once, when Itty Cora arrived at the mansion after closing his shop, Panikker from Parappanat, who acted on behalf of the Zamorin, was there, concluding a deal on pepper by handing over the advance,

'Your son? Heard that he is quite learned. I've just completed a deal on a hundred carts of pepper with your father and taken sixteen and a half quarters as advance. Can you tell me how much gold and silver I have in my purse?'

Though he did not like to be tested in this fashion, Itty Cora answered. 'Those who are lazy often find their pockets barren.' Panikker, who was known for his slothful nature, was hurt.

He asked, 'Are you mocking me?'

'You open the money packet, let us see.'

When Panikker opened the packet hanging on his waist, it was empty. As he stood with bulging eyes, Itty Cora comforted him, 'Close it and open it again.' Panicker did as directed.

'Seventeen gold sovereigns and a hundred and eight silver coins, right?' Panikker counted the coins and nodded in agreement. 'The feeling that you have money is more important than possessing money. If you feel that you don't have money, then there is no money. Even if the money is before your eyes, you will not see it. Calculation is just a trick. If you were really seeking information, I wouldn't mind answering. Why do you want to test me by asking me things which you already know?'

'Forgive me. I questioned you thinking you were still a boy. I should be your disciple.'

'No, this master-disciple relationship is peculiar to your culture. We merchants only sell, whether it is rice or knowledge.' Saying this, Itty Cora went in.

'Mapla, how lucky you are to have such a son! To be so knowledgeable at the age of twenty is indeed great. Anyway, Chirutheyi has reached a good place. Where is she now?'

'She is now the Kotha of Iyyala.'

'Great! She is skilled in song and dance. She will be a great success.'

The news that Chirutheyi was now the Kotha of Iyyala spread far and wide. Although her mother bewailed the fact that her daughter had become a whore, all the men in the land were eager to meet her. When Cora mapla started entertaining his overseas business partners and the royalty at Iyyala, Chirutheyi lost her shyness and gained experience. When Punnathoor *Ettan* Raja, the senior prince, hearing of her skill in music, dance, and poetry came to Iyyala and stayed there for two days, Chirutheyi's fame skyrocketed. Punnathoor thamburan was the first guest Itty Cora invited to Iyyala. Chirutheyi lit the lamp and invited the thamburan to enter. She put a tender coconut and a betel box before him and stepped back respectfully. The thamburan's gaze wandered all over her body and he thought to himself, 'Not bad, as good as the descriptions that had reached me.'

'Heard you are from a royal family?' he inquired.

'A Kotha doesn't have any relatives. I have only this granary. Consider me a low-born woman. You shouldn't bother about the ancestry of a *sannyasini.*'

'Do you mean that what you are doing is penance?'

'Of course. To make a different God appear before me each day!'

'Has anyone more powerful than I appeared before you?'

'How can I judge your strength before the duel begins? To arrive in armour doesn't prove your might.'

'You are outspoken. I'll cure you of that.' As the thamburan's eyes travelled over her body, Chirutheyi challenged him with a gesture. The thamburan put down the tender coconut that he had lifted to his lips. 'I haven't come so far to drink this.'

'Then let's go upstairs. I'll give you freshly brewed liquor and bran water.'

As Chirutheyi climbed the stairs, the thamburan got an eyeful of her abundance. Though he tried to control himself, his disobedient hand landed on her behind. She said, 'Don't be in such a hurry.' The shamefaced thamburan followed with his head lowered. Chirutheyi took him straight to the bedroom, seated him on the bed covered with silk, and gave him a goblet of liquor. He ignored the liquor and pulled her towards him. Though she pretended to struggle to free herself, she remained firmly in his grasp. She raised the goblet to his lips.

Drinking it in one gulp, the thamburan looked at her greedily. 'Can't control yourself, can you?' Chirutheyi asked.

'That's true. I've heard so much about you. My poison sac has been filling itself since then. Now the venom has inflamed my body and I can't bear to wait any longer.'

'Are you Thakshak, the snake king?'

'Not just Thakshak but a scorpion too. The poison has entered not just my head but also my body.'

'So don't delay the bite.'

The thamburan lost his venom after a couple of bites and slipped into a tired sleep. The next morning, he woke up and drank the rice gruel she gave him. As he relaxed

in the armchair on the veranda, Chirutheyi offered him a
betel leaf smeared with lime. The thamburan put it into his
mouth and stroked her shoulders.

'You are smart.'

'Did you doubt it?'

'No, not at all. I have just seen how smart you are. Itty
Cora told me that you are interested in poetry. I'd like to
hear you recite *Megha Sandesham*.'

'I was right last night when I said you have no sense of
discretion. Is *Megha Sandesham* suitable for this occasion?
You should listen to it when you are away from me and
think about me.'

'Then recite *Kumara Sambhavam*. That is ideal.'

'But don't imagine that *Kumara Sambhavam* has
happened. I took enough precautions before entering the
arena.' Chirutheyi recited the eighth sargam of *Kumara
Sambhavam*.

'He wasn't satiated with the copulation with Parvathi;
whose hair lay untied, sandalwood paste wiped out, sporting
disorderly nail marks on her body, and whose waist chain lay
broken.'

She gave a knowing glance and smiled mischievously.
The thamburan, who guessed her meaning, responded with
another sloka.

'When the rows of stars started fading, he felt sympathy
for his beloved; held her close to his chest and tried to close
his eyes.'

'Are you satisfied now?'

'Well, I'm satisfied but I don't think you are at peace.'

'No. I'm happy.'

After Punathoor thamburan's visit the scholars, singers,
and peers of the realm started frequenting Iyyala. Even while

entertaining her guests with song, dance, and literature, the Kotha managed the farm efficiently. She made Chakkappayi and the hundreds of labourers work hard. The cellars were always filled with bran, coconut, and pepper. As each of Itty Cora's ships dropped anchor at Ponnani, Chirutheyi would send out oxcarts laden with pepper from Iyyala.

The third year after Chirutheyi arrived at Iyyala, Itty Cora's father passed away. Itty Cora took over the business empire. He would return from foreign lands after six or seven months of travel. Then he would remain in town for four to five months. Even during this time, he would have to travel to Kochi, Kozhikode, and Madurai for trade. He would frequently go to the Iyyala house and participate in Chirutheyi's cultural gatherings. When Itty Cora spoke about Greek, Latin, and Arabic, literature those who knew only Sanskrit would listen in wide-eyed wonder. Once, when Itty Cora played a three-stringed violin that he had brought from Rome, Achutha Poduval, a renowned musician from Kochi, exclaimed, 'What is this wonder that is greater than the human voice?'

Itty Cora gave Poduval the violin saying, 'It's not that wonderful. In Rome, they are trying to make four-stringed violins.'

During that time in Tirur there lived Ezhuthachan, a poet. Itty Cora thought highly of him. Ezhuthachan reciprocated the feeling. Each time Cora came back from his travels he would invite Ezhuthachan to Iyyala. He was translating some books from Sanskrit to Malayalam. So when Cora spoke of similar Greek texts, he would listen with great interest. 'This sounds similar to our Vyasan?'

'Undoubtedly every country has a poet and the Gods they have created are in many ways similar to ours. If you really think about it deeply and do some calculations, they are all the same.'

'So, what about this Ram and Lanka?'

'I don't know about Ram, but I've seen Lanka. There aren't any demons there. Just people like us, though a bit darker. If you travel further east, you will see darker-skinned people. If you circumnavigate the seas and reach Babylon or Rome the people are whiter than anything we have seen. Everyone has their own gods and rituals. Nobody is completely right or wrong.'

Itty Cora was a bit disapproving of the fact that Ezhuthachan merely translated and did not write anything of his own. Once, he asked him, 'Instead of translating the writings of Namboodiris, why don't you write something yourself?'

Ezhuthachan smilingly replied, 'I translate to free these texts from the clutches of the Namboodiris, not to serve them. Shouldn't people who don't know Sanskrit be allowed to read these texts?' Later, Ezhuthachan wrote texts of his own.

When Itty Cora disappeared in the high seas after being defeated by the Portuguese, the authority of Adupputty mansion ended, though it is said that Iyyala Kotha and the granary lasted two more centuries. But no succeeding Kotha could match up to Chirutheyi.

12

The Black Pearl

I am black on the outside, clad in a wrinkled cover,
Yet within I bear a burning marrow.
I season delicacies, the banquets of kings, and the luxuries of
the table.
Both the sauces and the tenderized meats of the kitchen. But you
will find in me no quality of any worth,
Unless your bowels have been rattled by my gleaming marrow.
— A riddle of Saint Aldhelm

BY THE TIME I HAD FINISHED READING THE SECOND CHAPTER OF
Nakshathra Cora the chilly vodka had started burning inside me.
When Rashmi said, 'Why don't we take a break and eat something?'
we agreed. As Rashmi served us porotta and chicken, I noticed
the red weals on her neck. When she caught me looking, she said,
'This is the handiwork of our honourable minister. I had a narrow
escape because Rekha and Bindu pulled me away.'

'Madam Principal, you must lay down some safety rules for this game and the clients must strictly comply with them. Why do you take such risks?

'Scripter, we do have clear rules in the School but when people like Kuttan break them, there is nothing we can do. It is because of his protection that the police don't meddle with us.'

As I could not give them such protection, I did not say anything more. Finishing our meal quickly, we started reading the third chapter entitled 'The Black Pearl'.

It was from Itty Cora's time onwards that the pepper and ginger that grew in the forests of Kadangode began to be traded all over the country. Some planted large trees and grew pepper vines on them. When people were assured that pepper would always fetch a good price at Itty Cora's godowns, ox carts laden with pepper from different parts of the country started making their way towards Kunnamkulam. During those days, first-quality pepper would fetch ten sovereigns of gold per cart in Kunnamkulam. This pepper, picked and dried, would be filled in sacks to be sold in foreign lands. If Arabs or the Chinese happened to visit, they too would buy pepper. As he was close to the *Marikkar* of Ponnani, who commandeered the Zamorin's fleet of ships, Itty Cora's cargo-laden ships did not face any hurdles while setting off from the harbour.

Till Itty Cora came on the scene, the Arabs and the Chinese had a monopoly on the pepper trade of Malabar. The sea journey Cora's father made once a year to trade pepper was nothing in comparison with the trade carried out by the Arabs and Chinese. Though Cora's father, who had travelled up to the Roman Empire, was a good merchant, he was not very smart at the game of numbers and in handling different languages. Realizing his shortcomings, he had sent his son abroad for education. Itty Cora, who took over the business after his father's death, started putting to good use the knowledge he had acquired.

Realizing the possibilities of the pepper trade, he decided to expand his business. His first step was to increase the production of pepper in the country. He started large-scale pepper cultivation in the lands under his control. He brought the Parayas and the Malayars who formed the majority of the population into the pepper trade. All help was given to them from Aduputty mansion. Kandan Koran of Kattakamba was given complete responsibility of pepper cultivation.

Itty Cora called Kandan Koran 'The Black Pearl'. Kandan Koran was one of his closest friends, a friend from the days before Cora's father sent him abroad for higher education.

When Itty Cora took over the business he entrusted Kandan Koran with the pepper cultivation, and within two or three years Cora's godowns started overflowing with pepper. The households in Kunnamkulam sold him 1,000 measures of pepper a year. Itty Cora gave them a good price for it.

It spelt the resurrection of Kunnamkulam after the floods of 1341. Kunnamkulam grew as an important centre for business during Itty Cora's time. Itty Cora rebuilt all the churches and cupolas including Arthaat Church that had been destroyed in the floods. Though he helped the church and the priests in any way he could, he believed that he could deal with God directly without the mediation of either.

Kunnamkulam's development under the leadership of Itty Cora was peculiar as, contrary to the usual practice, the Parayas, Mulayars, and Cherumas also benefited. Earlier,

they had to eke out a living as landless labourers but they
now started earning well. With the money they made by
selling pepper to Itty Cora's godowns, they started to live
well. Itty Cora took the healthy young men from among
them on his ships. They came back with their purses full of
money and walked boldly through Kunnamkulam market.

The Cherumas who had lived like slaves to the
Thampurans, Nairs, and Namboodiris became Cora's men.
Itty Cora taught them that they did not need to fear anybody
as long as they could work. The aristocrats and bourgeoisie
started fearing them. The high born cautioned one another:
'He's Cora's man, careful.' Their women, wearing bright red
sarees, their hair decked with flowers, started coming to the
market to buy vermilion, *kohl,* and fragrant betel leaves.
No aristocrat dared lay a hand on them. But if Itty Cora
fancied any of them, he just had to inform Kandan Koran.
They would happily come to his room that night. They
considered it lucky to be fancied by Itty Cora, and even
luckier to bear his child. Out of the seventy-nine children
Itty Cora fathered, at least four or five were from among the
lower castes.

When the people became rich, the business enterprises
of the Christians in Kunnamkulam grew. Very soon,
Kunnamkulam became the biggest business centre between
the cities of Kozhikode and Kochi. New shops opened in
Parayil market. Varied commodities, from silks and tobacco
to gold, silver, and women, flowed to Kunnamkulam
businesses on their own. When they couldn't find a place to
open a shop, they used the front verandas of their houses.
Their women too entered the business world. People who
came from different parts of the land with their ox carts
laden with pepper filled their carts with the fare sold at
Kunnamkulam to sell back home.

As the production of pepper increased, Itty Cora needed more ships to transport it to foreign shores. His father had only had three ships. Itty Cora cut down good timber from the Machat hills in Kumbidikkadavu and constructed a permanent ship-building site. He appointed Cheralayam Thupran as the head carpenter and twenty carpenters to assist him.

Thupran's accurate calculations produced two-storeyed ships that were 56.5 measures long, 12.5 measures wide, and 8.5 measures high. The portion below was used to store heavy goods. When the ship was loaded with 120 measures of pepper, other cargo, food required for four months, and the oarsmen, it would sink down 5.5 measures in the water. The masts were tied to teak pillars on the upper storey. They could be retied according to the direction of the wind. There would always be oarsmen at the 24 oars placed on either side of the ship. The big room on the upper storey was the captain's room. There were four to five smaller rooms for the more important members of the crew and the slave women. Itty Cora's ships, quite unlike the Chinese ships that dropped anchor at Ponanni harbour, were more like those of the Portuguese that were built to withstand powerful waves and could be put to sea even in the most adverse weather conditions.

It was Itty Cora himself who provided Thupran with the model for these ships. Itty Cora was particular about employing only smart and hardworking people on his ships. It was impossible to manage trade with his fleet based on the pattern followed by his father, who had owned just three ships. Each group of tradesmen needed a captain, sailors, and labourers. It was Hydrose, who belonged to the family of the Zamorin's admiral Kunhali Marikar, who helped Itty

Cora. On Itty Cora's first journey, Hydrose was the second mate. Hydrose boarded the ship arrogantly believing that Cora, a mere boy, knew nothing about sailing. He got a taste of Cora's expertise the first night itself. When Hydrose and his assistants rowed blindly in the dark, Itty Cora guided them with the help of the stars. Till then, Hydrose had been ignorant about using stars to navigate. Itty Cora had tablets filled with information that Hydrose had never known existed. Hydrose believed that Itty Cora, who calmly gave directions while sailing on turbulent seas and who could speak the language of whichever land they reached, possessed supernatural powers. It was the tales that Hydrose spread about Itty Cora that earned him the name 'Nakshatra Cora'. Within two or three years, Itty Cora became the king of the pepper trade in Malabar. While the Zamorin merely had two or three ships, Itty Cora had two fleets with a total of eighteen ships that sailed the high seas. Each fleet was divided into two groups, with five and four ships each. They alternately set sail from Ponnani to foreign lands. Each fleet would return only after five or six months. Once it returned, repair work, reloading the ship with cargo, and setting sail depending on favourable weather conditions would take four or five months. When one fleet returned, the other would set sail. Even though one group was commanded by Itty Cora, two by his brothers Ukru and Tharu, and the fourth one by his closest friend Veliyankat Bapu, all the ships were owned by Itty Cora.

Itty Cora's ship was named Chai, written in Hebrew by joining the letters Chet (π) and Yod (ϑ). That was the icon.

The icon was on his mast too. It was the symbol of a secret society in some foreign land where Itty Cora had been a student. In Hebrew, the word chai means life. Itty Cora's ideology was to celebrate life. The numerical value of the word chai is 18. Itty Cora's men who accepted chai as the symbol on their flag came to be known as the 18th Clan. They had received eight secret commandments from their God.

Kandan Koran's people not only cultivated pepper, they also dried and packed the pepper brought to the godown and loaded it on the ships. Itty Cora considered them more important than his blood relations. He not only gave them good wages but also treated them as his equals. During Itty Cora's time, no one was barred from entering Adupputty mansion because of the accident of his or her birth. Itty Cora respected those who worked hard. He did not care for the aristocrats like the Nairs and Namboodiris, who lived a life of ease by exploiting the lower castes. Once, when Kaimal from Cheruvatheni came to visit Itty Cora, he saw Kandan Koran having lunch with Itty Cora at Adupputty mansion. He wasn't pleased.

As he was about to leave, he hinted to Itty Cora, 'Don't trust these darkies. They will start putting on airs if you give them too much freedom. You should learn to keep them in their place.'

'Kaimal, what is the colour of pepper?'

'Do we use pepper to line our eyes?'

'Then tell me, what is the colour of your eyeballs? Don't we see all the other colours with it?'

'I am not being critical, but you don't have a very good reputation among the Christians of Arthaat. They complain that though you are a good businessman you keep the company of low-born Chathans and Pothans. Don't forget that you Syrian Christians are originally Namboodiris who converted to Christianity.'

'What do you know, Kaimal? We eat because these Chathans and Pothans labour hard. Like pepper, they too are black pearls. If I get tainted by my association with them, so be it. By the way, the forefathers of the Christians of Kunnamkulam are not Namboodiris. We came here ages before Christ.'

Unconcerned with the disapproval of the high-born Christians and the Hindu aristocrats, Itty Cora grew closer to the black pearls. At the Adupputty mansion and in the Iyyala granary, Kandan Koran and Bappu enjoyed equal status with Ukru and Tharu. Chirutheyi entertained them all.

For the first *thiruvathira*, a full moon day of the month of Dhanu, after Itty Cora's father's death, Kandan Koran arrived with his people to plant pepper vines in the land near Iyyala farm. When he returned in the evening drenched in rain after a hard day's labour, Chirutheyi ran to him and dried his head with a cloth. Tall, dark, and well-built, Kandan Koran was physically stronger than Itty Cora, a handsome man with curly hair and a smile playing on his lips, always ready with a joke or a good story. Chirutheyi seated him on a straw carpet and served him rice gruel, vegetables, and dried fish in a brass bowl.

'Black Pearl, how many vines did you plant?' she asked.

'Nearly sixty, thamburatty. Mapla said to plant one thousand before the *njaatuvela.*'

'That's only twelve days away. Check whether the trees are good before you plant the creeper.'

'That's what we check first. How do you know about these things?'

'That is the way we Kothas are. We check the strength of the tree before we entwine ourselves around it.' She looked meaningfully at his broad chest and then quickly looked away.

He did not pay any attention. 'Why are you serving dry fish? Isn't there any fish in the Kumpuzha?'

'There is fish aplenty in the river. But I have no one to go fishing for me. The fish in Kumpuzha are smart. Bait doesn't hook them. You have to get down in the river to catch them.'

'It is not right to catch fish using a fishing rod. That's cheating. You have to go down in the water. Then huge fish will swim near you. Some of them will stay immobile. Their lifespan is over. They are praying to God. Catch them just below their necks. They will try to escape. Don't let them go.'

Chirutheyi served him more rice gruel. 'Won't God be angry if we catch that fish?'

'If the fish has lived its life, then we can catch it and eat it.'

'Who told you all this?'

'Cora mapla. He is an *avatar* of God.'

'God's avatar?'

'Undoubtedly. We saw it on Christmas night with our own eyes. A star shone brightly above Aduputty mansion at midnight. God came flying down from that star on a white horse. As soon as he came down, he asked, "Where is my son Itty Cora?" Mapla came running and stood before God. God hugged Itty Cora, kissed him on the forehead, and went back to the skies.'

That night, Kandan Koran narrated several stories about Itty Cora. In between the stories she writhed on his chest, like the fish in the Kumpuzha. While fishing, Kandan Koran whispered in her ear, 'Cora mapla has taught you all the wiles.

How will I ever repay this debt?' Silently, with a naughty smile, she laid her head on his chest. Even though he put in his best efforts till dawn, his debt only gathered interest.

The next evening, when Kandan Koran returned from work, he had a catch of five or six fish with him. Chirutheyi directed Chakkappayi and quickly prepared a fish curry for dinner.

'I didn't think you'd bring the fish today itself.'

'The grace of God. When I went for a dip in the river after work he was there under water. "You, Kandan Koran, catch four of these fish and give then to Chirutheyi." What can I do? And when I started to catch the fish, he added, "That girl took so much trouble last night. You should be grateful to her." I caught about eight fish. I'm trying to repay last night's debt.'

'Watch what happens tonight. You won't be able to repay my debt. To be called a black pearl isn't enough, you should be strong too. Tell me the truth. Have you seen Cora mapla's God?'

'Will anyone lie about God? But this God, contrary to what the Namboodiris say, doesn't wear silk; nor is he a vegetarian. Like our God, he drinks liquor and eats meat. He looks like the God on the cross Christians pray to. But the priests detest him.'

'Why?'

'It was this God who brought pepper to the earth, till then pepper was found only in the heavens. He cleverly stole it and gave it to the Coras of Kunnamkulam. He told them to sell it, make money, and live happily. He didn't give them pepper for nothing. The Coras gave something in return. They still continue to do so. It is because he refused to give it to the priests that they hate this god.'

'Then why do the Coras spend so much money on repairing churches?'

'That is the trick of a tradesman. It silences the clergy. In public, they are men of the Church but privately they worship the Pepper God.'

'How did your people join them?'

'That's the interesting part. Our ancestors were the pepper cultivators in heaven. God brought us along with pepper to the earth.'

'Is that why you are so dark?'

'Yes! We are the same colour as pepper. In heaven, pepper is known as black pearl. That's why Cora calls me Black Pearl.'

Chirutheyi murmured, 'Black Pearl,' and hugged him.

Till the monsoon ended with the Thiruvathira njaatuvela, Kandan Koran was in Iyyala. After planting a thousand pepper vines he went back and the week after that, when Itty Cora arrived, Chirutheyi told him about Kandan Koran's stories. He couldn't stop laughing.

'Was it all lies?'

'No, no. I was thinking about the story of the pepper in heaven.'

'Tell me.'

'The pepper in heaven was ten times as big as the pepper on earth; nearly the size of a grape, black, tinged with red. Its juice was very spicy with a bit of sweetness. You could never have enough of it. When God created Eve he fixed two peppers on her chest. When Adam and Eve were banished from heaven after the original sin, the peppers contracted in size and lost their spiciness and sweetness. Each child that falls on the earth from heaven seeks this pepper first.'

'I can smell a tall tale. Who made this up?'

'The Pepper God himself. Because he stole pepper for us, he was banished from heaven. Then he had to wander through earth and hell. When I come next, I'll tell you more stories.'

13

Chandamshu Chandrdhamkumbhipalah

Like the crests of a peacock
Like the gem on the head of a snake
Mathematics is situated on the forehead of the divine science.

GEORGE GHEVERGHESE JOSEPH DREW INSPIRATION FROM THIS SLOKA when he entitled his research text CREST OF THE PEACOCK.

Rashmi looked uncomprehendingly at Rekha when she saw the fourth chapter, 'Chandamshu Chandrdhamkumbhipalah'. When Rekha too looked blank, she turned to me. 'What does it mean?'

'To be honest, I don't know myself. I think it is some sort of black magic.' We started reading.

Itty Cora had a very good head for mathematics. The multiplication tables he devised 500 years ago are still in use. Itty Cora borrowed the peculiar intonation for chanting the tables from *madrassas* at Timbuktu. The children of Adupputty mansion were forced to learn by rote the multiplication tables up to 18, upwards and downwards. If the black pearls were Itty Cora's friends in matters of trade and agriculture, Namboodiris, Warriers, and Marikkars were his companions in the numbers game. When Itty Cora was in town, nearly every day someone would come to Adupputty mansion with a difficult mathematical problem. As Itty Cora was well-versed in Sanskrit and traditional Indian mathematics, he would come up with the answers in no time. But he wouldn't tell them the method he had used to arrive at the solution. Only after they admitted defeat despite repeated efforts would he tell them the solution. If Marikkar was excellent in navigational calculations, Namboodiri from Irinjalakuda and Neelandan from Ponnani excelled in other types of mathematical calculations. They learnt several complex concepts in mathematics and astronomy from Itty Cora. Based on the knowledge gained from Cora, Neelandan later wrote several texts in Sanskrit.

Because of his closeness to Cora, the Namboodiri from Irinjalakuda later settled permanently in Kanippayyur near Adupputty. His descendants became experts in, astronomy, mathematics, and astrology.

His brothers, Tharu and Ukru, and Neelandan from Ponnani were Itty Cora's favourite disciples. It was Itty Cora who appointed Neelandan, who was born in an impoverished Namboodiri family near Thirunavaya, as his accountant in the godown. Hearing of Cora's interest in the subject, Neelandan had gone to meet him with some mathematical tricks.

It was around this time that Itty Cora brought Chirutheyi to live in Iyyala. He had not yet taken up the reins of the business. He would gallop across the land on his horse, sampling different types of liquor and women. Luckily, he was home when Nelandan came to visit.

Neelandan presented a line from *Katapayadi,* an ancient Indian numerological system according to which each number has an equivalent alphabet, to Itty Cora, and respectfully stood aside.

Neelandan was nearly 40 years old but poverty had aged him, and he looked a lot older. Itty Cora told the travel-weary Neelandan, 'Go inside and eat some rice. We will look at this later.' As Neelandan stood hesitating, Itty Cora noticed the sacred thread on his chest, 'Oh you are a Namboodiri. Then perhaps it is better to starve than eat here.'

'I heard that the younger Cora is very interested in mathematics.'

'I'm not very interested in mathematics, but I am not uninterested either. My interest lies in women and the seas. Mathematics comes only after that. All right, what have you written? Read! Let me hear.'

'*Chandamshu Chandrdhamkumbhipalah.*'

Itty Cora was pleased.

'Oh, so that's the way it is. You are not a Namboodiri who merely does puja. Who taught you *Katapayadi?*'

'Irinjalakuda Madhavan Namboodiri.'

'Can you give the exact sum of *Chandamshu Chandrdhamkumbhipalah?*'

'3.14159 26536.'

'This is correct according to *Katapayadi.* But it isn't very accurate. We learnt to calculate the circumference and diameter of a circle a hundred times more accurately at Timbuktu. In Alexandria this is known as the Pi. Pi is a Greek alphabet. You aren't bad at mathematics. Will you have a tender coconut?'

'Yes.'

By then, the servants had brought a tender coconut and a couple of plantains on a banana leaf. Itty Cora and Neelandan then discussed many mathematical problems. Though Itty Cora answered Neelandan's questions within minutes, Neelandan, owing to his ignorance about mathematics in other parts of the world, couldn't answer Itty Cora's questions easily. But when Neelandan recited,

'Vyaasa vaarinidhinihithe
Roopahrudevasya
sagarabhihithe
Sthreesharaadi
vishamasankhya
Bhakthamranam swam prathkramaal kuryaal'

Itty Cora slipped into thought. When enlightenment dawned, unable to control his happiness, he rose and embraced Neelandan. 'Namboodiri, you are not an ordinary man. This is called the third series of Hypatia. I learnt it in Alexandria. But how can this theorem be proved?'

'What do you mean by prove?'

'That's the problem. In the Western way of thought it is not enough just to give a theory. It has to be proven, and only then will it be considered a theory, according to Hypatia. Have you heard about Hypatia?'

'No.'

'She was an extremely intelligent women who lived in Alexandria nearly a century ago. All the mathematical concepts in the world are based on Hypatia's theories. You just chanted what is known as Hypatia's third series. It is written thus:

'Pi = 4(1-1/3 + 1/5 - 1/7 + 1/9-. ...)

'Hypatia's principles have spread all over the world in Latin, Hebrew, and Arabic.'

'This you say is the third series, so what about the first one?'

'That is very well known. God has created the world based on this series. If you look at anything beautiful you will find this series in it. Count the number of petals in a sunflower, or the rings on a pineapple. The inconsistency is consistent. That's Hypatia's first series: 0, 1, 2, 3, 5, 8, 13, 21, 34, 55.

'If you add a number to the number preceding it, you will get the succeeding number. When you place it alternately you get the ratio of the petals of sunflowers. Now some Romans have come forward saying that they are the ones who discovered this.'

'This Hypatia was indeed intelligent. We have never thought of seeking mathematical patterns in objects around us,' Namboodiri said.

'Not just this. The numbers lying next to each other in this series have a definite ratio. This is called the Divine Ratio: .6180339887 ... That is the proportion of beauty in God's creations. Hypatia's limbs were in this divine ratio.'

'I would have liked to meet her!'

'So would I. But a thousand years have gone by. I was lucky enough to meet a beauty like Hypatia at Alexandria. It is said that good women and mathematics do not yield easily. They are initially recalcitrant. Afterwards you feel, "Oh, this was easy." She too resisted me in the beginning.

But I persisted and she fell for me. Even here I was lucky. I am not interested in mathematical problems that can be solved easily. How do you feel about such things?'

'It is not that I am not interested. But I have three daughters and a house steeped in poverty. I work in a temple near Thirunavaya. In my free time I play with numbers. There is a Zamorin who is very interested in mathematics. If you go to him with new mathematical problems he will give you something.'

'Both types of Namboodiris are at fault. Those who cheat the poor, make money, and are vassals of kings, and those like you who in spite of being intelligent don't put their intelligence to use and end up living a life of penury. Why don't you use your knowledge to earn some money? I am not asking you to do physical labour but the sort of work where your intelligence can be put to use. If I give you money now, won't it be over within two months?'

Neelandan looked pleadingly at Cora. Itty Cora let out another puff of smoke.

'I heard my father say that the accounts of the godown in Ponnani refuse to tally, no matter how hard they try. Why don't you try? It's work with numbers, after all.'

'My father wants me to conduct *yagnas* and become a *somayaagi* like my grandfather.'

'Be so by all means. I will help you in any way I can. But you must work too. I don't think you will become a somayaagi by merely performing pujas at a temple.'

Itty Cora spoke to his father and got Neelandan the accountant's job at the godown in Ponnani. Before he joined duty, Itty Cora's father did some plain speaking to Neelandan. 'I don't usually employ Namboodiris here. I agreed because my son wanted me to employ you. We do business to make profits. The Arabs and Chinese who come off the ships will try to trick you. The job of an accountant is not like that of a temple priest. Do not talk about what you see inside the godown. Understand?'

Neelandan nodded.

'You are a stranger to this land. You don't know our ways. In Cora country, nobody is given preference because of his caste. In the godown Kandan Koran and Neelandan are equals. We Coras don't enjoy women and liquor alone. You are welcome to join us if you wish.'

Agreeing to all the conditions, Neelandan assumed his duties. Though Itty Cora had spent a lot of money in refurbishing the Church, the priest of Arthaat Church disapproved of his association with non-Christians. Having hinted this to Itty Cora several times, he couldn't digest the fact that despite his warnings Neelandan was given employment at the godown. Believing it his duty to guide a straying lamb back to the fold, he went to Adupputty mansion one day. Itty Cora received him with a great show of hospitality. After eating and drinking, as they were enjoying the breeze on the veranda, the priest started advising Itty Cora.

'Even though your business is prospering, you do not fear God.'

'Why do you say that?'

'It's been three Sundays since you came to church. This is the fourth Sunday. You didn't come today either. That's why I came here. Do you imagine that wealth will give you everything?'

'No, what belongs to the Church is for the Church and what is Cora's is Cora's. You should just send word if you need anything.'

'It is not that kind of need I'm here for. You are getting close to Hindus and Cherumas. They haven't heard the call of Christ. If things go on like this, we won't be building a new church. I hear that you do things that are forbidden by Chandamshu Chandrdhamkumbhipalah, our religion. Your god-fearing forefathers always gave half their profits to the Church. Your father, each time he came from foreign lands, would come to church and give an account of his profit. Have you forgotten all that?'

Itty Cora did not answer. When he snapped his fingers, four or five people appeared, lifted the priest, and took him to the rooftop. They took off his cassock. When he cried out, they covered his mouth. Two men held his hands and legs. Ukru caught hold of a handful of hair on the priest's chest in his right fist.

'What is for the priest is for the priest and what is Cora's is Cora's. Get it?'

The priest stood silently, pleading for mercy.

'Have you lost your tongue?'

When the priest nodded, Ukru gave a mighty pull on the hair on the priest's chest. The priest cried out in pain. Ukru's hand was full of hair smeared with blood.

'Don't forget. What is for Cora is for Cora and what is the priest's is the priest's.'

Neelandan was more interested in mathematics and astronomy than in accountancy. But he did the work entrusted to him very meticulously. In his free time, he would read voraciously and solve mathematical problems. Once, when Itty Cora went to the godown in the evening, Neelandan was scribbling something.

'What are you working out so furiously? Are you calculating the number of pepper pods in the godown?'

'Kandan Koran brought a math problem yesterday. I can't understand it.'

'What is it?'

'That's the best part. He says like the twinkling white stars we see, there are also black stars. One white star for 18 black stars. His question is, in that case how many stars are there in all?'

'Have you found the answer?'

'No! I don't understand what he means by black stars.'

'Black stars can't be seen. They are burnt out stars. They don't have the brightness of a star that shines. Kandan Koran's people do everything in their lives in accordance with the stars. They say it's a continuation of the relationship they had in heaven. According to their calculations, the number of people on earth is equal to the number of stars in the sky. Black stars for black people and white stars for white.'

'But how do you find out how many stars there are?'

'Archimedes in Greece talks of such a calculation. How many grains of sand are needed to fill this earth? He says it's 1010 10: infinity. But for Kandan Koran's people, mathematics is also a system of belief. They have several sayings and chants based on this belief. Logic has no place there. But actually, the language of mathematics is the language of logic. It is because you are inquiring in that language that you are not able to arrive at the answer. No white star will burn out completely and become a black star. It is an ongoing process.'

'So what is the answer to Kandan Koran's question?'

'To get an accurate answer you have to understand two things: the zero and infinity. Infinity—that without an ending. If you add, subtract, divide, or multiply with zero, the answer is zero. It's the same with infinity—multiply or divide by infinity, the answer is infinity. How much is infinity into twice 18? Infinity! That's the correct answer to Kandan Koran's question.'

'That's the answer I too got. But we say it in a different way. If we add fullness to fullness or take away fullness the answer remains fullness. This is infinity. But Kandan Koran doesn't agree.'

'That's because you don't say it in Kandan Koran's language,' Cora said. By this time, Kandan Koran had arrived with a cart of pepper at the godown. Itty Cora invited Kandan Koran and seated him with Neelandan.

'What is the argument between the two of you?'

'Nothing! I asked him to tell me the number of stars in the sky. He's been bothering himself with it for two days! He said something about fullness.'

'Kandan Koran, if you sing your "Nachthra Song" Neelandan will understand.'

'How can I sing that song without asking God?'

'Go to the godown and ask God.'

Kandan Koran quickly lifted the pepper-filled sacks and made preparations in the front of the godown to ask God. Fifteen men and women from amongst the workers surrounded him. He seated his woman Kalikutty in the centre. After handing her a pot of liquor, they went around her thrice and then Kandan Koran began to sing. The rest of them sang with him. Kalikutty let her hair loose, downed the alcohol, and worked herself up into a frenzy.

Grandfather Cora's Grandfather Cora's Grandfather
Cora's Kalikutty (repeat twice), why is your face aflame?
(repeat four times)
Why are you shy when you see the stars blooming in the
sky? (twice)
Why are you shy when you go to sleep at night with
God? (twice)
Kalikutty whose breasts are firm and waist is trim despite
18 childbirths?
Undone hair beating the floor.
Drawing pictures in mud with your hair.
Pouring the milk from your breasts and loins in the
kalam. Lying down in middle of it gazing at God.
Tell me, Kalikutty, how many stars are there in the sky?
I can't see anything but the star necklace around the neck
of the black God and the sun in his ears.
How many fish in the star necklace?
Countless.
Does each white fish have 18 black eyes! Can't count.
Ask God, my dear Kalikutty.

We couldn't find God's answer to Kalikutty. The forty-three pages
of the book Benny had given us had ended. Rekha was disappointed
and searched eagerly to see if we had omitted any pages.

14

The Thorny Chairs of Torture

Everybody's worried about stopping terrorism.
Well, there's a really easy way: stop participating in it.
— Noam Chomsky

Hi Rekha,

Sorry, I haven't been able to mail you for the last few weeks, I was unexpectedly caught up.

The day I arrived in New York from Lima with Morigami, problems began. From the airport we went straight to Morigami's friend Masaki's house in Manhattan. Nearly twenty of her Peruvian friends were waiting there to welcome us. Everyone spoke about Lori Berenson, an American who was a prisoner in Peru. Lori's parents Rhoda and Mark Berenson, a teacher couple from New York, were at the party. In the latter half of the 1990s Lori had chucked her studies at MIT and gone to El Salvador as a freelance journalist. An extremely beautiful and intelligent woman who believed in Marxist ideology, she was easily able to get close to the leaders of the left-wing movements and earn their trust. Lori, who in 1990 started writing for leftist publications like *Modern Times* and *The Third World's Viewpoint*, had, by 1992, become the secretary and translator of Leonel González who was the leader of the Farabundo Marti National Liberation Front (FMLN), the strongest revolutionary organization in El Salvador. When the FMLN moved away from the ideology of armed revolt, Lori, who was an ardent Maoist, lost interest in staying on in El Salvador. When Leonel tried to sexually exploit her, she left El Salvador and moved to Lima in Peru. Lori Berenson had come in contact with the Tupac Amaru guerrillas when she had been working as Leonel's secretary. Nancy Gilvonio, a professional photographer and Nestor Cerpa's girlfriend, brought Lori Berenson to Peru. Nestor Cerpa was the second most important leader of the Tupacs after Victor Polay. But Lori didn't realize that she had been trapped in a very cleverly staged plot masterminded by Victor Polay and Cerpa.

As she was a freelance journalist from the US and because she was a glamorous and charming woman, she was soon able to enter the main Congress House in Lima and interview many prominent political leaders, including President Fujimori. On these occasions Nancy would accompany her in her capacity as a photographer. The interviews were just a front for taking as many pictures as possible of the Congress House so as to get a clear idea of the security systems in use. Very soon, Lori's rented house in Lima became an important hideout for the Tupac guerrillas. Victor Polay and Nestor Cerpa and others would stay there frequently and draw plans to capture the Congress. Unfortunately, Fujimori's secret police sniffed out their plot. The police arrested Lori and Nancy while they were travelling in a bus in Lima in the evening of the 30 November 1995. During the raid on Lori's house that night, three Tupac guerrillas and a police officer lost their lives. Several photographs of the Congress

House that clearly revealed plans for an attack were found in the house. Accused of aiding and abetting terrorism, Lori was sentenced to life imprisonment.

For years Lori was shut up in Yanamayo prison in the Andes, which was notorious for torture used on terrorists. As a result of the cruel torture she endured in prison, she lost her hearing in her left ear and suffered a serious injury to her spinal cord. It was owing to the intervention of human rights organizations like Amnesty International that Lori was moved from Yanamayo prison. Though Lori was given a retrial after the emergency was lifted following Fujimori's deposal from power, she wasn't acquitted; she was sentenced to twenty years of imprisonment.

On 17 December 1996, Tupac guerrillas led by Nestor Cerpa captured the Japanese ambassador's residence in Lima. They held hostage hundreds of diplomats, military commanders, and high-ranking officials, demanding the release of four hundred and sixty five Tupacs who were imprisoned in different jails in Peru. The fact that the third prisoner mentioned on this list was Lori indicates her importance in the organization and the extent of her influence on the Tupac movement. One hundred and twenty six days later, on 22 April 1997, Fujimori's special commandos carried out a lightning attack with the help of the US and freed the hostages. All the guerrillas who took part in Nestor Cerpa's action were killed. Slowly, the power of the Tupacs started to crumble. Victor Polay and other important leaders were arrested. Though several prominent intellectuals and thinkers like Noam Chomsky participated in efforts for Lori's freedom in New York that were spearheaded by her parents, it proved futile. The only respite was that from August 2000 onwards, for two years, she was moved to the female prison in Lima. In 2003 when she was thirty-three, Lori married her co-prisoner, Aníbal Apari Sánchez, a Tupac activist. It was to celebrate

the news of Lori's pregnancy that the Tupac sympathizers had got
together in Masaka's house the day we arrived.

Morigami was a research student in the Catholic University when
Lori had arrived in Lima. Though she had no visible links with the
guerrillas, they somehow knew that Morigami was against Fujimori's
anti-democratic government. As very few intellectuals and relatively
no one of Japanese origin were against Fujimori, Lori and Nancy
decided to establish contact with Morigami, thinking that it would
be helpful if such a person became involved in their movement.
They were merely acting on Victor Polay's orders. When Lori and
Nancy were arrested, they were on their way to meet Morigami,
having fixed up an appointment earlier. Morigami, a vehement
opponent of all violence in society, was shocked when she came to
know that the journalist who was on her way meet her had been
arrested for terrorist activities. As neither Lori nor Nancy uttered
Morigami's name in spite of being tortured by the police, she was
left alone.

It was when she went to Princeton for higher studies that Morigami
met Lori's parents, who were then in New York. Though Morigami
supported in spirit the movement that Lori's parents had launched
for her freedom, she never mentioned that it was when they were
coming to meet her that Nancy and Lori had been arrested. But
some of the Tupac guerrillas who were close to Lori knew this. They
believed that Morigami was part of the movement. Only Victor
Polay and Nestor Cerpa knew that Morigami had never met Lori.

By the time the party ended with everyone expressing their
good wishes for Lori to give birth to an intelligent and beautiful
daughter, it was 1 a.m. A member of cannibals.com was there with
Lori's parents throughout the party. We kept a close watch on each
other. As the guests started melting away, he whispered in my ear,
'I've come to see the prey earmarked for next Saturday. Have you
eaten the flesh of a Japanese woman?' I was shocked: Morigami was

only a little way from us, joking and laughing with friends. I asked him, 'There are around five or six Japanese women here. Who is the prey?' Replying 'I cannot tell you that,' he disappeared into the crowd. I was troubled. Morigami was the fleshiest of the lot. The other Japanese women were emaciated; when skin and bones were removed they would perhaps weigh around thirty pounds. An unknown fear overcame me when the unbidden thought entered my mind that I would perhaps be eating the flesh from Morigami's waist or thighs next Saturday night.

When Morigami left saying that she had work at Princeton, I went back to my old place. I had no news from her for two weeks.

Her cell was switched off and she didn't respond to my text messages or emails. Fearing that I would have to eat her flesh, I didn't go to the cannibal party on Saturday. Though I got a text from Morigami next Friday saying 'Meet 2mrw Masako's inn', my fears were allayed only when I met her in person. When she hugged me and kissed me on my cheeks, I held her close.

'What is this? Shall we go once more to El Parque del Amore?'

'You're talking nonsense, we happen to be in New York.'

'I'm serious. We can fly to Lima in the morning and come back after a week. I've urgent work there.'

Though her plans weren't clear to me, I agreed without further ado. We boarded a Chile Lan flight to Lima the next morning.

Morigami sent me to the apartment just after we landed at Jorge Chavez airport, saying that she had to meet a friend, and came back very late, at around 1 a.m. in the morning. Though I had Botticelli's Venus, FTV, and liquor for company, I was bored by the time she arrived. When she immediately changed her clothes and said, 'Get ready quickly, Cora, let's go to see El Beso,' I was relieved. In the cold dark night, we reached the Love Park at around 2 a.m. Parking her car near the gate Morigami clung to me and walked through the gates. The watchman asked the same question he had asked us the previous time. 'It's quite cold. Hope you've brought whisky with you?' Even though we hadn't, she nodded, and we walked in. When I asked her whether he would give us whisky if we hadn't brought any, Morigami laughed uncontrollably. Still laughing, she lay down on the left of El Beso. I sat next to her uncomprehendingly.

'Cora, that question is a secret code.'

'What does it mean?'

'He's asking me whether I am a prostitute. If I nod my head and say I have whisky with me, it means yes. No more questions are asked. When we return he has to be paid a percentage of what I earn. If I say I don't have whisky with me, he won't say anything, but the moment we enter the park he will inform the police. Usually, the police do not search this park, but they will be waiting outside. Then, we will be taken to the police station and subjected to a brutal interrogation. If they have any suspicion that we have connections with Tupac guerrillas or the Shining Paths they will not arrest us or take us to court. They will lock us up in a secret prison and we will never again see the light of day. There are several such codes that are used in Lima's city life. If, for example, a beautiful woman asks you for a cigarette in some shopping mall in Miraflores, she is asking you if you need her services for the night. If you give her a cigarette she will light it, say "Thank you," and kiss you. Then she'll behave as if she were your girlfriend of several years. Nobody will be suspicious.'

'Have we come here on this cold night to talk of these codes?'

'No, nor to experiment with a different technique to arouse you. Two people like us will arrive here shortly, a middle-aged man and a girl. The watchman will ask the girl, who will be clad in black jeans and a leather jacket, the same question that he asked us. She will nod, hug the man accompanying her, and lie down on her stomach on the right side of El Beso. That is the signal for us to recognize them. I'm lying with my legs lifted up a bit so that they can recognize us.'

'Who are they?'

'Tupacs. But they call themselves human rights activists who are working for Lori's freedom. They want to use our flat as a hideout for a few days.'

'Isn't that dangerous?'

'Yes. But we have no option. If we refuse, we will be killed.'

While Morigami was explaining all this, a slim, tall beauty and a middle-aged man had entered the park. The fair, heavily built man resembled former Venezuelan President Hugo Chavez. The girl took a small bottle out of her pocket and took a sip. After taking a close look at us, she lay down on her stomach and started swinging her legs. When Morigami was sure that it was the couple that we had been waiting for, she went to them and whispered *'Ccollanan Pachacamac ricuy auccacunac yahuarniy hichascancuta.'* The girl jumped up joyfully and hugging Morigami, responded, *'Ccollanan Pachacamac ricuy auccacunac yahuarniy hichascancuta.'* The man said the same words to me but I couldn't repeat them. As he stood, doubtful, Morigami said something to him in Aymara. Exclaming 'Cora Gonzalo's descendant,' he fell at my feet, crossing himself. While he was introducing himself as Mario, my eyes were on the girl with him. She looked barely twenty years old and was more beautiful than Morigami. As she bent forward, crossing herself and saying, 'Violetta Sanchez,' we heard police sirens outside. She looked terrified and hugged me, crying, 'Cora! Please save me, please save me.'

Morigami and I stood nonplussed. Mario patted her and tried to comfort her saying *'Ccollanan Pachacamac ricuy auccacunac yahuarniy hichascancuta.'* When Morigami looked at him questioningly, Mario explained.

'We are human rights activists campaigning for Lori's release from prison. Violetta led the demonstration demanding Lori's release with a black cloth tied around her face. We are trying to attain freedom by peaceful means for those who were detained during

Fujimori's dictatorship. The only connection Violetta has with revolutionary movements is that she had a distant relative, Eduardo Cruz Sanchez, who was killed in the uprising that captured the Japanese ambassador's residence. Yet the DIRCOTE police raided her apartment on Monday night. They raped Violetta repeatedly in front of her parents. When she fainted, they threw her out on the seashore. She is in shock. She wants a place where she can stay peacefully for a few days.'

'Don't worry. You can stay at my apartment. Don't go out too much. If anyone asks any questions, just say you're doing research under my guidance.'

'I don't know how to thank you.'

'It's nothing. The watchman will suspect us if we stay here talking for too long or if we go out hastily. We will stay for half an hour, pretend we've done what we came for, tip the watchman, and go out. First both of us as we entered first, then you. ...'

'But the vehicle that dropped us here has left.'

'So what? I'll start my car only after you come out.'

'Suppose we are stopped and questioned?'

'Let's pray to Tupac's jawbone that nothing like that happens. After all we have Cora Gonzalo's descendant with us.'

When we exited half an hour later, tipping the watchman ten sols, he told Morigami 'You don't look at all tired this time. Last time you came in like a horse and went out like a donkey.' When Morigami was out of hearing, he whispered to me, 'If you have to ride the same horse, why should you come here?' I shoved five sols into his palm, making him very happy. He asked, 'Do you see a pony behind you? Shall I arrange for a ride tomorrow night?' As Violetta reached the gate she hesitatingly tipped him ten sols. When the watchman accepted it with a joke, she cried out loudly and came running to the car with Mario behind her. Morigami quickly started the car.

The police stopped us when we reached Larcomar, and without bothering to look at Morigami's papers, asked us to accompany them to the police station. They took us to a dark interrogation room, and when a young police inspector bolted the door, Violetta fainted. Two policemen dragged her away. Before they questioned us, the policemen stripped us naked to check if we had any hidden weapons or drugs. Even after they found nothing on us, they did not allow us to wear our clothes.

The inspector looked mockingly at Morigami, who was trying to cover her nudity with her hands while the policemen were enjoying the spectacle. When she lowered her head pretending not to notice, two policemen lifted her hands up. Pinching her left cheek, the inspector started questioning her.

'What are you trying to hide? You are not a young girl to feel shy. Quickly tell us, are you a Shining Path or an MRTA?'

'I'm a professor of mathematics at Catholic University. I've no connection with these people.'

'What business does a teacher have in the Love Park at midnight? Are you teaching mathematics with your hips?'

'Can't you be more dignified?'

The inspector did not like the question. At a signal from him the police tied her hands at the back. The inspector caught her left ear and hair together, shook her violently, and slapped her hard. 'You college professors do not deserve dignity as you are good at deception. The truth will have to be dragged out of you.' Turning to his subordinates, he asked, 'Where is the "chair of thorns" that we used while questioning Guzman?'

The policemen placed a chair pierced with sharp nails in the centre of the room. Morigami stood looking at it, trembling.

'What are you staring at? This is the throne your president Gonzalva sat on. Sit on it, or speak the truth.'

When Morigami did not move, he roared, 'Whore! Sit on the chair,' and pushed her. She fell on the chair crying out loudly. The nails pierced her fair beautiful naked skin. She writhed on the chair, screaming. When she tried to get up the nails only pierced deeper.

I couldn't bear it. I shook off the policeman's hand and pulled her off the chair.

My unexpected move distracted the policemen, and in the fraction of a second Mario pulled a gun from one of them and started firing. Within minutes the inspector and three policemen lay dead.

While I somehow threw some clothes over Morigami, who was barely able to stand, Mario brought Violetta from the room next room to ours. We sped to Morigami's house.

I realized that busy cities are better than forests to hide in. In the days following our dramatic escape, the papers in Lima were full of news of an attack by Tupac guerrillas on the seventh police station at Larcorma that had left an inspector and nine policemen dead. Yet, we were unharmed. MRTA leadership took responsibility for the carnage and some of its members were arrested.

The Tupac arranged a doctor for Morigami's treatment. She had to spend the next week lying on her stomach. Violetta assisted the doctor who dressed Morigami's wounds twice a day. On the eighth day, she managed to lie on her back in bed. That night, surprising us, an important Tupac leader arrived at the apartment, masked. He did not reveal his name.

He greeted Morigami, '*Ccollanan Pachacamac ricuy auccacunac yahuarniy hichascancuta.*' Then he said 'Tomorrow, they are bringing Lori to Lima for a medical checkup. We will rescue her from the hospital and bring her straight here. You are responsible for her safety and you have to take her to New York.'

She nodded, still lying down. I trembled thinking of the dangers that lay ahead.

Cora with love.

15
Gonzalva Cora

Since it is impossible to know what's really happening
We Peruvians lie, invent, dream, and take refuge in illusion.
— Mario Vargas Llosa

Dear Rekha,

Two days ago, before her wounds healed, I had to escape from Lima with Morigami. It was a member of the secret police of Lima who had arrived masked as a Tupac leader. They had got information of a plot to rescue Lori, and he had come to our apartment to seek confirmation. Luckily, no one suspected our involvement in the murder of the policemen at the seventh police station. But when he saw Violetta Sanchez, in the flat his suspicions were confirmed. It was Violetta who had covered her face with a black cloth and led the demonstrators to the President's palace. None of us had any inkling that he was not a Tupac leader. When he insisted on meeting Morigami in spite of being told that she was ill, I thought he was aware of her condition. But when he left after discussing the plot to rescue Lori, not once mentioning Morigami's wounds, I felt something was amiss. He must have returned with a plan similar to the one they had used in 1995 when they had attacked the flat rented in Lori's name and captured Tupac guerrillas. The minute he left, the Tupac guerila who was guarding told us what had happened. We had no option but to escape immediately. Within fifteen minutes we somehow managed to dress Morigami, who had bandages on her buttocks and thighs, in a loose garment, lock the flat, and get out. Mario, who knew the by-lanes of Lima, drove us in a black Honda with tinted glasses. I sat in the front seat pretending to be an American tourist. Morigami lay on the back seat with her head resting on Violetta's lap. The bullets and guns we had taken from the police station gave us courage. Though the police stopped the car and searched us twice before we reached Peru Highway No. 1, known as the Pan American Highway, the going was smooth. As prostitution was legal in Peru, the police must have assumed that we were American tourists roaming around the city with call girls. Within an hour, we managed to get out of the busy city. We filled the car with gas, bought four bottles of Peruvian pisco and some food, and set out northwards. The Pan American highway was better maintained than most other roads in Peru. Although there were many steep inclines and bends on the way, along the coastline we got a good stretch of road for nearly four to five miles. As Morigami's car was in excellent condition, Mario was literally flying down the road.

It is four hundred and eleven miles by road from Lima to the Peru-Ecuador border town Agua Verde. Guayaquil, the biggest city of Ecuador, is one hundred and sixty eight miles from Agua Verde. It's from there that we booked tickets for the two of us to fly to New York. Luckily, we got tickets on the 8'o clock Lan Ecuador flight No. 516. It was a direct flight, and we would reach New York in seven hours. Our goal was to cross the border before evening.

Peru and Ecuador have a free transit agreement. Only my papers would need emigration clearance. As the emigration offices in Agua Verda and the one in the Ecuador border town of Huaquillas were notorious for corruption, we deliberately chose those routes, thinking that we could get across easily by throwing a few dollars around. If we were able to cross the border by evening, we could reach Guayaquil by midnight. Dropping us off at a budget hotel, Mario and Violetta could return, and we would fly to New York in the morning.

Half an hour after we left Lima, the tension in the car evaporated. Mario took a swig of the pisco and passed me the bottle. Once she received confirmation of the tickets, Morigami forgot her pain. She lay on her stomach on Violetta's lap and started humming, 'No llores por mi Argentina' from Evita. Sensing that Morigami's mood had lifted, Mario switched on music in the car. With Madonna's voice flooding the car I sipped pisco and passed the bottle to Violetta.

Unexpectedly seeing something in front, Mario hit the brakes. A Honda van was parked in the middle of the road and four or five people were standing in front of it with guns. I quickly took out my gun. The leader of the group came to me and asked, 'Where is Violetta?' When I looked helplessly at Mario, I saw that a thickset man had him in his grasp with a gun pressed against his head. They pulled Violetta and Morigami out and pointed guns at them. When the leader asked Morigami, 'Aren't you Violetta?', she shook her head. He leered at her, saying, 'Don't lie. Haven't you tattooed Violetta beneath your navel?' and lifted her gown. Though she had mating serpents tattooed below her navel, there was no 'Violetta' to be seen. The bandages on Morigami's body may have aroused their sympathy, for they let her go back to the car. The leader then pulled down Violetta's black jeans, and she covered her eyes with her palms. Beneath her navel, above a pair of tattooed serpents, was the name 'Violetta'.

'Give her to us and you can continue your journey undisturbed,' the leader told me mildly. Violetta looked at me pleadingly. I decided to use the techniques I'd learnt on the Baghdad war front. 'Okay. Take her. But what will we get in return?'

I pushed Violetta in front of them. The leader looked at me disbelievingly. As he stood hesitating, I jumped six feet in the air, twirled around, and rained bullets on them. Before they could understand what was happening, I kicked the gun out of the leader's hand with my left foot, and with my right foot kicked the face of the man who held Mario captive. I have to thank Victoria, who trained me in Baghdad, for being able to execute these maneuvers flawlessly. Mario repeated the miracle he had worked in the police station. But it was Violetta who took me by surprise by shooting down the opponents using the gun I had kicked out of the leader's hand. In the fight that lasted around ten minutes, two of their people died, and when the leader was wounded in his foot the rest of them fled. Violetta went close to the leader and fired three rounds point blank at him. His skull shattered, splattering blood in all directions. Unperturbed, she got into the car. Not wasting time, Mario started the car.

As Morigami lay down in the back seat, Violetta sat on my lap in the front seat. After a while she leaned back on my chest. Fondling her golden hair I whispered in her ear, 'Violetta, are you really a Tupac?' She laughed in response.

'Cora, you and I are Tupacs by birth.'

'Tupacs by birth?'

'Yes. You say that you are Gonzalo Cora's descendant. We believe that Gonzalo Cora established this society in 1572. He was the executioner who carried out the death sentence of the last Inca king Tupac Amaru in Cuzco in 1572. Realizing the gravity of the sin he had committed, he went to Machu Picchu and built a funeral pyre for himself.

'He went to all the Inca families in Cuzco and told them that he was going to commit suicide to atone for his sin. He asked them to spread the message and exhorted them to stand united to free Tupac's empire. On the eighteenth day he went to Machu Picchu. Tens of thousands of people climbed the mountain with Gonzalo Cora that day. He piled firewood up to his neck in front of the Second Sun entrance, set fire to it, and then begged Inti the Sun God for mercy. When he prayed loudly for forgiveness, Inti rose at midnight from the Lake of Titicaca. On the left of Inti was Pachacamac, the earth goddess, and on the right, Tupac Amaru. The three of them were in a golden chariot. The earth goddess moved close to the pyre. As they came closer, Gonzalo's ribcage cracked with a terrible noise. A tremendous earthquake followed. All the volcanoes of the Andes spat fire. The waves of the sea rose to the skies. There was thunder and lightning in Machu Picchu. By the time it began to rain, Gonzalo's funeral pyre had burnt itself out. Pachacamac's disembodied voice rose, "Tupacs will come to the earth again. You will cheat and kill them too." Tens of thousands of people climbed Machu Picchu that night. They bore witness to this.'

'Did a Tupac come again?'

'Yes, in the eighteenth century.'

'Tupac was born again in 1742 on 19 March in Surimana, Tungasuca, in the province of Cuzco. He was named José Gabriel Condorcanqui. He called himself Tupac Amaru II. The Peruvian freedom struggle began with him. Fighting for Peru's freedom and the liberation of the Latinos at the age of twenty-five, he said he was obeying the command of the earth goddess. He united the natives and in 1780 killed the Spanish Governor of Tinta, Antonio de Arriaga, and captured power. But within a short time, with the help of traitors, the Spanish army captured Tupac Amaru and his family. In the trial that was held in Cuzco, Tupac and his entire family were sentenced to death. His wife and children were beheaded before

Tupac's eyes. Tupac himself was killed in a brutal and barbaric manner.

'In the middle of the town, in May 1781, as tens of thousands of people watched with bated breath, a naked Tupac was brought from prison on the back of a donkey and led to the scaffold. Dancers and singers curtsied the Spanish government, and began to dance and sing. They made Tupac stand where everybody could see him and started to hurl abuses at him. They whipped him, exclaiming, 'Let him put his brains to good use in his next birth,' and forcibly fed him the feaces of the Queen of Spain that they had brought all the way from Spain. Then they brought him down to the open yard, made him lie down, and tied chains to each of his limbs. Each chain was fixed on the back of a horse. They planned to ride the four horses in four directions at the same time and pull Tupac's body apart. But they were not able do so. It is said that the earth goddess commanded the horses not to move. Finally, they gave up and took him to the same place where Tupac I had been beheaded, and cut off his head.

'The descendants of each of the Inca families that went to Machu Picchu in 1572 became part of the society. Many new people joined. Tupac society is still growing, having withstood torture and suppression for more than four hundred years.'

I had never thought that Violetta, who had been quiet all these days, could be so eloquent. Morigami was fast asleep in the back seat. Mario seemed to be of a taciturn disposition. We left Peru at around three and after five hours reached Chimbote, a small town nearly six hundred miles away. I feared that the police would be waiting to arrest us. But the Peruvian police aren't very efficient. We went to a small restaurant called Puma near the bus station that was open all night waiting for travellers. More than assuaging our hunger, we wanted to use the restroom and fill the car with gas. But we did not forgo ceviche, the national dish of Peru for which Chimbote was well known. Though ceviche, like the national brew pisco, was available everywhere in Peru, the fishing town of Chimbote boasted the tastiest. When we continued our journey, Violetta surprised me again by taking over the wheel from Mario while he sat in the back with Morigami.

We reached Trujilo before dawn. I heard Mario tell Violetta to drive quickly as it was the most important town in north Peru, and we had to be doubly careful in evading the police. Passing Chiclayo, Piura, and Sullana, we reached the important border town, Tumbes, at 5 p.m. Sixteen miles from Tumbes was Agua Verdes. Morigami sat up with difficulty. We had our travel documents ready.

Crossing the border wasn't as easy as we had imagined. Though we were ready to bribe the officials, the middlemen plagued us. Though we knew that the Peru-Ecuador border would be full of American tourists, we weren't prepared for such a long queue. As we stood at the end of a long line of tourists, a young Indian lady officer came out and spoke to Violetta. She took our papers and came back in minutes with the emigration clearance. We didn't have to offer a sol to anyone. Violetta hugged her in gratitude.

Mario took the wheel when we reached Ecuador. As we crossed the international bridge across Zarumilla river, I asked Violetta, 'Was she a Tupac?' Violetta nodded in assent.

'She said that she had heard a lot about me. The leadership had given her instructions to help us across the border. She has given us enough American dollars. Ecuador is a peculiar country. They don't have a currency of their own; like Panama, they use US dollars.'

'Does the Tupac leadership know of our journey?'

'Definitely. Once your tickets were confirmed I mailed them. They are taking care of our safety. Once we reach Ecuador we don't have to fear the Peruvian police. We have hideouts in several places. When Peru and Ecuador were at war the Ecuador government used to help us. Many Tupac camps started operating in Ecuador with the knowledge of the government. They are still active.'

After we crossed Zarumilla bridge, Mario stopped at a restaurant. We got burgers, fried chicken, and Coke. I saw two people watching us as we ate. One of them came up to us and spoke to Violetta in Quechua. She got up immediately and went to them. She came back and explained to us in a low voice. 'They've been deputed by the Tupacs for our security. They killed the spy who came to our flat last night. I don't think they gave him time to talk to the police about us. But some Shining Paths are on our trail. They are the ones who attacked us on the way. They have camps in Ecuador. So, it is better that we change our vehicle here. We will continue our journey in an old Chevrolet they have brought. The Honda will be safe here. They will follow us in another car.'

After our meal, we shifted our things into the Chevrolet. Though it was old, it was roomy and comfortable. We turned left from the Pan American highway to Guayaquil. The highway went straight to the Ecuadorian capital Quito. Though Quito is the capital, the most important city is Guayaquil. It is a big harbour city like your Mumbai. We reached Guayaquil at 10.30 p.m. Our stay was arranged at a hotel called El Noon, owned by the Tupacs. It was an old eighteenth-century building on the seashore near the harbour, but the interior was quite modern. As soon as we entered the suite on the second floor which overlooked the sea, Mario prepared to leave. Mario and Violetta had planned to leave that night, but Morigami stopped them. 'Violetta, why don't you go back tomorrow? I feel safer with you around.'

'You are in a safe place now. Why should you fear anything when you have Cora Gonzalva's descendant with you?'

'He too has his limitations. He's not superhuman.'

'Cora's people have some tablets inscribed with secrets. It endows them with magical powers.'

I couldn't control my laughter. She came to me and respectfully handed me a piece of paper she took from her pocket, on which was written 'Chandamshu Chandrdhamkumbhipalah'.

It is a line inscribed on Gonzalva Cora's tablet that Katrina also has with her. It is said to have miraculous powers.

'Do you have such inscriptions on your tablets?'

'I can't read any of it.'

'Didn't you try?'

'I did. It's in a strange language.'

After dressing Morigami's wounds, Mario and Violetta left. We went to the José Joaquín de Olmedo International Airport in Guayaquil in a van arranged by the Tupacs. We boarded the flight without further delay. Though her wounds had started to heal, Morigami found it difficult to sit.

'Can you sit up for seven hours?'

'Have to manage somehow.'

'When was Cora Gonzalva made to sit on the chair of thorns?'

'Not Cora but Abimael Guzmán, the leader of Shining Paths. The Shining Paths called him Chairman Gonzalo. When they arrested Gonzalo, a psoriasis patient, from a dance teacher's house they took him straight to the seventh police station and made him sit on the chair of thorns. His wounds took a year to heal.'

'A year?'

'In Yanamayo jail they gave him a chemical, telling him it was an ointment for his wounds.'

Morigami swallowed her painkillers. The Aymera Indian airhostess helped her. It was evening when the flight landed at JFK airport, ten minutes after the scheduled time. We had finally extricated ourselves from the unholy mess we had landed ourselves in. I kept thinking of the words Violetta had shown me. Had they been in Aymara or Quechua, Violetta would have known their meaning.

'*Chandamshu Chandrdhamkumbhipalah*'. Have you heard of it, Rekha?

Cora with love.

16
Sora Again

Perhaps the mission of those who love mankind is to make people laugh at the truth, to make truth laugh, because the only truth lies in learning to free ourselves from an insane passion for the truth.

— *The Name of the Rose*, Umberto Eco

WE HAD BEEN TOO BUSY GATHERING INFORMATION ABOUT ITTY Cora to hold soirées at the School for some time. But when Femi called to say that we must have a session that week, Rekha agreed. Having finished reading the first half of Morigami's blog and four chapters of *Nakshatra Cora*, I suggested that we discuss 'Itty Cora and the History of Kerala Mathematics', and Rekha agreed. As an expert on the subject we invited a retired professor from Kochi University, Professor Y.R.S. Vaidyanathan, who was known as Swamy. Apart from our usual guests, Femi and Brain, we invited

Benny and Advocate Mani, who was doing research on the history of Kunnamkulam.

As decided earlier, with the exception of the new guests, we were all dressed in traditional Kerala attire. Rashmi and Bindu wore *adikkachas* as undergarments and over them *arakachas* around their waists and *mulakachas* to cover their breasts. They had tied their hair up high and adorned it with jasmine and champa flowers. These garments were part of the 'Kotha Collection' that Bindu had designed for her upcoming fashion show in Kochi. Rekha had draped around herself the showpiece of the collection: the eighteen muzham kaachi, which was a length of silk with elaborate designs. If worn properly, the light red cloth revealed the exact contours of the body. Femi sported another piece from the same collection, an archakacha, a garment worn by the women of north Kerala when they went to war. Luckily, there was no menswear line in the collection, and Brain and I got away with wearing mundus and throwing smaller veshtis around our shoulders.

Swami was an Iyengar who had recently settled down in Kochi. He considered himself the next Ramanujan. But he wasn't as intelligent as he thought himself to be. He had gained a reputation for himself in academic circles by giving scholarly talks about the history of Indian mathematics. Advocate Mani, who was a practicing lawyer at the high court, had researched the history of Kunnamkulam with the sole intention of giving prominence to his own ancestry. After introducing everyone and offering drinks, Rekha commenced the discussion.

'The topic chosen for discussion today is the connection between an international pepper trader from Kunnamkulam, Francis Itty Cora, who lived in the fifteenth century, and the development of mathematics in Kerala. To make this discussion fruitful, we had mailed you all the information we have been able to collect about Itty Cora. We hope all of you have read the scanned copies of the first four chapters of K. Porinju B.A.'s *Nakshatra Cora alias Cora the Sailor.* As the school does not believe in formalities, let's begin.'

Swami assumed that everyone was waiting eagerly to hear him speak but by the time he opened his mouth, Femi, who was sitting near Brain on the sofa, began talking. 'When I read Rekha's mail the first thing that struck me was the inherent misogyny. Hypatia's tragedy is the tragedy of all women. Itty Cora, who later presented Hypatian principles to the world as his own, is just another example of the unfairness of a male-dominated society.'

'Femi,' Rekha said, 'I don't think we should approach this topic from a feminist perspective. I'm not saying that it is irrelevant. But we have to explore Itty Cora's contribution to the Kerala School of Mathematics that is being seriously discussed today in international circles. We have invited Professor Vaidyanathan and Advocate Mani for that purpose. A historical analysis is also necessary. As the principal of the School, I would suggest that this is the direction that the discussion take.'

The minute Rekha stopped, Swami moved forward on his seat and started to speak. 'Friends, even though this isn't an academic seminar, as the topic chosen is the history of mathematics, we should approach it with gravity. History is pure. No one should attempt to pollute it. But one must ever search for new knowledge. When we embark on that quest, the first step is to clearly establish the facts that are already known. The contributions of Sangama Grama Madhava, Parameshvaran, Neelakanda Somayagi, Jyeshthadevan, and Achutha Pisharady who lived in the fourteenth, fifteenth and sixteenth centuries, are being discussed in international academic circles under the umbrella term 'Kerala School of Mathematics'. Among them, the most important are the contributions of Sangama Grama Madhava. He is thought to have established this school. He lived from 1340 to 1425 in Irinjalakuda near Thrissur. He was the author of *Karanapaddhati*. His contemporary Parameshwaran

(1370 – 1466) lived in Alathiyoor village on the banks of the Bharathapuzha. He authored *Drigganita,* a text on astronomy, and wrote a commentary titled *Sidhantha Deepika* for Bhaskaracharya's principles contained in the text *Mahabhaskareeyam.*

'Neelakanda Somayagi (1444 – 1544) was his son. He wrote *Aryabhatiyabhasya,* a commentary on *Aryabhatiyam.* His most important contribution is *Tantrasangraham,* an explanation of Sangama Grama Madhava's principles. Jyeshthadevan (1500 – 1600) wrote *Yukthibhasha,* a Malayalam text explaining the theories of Madhava and Neelakandan. Though Isaac Newton is credited with having discovered calculus, it is now accepted that Madhavacharya had discovered it two hundred years before Newton. I've heard a lot about all these stalwarts who belonged to the Kerala School of Mathematics. But this is the first I'm hearing of an Itty Cora. Who is this Itty Cora?'

Swami stopped and looked questioningly at us. Benny indicated that Mani should explain. He put down his glass and started to speak as if he were presenting a case before the magistrate. 'Swamy, I expected this question. If you raise a doubt about the existence of Itty Cora then there is only emptiness left, a void which resists the discovery of knowledge. I know the history and geography of Kunnamkulam. We, the people of Kunnamkulam, know that a man called Corappappan existed. But if you research the history of this place, you won't find his name. Who wrote the history of Kerala? Namboodiris, Panickers, Nairs, and Warriers. Do they know the history of our land? They hung around temples and palaces and wrote a history to please the royalty. Don't go by that prejudiced perspective and ask questions like, "Who is this Itty Cora?"'

'That's not what I implied. The history of the Kerala School of Mathematics doesn't mention Itty Cora.'

'It won't. You mentioned a lot of names now. Who are they? I'll tell you. This Sangama Grama Madhava was a Madhavan Namboodiri from Irinjalakuda. In those days, what was "Koodal" in Tamil was "Sangragramam" in Sanskrit, and what is referred to here is the area around Koodal Manikyam temple. Parameswaran, Neelakandan, and Jeshthadevan are all Namboodiris from Thirunavaya, and they included Achuta Varyar for form's sake. Swami, this is the history of Namboodiris and not the history of the Kerala School of Mathematics.'

'Advocate! Don't lose your temper, let's all calm down,' I said. I poured everyone the nico chilly vodka that Benny had prepared in advance. Bindu brought fried mutton and hog plum pickle on a tray. She walked with difficulty as her garments were too tight, and Benny laughed.

'Oh! It's difficult to walk in these clothes, isn't it? Women who lived in those times must have had so much trouble.'

'No. I'm just not used to them. They're ideal for our climate. I'm presenting this collection at the Lakme fashion show in Kochi next week. What do you think?'

Benny felt her breast cloth and said, 'It's good quality cloth. I didn't realize it was so fine.'

'It's a combination of Egyptian cotton, linen, and Mysore silk. This piece is priced at 17,700 rupees. But I haven't put price tags on what Rekha and Femi are wearing. Price on request. Those are my showstoppers.'

As the conversation swerved from Itty Cora to fashion, Femi intervened eagerly. 'Is it your first fashion show?'

'No, my third. The first was last January at the Taj in Mumbai.'

'Who sponsored it?'

'Lakme. Then, in August, I had a show at Park Sheraton in Chennai. After that show, I got offers to design costumes for movies. The Kochi show is the first show of the year. Lakme is sponsoring.'

'We must make it a grand success. Kochi must be brought on par with Mumbai and Bengaluru in the Indian fashion scene.'

'Femi, we have good designers and models here, but we don't have an organized fashion industry. Mallus have a very conservative outlook.'

'We should change our attitude.'

I couldn't believe my ears. Usually, feminists in Kerala vehemently denounce beauty competitions and fashion shows. They take to the streets protesting against the artificial norms of beauty that male-dominated society foists upon them. I was surprised to find Femi arguing for the fashion industry. As I gazed at her breasts which refused to be contained in the mulakacha, Rekha pinched me on my thigh. Seeing that we were digressing, she stood up and said:

'Friends, let us come back to Itty Cora. We can have another session to discuss fashion. I've something to say about Itty Cora in connection with what the Advocate and Swamy said. First, let us take Swamy's question, "Who is this Itty Cora?" That is the core of our discussion today. According to the established history that Swamy has learnt, Itty Cora doesn't exist. He will not find a place in such histories. As Advocate said, in Swamy's Kerala School of Mathematics, there are only Namboodiris. I recently came across a website on the Namboodiris in Kerala. It's created by a group of Namboodiris who work in the US. If you read it you will get the impression that Namboodiris were the sole inhabitants of the Kerala cultural space at all times in the history of the state. They have made E.M.S. and V.T., who fought against the injustices prevalent in the Namboodiri community, are icons of their glory! The same has happened to the history of the Kerala School of Mathematics. The Namboodiris claim to be masters of mathematics and astronomy by completely ignoring the contributions of the Thachans, Moosaris, and Panickers, who applied mathematics in their chosen fields of work, and that of Jewish traders like Itty Cora. There are no genetic differences between Namboodiris and the rest of the species, then why is it that all the intellectuals of a society are Namboodiris? The question "Who is Itty Cora?" is a product of the intellectual suppression of the lower classes by the hierarchical caste system.'

'Rekha, I've never heard of Itty Cora in connection with mathematics. That is the reason I asked the question. Agreed, there lived such a man in the fifteenth century. What are his contributions to mathematics? Are any theories or texts attributed to him? Is he mentioned in other texts? None of these questions are answered in the notes you sent me. *Nakshathra Cora* is not an authentic work. It is an apocryphal work based on hearsay. Even this book doesn't say that Itty Cora was a mathematician.

'The Kerala School of Mathematics has a verifiable, accurate history. Sangama Grama Madhava has been accepted internationally. Many people support the view that Madhava's Kerala School discovered calculus two hundred years before Newton. Foreign universities including Princeton teach it as the Madhava-Leibniz series. When matters are proceeding so smoothly, why do you insist on dragging this Itty Cora into the picture?'

'Swami, it is convenient to maintain status quo in history as it is in science. But with status quo, there is no growth. We don't claim that Itty Cora is a mathematician. Corappapan was an international pepper merchant from Kunnamkulam. But Itty Cora has an important role in the growth of the study of mathematics.'

'Do you have any evidence to prove it?' Swami addressed his question to Rekha, but it was Bindu who answered.

'Swamy, we are in the process of collecting proof. The papyrus scrolls on astronomy and mathematics believed to have been lost when Hypatia was murdered were taken by Orestes from Alexandria to Timbuktu and preserved there. Hypatia's theorems were taught in the universities that flourished during Prophet Muhammad's time, as the Catholic Church did not exert any influence in those places. These theories spread from Timbuktu to the Maghreb and to other

Arab countries. The Italian Fibonacci learnt Hypatian theorems from the Maghreb, and after returning to his country, appropriated them as his own. It is Hypatia's first series that is now celebrated as the 'Fibonacci numbers'. Itty Cora reached Timbuktu two hundred years after this. He studied in Timbuktu for a year and for another two years in Alexandria, and imparted the knowledge he gained to the Namboodiris who worked for him in Kunnamkulam. The Namboodiris, who feared that the Greek language might pollute them, translated it into Sanskrit and wrote it down on palm leaves and tablets.'

Swamy interrupted Bindu's lucid recital of this alternate history: 'When Neelandan meets Itty Cora for the first time in *Nakshatra Cora* doesn't he recite "Vyase Varidhi"?'

This question made me realize that Swamy was extremely intelligent. Bindu paused for a moment to think and then continued, 'Swami, Porinju may have made some mistakes. He wrote *Nakshatra Cora* in the 1930s. He must have started work on the book three or four years before that. The sources he had for information on Itty Cora were very limited. Porinju's raw materials may have been based on the myths and the information given to him by some priest defrocked by the Catholic Church. I think he has tried to present the information he gathered as honestly as possible, but the possibility of Neelandan reciting "Vyase Varidhi" to Itty Cora on their first meeting is very slim. I have heard another story where Itty Cora gifted Madhavan acres of farmland when he read out the theories Itty Cora had taught him and he had translated into Sanskrit with Neelandan's help. That is said to be the reason why Madhavan left Irinjalakuda to settle down in Kanipayyoor.'

'Sorry, but you are playing havoc with our history. These are not things that can be accepted lightly. Sangama Grama Madhava and Neelakanda Somayagi have been recognized widely through their works, and these are established historical facts. You are trying to upset an authenticated version of history with a perspective based on hearsay.'

I couldn't allow Swamy's allegation to slide lightly as it was the basic rule of our soirées that everyone's opinion should be respected. Rekha gestured to me to let it go. But I made my disapproval clear: 'Swamy, these are not mere rumours. It is the other side of the established history of the Kerala School of Mathematics. Everyone has the freedom to believe variant versions of accepted history. The evidence is being collected. You can argue that the evidence is incorrect or insufficient. But you cannot question the motive behind it.'

Swami subsided into the sofa for the time being and Bindu continued, 'Itty Cora too was well versed in Sanskrit. He provided employment to the Namboodiris who came to him for financial help. Along with that, he taught Hypatia's theories to those who were interested. These theories are now being celebrated as the discoveries of the Kerala School of Mathematics. Around the same time, these theories were being disseminated across Europe through the secret Hypatian Schools that were established in the Maghreb and Europe. They later came to be attributed to Fermat, Fibonacci, Laplace, and Fourier. The arguments we are raising here are relevant not only for the Kerala School but the global history of mathematics.'

When Bindu fell silent, Brain spoke for the first time.

'I am not a historian of mathematics, but I don't think that this possibility can be easily discarded. But, as Swamy asked, what is the corroborative evidence, Bindu?'

'Gheverghese George Joseph in his book *The Crest of the Peacock* argues that the theories of the Kerala School reached Europe through Jesuit priests. That is completely contrary to the Itty Cora argument. But G.G. Joseph's view has not been fully accepted by the Europeans. They will use it to undermine the Kerala School but they will never recognize the Hypatian School either. If they do so, they will have to rewrite the entire history of European mathematics. Similarly, the Catholic Church will never recognize the Hypatian School. Though both are pagans, they would prefer Sangama Grama Madhava.'

Benny poured one more round of nico chilly vodka. He filled Bindu's glass last. She gulped it down.

'I didn't really understand what this girl said. Are you trying to say that this Corappappan was such a great man?'

'Any doubts, Benny? He was our Kaaranavar. It was one among his seventy-nine children who established our ancestral house in Narikatt. We have two priests in the family.'

Rashmi looked excitedly at Advocate, 'Is your house the First House of the 18th Clan?'

Advocate pretended to receive an urgent call on his cell and went to the balcony. I felt something was amiss. Femi started to speak, making the most of the opportunity, 'We have reached a point where this discussion cannot proceed without more proof. We have to collect more evidence to prove Bindu's argument. But, considering the available proof, we can't discard the theory. We must collect more authentic evidence about the Hypatian School in Timbuktu and the ones in Europe and Algeria. We should meet after doing some more research. We must problematize the anti-women perspective that begins with the life of Hypatia.'

We agreed to part.

17
An Offer Refused

Long live Iraq! Long live the Iraqi people! Down with the traitors.

— Saddam Hussein

Dear Rekha,

I went straight to Princeton University with Morigami from JFK. She needs someone's help for a few days. It's just an hour's drive from New York to Princeton in New Jersey, but we had to take a taxi to Masako's house and get our car before proceeding to Princeton. It was late evening by the time we reached. Morigami stays on campus in the Laurence Apartment complex. The atmosphere is calm and serene. If you've seen the movie *A Beautiful Mind,* it has the same ambience.

Though it is a studio apartment, Morigami has done it up beautifully. I felt a sense of relief when I reached the mild winter of New York from the sweltering heat of Ecuador. Morigami got her keys from the housing department, and the instant she entered the flat, she kicked off her shoes and lay down flat on her stomach on the bed. She was asleep in no time. The long flight had exhausted her. As her refrigerator was well-stocked, I cooked dinner and then woke her up.

'Cora, you've been through lot a trouble.'

'I had no option.'

'You've to stay with me at least a week. I've thought of a way in which you can make good use of the time you spend here. Go get the palm leaves and tablets you have. I've brought everything Katrina gave me. We'll examine them closely. After I report to the department tomorrow, I just need to go to the library once in a while and update my blog on Itty Cora.'

I dressed her wounds that night and found that the Tupac doctor's medicines were effective. Her wounds were healing.

The next day I accompanied Morigami to Fine Hall, the fourteen-storey building in which the mathematics department functions. It is the biggest building in Princeton University. We went to meet Morigami's research guide, Professor Carlo Rocca, who had his office on the eighth floor. When she introduced me as Francis Itty Cora's descendant, he exclaimed, 'Mr Itty Cora, welcome to Princeton! Morigami, you are really lucky to meet the descendant of a man who is believed to have lived five hundred years ago and is the subject of your research. Where did you meet him?'

'Peru, but Itty Cora was born and brought up in the US. His mother migrated from Florence. He's an Iraq war veteran.'

We spoke to him for a while. The professor told me to stay on a bit and help Morigami with her research. I tried to mask my feeling of intellectual inferiority. Morigami did not want the professor to know about her injuries and quickly stepped out of his office. She borrowed some books from the library, and we came out of Fine Hall.

Next, we went to meet Professor Paul Krugman of the economics department. She had told me that he was an important economist who attacked Bush's financial policies in his column in the *New York Times*. Though Morigami introduced me as an Iraq war veteran, he treated me with sympathy. Only after detailed introductions were made did we speak about the Iraq War.

'Itty Cora, how do you see the Iraq War now?'

'I went to Iraq as part of the special recruitment conducted by the Pentagon to implement the Salvador Option. I was in Baghdad in the 372nd Military Police Company. Linda England and Charles Garner were in the same company. I was trained in the camp connected to Abu Gharib prison. Then they sent me to Fallujah. I was quite enthusiastic in the beginning. Flowing liquor, good-looking Iraqi girls, the freedom to do whatever one wanted; we were celebrating life. Now I feel that it was wrong. It could certainly have been avoided.'

'Why?'

'Saddam did not possess any weapons of mass destruction as we thought or said he did.'

'This afternoon, the war journalist Jose Anderson is giving a talk on US policies in Iraq in Robertson Hall in the Woodrow Wilson International Affairs Department. Anderson is a friend of mine. I think he will find it quite helpful to have a veteran like you with him. Will you help him?'

I was not used to speaking at university seminars, and looked at Morigami. She nodded, and I agreed.

We went back to the apartment, rested a while, and reached Robertson Hall at a quarter past two. The seminar was scheduled for 2.40 p.m. The notice board outside the hall sported the notice: 'IWV Itty Cora will also speak in this seminar.' Josse Anderson was waiting for us. After formal introductions, he came straight to the point.

'I need your help during the second session of the seminar. I'll invite you to talk about your experiences in Iraq.'

The seminar started bang on time. As the topic was Iraq, the hall was overflowing with listeners. Several prominent people, including Paul Krugman, were in the audience. After the first session, Anderson invited me on stage.

'Mr Itty Cora, can you share your experiences on the Iraq war front with us?'

As I was drawing to a close my narration of the most terrible experiences in Iraq, someone from the audience asked, 'Mr Itty Cora, didn't you have even a single good experience in Iraq?'

'Just one. I saw Saddam Hussein in person.'

'When?'

'After Saddam's arrest, once Donald Rumsfeld had come to meet him in prison with Bush's compromise formula. When Saddam was brought to meet Rumsfield, I was on sentry duty outside.'

'What did they talk about?'

'Such conversations are always held behind closed doors. Sentries are not privy to them. But I remember the expressions on their faces as Rumsfeld came out: a fox bidding farewell to an old, wounded lion.'

As I went back to my seat, Anderson continued. 'That conversation was later somehow leaked and published in the Egyptian Magazine *Al-Usbu*. It came out in their second edition of May 2005 titled, "A Rare Conversation between Saddam and Rumsfield".'

Anderson clicked his laptop, and the transcript of the conversation appeared on the screen.

Saddam – Donald

Rumsfeld: I have come to meet you to talk with you about the situation in Iraq. We have been in communication with some of your supporters inside and outside Iraq and they have advised us to listen to you.

Saddam Hussein: And what is it that you want? Your forces have occupied the territory of noble Iraq; you brought down the ruling regime without any legal basis; you attacked the sovereignty of an independent, free, sovereign country; and you committed crimes that history will record as testimony against your bloodstained civilization. So what more do you want?

Rumsfeld (trying to conceal his anger): There is no call for going into the past. I've come specially to present you a clear and specific offer, and I want to hear from you a clear and specific answer.

Saddam Hussein (mockingly): I suppose you've come to apologize and return authority to the Iraqis.

Rumsfeld: We have nothing to apologize for. You were a danger to your neighbours. You were trying to acquire weapons of mass destruction, and you exercised dictatorship over your people. So, it was natural for us to extend our help to the people of Iraq to rid themselves of the hardships they had faced for more than thirty years.

Saddam Hussein: I know that you're ignorant of history and I know that your president is no less ignorant. But it seems that you've been telling lies for so long that you have come to believe them yourselves. If you mean by 'our neighbours' the Zionist entity, then, yes, we really were posing a danger to it and preparing to liberate our plundered land in Palestine. This is the trust of every Arab person, not just Iraqis, for that land is Arab and its people are Arab and the Zionists have done nothing but occupy the land. They came from every corner of the world with your help and that of the old colonial powers. But if you mean Kuwait, I would like to ask you: have you withdrawn from Kuwait yourself?

Rumsfeld: These are security issues. Besides, between us and Kuwait and the other Gulf states, there are security agreements. We came in based on their request to defend them from your threats.

Saddam Hussein: Isn't it funny to entrust the wolf to guard the sheep? The Kuwaiti people are an Arab people, and Kuwait is Iraqi territory. So, I would ask you to go and read up history well, except that I am sure that you will never be able to grasp it.

Rumsfeld: Enough of this chatter. I am offering you ...

Saddam Hussein (cuts him off): Before you offer me your rotten goods, I want to ask you: did you find any weapons of mass destruction?

Rumsfeld (confused): We haven't found any so far. But we definitely will find them one day. Do you deny that you were intending to make a nuclear bomb?

Saddam Hussein: We have had no weapons of mass destruction since 1991. We were speaking the truth to the International Inspection Team and we were speaking the truth in our letters to Kofi Annan. And you knew that, but you were looking for any false excuse to occupy Iraq and overthrow the legal regime.

Rumsfeld: The Iraqis welcomed us, and the reason was the bloody practices of your regime for all the years you ruled Iraq.

Saddam Hussein: I ask you, Mr Rumsfeld ... enough lying. It is because of you that the earth of Iraq has become soaked with blood. You plotted against us and you came with some traitors to take over the great land of Iraq.

Rumsfeld: Those you call traitors were chosen as their leaders by the Iraqi people through democratic means and free and fair elections, which never took place while you ruled the country.

Saddam Hussein: I know that you came with a band of traitors with Jalal al-Talibani in their front ranks (laughs mockingly). Great Iraq being ruled by al-Talibani and al-Ja'fari, isn't that ridiculous? And what kind of elections are you talking about? Is it possible to hold free elections, as you call them, when our country is occupied? Mr Rumsfeld, we have learned from history that occupiers come only with their lackeys and agents; you want after that to convince me that the people of Iraq are enjoying freedom and democracy? You must really be delirious.

Rumsfeld (trying very hard to control his anger): You are in isolation and don't know the facts of what is going on outside. The Iraqi people have been freed from your oppression. If they saw you or any of your men on the street, they would destroy you!

Saddam Hussein: And I bet you that if the Iraqi Resistance learned where you were, you wouldn't be able to get out of Iraq alive. I want you to convey some advice to your stupid president: you must tell him to save what remains of his troops. Death is stalking them and history will not forgive him.

Rumsfeld: I came to talk with you about the 'terrorist' operations that your men are inciting and carrying out. They recently carried out a foul attack against Abu Gharib prison where more than fifty Americans were killed or wounded, and they killed a number of those in custody on various charges as well. Your men are getting help from terrorists in every corner of the world and they are threatening the democratic experiment in Iraq.

Saddam Hussein: What exactly is it that you want?

Rumsfeld: I'm making you one offer, and that is that you will be released and can freely choose for yourself a place of exile in any country you like, on the condition that you go on television and issue a condemnation of terrorism and order your men to stop these acts.

Saddam Hussein: Have you obtained the agreement of your president to this offer?

Rumsfeld: Yes, this offer was arrived at in a meeting in which the President, Vice President, Secretary of State, and Chief of Intelligence took part. And I have been authorized to inform you of this offer.

Saddam Hussein: It's a paltry offer.

Rumsfeld (with a sigh): We're also ready to bring elements close to you into the government.

Saddam Hussein: And what else?

Rumsfeld: You will be given generous financial assistance and security protection for yourself and your family in the country of your choice.

Saddam Hussein: Do you want to hear my conditions?

Rumsfeld: I would love to.

Saddam Hussein (with an air of superciliousness): I want you first to set a timetable for your withdrawal from Iraq and your government to commit itself to it before the world and to begin the withdrawal immediately.

Second, I ask you to release immediately all the Iraqi and Arab prisoners in the prisons you have set up. Third, I ask you to pledge full compensation for the material losses inflicted on the Iraqi people as a result of your aggression against our country since the Mother of all Battles in 1991 until today. And I accept the assistance of an Arab and international committee in estimating the extent of those losses.

Fourth, I ask that you return the money that you and your men have plundered from the treasuries of Iraq, and its oil, in particular by that criminal L. Paul Bremer with his gang of traitors and renegades.

Fifth, I demand the return of the artifacts that you have stolen and given to the archaeological artifacts mafia. These are treasures that are beyond all monetary value, because they carry the history of Iraq and its civilization. It's true that you don't have any civilization or history and that the lifespan of your country is no more than a few hundred years, but all that must not serve to justify your theft and your hatred for the civilization of Iraq and the wealth of Iraq.

And sixth, you must hand over the weapons of mass destruction if you have found any, and return to us the lives of all the martyrs whose lives you have taken, and the honor of the noble women of Iraq whom you have dishonoured.

Rumsfeld: Is this some kind of joke?

Saddam Hussein: No! This is the bitter reality ... which you know, Mr Rumsfeld. You have committed the greatest crime in history against a peaceful Arab country. We met in the 1980s. Do you remember your offers?

Rumsfeld: Enough of the past. We are reassessing our position towards you and towards a number of powers that have been hostile to us in the past. We have decided to hold dialogue with moderate Islamists, and we have no objection to their coming to power through the ballot box. More important than that, we have decided to open channels for dialogue with 'terrorist' organizations like the Hamas, Islamic Jihad, and Hezbollah, and also with other fundamentalist organizations in the world. We even plan to contact the Taliban movement in Afghanistan to examine the possibility of their participation in power, in exchange for their giving up arms.

Saddam Hussein: So you have begun to rethink your erroneous course?

Rumsfeld: It is a natural development of events. We are striving to spread democracy in all countries and movements subject to tyranny.

Saddam Hussein: May you prosper if you are speaking the truth. I know your real aim, though. If you were really speaking the truth, then you and your allies would begin immediately by withdrawing from Iraq. And you would also have to depart from your position of support for 'Israel'. But I know that your president is stubborn and arrogant and is not telling the truth.

Rumsfeld: He is a democratically elected president, not a bloody ruler like you.

Saddam Hussein: Terror is your product and lying is your method.

Rumsfeld: This offer is a historic opportunity for you. You will be released and we will consult with you in everything related to the running of Iraq. If you refuse this offer, the opportunity will be lost.

Saddam Hussein: I am not looking for opportunities. I am not looking for a way to save my neck from the gallows that you have set up for all of Iraq. If I wanted that, I would have accepted the Russian offer and saved my sons and grandsons from martyrdom. I don't know what has become of my family and my daughters and grandchildren. But believe me, I am concerned with every Iraqi citizen and the future of great Iraq more than I am concerned with myself and my family.

Through your men, you previously made me an offer that if I declared that the weapons of mass destruction had been smuggled to Syria, in return you would release me. I rejected that then and I reject it again now.

Rumsfeld: I don't want a rejection from you. I want you to think about it. We are continuing our reassessment of our stances at present. We want to stop the bloodshed on both sides. And therefore, we have made this offer out of a position of power and not of weakness.

We asked Jalal al-Talibani to make a statement denying any intention of executing you as a sign of good intentions on our part. We are ready to reassess our entire position on the political arrangement in Iraq as a whole and to discuss this matter with you and with your men.

Saddam Hussein: Are you ready to withdraw or not?

Rumsfeld: We can possibly discuss redeployment. Our forces have prepared bases for a long stay. We could perhaps withdraw from the streets and cities, but we will remain in the bases for some time.

Saddam Hussein: Then you want a new stooge to add to the line of stooges. No, Mr Rumsfeld. Don't forget that you are talking with Saddam Hussein, the President of the Republic of Iraq.

Rumsfeld: But you have lost power.

Saddam Hussein: I have nothing left but honour, and honour cannot be bought and sold.

Rumsfeld: But life is priceless.

Saddam Hussein: There is no value to life without honour. You robbed Iraq of its honour when you trampled on its land, and we will regain our honour whether Saddam Hussein remains or dies a martyr.

Rumsfeld: Your supporters with whom we have been holding discussions told us that you were the first and last decision-maker. Were they expecting this reaction from you?

Saddam Hussein: Definitely, they know that Saddam Hussein cannot back down at the expense of his homeland and honour.

Rumsfeld: History will hold you responsible for the blood that is being shed in Iraq.

Saddam Hussein: Rather, history will judge you for your crimes. I warned you before that you would commit suicide on the walls of Baghdad. And here you are, paying the price. I want you to go to London and read the records of the British Foreign Office and learn something about the struggle of the Iraqi people against your British friends, who are now repeating their mistakes and fighting with you. The Iraqi people are a stubborn people who do not fear death. The resistance is stronger than you imagine. So I promise you that you will have to face even more.

The audience in Robertson Hall devoured the text with their eyes in pindrop silence. But no one was willing to speak about it. People walked out silently. As I was returning to Morigami's apartment, someone called out, 'Itty Cora, do you remember Saddam's face that day?'

'Yes, he looked like a wounded old lion.'

Cora with love.

18
N Is a Number

In our century, in which mathematics is so strongly dominated by 'theory doctors', he has remained the prince of problem solvers and the absolute monarch of problem posers.

— Dr Ernst Straus about Paul Erdos

Dear Rekha,

When we returned after the seminar in Robertson Hall, Morigami showed me everything she had collected about Itty Cora: hundreds of books, thousands of photocopied pages, a sketch of Palazzo Cora in Florence, replicas of a few Raphael paintings, copper tablets, and palm leaf manuscripts she had got from Katrina, a heap of CDs, and a DVD of the documentary *N Is a Number*.

I first looked at Katrina's tablets and palm leaf manuscripts. The copper tablets were similar to those that I had. Not being able to understand the geometric shapes and words in an alien tongue, I turned to the DVD.

'Is this a movie about Itty Cora?'

'No. It's about Paul Erdos, the biggest mathematician of the twentieth century. The Hungarian pronunciation is Pal Eardoche. He is the one who started me on the quest for Itty Cora.'

'How?'

'He is my guru. I met Pal Erdos when I went to Budapest in 1992 for the BSM. BSM stands for Budapest Semesters in Mathematics. In 1985, Erdos started the Hungarian Academy of Sciences. It's a prestigious course for students before they embark on serious research. Eminent professors from Alfred Renyi Institute of Mathematics and   Eötvös Loránd University teach this course. The BSM is very useful if you want to get a place for research in universities like Princeton. It certainly helped me.

'Pal Erdos was born into an intellectual Jewish family in Budapest on 26 March 1913. His parents, Anna and La Jose Erdos, were mathematics teachers. When his mother was in hospital giving birth to Pal, his sisters Magda, aged five, and Clara, aged six, succumbed to the scarlet fever that was raging across Europe.

'La Jose was forced to join the army, as there was compulsory military conscription during the Austria-Hungary war. He was captured by the Russians and taken to Siberia. Anna was devastated but survived, owing to her indomitable will. She was afraid to send Pal, who was a weak child, to school for fear that he might fall ill, and so she educated him at home. Six years later, when Pal's apuka came home from Siberia, things began to go well for the family. Pal, who was an exceptionally bright child, was introduced to the world of mathematics by his parents. By the time he was three, he was already multiplying and dividing numbers. At the age of ten, La Jose showed him the world of prime numbers. Pal, at the age of eleven, started writing for *KoMal*, a mathematical magazine published in Hungary for higher secondary students. Though there was a six per cent cap on admissions of Jews to universities in Hungary,

Pal secured a place in Budapest Science University. It was during his time at the university that an incident which became a milestone in his life occurred. In 1850, Chrbychev had presented extremely complicated proof for Joseph Bertrand's 1849 theorem, which stated that there is always a prime number between one prime number and its double. Pal Erdos proved this theory in a very simple manner. This earned him a doctorate from Budapest University in 1934. To get a doctoral degree in mathematics at the age of twenty-one is no mean feat. Soon after, he got a fellowship in Manchester for higher studies. While Erdos was a research scholar in Manchester, Hitler was embarking on his Jew hunt. When he realized that he could never go back home, he moved to the US. He reached Princeton in 1938, but his hedonistic life forced him to leave. Then he started on his journeys. Now you watch *N Is a Number*. We'll speak later.'

N Is a Number: A Portrait of Paul Erdos is produced, directed, and edited by George Paul Csicsery. But it is John Knoop's camerawork that is a marvel. The camera has picked up every nuance of the anarchic life led by the eccentric intellectual Pal Erdos. Pal and many of his scientist friends appear in this movie that was filmed in four countries. It has won several honours at international film festivals in Berlin, Montreal, and Chicago. After watching the movie I felt that I'd known Pal a long time. But I still didn't understand how Pal had introduced Morigami to Itty Cora. She explained, 'When I was a student at Catholic University in Lima, I was placed first in an exam conducted by the Mathematical Association of America; that is how I got selected for the BSM. I flew to Europe for the first time in September 1992. As there were no direct flights from Lima to Budapest, I flew to Frankfurt and then on to Budapest. The East European countries were celebrating the downfall of communism.

'Budapest includes Buda that lies on the west of the Danube, and Pest on the East. Our university was in the metropolitan area of Pest. My roommates were Betsy from Chicago and Nikita Sabo from Holland. Though my stay was comfortable, I found it hard to master the Hungarian language that had fourteen vowels in it. Pal was our course director, but even a month after the course had begun he hadn't come to teach us. No one knew where he was or when he would arrive at the institute. But the other teachers were excellent. My electives were number theory, combinatorics, and topology. We had to learn elementary problem-solving, the history of mathematics, and the Hungarian language. Though combinatorics was a bit complicated, it wasn't very difficult for me as the lessons were in English. As even the signboards in Budapest are in Hungarian, the greatest challenge was to learn the language. You had to learn their language to survive in that country.

'In the evenings Betsy, Sabo, and I used to go shopping or to operas or classical concerts. Sabo knew a little Hungarian, so we found it easy to move around. In our free time we boarded the Blue Line or the Red Line on the Millenium Metro and went sightseeing in Buda and Pest. We visited Statue Park, Margaret Island, the Hungarian Museum, and Buda Castle. My favourite of the nine bridges across the Danube was Szechenyi, a hanging bridge built in 1849. It was the first bridge built across the Danube in Budapest. It is a cultural symbol of Budapest. It is lovely to watch the Danube from Szechenyi, when the sun sets in Buda.

'On weekends the BSM students used to go to Prague, Kraków in Poland, and other places in Hungary from Keleti, the railway station in Budapest. The fervour of the Velvet Revolution was dying out in Prague. Havel resigned as president during this period and Czechoslovakia decided to split into the Czech Republic and Slovakia. We started for Prague on 7 November 1992 by the Saturday morning Budapest-Berlin (EC174), which left at 9.30 a.m. We reached Prague at four in the evening. As the train did not stop at Praha hlavni nadrazi, the most important station, we got down at the next station, Praha-Holesovice. Prague was silent.

The shops were shut. There were no buses or taxis. Black flags dotted the place. There were silent processions everywhere. Alexander Dubcek had died that day. He was injured in a car accident on the first of September and died on the seventh of November. Have you heard of the Prague Spring? Dubcek had tried to give a humane touch to Russian communism. The Prague Spring began on 5 January 1968 when he was elected the first secretary of the Communist Party of Czechoslovakia. Brezhnev suppressed it cruelly and on 20 August 1968 the Russian army entered Prague, arrested Dubcek, and flew him to Moscow in a military helicopter. When he returned on 28 August, he was almost unrecognizable; even his voice had changed. It was said that he had been fed radioactive strontium in his soup. Anyway the Prague Spring came to an end. Very soon Dubcek's position in Czech politics declined. When the Velvet Revolution brought the communist regime down in 1989, Dubcek was unanimously elected speaker of the Czechoslovakian Federal Assembly on 28 December 1989.

'We spent the whole day in the hotel. Watching the TV news flashes about the death of Dubcek. Volga, a teacher, remarked, "It may just be your luck that Dubcek has died. Now wherever he is, Pal Erdos will definitely come here." Erdos detested both Jo (Joseph Stalin) and Uncle Sam, liked Dubcek. As Volga had predicted, Erdos who was in London reached Bratislava, the capital of Slovakia the next day for the funeral.

'As Prague was in mourning, we returned to Budapest on Sunday without having done any sightseeing. The students were happy when the combinatorics teacher Yousuf Alavi announced that Pal Erdos would come straight to Budapest after the funeral. Hungarian television ran a live telecast of the funeral. Former Czech President Havel was conspicuous by his absence at the funeral, which was attended by dignitaries from over fifty countries. We couldn't get a glimpse of Pal Erdos on TV, as a large number of politicians were present.

'The next day, the institute wore a festive look. By 3 p.m., all the teachers and students got into a van on which the letters BSM were inscribed in a large font, and set off for Budapest Ferihegy International Airport that was eight miles away. As the fourth flight from Bratislava landed, a visibly tired Pal Erdos—he was seventy-nine at the time—came out with the Cambridge mathematician Béla Bollobás and his wife Gabriella Bollobás. Though he was ravaged by age and carelessly clothed, there was a glow on his face. I waited a while for the crowd to melt before going up to him. He looked at me carefully. I was the only person of Japanese origin there.

'"Nippon epsilon, your name?"

'"Hashimoto Morigami."

'He patted me on my back like a grandfather would and got into a car with the Bollobáses. My heart told me that I had met the guru I was searching for.

'He led a very strange life. He had no family, job, or home. Even the position as course director of the BSM was an honorary one. He led a nomadic life moving from one university to another, from the house of one mathematician to the next, flitting across continents for conferences, living out of two suitcases. Pal Erdos travelled all over the world. He couldn't perform the routine mundane tasks that ordinary people carried out in their daily lives. He never bothered about money. He didn't even wish to prove new theories and gain accolades. But he was the God of problem-solving. His life flowed from the intricacies of one problem to the next. There is no area of mathematics that he left untouched. He published more than a thousand mathematical texts. Four hundred and ninety-three mathematicians have co-authored texts with him.

'The next day, it was Pal Erdos who taught us combinatorics. He began by talking about *Bhagwati Sutram,* a Jain religious text believed to have been written in India in the fourth century. When he said that combinatorics originated in India, I saw some mathematicians casting surprised looks at one other. He said that he had once gone to India for a series of talks in the universities and given the remuneration he received to the widow of Ramanujan, an Indian mathematician who had died young. In very simple and entertaining Erdos language—language in which the words *Super Fascist* referred to God, *epsilon* meant children, slaves were men, bosses implied women, noise was music, and *captured* and *liberated* stood for married and divorced respectively—he spoke about the basic principles of combinatorics. After listening to him, I lost all my fear of the subject.

'Pal Erdos spent three more days in Budapest. He stayed in an apartment as a guest of the university. After his mother's death in 1973, he had never stayed in his own apartment in Budapest. Though he was known to be a confirmed bachelor with no interest in anything other than mathematics, I wanted to meet him alone. I went to meet him on the evening of his second day at the university. He was on his balcony gazing at the Danube.

'He said, "Nippon epsilon, welcome! Welcome!" I was struck with the thought that this frail man was considered the emperor of mathematics. As I sat down hesitantly, he took a piece of paper out of the pocket of his faded coat and gave it to me. It was a mathematical problem.

'"Is there a power of two that contains every digit from zero to nine the same number of times?" he asked

'I couldn't grasp the question at once. Maybe it was because I was nervous in the presence of the world-famous mathematician.

'"$20 if you can find the answer in ten minutes."

'When I heard the amount of the prize money, I assumed it was an easy question. I'd heard that he offered higher prize money for more difficult questions. It was considered an honour among students of mathematics to receive a cheque signed by Erdos. Many never cashed the cheques, preferring to frame them as memorabilia.

I stared at the question; within minutes the answer formulated itself in my mind. I looked at him boldly and said, "No".

'"How did you arrive at this answer?"

'It was a sample Erdos problem that was used to make beginners think. If all the numbers from 0 to 9 in a number that includes all these numbers is added in whichever order they may be, the answer will be $0+1+2+3+4+5+6+7+8+9 = 45$. Now imagine that these numbers are repeated several times. If they are repeated several times the answer will be $K(0+1+2+3+4+5+6+7+8+9) = 45K$. Whatever might be the value of K, it will be divisible by 3. Any number that is a multiple of 2 is not divisible by 3. Once you get the answer it seems simple but I can't describe to you the tension I went through before I arrived at the solution.'

'Did he give you a signed cheque?,' I asked her.

'Not then, but the next day in class. I was one of four students who received a signed cheque from Erdos during his stay at the university. When I answered his question and explained it, he hugged me. I was only twenty then. Youth was coursing through my veins. You know that I don't consider it wrong to use my body for academic advancement. I prolonged the embrace for half a minute. I don't know whether he even noticed that I was a woman. We spoke for nearly half an hour. He was really surprised when I told him that I was from Peru.

'"I thought you were from Japan."

'"Half Japanese. My maternal grandfather emigrated from Okinawa. I was born and brought up in Lima."

'"Did you join the BSM to learn combinatorics?"

'"No, what I really like is the history of mathematics."

'"That's good. It's the first time a student who is interested in the history of mathematics has joined the BSM. Usually, the students are interested either in combinatorics or graph theory. I'll give you an interesting assignment."

'He took a photograph of Alexander Grothendieck out of his suitcase and gave it to me.

'"Epsilon, this is the French mathematician Alexander Grothendieck. Since 1991 his whereabouts are unknown. It is said that he is somewhere in the south of France. He is a friend of mine. He and I and some others are members of the secret Hypatian School. Today, it is just a school of thought, not a formal organizition. But up to the eighteenth century, these schools were very well organized. Till the Catholic Church rid itself of its enmity towards mathematics and science, people working seriously on these subjects usually had some connection with these schools. You should go and meet Alexander Grothendieck. He has documents about an Indian pepper merchant who lived in Florence in the fifteenth century. He once told me that these documents have great importance in the history of mathematics."

'"Who is this pepper merchant?" I asked.

'"A Francis Itty Cora. He was a native of Kerala in India, but from the beginning of the sixteenth century he lived in Florence in Italy. I've collected a lot of information about him. If you are interested, come and meet me before I leave."

'I took Grothendieck's picture and left.'

It was getting late; we had dinner. As I dressed her wounds, she cracked a cruel joke.

'Itty Cora, you are now like Pal Erdos. If you write a test to qualify for the papacy, you will score cent percent marks.'

I was furious. I pinched her ear hard and she sulked.

Cora with love.

19

La Computadora!

Harastharasthrunya Nidhuvanakalaha,
Moukthikanam Visherno,
Bhoomow Yatha Sthree Bhagashayana
Lagthah Panchamoshancha Drishtaha
Praptha Shashatussukosham Ganakah Dashamaka
Samgreehithaha Priyena
Drishtam Shalkam Cha Sootre Kathaya Kathiraiyer
Moukthkaireshe Harah

Dear Rekha,

Morigami was very happy when I gave her the tablets and palm leaves I had at my place in New York. As she lay on her stomach examining the treasure trove carefully, I sat beside her on her left.

'Cora, there are marked differences between these and the scripts Katrina gave me, both in geometric shapes as well as in the text. Alok Chandra Chaterjee, who is doing research in computer science at the University of Chicago, is coming to Princeton tomorrow. Alok is a friend of mine; ours is a friendship of bodies. He knows many Indian languages including Sanskrit and Pali. Shall we ask Alok to take a look at these?'

'As you please. But be careful. Don't lose them.'

'Never! I won't part with the originals. I'll give him scanned copies. Alok is trustworthy.'

'You can't be sure. It is, after all, a friendship based on sex.'

'It's not a relationship I have with many people. It is quite unlike the companionship you develop with a person you share a drink with. This is something shared by two people who faithfully celebrate the friendship of their bodies. I'm not talking of male chauvinists or men who occasionally slip out of their marriages. I'm talking about people who think deeply and live freely. Alok is such a person.'

'Okay, as you wish.'

'Both of us are working hard to get an Erdos Number One. In the field of international mathematical research, people who co-author academic papers or texts with Erdos are said to have an Erdos Number One. There are four hundred and ninety three people who have got this number. People like Béla Bollobás, a close disciple, have co-authored four or five academic essays with him. People who co-author articles with those who have co-authored papers with Erdos are said to have an Erdos Number Two. It's a sort of chain that may go up to Erdos Numbers Three, Four, or Five. Most of those who have won the Nobel Prize, the Field Medal, or the Crafoord Prize would fall within the Erdos Numbers One to Four. Many are still publishing their research findings based on the research they did with Erdos before his death as they have his authorization letter to do so. I've got an authorization letter from him too, which means that I can publish my thesis titled "Francis Itty Cora: The Link between Eastern and European Mathematics" by Pal Erdos and

Hashimoto Morigami, once my research is over. Alok is in the same position. Erdos gave him an assignment in combinatorics when he joined the BSM in 1994.

'I met Alok four years ago. Alok, who got his doctoral degree in computer science from IIT Kanpur, was in Princeton for only under a year. Like Pal Erdos, Alok too was not given an extension for his fellowship because of his anarchic lifestyle. But the time he spent at Princeton was enjoyable. He doesn't fit your set notions of a computer scientist. He looks like a college student. His day starts at twelve noon and ends at 2 a.m. There is no intoxicating substance that he hasn't tried. But he dresses neatly, uses a jasmine-scented perfume, and converses entertainingly with a slight Indian accent. He tries to make a joke out of everything. He pulled my leg soon after I met him.

'"Morigami, you are Peruvian. You must be knowing Spanish very well."

'"A bit."

'"Tell me, what is the gender of the computer? Is it la computadora or el computador?"

'I hadn't ever thought about the gender of the computer. In Spanish, all nouns are gendered. Not wanting to appear foolish I said, "It's la computadora."

'He immediately asked me, "Why?"

'As I stood silent, he replied.

'"It is because the computer is like a beautiful woman. Even if the hard disk is full of data, someone has to log on for the machine to work. You compare many models before you buy one. Then you spend more than half your salary buying accessories for your system. Within no time it becomes obsolete, no matter how good the configuration is. Then you feel that you should have waited a while longer to get a better model. If you make a tiny mistake while using it, your computer sulks like a touch-me-not."

'I laughed at his joke. He sees everything from an Indian perspective. I told him that his observations couldn't be applied to women all over the world. Women here are not touch-me-nots. Once the relationship is over they will bid goodbye and part in a dignified manner.'

'"In that case there is a chance that we can be friends."

'"Why?"

'"I don't believe in love. I believe only in love-making."

'The friendship of our bodies began that night when I defeated him in the first game. He couldn't keep up with my pace. He kissed me on both my cheeks, calling me his "La Computadora". He said all my moves were as perfect as if they had been programmed in a computer. He has called me "La Computadora" ever since. As he was leaving he told me, "Morigami! Your P number is one."

'The P number is not as complicated as the Erdos number. It's a scale of ten to one where one is the highest and the partner rates you based on your performance. Alok lifted me up and put me down, bidding me goodbye.

'When he was in Princeton, Alok used to come here often. He would text me ten minutes before his arrival saying, "Dear *La Computadora,* may I come and log on?"' It could happen at midnight, mid-afternoon, or at 4 in the morning. But he has never texted me when it would be inconvenient for me. If I replied saying, "Welcome, the system is on," he would be at my apartment within minutes. I told you that Alok knows Sanskrit. Each time he came to meet me, he would recite a verse and explain the meaning to me, but only if I defeated him in the game. I've recorded some of his verses:

Harastharasthrunya Nidhuvanakalaha,
Moukthikanam Visherno,
Bhoomow Yatha Sthree Bhagashayana
Lagthah Panchamoshancha Drishtaha

Praptha Shashatussukosham Ganakah Dashamaka
Samgreehithaha Priyena
Drishtam Shalkam Cha Sootre Kathaya Kathiraiyer
Moukthkaireshe Harah.'

Though I couldn't understand its meaning, I liked the rhythm of the chant. I was surprised to know that a dry subject like mathematics had a rhythm and music of its own. But when Morigami explained the meaning it became more interesting.

'This is a simple problem from *Leelavathi* written by Bhaskaracharya who lived in the twelfth century.

'While passionately making love, the beloved's pearl necklace broke. One-third of the pearls fell on the floor, one-fifth on the bed, one-sixth got entangled in her hair, one-tenth of the chain was in her lover's hand, and six pearls were left on the string which had held them together. How many pearls were there in all? Now, a primary school student can easily find the solution to this problem.

'$6 = x - (x/3 + x/5 + x/6 + x/10)$

'The answer is 30 pearls. But all Alok's problems were not this easy. Some were as complicated as Erdos's problems.'

'What happened after you got Alexander Grothendieck's photograph?' I asked.

'By the time I returned, everyone in the campus knew that I had gone to visit Pal Erdos. Betsy asked me with a naughty smile whether Erdos was all right after my visit. Sabo acted as if I had committed a crime. She said that he was a frail old man and I should not have disturbed him. She feared he would have an emotional attack. I was angry and shut myself in my room. My frayed emotions settled down only when Erdos handed me the cheque in class the next day. He called me, "Mr Hashimoto Morigami" and when Yusuf Alavi corrected him, he apologized, "Sorry Nippon Epsilon ... I thought you were a boy."

'That evening when I went to his apartment, he spoke to me for a long time. He had no one to call his own after his mother died in 1973. He was a Benzedrine addict and believed that it stimulated his intellect. I think on that day also he was under the influence of Benzedrine. When I went in, Béla Bollobás's wife was sitting a little apart from the others and sketching Erdos. I later learnt that she had acted in Hungarian movies in her youth. Gabriella smiled perfunctorily at me and continued with her sketching. The sketch later served as the model for Erdos's bust sculpted for the Isaac Newton Institute of Mathematics in Cambridge. Erdos signalled to me to sit on his left. Then, he looked silently into the distance before speaking to me in a low voice.

'"Mathematics is an inexplicable wonder that is above time, place, or language. It is the basis of all creation, sciences, and arts. When we delve into the history of mathematics we arrive at the genesis. Not the Genesis in the Bible, but the Genesis of Erdos. I believe in the holy book that contains the essence of this universe. It is called *The Book,* a text which contains all the principles of mathematics. Mathematicians are trying to analyze all the unopened pages in that book. The historian of mathematics has to find out who has opened each page and who has read it. I believe that there has been a parallel development in the study of mathematics in different cultures around the world. Like other sciences, mathematics too must have developed out of the needs of the people. The claims that some cultures discovered the zero or we discovered numbers or the decimal are empty claims. Mathematics was developing in the Maghreb countries and in India and China along with Europe. When you research the history of mathematics, it is more important to find out which social condition produced a particular branch or principle of mathematics rather than who discovered it. Any discovery may have more than one claimant. There is a lot of discussion on the connection between the Kerala School and European mathematics.

I don't think these discussions are on the right track. Though the contributions of Aryabhatta, Bhaskara, and Madhava cannot be ignored, I can't subscribe to the view that Europeans appropriated all their discoveries. It is not impossible that similar things happened in different societies at different times. Not all the people who have contributed to mathematics are mathematicians. There are businessmen, musicians, revolutionaries, and sports stars among them. When the US was hunting down communists, the emigration officials once asked me what I thought about Marx. Fearing that I would be misunderstood if I replied that Marx was one of the best mathematicians the world has ever seen, I said, "I'm not competent to judge but no doubt he was a great man." Still, they denied me a visa thinking that I was a Marxist. Usually, mathematicians who work in other areas remain unrecognized.

'Francis Itty Cora is one such unrecognized person. No contribution of Itty Cora's has been documented in the recognized history of mathematics. Yet, he was not a mere pepper merchant. In the beginning of the sixteenth century, he along with Raphael ran the secret Hypatian School in Europe. Cora, who had studied at a Hypatian School in Alexandria, was a pepper trader to the public but was in reality a Hypatian mathematician. In the Hypatian School at his Palazzo Cora on the banks of the Arno in Florence, all the principles of Hypatia were imparted to the students. Fermat's Last Theorem, which is considered a wonder and challenge for mathematicians, was said to have been taught there.

The Hypatian School called it Cora Theorem.

'It is said that in 1637, Fermat wrote his famous Last Theorem in the margins of a page in a copy of the *Arithmetica*. This is not credible.

'Fermat, who published in great detail all his other theories, wouldn't write an important theorem he had discovered in the margin of a book. And the copy of *Arithmetica* in the margins of which he wrote this theorem is lost. Grothendieck has enough proof to prove that this theory was Itty Cora's. But Itty Cora took contrary positions in many other matters. Even while he was running the Hypatian School, which propagated ideas that were against the Catholic Church, Cora was a procurer for Lorenzo de Medici and Pope Alexander VI. It is said that Itty Cora was a leading figure among those who orchestrated the sexual anarchy that was rampant in European palaces. It was rumoured that Cora, who respected Hypatia as one of the foremost mathematicians in the world, would bring beautiful women to his palace, strip them, and subject them to barbaric acts in the name of Hypatian rituals. Many records documenting this are available in the libraries of Medici and the Vatican. Grothendieck claims that there are documents pertaining to Itty Cora in Milan, Kenya, the Seychelles, and Istanbul. But the professors of an Indian university I once visited said that they knew nothing about Itty Cora.'

'Completely confused, I asked Pal Erdos whether Itty Cora was a rational mathematician or a superstitious pagan.

'Epsilon, your question is justified. Many of the details available about Cora are contradictory. Many may be mere fables. Some people display peculiarities in their behaviour that may at first sight appear contradictory. Our aim is to discover the truth about Itty Cora. You will get important information about Itty Cora from Alexander Grothendieck."

'I kissed his withered cheek and returned to my room, never to see him again.'

Cora with love.

20
Fermat's Last Theorem

Cubum autem in duos cubos, aut quadratoquadratum in duos quadratoquadratios et genaralit nullam in infinitum ultra quadratum potestatem in duos eisdem nominis fasest dividere cuius rei demonstrationem miriabilem sane detexi. Hanc marginis exiguitas non caperet.

It is impossible to separate a cube into two cubes or a fourth power into two fourth powers, or in general any power higher than the second into two like powers. I have discovered a truly marvellous proof of this, which this margin is too narrow to contain.

— Fermat's Last Theorem

AFTER READING ITTY CORA'S LAST EMAIL, REKHA CLICKED ON Morigami's blog. She realized then the significance of the threads she had left unread as she had not made the connection between them and Itty Cora. Rekha clicked on Fermat's Last Theorem.

Morigami's World of Plus and Minus: Fermat's Last Theorem

As most of the readers of this blog would be interested in mathematics, I don't think it is necessary to give an in depth explanation of Fermat's Last Theorem. Fermat's Last Theorem states, 'It is impossible for a cube to be the sum of two cubes, a fourth power to be the sum of two fourth powers, or in general for any number that is a power greater than the second to be the sum of two like powers. In mathematical language if an integer n is greater than 2, then the equation $an - bn = cn$ has no solutions in non-zero integers a, b, and c.

This looks deceptively simple but is quite difficult to prove. A British mathematician Andrew Wiles in 1995 proved this theorem, which had remained a challenge for three and a half centuries. It is said that Fermat in 1637 wrote this theorem in the margins of a Latin translation of *Arithmetica*. He added that the proof he had discovered wouldn't fit into the margin. That copy of *Arithmetica* isn't available now, and he has not documented this proof anywhere else either. It is not plausible that Fermat who wrote in great detail to other mathematicians discussing his theorems, would have failed to record the theorem and its proof elsewhere. Therefore, it is debatable whether this theorem that won Andrew Wiles several awards including the Wolfskehl Prize can be attributed to Fermat.

Pierre de Fermat was born in 1601 into a rich family that was into the wheat and cattle business in Beaumont-de-Lomagne in France. He had not studied mathematics formally. Though he was greatly interested in mathematics, it was in law that Fermat graduated from Orléans University after his school education in Toulouse. He joined the lower chamber of the Toulouse Parliament on 14 May 1631 and rose to the post of chief magistrate of criminal courts in 1652. In those days judges in France did not mingle with the general public, and hence Fermat devoted all his leisure time to the study of mathematics. As part of his legal education he had acquired deep knowledge of Greek and Latin, and so was able to study the mathematical texts of Archimedes, Apollonius, and Diophantus. As a result, he gained the friendship of mathematicians in France with whom he held discussions and exchanged letters on this fascinating subject.

In the early days, Fermat's contributions were connected with Apollonius's 'Plane Loci'. Descartes, the father of geometry, was Fermat's contemporary. Fermat continually engaged in debates with Descartes, Frenicle de Bessy, Beaugrande, and Mersini, who were some of the foremost mathematicians in Paris. Though his contributions to algebra, geometry, and probability theory are valuable, mathematicians including Descartes declare that they are limited in scope.

There were allegations that Fermat used his vast knowledge of the classical languages to glean information from ancient mathematical texts and appropriated it as his own, and that was why he failed to prove his theorems. He never presented his mathematical findings before the academic world, but would pose problems and challenge other mathematicians to find solutions. This practice of Fermat's gave rise to many accusations challenging his contribution. Though it is indisputable that Fermat had deep knowledge of mathematics, it is a fact that manipulation had a great role to play in the intense academic competition that existed among scientists. The allegation that Fermat did not discover Fermat's Last Theorem is as old as the publication of this theorem by his son Samuel in 1670.

Bachet's 1621 translation of *Arithmetica* is the most popular translation of the book in Latin. It is said that Fermat wrote this theorem in the margins of a copy of that book. On 12 January 1670, five years after Fermat's death, Samuel republished this book along with Fermat's notes. Samuel claimed that the copy Fermat had used was lost. Just like Fibonacci, who studied the Hypatian series in Algeria and passed it off in Italy as his own, Fermat might have seen this theorem and written it down in the margins of the book, planning to use it later.

As the number theory did not have any practical use, except as an intellectual exercise for mathematicians, no one paid much attention to it even after its publication in 1670. Proving that the area of a right-angled triangle will never be a square, Fermat gives the equation $n = 4$, somehow demonstrating it for the same value. Even Euler presented a slightly weak proof of it for the value $n = 3$. In 1825, Legendre and Johann Peter Dirichlet, together with the support of Euler's proof, proved this theorem for the value $n = 5$. Fifteen years later, in 1839, Gabriel Lame established that this theorem held good for the value $n = 7$ also. But it was Sophie Germain, the most brilliant female mathematician the world saw after Hypatia, who put forward the idea of a common proof for Fermat's last theorem and published her findings.

Sophie Germain was born into a middle-class business family in Paris on 1 April 1776. She displayed a keen interest in and aptitude for mathematics at a very young age. As young women from aristocratic families were not allowed to enter the world of knowledge, Sophie's parents tried to dissuade her from pursuing higher studies, but she refused to comply. When Sophie was eighteen years old, in the year 1794, Ecole Polytechnique was established in Paris to train mathematicians and scientists. As women were denied admission, Sophie sent a research paper to Joseph-Louis Lagrange, a teacher at the Ecole Polytechnique, in the name of Lee Blanc, a former student. Lagrange, who was a famous mathematician, was amazed by the paper and demanded a meeting with the writer in person. When he found that Lee Blanc was in reality a girl, an astonished Lagrange introduced Sophie to the mathematicians in Paris and welcomed her into the world of serious academic research.

It is said that the gorgeous Sophie used her beauty to her advantage and became close to Lagrange. She continued this relationship throughout her life. Be that as it may, basing her studies on Lagrange's examination of the number theory, Sophie tried to discover a general proof for Fermat's Last Theorem. As a result of her diligent efforts, she was able to prove that Fermat's Last Theorem holds true for all prime numbers below 100. Had Sophie not died of a fatal disease on 27 June 1831 at the age of fifty-five, she would definitely have produced more accurate proof of Fermat's Last Theorem.

In 1823, and later in 1850, the French Academy of Sciences proclaimed a huge reward for anyone who proved Fermat's Last Theorem. Though the Academy of Brussels proclaimed a third award in 1883, no one in the nineteenth century could develop any of Sophie's discoveries further. In 1908, the German industrialist Paul Friedrich Wolfskehl proclaimed a prize of one million marks for proving Fermat's Last Theorem. The lure of fame and money provided by these awards resulted in the publication of thousands of incorrect proofs of the theorem. In the famous mathematical historian Howard Eves's words, 'Fermat's Last Theorem has that peculiar distinction of being the mathematical problem for which the largest number of incorrect proofs has been published.'

Fermat's last theorem remained a challenge even in the twentieth century despite several important discoveries in the world of mathematics. Finally, it was in 1995 that the British mathematician Andrew Wiles conclusively proved the theorem, relying on the most complicated techniques of modern mathematics. Andrew began his efforts to prove Fermat's Last Theorem, taking inspiration from the discoveries of a wonderfully gifted genius, Evariste Galois (1811 –

1832) who lived in Bourg-la-Reine in France and was a contemporary of Sophie Germain's. Andrew Wiles used the permutation theory of Galois, which later came to be known as Galios's theory, Sophie Germain's discoveries, and also all the theorems of geometry and modular theory. Afraid that his discoveries would be appropriated by other mathematicians, Wiles did his research very secretly and presented his proof before a host of eminent mathematicians on the 21st, 22nd, and 23rd of June in 1993 at the Isaac Newton Institute of Mathematics in Britain. He established that Fermat's Last Theorem was correct by proving the Taniyama Shimura conjecture about elliptical curves. But a grave error in Andrew Wiles's proof was pointed out at the time. Undaunted, Wiles, with the help of his student Richard Taylor, worked hard for a year, and in September 1994 made his proof error-free. In 1995, this proof was published in the *International Mathematical Association Journal*. Andrew Wiles won all the important prizes for mathematics including the Wolfskehl Prize and the Crafoord Prize. As he had crossed forty he was denied the Field Medal, which is the Nobel equivalent for contributions in mathematics, but he was given a special memento made of silver. Fermat's Last Theorem, which had posed a challenge for three-and-a-half centuries, finally surrendered before man's intellect.

This is the accepted history of Fermat's Last Theorem. However, there is evidence that this theorem was taught much before Fermat and was born in the secret Hypatian School at the Palazzo Cora in Florence. It was also taught in all the Hypatian Schools like the ones in Fez and Alexandria.

The astronomer Abu Mahmud Hamid al-Khidr al-Khujandi, who lived in Ray town in Iran (present-day Tehran) between 940 and 1000 CE, has presented the same theorem in a different way in his texts. He pursued his higher studies at Timbuktu in Mali. This theorem is mentioned in some ancient manuscripts obtained from

Sankore madrassa in Timbuktu and documents obtained from the library in Topkapı Palace in Istanbul. It was as a result of deliberate efforts by the Catholic Church to cleanse history of all mention of Hypatia that many such documents disappeared. Evarist Galios, who became famous through Galios's Theorem, was a descendant of Adriana Cora, a Frenchwoman who was the hostess and mathematics teacher at Palazzo Cora when it was torched in 1556. Adriana Cora was the youngest of Cora's seventy-nine children. Adriana's mother Mariana Medici, along with Louisia, was one of the important hostesses at Palazzo Cora during Itty Cora's last years. But Mariana Medici did not really belong to the Medici family. Itty Cora had brought the beauteous Mariana from Paris in 1510 to seduce Cardinal Giovanni Medici, the second son of Lorenzo Medici, and lure him away from his immoderate obsession with homosexuality. Though Mariana couldn't accomplish the task set for her, she was able to exert considerable influence on the Cardinal. Till he assumed the papacy under the name Leo X, Mariana Medici lived in the palace. On 11 March 1513, when Cardinal Giovanni was elected Pope, Mariana was given a tenth of his private property on the condition of silence and sent to Palazzo Cora. At the time of the Pope's ascension ceremony on 13 March, Mariana was entering the fifth bedroom of Palazzo Cora. The twenty-two-year old Mariana was the last woman in Cora's life. Cora was then fifty-seven years old. On 3 January 1515, Mariana gave birth to Cora's seventy-ninth child—Adriana Cora.

Though each one of his seventy-nine children were extraordinarily intelligent and capable, it was Adriana who had inherited Cora's genius in mathematics and astronomy. Adriana studied Hypatian mathematics and became a teacher at the secret Hypatian School at the age of fourteen, and was able to attract students from all over Europe. Though many aristocrats wanted to marry the beautiful

Adriana, she preferred to evade the knot of matrimony, act as the main hostess of Palazzo Cora, and pleasure the men who sought her hand.

Adriana gave importance to the celebration of sexuality in the man-woman relationship and dedicated her life to teaching Hypatian mathematics and propagating Hypatian philosophy.

Seeing Adriana's growing influence in Italian society, the Catholic Church spread the rumour that she was a witch. The church was also instrumental in making people believe that Palazzo Cora was a den of black magic and prostitution. On 17 January 1556, a violent mob of Christian fanatics burnt down Palazzo Cora. Adriana escaped, disguising herself as a man. Even in her haste to escape she did not leave behind Itty Cora's copper tablets and palm leaf manuscripts.

Adriana somehow managed to reach Pisa and escaped on a cargo ship bound for Marseilles in France. Pierre Nicholas Galios was the captain of that ship. Within a short time, the intelligent captain realized that Adriana was not a man. When he questioned her, she told him a lot of colourful lies. She said that she had worked as a mathematics teacher at the Medici Palace and the dirty power politics inside the palace had succeeded in throwing her out. She added that she was now on her way to meet Catherine Medici, the Queen of France. Though she was older than him by four or five years, Galios became attracted to Adriana's beauty and expressed a desire to marry her. When Adriana refused, saying that her only interest lay in mathematics, he begged her to marry him promising his ship to her as a wedding gift. Adriana scorned his attempt to entice the daughter of Cora, who was the greatest ship-owner the world had seen, with the promise of a single ship. As the ship which started from Pisa in the afternoon continued its journey across the Mediterranean at night, the spurned Galios forced Adriana into his room and when she resisted, stripped her naked and crushed her in

his arms. When she realized that he would overpower her, she said
that she would marry him if he agreed to one condition. Hearing
this, Galios laughed, 'The queen who admits defeat in battle cannot
put forward conditions.'

'Not as a right but as a plea.'

'I am willing to obey not one but a hundred conditions to make
you my own.'

'You must allow me to learn and teach Hypatian mathematics
and astronomy all my life.'

'If you can satisfy my libido, you can learn and teach whatever
you want.'

Galios, not waiting for her assent, satisfied his sexual urge and lay
back fatigued, then Adriana confessed the truth.

'My sweet Cora, you are a liar!' Galios said.

'I did it to save my life or you may have killed me for being a
witch.'

'Do you feel reassured now?'

'Yes, but as you are doing business with the Roman Empire, you
will not find it easy to comply with my demands.'

'Why?'

'Though the Hypatian theories I teach are scientifically proven,
they are against the beliefs of the Catholic Church. It is because we
taught her theories that the Christian fanatics burnt our school last
night. They would have burnt me alive if I hadn't escaped. They say
that we are pagans and practitioners of black magic.'

Galios fell silent. Then as if he had arrived at a firm decision he
hugged Adriana saying, 'My sweet Cora, do not be afraid. I agree to
all your demands.' All through his life Galios called her 'my sweet
Cora.'

Adriana's secret Hypatian School functioned well for a long time
in Marseilles. Though after marriage Adriana took Galios's name,
her school was known as the Cora School and the mathematical

theorems taught there were called 'Cora theorems'. In the sixteenth and seventeenth centuries, Hypatian philosophy survived the repression of the Catholic Church due to the efforts of the Cora School. By the end of the seventeenth century, for reasons unknown, the Galios family moved from Marseilles to Bulgaria. It is from the documents Grothendieck obtained during his inquiries about Evriste Galois that we get this information. When Grothendieck challenged the accepted history of mathematics everyone called him insane.

Born on 25 October 1811, Evariste Galois performed wonders in mathematics in his short lifespan of twenty years. Galois discovered Group Theory, the basis for Galois's theorem that became an important branch of abstract algebra. He was active in politics and was at the forefront of Republican protests against royal governance, and pursued his research in mathematics during his free time. Galois was the best mathematician among Adriana's descendants.

Galois had to suffer many setbacks in his life because he stood up for Hypatian philosophy. Though he was an incomparable genius, he was denied admission at Ecole Polytechnique. In the oral examination conducted in 1828, when he first applied, the examiner failed to comprehend the Hypatian theorems Galois spoke about. It was when he applied again in 1829 that an interesting debate arose in connection with Fermat's last theorem. Galois was asked to explain Fermat's last theorem for his oral exam. After writing the theorem and its proof on the board and explaining it, he said, 'This theorem has been taught for hundreds of years at the Hypatian School. We call it the Cora Theorem. People connected with the Catholic Church are spreading a lie when they insist that this was discovered by Fermat.' When an enraged examiner cursed him, Galois threw the duster in his face and walked out. Though he later joined Ecole Normale Superieure, which was a step lower than Ecole Polytechnique, he was expelled because of his political activities.

Galois was persecuted because of his belief in Hypatian philosophy. His father Nicholas Gabriel, the mayor of Buglaria, committed suicide after falling out with the Catholic Church. His girlfriend Stéphanie-Félicie Poterin left him because she believed that he practiced black magic. A desperate Galois challenged Stephanie's fiancé Pescheux d'Herbinville to a duel. Galois was fatally wounded in the lower abdomen in the duel fought on 30 May 1832, and as he lay dying with his head resting on his brother Alfred's lap, he said, *'Ne pleure pas, Alfred! J'ai besoin de tout mon courage pour mourir à vingt ans.'* (Don't cry, Alfred! I need all my courage to die at twenty.)

When history records that in 1995 Andrew Wiles proved Fermat's Last Theorem, what is silenced is the great tradition of Hypatian mathematics.

21
Cora Poottu

Those who consider the Devil to be partisans of evil and angels to be warriors of God accept the demagogy of the angels. Things are clearly more complicated.

— Milan Kundera

THERE WAS NO NEWS OF BENNY FOR A FEW DAYS. HIS CELLPHONE WAS either busy or turned off. If it rang at all, the call would be cut off. Then, last morning, just as I was wondering what had happened to him, he came to see me.

'What happened to you?'

'Things are in a mess. I've brought something to set fire to our insides. We'll talk after we've downed some of it.'

Benny took the bottle out of his bag and within minutes, the nico chilly vodka was ready. By the third peg he became loquacious. Our conversation naturally turned to Itty Cora.

'You tell me something. How am I going to benefit from all this? You can write your story and have sex with all the three women. But what do I get? Tell me that.'

'Why do you say that, Benny?'

'I've to say it. Those women are in it for the money. Let them make money. I'll do whatever possible to help them. But I'm not getting anything out of it. I may not belong to the 18th Clan but I am from Kunnamkulam. I do not work for free.'

'What do you want?'

'Haven't you got it yet? I'm like the vendor in a sweetshop. That girl calls me morning, noon, and night, asking for information. Who am I? The CBI or CID? And the only thing I get in return is sweet talk. Do I benefit in any way? No.'

'Don't worry we'll find a way. I'll call Rekha.'

'You don't interfere. I've spoken to her. I said, "Girl I've seen a lot of these dramas. If you want more information you'll have to teach me in your school." She just put down the phone. You tell me. Why can't she admit me to her school? If she can teach you, then why not me? Does she think I won't pay their fees?'

'Don't get upset. Rekha hasn't said that she won't admit you into her school.'

'She hasn't said she will either.'

'Haven't you heard that silence is consent? But there are some formalities with regard to admission in the school. A new client needs to be recommended by an existing one even to be a guest. They are quite strict about the fees also.'

'Money is not an issue.'

'Then it's easy.'

I called Rekha and fixed an appointment for Benny that night.

Her laughter echoed over the telephone.

'I thought he was quite upset when I spoke to him yesterday. I heard a lot of Kunnamkulam expletives over the telephone.

He said he was on his way to Kochi. But I had an important guest. That is why I disconnected the phone. When he had called earlier he had told me about a D'Souza from Goa, who was coming to Kunnamkulam for Christmas. He has some connection with Itty Cora. It is good that Benny is coming over. I'll get all the details from him. You come in the morning. I've lots to tell you.'

Benny had a mischievous smile on his face.

'So things are settled. But who is this D'Souza from Goa?'

'I thought I'd told you about him.'

'Did you say it just to bait Rekha?'

'No, no, I intended to tell you too. But I was waiting for more information.'

'Don't try to fool me, tell me in detail.'

'This Christmas, the custom of Corakku kodukkal will be observed at the First House in Kunnamkulam. The girl is from Goa—Leena D'Souza. Her father, Alfred D'Souza, is a shrimp exporter operating from Mangalore and Goa. They come to Kochi occasionally. Alfred's mother Anna was an old flame of Tharu's. Everyone from that family except the children will be here for the ritual. They're filthy rich.'

'Will Anna be there?'

'She died ages ago. Alfred, his wife, and daughter will be coming from Goa. Moses and family are coming from Chennai. I don't know how Moses and Alfred are connected. I've figured out how we can participate in this ritual.'

'How?'

'None of these people has been to Kunnamkulam before. They will go straight to Hotel Elite from Cochin Airport. If we manage to dupe them, we can achieve our goal.'

'Tell me more.'

'I've thought of a way. There's a boy I know who works at the reception desk at Hotel Elite. He told me that rooms 421 and 422 on the fourth floor have been booked for the Goans. I immediately booked number 423 in Mrs and Mr Pereira's name. You should check in at the same time as them. Meet them at the reception desk. Convince them that you too have come for the ceremony at the First House. Then, it is up to you and Rekha.'

I quite liked Benny's plan, but it was risky. If Georgekutty or the guys in the Ukroo, Tharu, Cora group got to know of it, we wouldn't get back to Kunnamkulam alive. As he finished his drink and enthusiastically made his way to the school, I called Rekha and told her the plan. But she wanted to know more about Benny.

'He is not a troublemaker, is he?'

'No, he is okay.'

'I am a bit wary of such raw guys, and since Rashmi and Bindu are away, it's a solo performance that I've planned in the Body Lab.'

'Just enjoy it, Rekha. Tell me all about it tomorrow.'

When I reached the school in the morning it was Benny who opened the door. He looked freshly bathed. I asked him where Rekha was, and he led me to the Body Lab. She was lying on the floor motionless, with her left hand folded under her. Her nightie was raised above her knees. She couldn't talk. Benny smiled at me, as I stood astounded.

'She made me sweat it out last night and in the morning she mocked me. Fed up, I pinned her down in the Corapoottu. Cora's lock is an important adavu displayed at the Onathallu in Kunnamkulam. The left hand is twisted backwards and the opponent is forced to bend down and the eighth rib pierced with the forefinger. Then, the loser is hoisted on the victor's shoulder and slammed on the floor. The victim is rendered immobile and loses the ability to speak till the clasp is unlocked. Only the person who locked the victim can unlock it. You have to kick the victim beneath the buttocks twice with your right foot and poke him on the left side beneath the tenth rib with your forefinger, then lift and twirl him thrice and put him down on his stomach. You need to have an in-depth knowledge of the nerves and vital spots in the body to do this.'

When I saw Rekha looking at me helplessly, I told Benny to set her free. He freed Rekha immediately and pulled her to her feet.

'That was to punish you for your arrogance.'

Rekha stormed into the bathroom, saying, 'I didn't know what you were up to, or I wouldn't have stood still and let you have your way.' Wanting to celebrate, Benny ordered food. By then, Rekha had come out. As Benny was the one paying for the entertainment, Rekha sat next to him. Benny, who had overcome all his nervousness, draped a rather proprietary arm over Rekha.

Rekha complained, 'My back still hurts. Hope there aren't any aftereffects.'

'Don't worry.'

'Benny, tell me how did it get its name?'

'The Cora name is associated with all sorts of things in Kunnamkulam. This may be something he learnt during his travels, or he may have devised it himself. There is also the Corakuthu. That's again demonstrated during the Onathallu; a poke under the navel with the thumb. If an expert does it, the victim will faint. Men with a weakness for women are mockingly called "the Coras". Fair cherubic boys are called Cora Kuttikal. Then there is Corappanam, the money they use as capital; Corapattus, the songs sung in his memory; and Corakku kodukkal, the ritual of offering a maiden to Cora.'

Rekha started talking about Leena D'Souza. Benny had given her all the details the previous night, and both of them had come up with a carefully detailed plan.

'I intend to send Bindu to Kunnamkulam as Mrs Pereira with you, Scripter. Susannah, George, and Kunhippalu would recognize Rashmi and me.'

'Yes. Bindu can easily carry off the part.'

'On 23 December, when the D'Souzas come out of the airport, you have to follow them. Make sure that you reach the hotel at the same time as they do.'

'Anna's husband had a relative who worked as a railway engine driver in Shornur. He was the one who arranged Anna's marriage. He was a Pereira. His family migrated to Australia before Independence. You must pretend to be his son and daughter-in-law.'

I felt I was being locked in a Corapoottu. Most people in Kunnamkulam know me well. If I was discovered, it would mean death. Rekha who sensed my hesitation tried to boost my sagging courage.

'Don't worry. Benny will teach you all the *adavus* to beat your opponents, and his men will be around if you need help.'

We discussed the plan thoroughly in the afternoon with Bindu.

Bindu and I mentally prepared ourselves and waited for 23 December.

D'Souza and family landed at Cochin International Airport on 23 December. They came by the 11 o'clock Jet Airways flight. The UTC had sent a black Innova to pick them up. Rekha stood close to a man holding a placard which read 'Welcome to Mr Alfred D'Souza and family'. She told us the number and model of the car the D'Souzas got into.

Rashmi drove our car. In the back seat Bindu, dressed in a short sleeveless dress, and I in a pair of shorts playing Pereira's part, sat listening to music. After the journey, which lasted an hour and fifteen minutes, we bid Rashmi goodbye and entered the hotel to see Alfred talking to the receptionist. Leena and her mother were sitting in the lobby. Alfred seemed reserved. Though I smiled broadly, he did not return my smile. But Bindu succeeded in striking up a conversation with Leena, who was clad in black capris and a red T-shirt with 'Discover Me' written boldly on it. She smiled and greeted her, saying, 'I'm Angela Pereira.'

'Leena D'Souza. Are you from Goa?'

'No, from down under. Sydney.'

Leena's smile widened at Bindu's response. Unfortunately, Alfred arrived just then with the room key. Leena and her mother followed him to the lift. Bindu came and stood behind me at the desk. The young receptionist asked, 'You Benny's friends? Let me know if you need anything.'

The minute we reached our room, Bindu called Rekha and Benny. 'Slow and steady' was Rekha's advice. Benny reassured her, 'My people and I are at Thrissur. Don't worry.'

As I relaxed on the bed, Bindu positioned herself on the sofa. I told her that she looked more like an Anglo-Indian than Leena and her mother.'

'We will go and meet them in the evening.'

But Bindu said, 'We won't need to go to them. They will come to us.'

As Bindu had predicted, when Alfred was relaxing after a heavy lunch, the mother and daughter came to our room.

They were interested when we told them that we had come for a religious ceremony at Grandfather Nicholas Pereira's ancestral house. When Bindu mentioned that it was a secret ceremony, the mother asked, 'You mean the "Cora function"?'

Though they hesitated at first, they admitted that they too had come for the ceremony scheduled for the next day. They said that Moses and family had cancelled their trip, but they were happy to have met us.

By the time we finished dinner, Bindu and I had become their close friends and relatives. Alfred, who was embarrassed by the ritual and all it entailed, was comforted when he was told that Angela had undergone the ritual eleven years ago, and that we had come to make arrangements for our daughter to be offered to Cora next year.

By 11 p.m., three people from the First House had come to meet us and explain the rituals in detail. They told Bindu and I to comfort the parents if they found the rituals upsetting, as was known to happen.

When Leena's mother said, 'Don't worry, Angela has enough experience,' they looked at her strangely, but Bindu pretended not to notice.

As we shut our bedroom door at the stroke of 12, I felt that I should make the maximum use of this night that I hadn't paid for. After downing three pegs of the bottle of the cashew feni that Alfred had gifted us, I felt that I was indeed Pereira from Australia. I think Mrs Pereira was also quite sozzled. Bindu, who usually complained that I was a pervert, crossed all boundaries of perversion that night in bed with me. We lay locked in an embrace, waiting for Cora's rituals to begin.

22

Grothendieck and I

The ethics of the scientific profession (especially among mathematicians) have degraded to such a degree that pure and simple theft among colleagues (especially at the expense of those who have no position of power to defend themselves) has almost become a general rule and is in any case tolerated by all even in the most flagrant and iniquitous cases.

— An excerpt from a letter by Alexander Grothendieck to the Royal Academy of Sciences refusing the Crafoord Prize

AFTER SPEAKING TO BINDU, REKHA LOGGED ON TO CHECK IF THERE were any emails from Itty Cora. Seeing that he hadn't written to her she went to Morigami's blog. Though she clicked 'Grothendieck's Mathematics', she was disappointed to see that it only contained Grothendieck's theorems and their explanations. She realized that she didn't have the intellectual capacity to comprehend them and clicked on the next thread.

Morigami's World of Plus and Minus

Grothendieck and I

Alexander Grothendieck is a mathematician who influenced me as much as Pal Erdos did, or perhaps even more. He brought about a complete transformation in my life. Till then, I had approached mathematics as a science and analysed it logically. It was Grothendieck who guided me to the politics and hypnotic mysticism of mathematics. He was able to dismantle all my notions about life and society. After meeting Grothendieck, Morigami became a very different person.

Before I went to Budapest I gathered as much information as possible about him. I got to know the person from the books available in the Institute library and from what the teachers told me about him.

Alexander Grothendieck was born on 28 March 1928 in Berlin to a Russian Jew, Alexander Schapiro, and Hanka Grothendieck, who was a Protestant and communist from Hamburg. He had a miserable childhood. His parents were anarchists who both had children from previous marriages. Schapiro, who belonged to a conventional Jewish family from Ukraine, was arrested at the age of seventeen for participating in anti-Tsarist activities and was incarcerated for more than ten years. Escaping from Russia to Berlin, he assumed a new identity as Alexander Tanaroj and worked as a street photographer. It was then that he met Hanka and married her. Born in a prosperous family in Hamburg, Hanka was drawn to revolutionary politics and was working in connection with some terrorist groups in Berlin. Both of them used to write academic articles as well as fiction in many leftist publications in those days.

In 1933, when the Nazis took over Germany, Schapiro and Hanka fled to Paris, leaving a five-year-old Alexander with their friend

William Heydorns' family in Hamburg. No information is available about their lives for the next five to six years. It is believed that they participated in the Spanish Civil War and fled to Paris on Franco's victory. As they were associated with leftist terrorist insurgents, Parisian society looked upon them as dangerous foreigners.

In 1939, when the Second World War broke out, feeling that a Jewish boy was not safe in Hitler's regime, William Heydorn got in touch with Schapiro through the French Embassy and sent Alexander, who was just eleven years old then, alone on a train from Hamburg to Paris. It was sheer luck that the Jewish boy from Germany, which was in the throes of Nazi fervour, reached his parents safely. Shortly after Grothendieck reached Paris, Schapiro was arrested. Imprisoned without a trial, he was never able to see his wife or child again. Sent from one Nazi camp to another, Schapiro finally died in Auschwitz in 1942. But Grothendieck and his mother came to know of his death only by the end of 1945.

Grothendieck, who hero-worshipped his father, was devastated by the news of his death.

During the War, Grothendieck and his mother lived in several refugee camps in France. In 1940, while he was in a camp near Mende, Grothendieck with a childish desire to kill Hitler tried to escape from the camp but was caught. He was subjected to cruel torture and before long was separated from his mother. The camp officers alleged that his mother was spoiling him, and Hanka was moved to another interim camp and Alexander was sent to a children's home in Le Chambon, run by a Swiss agency. The mental and physical torture in his childhood resulted in Grothendieck developing a political perspective that forcefully protested against war and violence.

The children in Le Chambon were given formal education. Though he received a tolerably good education from a school run by a Protestant priest for refugee children, Alexander was disappointed with the repetitiveness of textbook mathematics. In 1945, when the war ended, Hanka and her son settled down in Mizar Guze, a village on the shores of the Mediterranean near Montpellier.

Hanka eked out a living working in vineyards, but luckily her son won a scholarship to Montpellier University. The conventional educational system at Montpellier did not satisfy Grothendieck. The teaching community that laboured under the misconception that there was nothing new to be discovered in mathematics disappointed him. In 1948, he won a scholarship to pursue higher studies in Paris. But when he attended a couple of seminars at Ecole Normale in Paris, he realized that he lacked the intellectual foundation that was essential to participate in such seminars and he moved to Nancy University, which was then considered the hub of mathematical study in France. It was during the years from 1950 to 1953 that his mathematical talent was honed.

At Nancy University, Grothendieck did research under Laurent Schwartz and earned his doctoral degree with honours. The only confusion was regarding which of the six theses he had submitted should be awarded the degree. Though he got a doctoral degree, he couldn't find permanent employment because he was not a French citizen. As military service was mandatory for French citizenship, he did not apply for citizenship but accepted a teaching position at Sao Paulo University in Brazil. He later worked and pursued research in several eminent universities like Princeton and Harvard, and in 1956 when he returned to France, he was considered the most important mathematician in the world. By then, he had published several research articles on topology, algebraic geometry, functional analysis, and category theory. But Grothendieck was not a famous problem-solver like Pal Erdos or John Nash. He was known as a theory builder. He preferred to analyze problems not at the micro level but from a more comprehensive perspective. I wondered how Grothendieck, who has such a different view of mathematics in particular and of life and society in general, had become Paul Erdos's friend.

Grothendieck's plenary talk at the International Conference of Mathematicians held in Edinburgh in August 1958 shot him to the pinnacle of fame. His new perspective that connected algebraic geometry and topology determined the direction of future research in mathematics. The same year, a wealthy physics professor wanted to establish a research institute in Paris based on the model of the Princeton Institute of Advanced Studies, and he entrusted Grothendieck with the responsibility. Grothendieck was able to make the Institut des Hautes Études Scientifiques (IHES) a premier institute of research. But problems within the IHES compelled Grothendieck to bid farewell to mathematics in 1970. Like Pal Erdos, Grothendieck was also very close to his mother.

Hanka was with Grothendieck in Paris, and followed him when he moved to Nancy. Hanka, who was proud of her son's abilities, took care of all routine matters, leaving Grothendieck free to pursue his passion for mathematics.

In spite of his complete involvement in research, Grothendieck took good care of his mother, who was tubercular. But he was not very careful in his own life. His life echoed his friend Erdoch's anarchic one. It was his middle-aged landlady who bore Grothendieck his first son, Sergi. Though he was involved with several women till his mother's death in 1957, none of these relationships ended in marriage.

After his mother's death Grothendieck married Mireille, who was a few years older than him. The marriage was initially a happy one, and they had three children—Johanna, Mathew, and Alexandri. The family travelled widely. During this period, which can be called the golden age in Grothendieck's life, Mireille took care of everything. In 1966, he won the Field's Medal. Mireille filled the void left in his life by his mother's death, but she could never be a good lover or give him any sort of intellectual support. Neither could she wean him away from the anarchism that ruled his life. She found it extremely difficult to adjust to his lifestyle and political beliefs. Finally, when Grothendieck resigned from the IHES in 1970 protesting against NATO's military involvement in Vietnam, Mireille, who couldn't understand the subtleties of the politics involved, separated from him.

Justine Skalba, a research student he met in 1972 while on a lecture tour in American universities, was the next woman in his life. By the time he met Justine, Grothendieck had completely moved away from research. Whenever he was invited to give a talk on mathematics, he would accept on the condition that he would be allowed to deliver a political discourse as well. Justine lived with him for hardly two years, yet she was the one who was able to understand him more than anyone else could. An active participant in the wave of counterculture that was sweeping across Europe in the 1970s, Grothendieck bought a large house in Paris to set up a commune, and started staying with hippies. Justine found it impossible to live with him. In 1973, she left for the US with their son Johnny.

Though Grothendieck was sympathetic to the movement for freedom initiated by students and intellectuals that was gaining momentum all over Europe in the last years of the 1960s, he wasn't willing to limit his political involvement to the intellectual arena. When the US was attacking Vietnam, he spent three weeks in Hanoi declaring his support for the resistance. There, he vehemently condemned NATO's military attacks. But his belief that colleagues and students would stand by him was misplaced. 'Survival', the group he established to propagate his political ideologies, did not exert much of an influence on even the community of mathematicians. The anarchists of counterculture did not respect him as the mathematicians did. I feel that Grothendieck withdrew from public life unable to bear the rebuffs his political ideology received even when he was at the peak of academic success.

After moving away from the IHES and research, he accepted a faculty position at Montpellier, bowing to the wishes of his friends. But he put forward a condition that he would not guide any research projects. He stayed in a remote hilly area, which did not even have electricity, and only rarely did he come to the university. He gradually reduced the number of visitors he received, but continued to communicate with some friends through letters.

During this time, he grew doubtful about the pertinence of the history and principles of mathematics, and the validity of science itself. We should read Grothendieck's inquiries into the life and the principles of Galois in relation to these suspicions that arose in his mind. Unfortunately, he destroyed the 1,500-page long manuscript he had written about Galois. *Reapings and Sowings: Reflections and Testimony of the Past of a Mathematician,* written during the period 1983 – 86, was the only work that was published. It gained attention more for revealing the extent of deceit and plagiarism rampant in mathematical research in the twentieth century than as an autobiography.

Before he retired from Montpellier University in January 1988, he was awarded the Crafoord Prize. The prize was instituted in 1980 by the Swedish industrialist Holger Crafoord and Anna-Greta Crafoord. This prize is awarded for contributions in subjects like astronomy, mathematics, earth science, and zoology, which are not considered for the Nobel Prize. The recipients are chosen by the Royal Swedish Academy of Sciences. It is a Nobel equivalent, and the prize is given away by the Swedish king himself.

But Grothendieck refused the prize. *La Monde* on 5 May 1988 printed the letter of rejection that he wrote to the Swedish Academy. Following this, Grothendieck changed his residence to escape an onslaught of visitors. Though he remained in touch with a few friends, the world lost all contact with Grothendieck after August 1992. It was in these circumstances that Pal Erdos asked me to go and meet Grothendieck. I couldn't figure out how Grothendieck was connected to Itty Cora. I also failed to understand why Pal Erdos held the Catholic Church responsible for Grothendieck's withdrawal from society.

When I boarded the train from Budapest, I had no idea how I would find Grothendieck in France. The only saving grace was that my classmate Jim Corda, who was accompanying me, spoke French fluently. But he was not interested in meeting Grothendieck. The history of mathematics held no appeal for him. He went with me because my body lured him. It was the first time I was using my body to attract a man with the purpose of manipulating him for my ends. I was able to cleverly prolong his waiting, but don't think that I cheated Jim. Before we returned from Montpellier, we celebrated at La Clara, a beach resort on the Atlantic Shore.

Changing four trains, we reached Montpellier on the third day at 11 a.m. It is a beautiful town on a hilltop barely five miles from the Mediterranean Sea. Montpellier means the 'naked mountain', a hill devoid of trees. It was 2 p.m. by the time we freshened up at the hotel room and reached the mathematics department of Paul Valery University. Though Jim spoke to a couple of middle-aged teachers, it was futile; they claimed that they had no idea where Grothendieck was. Though we told them that we had just completed the BSM course at Budapest and had a letter for Grothendieck from Pal Erdos, they were unmoved. When I started to cry and said in the little French I knew that I couldn't go back without meeting Grothendieck, an old professor came to me and asked, 'Are you Sayako's daughter?' I nodded. He said, 'Your poor mother! Is she still in Tokyo University?'

'Yes.'

'Is this the first time you are coming to meet your father?'

'Yes.'

'Don't cry. Tomorrow is Friday. It's my day off. I will take you and your friend to your father.'

I wiped my tears and looked at him gratefully. I was really in tears by then. Jim, who had no idea that I was lying, looked at me sympathetically. We returned to our hotel, promising to come back the next day. Seeing Jim's sympathy, I couldn't bear to confess that it was a lie and so had to act sorrowful throughout the night. The next day, the professor took us in his car to Carpentras, which was some distance from Montpellier. As the terrain was hilly the journey took nearly one and a half hours. Carpentras, a small hill town, had a sweets market every Friday morning. We bought a packet of Grothendieck's favourite Berlingot chocolates and set off for Les Morion. As it was a steep descent, we reached quickly. The professor stopped in front of an old building by the side of a winding road. He said, 'This is where Grothendieck lived until a couple of years ago. The house still belongs to him. But no one stays here now. If we climb up a bit, we will reach a Celtic village. He lives there now. It's a village with no modern amenities, not even electricity.'

Jim and I followed the professor. We climbed the slippery hill, and by afternoon reached the village. We saw Grothendieck sitting on a granite bench outside a thatched house that looked like a cave, along with two young girls aged around seven or eight. He was wearing a coarse black garment that covered everything except his face. He was teaching the children to divide and multiply using pebbles. When they saw us, the children went inside. Grothendieck, who looked displeased to see us, asked the professor who we were. Ignoring his annoyance, the professor went up to him, gave him the packet of Berlingots, and asked him, 'Monsieur Gro, do you remember Yutaka Taniyama?' Grothendieck thought for a while. Then he looked at me carefully. I had no idea who Yutaka Taniyama was. He muttered in a mixture of French and English. 'In your eyes,

I can see Yutaka Taniyama. I can see Goro Shimura and Yutaka's girlfriend Misako Suzuki. I can also see my dear Sayako. Tell me, are you my daughter?' I once again became a prisoner of my own deceit. I couldn't say no. As Grothendieck held me close and kissed my forehead, I wept. As we stood silent, the professor told Jim he would come back the next day and left. 'When she heard that your uncle Yutaka Taniyama had committed suicide, your mother, who was with me in Paris, wept uncontrollably. She wept again when Misako committed suicide barely a month later. But that was the last time she cried.

'We promised each other that no matter what happened to our relationship, neither of us would commit suicide. We had to part shortly. Many told me about my smart daughter growing up with Sayako in Tokyo. We had to wait so long to meet. Tell me, is your mother well?'

I nodded.

As he kissed me again, a pungent odour from his garment assailed me. I gave him Erdos's letter. He read it anxiously.

'I expected it to be from Sayako. Never mind. You are lucky to be Erdos's epsilon. I will definitely tell you Itty Cora's story. Unfortunately, I destroyed all the mathematical documents connected to him when I was mentally unstable. I cannot give you any proof. The book I wrote about Galois wasn't published.'

We stayed with him that night. He told me everything that he knew about Itty Cora.

23
La Sans Pareille

I believe that you can reach the point where there is no longer any difference between developing the habit of pretending to believe and developing the habit of believing.
— *Foucault's Pendulum*, Umberto Eco

I WOKE UP TO THE SOUND OF FRANTIC KNOCKING. I THOUGHT I HEARD someone call out 'Angela'. Thinking it might be Mrs D'Souza, I slid out from Scripter's embrace, donned my nightgown, and opened the door. But when I opened the door, I saw a middle-aged woman accompanied by four or five masked men. They moved fast, and before I knew what was happening, they had stuck a plaster over my mouth and tied my hands together. The men were merely obeying the lady's orders. She pulled Scripter up from bed and made him stand in the middle of the room. 'You bastard! You are the one stirring up trouble.'

As he stood silently with his head bowed, she punched him under the navel with her right fist her thumb pointing outwards. He crumpled down in pain. No sound came from him as they had stuck a tape over his mouth too. It was a very well planned attack, and everything happened within minutes. The woman did not speak again. They blindfolded me and asked me to walk. I don't know what they did to Scripter.

They took me to a room on the fifth floor of the hotel. They stripped off my nightgown and started examining every inch of my naked body. As Rekha had warned me about a possible body examination, I had a fake tattoo of twin serpents below my navel and a mark behind my left ear symbolizing that I had been offered to Cora.

They examined me very carefully. Suddenly, I knew that the probing fingers moving clinically over my body were those of a man. I was paralyzed with fear. I heard someone tell the man who was examining me, 'Pranji, check if all four signs are there.'

I didn't know what the third and fourth signs were (I still don't). Nearly a quarter of an hour later, they pulled the nightgown over me and took off my blindfold. I saw that there were more people in the room. I think that the person who had examined me was a seventy-year-old man. From the conversation floating around him, I knew that his name was 'Pranjiettan'. Fortunately, he patted me on the shoulder and said, 'She is Cora's woman. Mariyamma, who told you they are imposters?'

'George. He said they are associated with the women who had come to meet Susannah.'

'He must be mistaken. All the four signs of Satan are there on her body. But I can't remember when she was offered to Cora.'

'Pranjietta, are you losing your memory as you grow older? This is why I tell you to keep a tab on all this. It's not enough to maintain accounts of Cora's money alone.'

'I have maintained accurate records of each woman who has entered the room to be offered up to Cora. But this girl's name is not mentioned. Now, girl, you tell me, which year were you given to Cora?'

As I stood trying to think up a plausible story, Scripter was led into the room. He had been cruelly tortured and blood was flowing from his mouth and nostrils. When they felt that something was amiss, everyone except Pranji and Mariyamma left the room.

'Pranjietta, I think he has been brutally beaten. Now he is neither speaking nor breathing.'

'I told you to be careful, you bastards.'

'It happened. What do we do now?'

'Is he dead?'

'Not yet.'

Pranji held his fingers under his nostrils. Then he lifted Scripter's eyelids. Mariyamma asked, 'Trouble?'

'No,' he said. He caught hold of Scripter's lower abdomen and pulled hard. Scripter howled as if he had been whipped. Pranji pushed him on to the cot. All of them looked in admiration at Pranji.

'Don't stand and gape. Go fetch Dr Lazar.'

Mariyamma helped Scripter lie down on the bed. By the time she wiped his face clean, the doctor had arrived. I think he also belonged to the 18th Clan. Though I asked him whether Scripter should be taken to a hospital, he did not answer. He dressed the wounds and gave Scripter an injection. A little later, he opened his eyes.

'Dr Pereira, forgive us. It was a misunderstanding. We are convinced that your wife is Cora's woman. But I can't find her name in the records. Do you remember the year she was given to Cora?'

'My grandfather Nicholas Pereira was an engine driver working at Shornur railway station. We too are of the 18th Clan. But I was born and brought up in Australia. Angela was made Cora's woman after marriage.'

'Do you remember the year she was brought here for the rituals?'

'It was not in Kerala that Angela was offered to Cora.'

'How can that be?'

'Though Kunnamkulam is Corappappan's nerve centre, these rituals are conducted in many other places. You may not be aware of it. The rituals might have minor differences. Angela was given to Cora in Tarlabari in Istanbul.'

When I realized that Scripter was living up to his name, I was relieved. Pranji and Mariyamma listened intently.

'My grandfather Nicholas Pereira, like other Indians of the 18th Clan, also believed that the myth of Corappappan and the rituals connected to him were peculiar to Kunnamkulam. It was this thought that troubled him when he migrated to Australia. He continued to send Cora's money to the First House and observed many rituals. He taught his children and grandchildren Kunnamkulam Malayalam. When my father's eldest sister Sophie reached puberty, they brought her to Kunnamkulam from Sydney and conducted the rituals observed on Christmas Eve. As they did not have the money for the airfare, they travelled by ship; the journey lasted for weeks.

'Sophie was given to Cora that night. In the light of the oil lamp, a small spider climbed up the body of the inebriated fourteen-year old girl. Though she pushed it away, it climbed up her thighs. As she tried to push the spider away, it transformed into a strong, handsome youth emitting the fragrance of a wildflower. Having celebrated the night, before he changed into a butterfly and flew away, he kissed her and asked, "Are you happy? Do you want anything else?" She gave a surprising answer.

'"I am happy, but not satisfied. How can I, living as I do in Sydney, see Cora again?"

'"You can't. A woman can see Cora only once in her lifetime. But I am present in every nook and corner of the world. An Itty Cora is there asleep within every man. It is up to you to awaken the Cora in him. I've just taught you the primary lessons. The rest you have to learn by yourself."

'"If I have a daughter, should I bring her here too?"

'"No, these rituals are observed in many parts of the world. They might vary slightly. But the name Cora remains the same."

'The girl who sorrowfully watched the butterfly fly away in the morning brought great good fortune to our family. When he returned to Sydney, Nicholas got the contract for a new railway line. Within three to four years, they became rich. Sophie married the son of a rich man in Sydney, Mayor John Andrews.

'My father was born after all this happened. He was interested in the business from a very young age. He had great faith in the Corappappan myth. Mamma did not belong to the 18th Clan; neither did she become a member after marriage. Maybe Corappapan was unhappy because of that; anyway, the shipping company lost money. When I took over after Appa's death, I inherited a mountain of debts and an old cargo ship.

'As I was struggling to find a way out of this, I thought about Corappapan. I went to meet Aunt Sophie. She was happy to help me. She said, "Oh, you've finally remembered Corappappan. Wherever we are, the 18th Clan must never forget Corappappan. Your father forgot him, and that is the reason for his misfortunes. What you should do is get married and offer your wife to Cora. I don't know if the rituals are still performed in Kunnamkulam. My daughter was given to Cora in Tarlabasi in Istanbul.'

'I married Angela, who was distantly related to Aunt Sophie. The next Christmas after our marriage, we went to Tarlabasi in Istanbul to offer her to Cora. It is a rough area near the European side of Turkey. The First House is in a street where the Jews have their shops. Prostitution being legal in Turkey, there is a brothel, or genelev as it is called in Turkey, on the upper floor of the First House. As Aunt Sophie had made all the arrangements, we had no difficulties.

'She had told us that other than the language used, there were no differences in the rituals. Before Corappappan flew away as a butterfly, he wrote *"La Sans Pareille"* beneath the serpents tattooed on Sophie's navel. The head of the house told us that it was a rare occurrence. It is true Angela's beauty was then unparalleled.' After returning to Sydney, we changed the name of the shipping company to *La Sans Pareille*. Next year, Angela gave birth to Sophie—we named our daughter after my aunt. We deal in coal in Australia, and we have fourteen large and four small ships. Sophie will probably attain puberty next year, and we intended to give her to Cora in Tarlabasi. But unfortunately, Aunt Sophie passed away last September. When we inquired, they said the next Christmas Eve had been booked for the billionaire Christopher Onasis's daughter. It was then that we got to know about Mr D'Souza's daughter. We came to see Corappapan's birthplace, and if possible, arrange for our daughter's ceremony next year.'

Scripter brought his marvellous tale to a close.

'Pereira, I really can't believe what you've told me. It's probably ignorance on my part. You talk about Australia and Istanbul, but though you say you were born and brought up in Australia, how do you speak such perfect Kunnamkulam Malayalam? Anyway, Mariyamma, take them to their room. Let the rituals scheduled for the morning go on as planned. We will see if there are any problems. I still don't understand why George panicked.'

They brought us back to room 423. Maybe they felt we were not dangerous, so they didn't blindfold us. Mariyamma spoke to us quite kindly.

'Don't let anyone know what happened here. Be ready to go to the First House by 9 tomorrow.' When Mariyamma and her goons departed, it was 4 a.m. We tried calling Rekha, but her cellphone was switched off. Benny wasn't answering his phone either. Relieved that we were safe, we drank some feni and lay back on the bed. Scripter's eye had swollen up.

'Does it hurt, sweetheart?'

'Not really, like my story, I was faking most of it, or else they would've killed me'.

'You should have seen yourself when they brought you in, bleeding all over. You and your *La Sans Pareille*. Suppose they'd examined me again to check?'

'When I was narrating the story they would only have been imagining your naked body, which is still perfect even though you have an eleven-year old daughter. I was sure that they would be too engrossed in the story to examine you again.'

'If they had decided to check once more, my face would have been as swollen as yours is. Where did you get the French words from?'

'That's another interesting story. If you hear it, you'll really get them tattooed on your navel.'

'Let me hear the story first, then I'll decide.' Scripter started yet another yarn.

'Simonetta Vespucci, a lady three or four years older than Francis Itty Cora, was known as *La Sans Pareille* in Florence. She was an unparalleled model of female perfection. She's the model for Botticelli's *Birth of Venus* and his paintings of Cleopatra and Venus. Simonetta came to Florence as the bride of Marco Vespucci, a distant relative of Amerigo Vespucci, and in time became available to the rich and the famous in Florence. When Itty Cora took over the business after his father's death and came to Florence, Simonetta was the mistress of Lorenzo Medici's brother Guilano. It was Guilano who first called Simonetta *La Sans Pareille*. Simonetta secretly invited the rich handsome foreigner who had come for pepper trade to her palace.

'When Itty Cora went to her room Simonetta was in bed, pretending to be asleep. As he stood perplexed, he saw a small golden snake crawling up the leg of the cot. Even as Itty Cora leapt forward she got up, took the snake in her arms, and held it against her breast. Like an obedient child, it slithered around her neck and lay with its head between her cleavage. Cora looked from Simonetta's enticing smile to the shining eyes of the serpent.

'"Are you afraid of the snake? Or are you calculating my price? Itty Cora? He who can buy the world?"

'"I've never been afraid in all my life. The price must be decided by the seller, not the buyer."

'"Though you are just a boy, you are smart. Isn't it the arrogance born of the knowledge that you have the money to buy whatever you want, howsoever expensive?"

'"You can think so if you wish. I've got four ships of pepper, gold, and precious stones."

'"I don't want any money. You can have me if you remove this snake from my bosom."

'"Yes, I will."

'Itty Cora pulled her towards him, and as the snake tried to raise its head, he caught it in his right hand and twirled it in the air thrice before dashing it to the ground. Its vertebrae shattered noisily. Plucking off its head with his sharp nails, he put it into his mouth. Simonetta looked with horror at Cora, who was eating the snake alive.

'"Are you a cannibal too?"

'"No. I only eat animals that can bite me back."

'"I am an animal that will bite back; come, let us start feasting."

'Itty Cora liked her. He carried her to bed. Before leaving the next morning, he gave her the title reserved for his favourite woman, *La Sans Pareille*. He himself tattooed the words beneath the entwined serpents on her navel.

'Itty Cora never saw Simonetta again. On the night of 26 April 1476, twenty-two-year-old Simonetta Vespucci died of consumption.'

His tale coming to a close, Scripter lay with his head resting on my breasts.

'Do you feel like getting the tattoo now?'

'No. I don't want to die at twenty-two.'

'If we are discovered, we'll be dead tomorrow.'

'Be optimistic.'

24
The Gospel of Cora

I don't believe in God, but I'm afraid of Him.
— *Love in the Time of Cholera*, Gabriel Garcia Marquez

As soon as Rekha woke up, she tried calling Bindu, Scripter, and Benny. All of them had switched off their mobiles. It was just 6 a.m., and Rashmi was fast asleep. Without waking her, Rekha checked her inbox. Cora had sent her an email.

Dear Rekha,

You must be peeved because I haven't written to you for a couple of days. That must be the reason for your silence. I don't want to see you sulking, and that is why I didn't want a video chat. You must be thinking I am prolonging our meeting unnecessarily. But to put an end to all your misgivings, I will be reaching your country tomorrow morning—on Christmas day. Wait for some wonderful surprises. I'll reach Kochi at 3 a.m. on the connecting flight from Mumbai.

Cora with love. (Please check your bank account)

Rekha couldn't believe it ... An end to a wait that had lasted
months. When she checked her bank account she got another
shock. Itty Cora had transferred $4,000 more than the amount she
had asked for to her account. When Rashmi woke up and got to
know the good news, she too was thrilled. They wanted to share it
with Bindu.

'We shouldn't have sent them there.'

'Rashmi, I just hope they get back fast.'

'Don't worry it's just after 6. Bindu and Scripter must be tired
after last night's celebrations. Try Benny once more.' But Benny's
mobile was still switched off. Then she clicked on Morigami's blog.
There was a new thread, 'The Gospel of Cora'.

As Alok has translated the documents I got from Katrina
and Xavier Itty Cora, my inquiries about Francis Itty Cora
are drawing to a successful closure. In the documents that
Alok has titled the 'Cora Code', there were two major
sections; 'The Gospel of Cora' and 'Cora's Journal', with
some sections inserted in between. Scientific examination
revealed that the first two parts were more than five hundred
years old. One of the tablets contained a map used in the
fifteenth century, and the other a geometric shape that was
earlier known as the 'Witch of Amnesia'. The translation of
the 'Gospel of Cora', which is believed to have been written
by Cora himself, follows.

The Gospel of Cora

People of the 18th Clan! I am your father—Corappappan.
You have no God, church, or priest other than me. Seventy-
nine children I fathered with eighteen women in eighteen
countries. Their children, grandchildren, nephews, and

nieces—my blood courses through your veins. But you cannot belong to the 18th Clan by mere accident of birth. It is the life you lead that decides whether you are of the 18th Clan. This gospel teaches you how a member of the 18th Clan should and should not behave.

I don't really know whether you can call it a gospel because I have nothing to say about God or Christ. Those who came before me have spoken of that. I wish to speak only about Hypatia and mathematics.

Hypatia is neither the daughter of God nor is she a prophet. She never performed miracles; did not bestow sight on the blind, change water to wine, or feed a thousand people with six pieces of bread. She did not lead the sinner to salvation. Yet, she was a saint to thousands of her students.

The daughter of Alexander of Theon was perfection incarnate, a wonderful creation whose limbs were in the divine ratio. No woman as beautiful as Hypatia was born on this earth before or after her. She preserved her beauty with a strict regime of physical exercise. Hypatia, who was as beautiful as the Nile, believed in complete freedom of the self, and therefore consorted with different men, explored all avenues, and celebrated life in every possible way.

She was as intelligent as she was beautiful. A mathematics teacher in Alexandria, she was equally skilled in science, music, literature, and politics. She lived in an octagonal house called 'Geometrica', which was equipped for stargazing. On moonlit nights she drank chai with blue lotus petals dissolved in it, smoked the herb datura, and studied the stars. Though she enjoyed all types of stimulants, she derived real intoxication from her inquiries into the mysteries of the universe.

Hypatia was much more than a mere teacher or scientist. Involved in all aspects of social life, she spoke the language of logic and reason. She protested against superstition. Yet, she was crucified. Fanatical followers of Jesus Christ brutally murdered her. Hypatia's blood flows in the veins of all of you of the 18th Clan.

I have not seen my mother. She died on the same Christmas Eve that she gave birth to me. The day I returned home after completing my education at Alexandria, my father gave me a small packet covered in red silk. It belonged to my mother. In it was a text written in the Grecian script which my father could not read. It contained the Hypatian genealogy. According to it, my mother had in her veins the blood of Hypatia, who was crucified a thousand years ago. It is said that three beautiful women arose from the blood of Hypatia when she was killed in the Caesareum at Alexandria. My mother was a descendant of one of those women.

When I met Raphael later in Florence, he too traced my ancestry to the same story.

Though descendants of Hypatia, we are traders. Raphael's people were artists and painters. There is a third category that consists of scientists and rulers. This gospel is meant for my descendants who are traders: for the 18th Clan which is riddled with the sins of avarice, greed, deceit, and subterfuge; the people of the 18th Clan who are unable to love their neighbours like they do themselves, who cannot turn the other cheek when slapped, or refrain from perjury.

In the Gospel of John, it is said that in the beginning there was the word. I believe that is true. I am writing this gospel because I believe in the power of the word. You can call this gospel, one that has been written in eighteen languages for eighteen households in eighteen countries, chai. In Hebrew chai means life itself. Liquor brewed with sweet cumin seed is called chai. Try to live according to chai. You will come to understand that it is not difficult. Chai will lead you to ultimate freedom, prosperity, and happiness. Eat, drink, fornicate, and celebrate life like a carnival. Paradise is here on earth. Do not fear Hell.

Do not doubt the concept of the Genesis. Do not question or insult the sons of God or the prophets because they have worked for the amelioration of humankind. Many have misinterpreted their efforts, but they were intended to make human beings intrinsically good. Allow those who can abide by their laws to live accordingly. But their laws are not for traders like us.

Though I am your God, Son of God, and Prophet, in public you have to feign faith in God. Attend church regularly. Pretend to respect the priest. Always talk about peace, brotherhood, and the will of God. This is an important trick of our trade. Your words and deeds need not be one. But the world should think it so.

The vocation and the life of the 18th Clan is trade. It is true to say that we live to trade and not vice versa. The law of trade is our law. Do not involve yourself in other professions that demand labour and waste your time. Use your intelligence to make others' labour your own. Buy anything you can and sell it at a higher price. Your focus should be only on profit. Pepper, gold, and women are commodities to be bought and sold. All is fair in trade: you can entice, lie, cheat, or kill to make a profit.

Mathematics is the foundation of all the tricks of any trade. You of the 18th Clan should at a young age diligently learn the primary concepts of Hypatian mathematics. Tables have been created in all languages for that purpose. There are other texts for those who want to make a higher study of mathematics. Hypatian principles of mathematics and astronomy can be used to explain all the wonders of the world.

One-tenth of the profit you make is Cora's money. Each member of the 18th Clan should faithfully entrust it to the head of the First House. What he does with the money is a secret. I've told the present head of the First House what he should do with it. He will impart the knowledge to the next generation. Those who fail to remit Cora's money will be severely punished. The nature of the punishment is also a secret.

Do not enjoy liquor or women alone. Do not eat dinner alone. Do not sleep alone on a cot. Do not tie the single cloth around your waist. Do not travel in a single ship for purposes of trade. Joy is meant to be shared.

Cora's woman is as important as Cora's money. When a girl of the 18th Clan attains puberty, she should be given to me on Christmas Eve to be made Cora's woman. There are certain rituals to be observed that will remind you of Hypatia's crucifixion. No one should ask or divulge what happens in the cellar at night. Once the girl is taken to the room, it should not be opened till daybreak. If a girl who is not of the 18th Clan is married into the clan, she should observe these rituals and become one of us.

Love, altruism, and romance are all false notions. They will only serve to shackle your advancements in business. A trader should be able to accept or reject anything without emotion. Transform romance to lust and celebrate life. Be careful not to let a drop of love or kindness enter your heart.

Do not form attachments with anyone, not even your parents. If you do get close to anyone, remember that it will lead to love and love will lead to failure and loss. Love will cloud your senses like opium. Desist from love and affection. Hatred is the best emotion. Through hatred, you can avoid liabilities and loss.

Only a good actor can be a good tradesman. Smile even while you slit another's throat. People should feel that you are lending a helping hand even when you are cheating them. When you lie, assume the demeanour of a saint. Never let your expression betray your anger.

When you buy slaves for your ship, always look carefully at their hands and thighs; only those with strong thighs will be good oarsmen. Do not nurture weak slaves. Sell them when you reach shore. Kill the disobedient slave and throw his body into the sea. When you buy a slave woman, examine her hips. A woman with weak hips will give you illness, not pleasure. A woman with Cora's sign on her body is Cora's woman. Never make her a slave.

Religious exhortations about life after death, sin, good, and evil make us prisoners of fear. They inflict taboos on us. They deny the natural urges of the human mind and body. I doubt whether even Christ was able to abide by these rules.

To say that no man is like another is truer than to say that all men are not similar. Never-ending desire leads us forward. That is the basis of mankind's incessant evolution. All progress is driven by the insatiable greed for money, sex, and power. Any religion or philosophy that does not recognize this greed will be swallowed up by time. I learnt these basic principles from the Hypatian School in Alexandria. It was owing to her belief in this philosophy that religious fanatics cruelly murdered Hypatia thousands of years ago.

Life for the 18th Clan is a celebration. Celebrations can be of three kinds: celebration of food, celebration of drink, and celebration of sex. Most often, all three celebrations go hand in hand. Though there is nothing on earth that cannot be eaten, the best food is the flesh of humans. Flesh from the thigh and liver of a fallen rival is the tastiest. Unfortunately, as wars are not a frequent occurrence, we have to hunt our prey down.

Choose a black girl who has not yet attained the age of eighteen as your prey. Carve out flesh from the thighs and hips of the victim murdered at twilight. Cook it with pepper and eat it before midnight. Do not consume human flesh more than once a week. For the 18th Clan, liquor is of two types. Chai, a strong liquor made out of sweet cumin seed, and *nymph,* a lighter drink made from paddy and datura. A woman who drinks chai will be as strong as a horse. Never try to control her. Surrender to her. Nymph distilled at home will not intoxicate you immediately. But once ignited, it will take a long time for the flames to be extinguished.

The greatest celebration of the 18th Clan is the celebration of sexuality. Though family and morality have no place in the pursuit of this celebration, they are not to be publicly rejected. Romance is a ploy to keep a mate who attracted you because of beauty or strength tied to you. Family is a trick used to chain your mate to you. The codes of morality are derived to legitimize possessiveness. All this will greatly curtail your freedom. That is why all these concepts are unimportant for the 18th Clan, for whom freedom is most important. We will denude in imagination any woman we meet; we will tell her straightaway if we like her. If she doesn't accept our overtures, it is not wrong to force her. A woman similarly has the right to take any man she likes to bed and to resort to force if he refuses her.

Business is war. Each war has many secrets. The intelligence to hide your own secrets and discover those of others will spell success. We use many codes for this. These codes must never be revealed to others. Each member of the 18th Clan must take an oath of secrecy when he or she comes of age.

The discovery of the truth is not our goal. There are others who have made it their vocation. Our inquiries into science, mathematics, and the world are motivated solely by our vocation as traders. The discoveries and inventions we make are used only for making more profit. You can trade this knowledge or you can use it to improve your business. All our actions are motivated by the desire to overtake our rivals in trade.

The 18th Clan has two goals: make the maximum profit out of trade; use the money you earn to make life a celebration.

After reading the gospel, Rekha looked at Rashmi.

'No wonder the 18th Clan is so powerful. Its net is spread all over the world. We will never be able to discover all its links. But I still don't understand how others passed off Hypatian philosophy as their own.'

'Why do we need to know? Unlike Morigami, we are not doing research in the history of mathematics. Like Itty Cora, we must find out how we can make money out of this. For that we must discover the secrets behind Cora's money.

'When Itty Cora withdrew from the world of business after losing his ships in the altercation with the Portuguese, he must have been extremely rich. That money wouldn't be kept in a single place. It must be hidden somewhere in the vicinity of these eighteen houses. The profit given as Corappanam to the head of the First House must in itself be a vast amount by now, after adding up cumulatively for five hundred years. We are interested only in this money. But we need Morigami's help to find out more about it. I don't think the members of the 18th Clan in Kunnamkulam have much information.'

Rekha's mobile sang 'Cut my life into pieces'. It was Benny. 'Any news?'

'No, Rekha, both of them have switched off their mobiles.'

'Are they in trouble?'

'Not likely. I'd told them to call me if they needed anything. I saw George's car roaring into Elite this morning.'

'Is the minister's son there too?'

'I'm not sure. He had some function in Kochi yesterday. He may have come here. Don't worry, twenty of my people have surrounded the First House.'

25
The Holy Seed

Nakupenda pia nakutaka pia mpenzi
wee!
I love you too and I want you too, my love!
— Michael Jackson, 'Liberian Girl'

CONSOLING HERSELF WITH THE THOUGHT THAT BENNY WOULD handle the situation if Bindu or Scripter were in trouble, Rekha clicked the next thread of Cora's Journal in Morigami's blog.

Morigami's World of Plus and Minus

This is *Coco de Mer,* the sea coconut. Its botanical name is *Lodoicea maldivica.* It is the seed of a coconut-like tree and found only on the islands of Praslin and Curieuse in Seychelles. A fully grown Coco de mer is around half a meter in diameter and weighs about twenty to thirty kilograms.

Coco de mer is the biggest seed in the world. Coco de mer trees grow up to a height of thirty meters and the seeds take around six to seven years to mature. Like the nutmeg, the Coco de mer also has male and female trees and the black parrots that are found only in the Seychelles carry out pollination. The Coco de mer and black parrots, which are under the threat of extinction, are preserved in the Vallée de Mai, known as the Paradise of Seychelles.

Till 1768, when the Coco de mer tree was found in Praslin in the Seychelles, it was believed that the seed belonged to a divine tree growing under the sea. Itty Cora brought this seed that was thought to possess miraculous powers to Europe. It was the Coco de mer that opened the bedchambers of the royal palaces in Europe to an ordinary pepper trader like Itty Cora.

It was the peculiar shape of the Coco de mer that looked like two big coconuts joined together that made this seed so precious. A fully grown Coco de mer resembles the hips of a woman. This is the reason why the seed was connected with the myths arising from the belief that all the energy in the world emanates from women. Many rituals were built around this seed.

The Coco de mer was respected in public as the holy seed that granted prosperity and good fortune to the European royalty, and in private venerated as a sex toy that gifted virility. Though the Catholic Church denounced it as a seed of sin that Satan had thrown on the earth to tempt man, Popes like Alexander VI bought it for a high price. Many statues and curios made out of Coco de mer during the Renaissance are preserved in museums around Europe. Alok insisted that the holy seed mentioned in Cora's journal was the Coco de mer because there was a picture of the Coco de mer on the map engraved on the copper tablet.

Alok has not translated the texts verbatim. As many parts of Cora's journal had decayed with time, he omitted sections that he could not comprehend and in some places made his own additions. So, Cora cannot be credited with sole authorship of these texts.

Cora's Journal

I am a merchant. I travel all over the world to sell pepper, ginger, cardamom, and nutmeg. My journeys begin from Kunnamkulam where I was born, and they end in Florence. In between, we drop anchor at various ports to buy and sell cargo. As each voyage is a quest for new knowledge, a route once traversed is not taken a second time. All my travels were in search of novelties: new routes, new ports, new countries, new people, new liquor, and new women ... All my journeys ended in Florence because Florence is the centre of all that is new in the world. Florence, the intoxicating city of the Greek goddess of spring, Flora. The most beautiful and intelligent women who are experts in celebrating the body are to be found in Florence. Like all rivers flow into the sea, these beauties flow to Florence.

The River Arno, which flows through Florence, joins the sea at Pisa. Till a while ago, Pisa was a good port to drop anchor. But now, it has become dangerous. The soil has eroded, ruining the port. It is difficult to go to Florence from Pisa, sailing along the turbulent Arno.

We drop anchor at Livorno and go to Florence in horse carriages, leaving more than half the crew on board to guard the ship. By the time we get to Livorno, the horse carriages from the Medici Palace will be waiting for us at the port. They know that Itty Cora will arrive in the second or third week of every April. We have never needed to wait for a horse carriage. All the cargo we bring, whatever it might be, is for the Medici Palace. Pepper, ginger, nutmeg, and cardamom are loaded in the carriage behind. In the first carriage that is specially decorated, a slave girl chosen to be gifted to Medici is seated with the holy seed in her hands. Having loaded urns containing the centuries-old chai from Babylon in the same carriage, I proceed in front on a white horse to the Medici Palace.

We reach the Medici Palace in Florence within three to three-and-half hours. During the time of Lorenzo Medici, he himself would come out to receive us. Though each time the slave girl would be a different colour and shape, she would always have the holy seed anointed with olive oil in her hands. Lorenzo Medici, who had an angular face with a flat nose, would always look curiously at the holy seed and kiss it before planting a kiss on the slave girl's lips in welcome. He would always remark to the slave girl, 'Your lips are a bit wider than the holy seed.'

The secret behind the holy seed is actually the secret behind my success in business. No one knows where I get it. People believe that there is a world under the sea, and that the holy seed grows there. Believing in its miraculous powers, they give me the price of a shipload of pepper for a single seed. Maybe it is because of the miraculous power of the holy seed that I was able to taste success repeatedly in my trade.

I saw the holy seed quite accidently during my first voyage across the sea for trade. As we were rowing southwards in the sea between Mozambique and Malagasy, we thought we saw a woman's body rising and falling in the waves. Hydrose and the other sailors reminded me that this was Satan's sea and one shouldn't pay any attention to the strange sights exhibited by the sea or the skies. It's a dangerous part of the ocean which sailors call the 'Agulhas'.

My father's friends from Malindi and Mambuta had explained in detail how the Agulhas should be crossed. It should be past twilight before one crosses it. Satan can come in different guises. He hates the whites who are people of God. That is why the Whites are never able to cross the Agulhas. We are not troubled much by Satan. Yet, he should be given his due. Before embarking, the captain of the main ship should throw a cross, which is the symbol of God, into the sea. Then he should sever the heads of three sheep and a black cat and say loudly in Swahili, '*Nakupenda, Nakupenda, Nakupenda ... Iblisi,*' (I love you, I love you, I love you, Satan) and throw them into the sea. A black slave girl should be tied naked to the mast of the main ship on the deck. Then, if you row forward without stopping or looking at either side, you will cross the point before noon the next day. The slave girl may or may not be taken by Satan. If left behind, she can be beheaded and eaten at night. As we were crossing the Agulhas, following their instructions, we saw a woman's body floating half-submerged in the water. When the sailors told me that it might be the body of a slave girl taken by Satan from some ship that had gone ahead, I refused to believe them. I tied a rope around Cheero, who was by me, and threw him into the sea, asking him to find out what it was. I told Hydros, my second mate, 'If she's dead, we will have a delicious dinner; if not, our after-dinner games will be grand.' Though he laughed with me I saw the shadow of fear cross his face. But what a surprised Cheero swimming through the strong waves brought back was not the body of a woman, it was the twin coconut which later brought me all sorts of good luck. We started calling it the 'holy seed' much later.

The twin coconut Cheero brought from the sea looked like the waist of a young and naked black woman. Everyone looked at it in wonder. We had never seen such a coconut in all our lives. Cheero, frightened, thrust it into my hands.

I examined it closely. Each of the twin coconuts weighed four times an ordinary one. As it hadn't been in water for too long, the fibre wasn't spoilt. It was fresh. When I wiped it with a cloth, it really looked like a female body cut in half.

I took it and went to Suchoyi, the black girl who was tied to the mast. As I tried to hold the twin coconut to her waist, she screamed, 'Hapana! Hapana!' (No! No!). Then, she told us the story of the holy seed.

'Master, this is the holy seed. The seed that grows in God's garden that lies under the sea. Only one seed will be borne by a tree in a hundred years. It takes another hundred years for it to mature. Sometimes, God throws a seed or two on the earth. Those who get it are extremely lucky. The grandfather of our emperor got one. It is still preserved in the palace. When I was a slave in the palace, certain rituals used to be observed. It was placed near the waists of queens and princesses to enable them to bear many intelligent and beautiful children. Slaves like us are not even supposed to touch it.'

'What will happen if you touch it?'

'I don't know.'

'You too will become a princess.'

Everyone around burst out in laughter. I decided to make her a princess. I pretended to perform some rituals holding the twin coconut to her waist, and untied her and took her to the captain's room. I smeared olive oil on the twin coconut after wiping it clean and gave it to her.

'If you know what the princesses at the palace do with it ... do it now.'

She hesitated at first, but she had to obey my commanding glance. She held it close to her waist and chanted in Swahili. Her hand that moved slowly at first gradually gathered momentum. Then she moved like one possessed, her hair flew all over her face and her dark voluptuous body streamed with sweat. When she finally fell on to the bed, she had lost consciousness. She had ceased to be a slave. I felt an aura slowly develop around her.

There was a procession of miracles after that. The sea never turned turbulent. The westerly hurricane that usually scares people as they cross the point did not appear; the waves, which usually rise as high as mountains, lowered their hoods.

At Chikua, the first port we drew into in, the king himself came to receive us. He gave us a copper urn filled with gold coins in return for the pepper we gave him, and requested us to stay with him at least a week. On the fifth day, he surprised us yet again. He requested us to allow him to make the black slave girl we had brought with us his queen.

We joyfully agreed, and on the seventh day we set sail after Suchoyi was crowned the queen of Chikua. By then, the crew and I had started to have implicit faith in the miraculous powers of the seed. I decided to present it to a very important person.

I never presented the holy seed to anyone till we reached Florence months later, after trading our cargo at Lisbon and Istanbul. We reached Florence on Wednesday,

14 April 1478. As my father had never travelled beyond Rome, none of my crew knew anything about Florence. I too had only heard about Florence when I was a student in Alexandria. I had heard about the young Lorenzo Medici who controlled Florence, which was the centre of all that was new in the world. It was also famous for its beautiful women. As Medici's bank controlled the finances of the Roman Empire, we had to befriend Medici to establish a monopoly on the perfume trade.

When I was in Rome I had come to know that Medici hadn't been allowed to marry his childhood sweetheart Lucrezia Donati, and had had to bow before the authorities and wed the rich, conventional Clarice, who couldn't accept Lorenzo's modern outlook. Like his younger brother Giuliano, women were Lorenzo's weakness.

As our friends in Rome had warned us that it was dangerous to sail from Pisa to Florence, we dropped anchor at Livorno and went by horse carriage to Florence—two carriages loaded with pepper and perfume were led by Hydrose, and I was in a third carriage with the two slave women we had bought at a high price from Istanbul and Babylon, and the holy seed. We had to wait two days at the palace entrance for an audience with Lorenzo. Though they knew that we were spice traders from the East, it was only on the third day that we were summoned to the palace. When we went inside, Giuliano was with Lorenzo. Putting his hands around the slave girls, Giuliano asked, 'Have you brought anything else?' As I gave him the holy seed, he mocked me saying, 'I want living toys.' Not heeding my words when I said the seed had the power to even save his life, Giuliano walked away with the slave girls, but Lorenzo took the holy seed from me and looked at it with curiosity. I told him its story.

He happily accepted the holy seed. He bought all our cargo and arranged for us to stay in the palace, asking us to join him in the Easter celebrations. He bedecked the holy seed and gave it pride of place in the palace. Surprised at its shape, his wife Clarice Orsini questioned me about the holy seed. Clarice, who was fatigued by the age of twenty-five as she had given birth eight times, was quite interested to hear Suchoyi's story. She requested me to bring her a holy seed secretly when I next visited them.

We saw the beautiful city of Florence. When I saw the small palaces on the banks of the Arno, I too had a desire to possess one. On 24 April, a Good Friday, we went to the biggest church in Florence, Santa Maria Cathedral, which is called Duomo. It had the highest steeple I had seen in my life.

A plot was being hatched to murder Lorenzo and Giuliano on the twenty-sixth, which was Easter Sunday. The plot, which later came to be known as the Pazzi conspiracy, was masterminded by Jacopo de Pazzi. He belonged to the Pazzi family, who were Lorenzo's rivals in banking, and was backed by the traditionalists including the Pope. While we were celebrating Easter on a decorated boat in the Arno, Lorenzo and Giuliano were attacked in Santa Maria Cathedral. Giuliano was cruelly murdered, but Lorenzo managed to escape with wounds. The plot to kill Lorenzo was foiled, and the people of Florence captured all those who were involved in it. They stripped Jacopo de Pazzi naked and dragged him through the streets before killing him and throwing his body into the Arno.

When the riots had been quelled, Lorenzo inquired about Itty Cora, the trader from the east. He held my hands in his own and thanked me, 'It was your holy seed that saved my life.' I think he believed that Giuliano would still have been alive had he not mocked the holy seed.

Having succeeded in opening the door to Lorenzo's heart, my success was assured. All the dignitaries of Florence quickly became my friends. I soon held the monopoly of the perfume and pepper trades. There were many who secretly asked me for the holy seed. Each time I sailed, I searched for it. I've never gone without getting one, sometimes even more than one.

Suddenly, Rekha's cellphone received a message from Bindu: 'Need urgent help, start immediately.' Rashmi and Rekha started for Kunnamkulam almost at once. As Rekha was tense, it was Rashmi who took the wheel. Trying to calm Rekha down, Rashmi hummed, *Nakupenda pia, nakutaka pia, mpenziwe.*

'Hey, haven't we heard this before?'

'We read it in Cora's journal. He wrote, *"Nakupenda Nakupenda Nakupenda Iblizi"*. This is not that. It's a solo number from Michael Jackson's *Bad*—'The Liberian Girl.'

'I hope those iblises don't hurt Bindu.'

26
Cannibal's Feast

*About morals, I know only that what is moral is what you feel
good after, and what is immoral is what you feel bad after.*
— Ernest Hemingway

THOUGH MORIGAMI GLEANED PLENTY OF INFORMATION FROM THE
documents Alok had translated for her, Professor Carlo Rocca
thought it advisable for her to visit Kerala before she submitted
her dissertation. Professor Rocca made all the arrangements. He
arranged for her to speak on 'The Kerala School and the History
of Non-European Mathematics' at the recently established Kerala
School of Mathematics at Kozhikode, the Department of History
at Mahatma Gandhi University in Kottayam, and the Ramanujan
Institute for Advanced Studies in Mathematics in Chennai. But
Morigami needed permission from the Peruvian movement to
travel to India. She was denied permission initially on the grounds
that Alberto Fujimori's trial was in its final stages in Lima, and

that Morigami's presence was needed in New York at all times. But Morigami persisted, saying that the trip was crucial for her research and that she had been scheduled for talks at three important Indian universities. It was only because of her persistence that she was granted permission.

Initially, Itty Cora wasn't inclined to accompany Morigami to India. It was when Professor Rocca himself persuaded him that he agreed, and that too on the condition that he would travel only after 22 December. As they went to bed after dinner, Morigami asked him the reason.

'Why do you insist on going after the twenty-second?'

'The annual feast is on the twenty-first. You can join me if you are interested.'

'You mean the cannibal feast?'

'Yes!'

'My God! Should I come?'

'I won't force you. But I can promise a wonderful experience.'

She lay awake a long time, thinking about his invitation. She felt revolted when she thought of human flesh in her mouth. But then she remembered the initial revulsion she felt during oral sex. She also recalled exploring the different ways of kissing that yielded untold pleasure. If we can eat the flesh of other animals, why not humans? She felt that there was more justice in killing to eat rather than taking a life for money and power. By the time she made the decision to attend the cannibal feast after much deliberation, Itty Cora had slipped into deep slumber. Without waking him, she bit his lips, cheeks, ears, and neck till he woke up in pain.

'I have decided to come with you on Saturday. I was getting some practice.'

'Clever,' murmured Itty Cora and covered her with kisses. On the morning of 21 December, Itty Cora and Morigami arrived at the secret meeting place of cannibals.com. Members called it Cannibal's

Club. Itty Cora had taken permission from the president of the club to enrol Morigami.

Cannibal's Club was housed in a huge three-bedroom apartment far away from the busy city. Arthur James, a fair sixty-year old retired share broker, was the president. The board outside the apartment read Arthur James Inc., Brokers and Investment Consultants. The green-eyed Arthur and his slim, svelte secretary Agnes welcomed them.

'Welcome to Cannibal's Club, Ms Morigami. I've heard a lot about you. A couple of members of this club are from Princeton. I know that people like you are not hard up for funds and we have decided to enrol you as the thirty-second member of this club, believing that you will settle your monthly dues regularly. You must not divulge the secrets of this club to outsiders. Usually, people who violate this condition end up as our prey at the next feast. Please do not allow that to happen to you.'

Morigami nodded in assent and sat next to Itty Cora on a sofa. Agnes offered everyone drinks. Arthur James pulled hard on his pipe and leaned back.

'I hope you have taken this decision after giving it a lot of thought, Morigami.'

'Certainly. Itty Cora has explained everything to me.'

'Have you eaten human flesh before?'

'I've never had a chance. But I've often yearned for it.'

'When? During sex?'

'Yeah.'

'Cheers for being frank, and congratulations on your bold decision. Have you come ready to eat human flesh this evening?'

'Of course.'

'Then listen carefully to Agnes. You are going to eat the tastiest and healthiest food you have ever eaten in your life. Once you taste human flesh, you will not want to eat anything else. You will never tire however much you physically exert yourself. You will never feel fatigued when you celebrate your body, no matter how long the celebration lasts. Yet, as it is impossible to eat human flesh daily, we give mutton or beef its colour, smell, and taste and satisfy ourselves with it. We make the essence here. But that isn't enough. To retain the vitality the consumption of human flesh gives us, we must rejuvenate our bodies by participating in the weekly feast.'

'When you become a cannibal, you will experience several physical and psychological changes. You will develop a different perspective on society. After today's feast, you will see every human being as a potential prey. You will conjure a mental image of chewing on the fleshiest part of the person who is in front of you. You will completely free yourself of the framework of morality and decency imposed by society. You will feel that limitless energy is being produced within your body. The desire to conquer everyone will arise in your mind. Your sexual urges will increase manifold. You will be insatiable. Even after you grow old you will be sexually active if you remain a cannibal. Unfortunately, it hasn't succeeded in your friend Itty Cora's case. But many who had lost their sexual vigour have regained it here.'

'Why doesn't it work for Itty Cora?' Agnes smiled silently at Arthur James.

'That is something I cannot understand. Maybe it is because he has not found a good mate for himself. Why don't you both try after the feast tonight? Wish you all the best, Cora!'

Arthur pulled on his pipe once more and handed Morigami the papers he had kept ready. As she started to sign, Itty Cora stopped her.

'The law says that you have to sign in your own blood.'

'This is like joining the Shining Path.'

'The two are not very different.'

Agnes inserted a needle into Morigami's vein and pulled some blood into a tube. Morigami dipped the steel pen James gave her into the blood and signed the papers.

'Next, we have the rite of transforming you into a cannibal. It is performed in the next room for people who haven't consumed human flesh before. Come, let's go there.'

In the room, there was a small dining table with three chairs around it. A fridge stood close to it. A fire was burning in the fireplace on the west side of the room. Arthur James seated Morigami at the table and placed cutlery in front of her. Agnes placed a bottle of vodka and a plastic container she took from the fridge in front of Morigami.

'Please open the container.'

Morigami opened it slowly ... She withdrew her hand quickly.

'Don't worry. It's the palm of the prey that was slaughtered last week. Put it on a plate and cut off a piece. If you want to eat it raw, season it with salt and pepper, or you can roast it over the fire in the fireplace. Once you eat human flesh, wash it down with vodka, and kiss your lover, you officially become a cannibal.' Itty Cora thought that he saw a shadow of revulsion cross Morigami's face. To reassure her, Itty Cora carved the small finger off the palm, dipped it in salt and pepper, and popped it into his mouth. Seeing him do so, Morigami overcame her initial hesitation. She took a gulp of vodka and picked up the fork and knife. But cutting off the finger wasn't as easy as it seemed.

Seeing her struggle, Agnes advised her to position her fork at the third joint of the finger and cut it off.

When she obeyed, she found that it was as easy as plucking a flower. Morigami seasoned it well with salt and pepper and looked questioningly at Itty Cora, deliberating whether to eat it raw. Before Cora could say anything, Arthur James intervened, 'You are eating human flesh for the first time. Roast it before you eat.' Morigami pushed a metal rod into the finger and placed it over the coals in the fireplace. The smell of burnt human flesh permeated the room. Morigami gave the metal rod to Agnes and retched. Itty Cora forced some vodka down her throat. When she had emptied her glass, Arthur held another glass to her lips. When the third peg of vodka had inflamed her senses, she felt that the smell of roasted human flesh wasn't intolerable. She happily accepted the roasted finger Agnes gave her and chewed it down. Not satisfied, she cut off the thumb and dipped it in salt and pepper. Arthur, Agnes, and Itty Cora stood around her clapping, and sang, 'Lovely! A new cannibal is born.' Morigami grabbed Itty Cora and kissed him greedily. As she withdrew, panting, Arthur James shook her hand. The initiation being over, Arthur James moved to the next stage.

'The prey for this evening's feast is in the next room. She is a Costa Rican rock singer who has settled down in Chicago. We brought her here for a music programme. We have to use such ruses to capture tasty prey. She has just turned twenty and has a lot of flesh on the thighs, waist, and breasts of her six-foot-tall body. It is only by luck that we have such a good prey for this feast at which thirty permanent members, including the newly inducted Morigami, are to participate.'

Arthur James took them to the next room. The naked prey was lying unconscious in the middle of the room on her side. Arthur laid her flat so that Morigami could see her properly.

'We are slaughtering her for the feast tonight. Dr Andrews has examined her and declared her fit. All medical tests including the Elisa test have been conducted. They are all clear. We never take any risk. The killing will take place just before twilight. Till then, the prey is under sedation so that members can take a look at her. Each member can book the part of the body they'd like to eat. Look at the marks made on the prey's body—those are the parts which have already been reserved.'

As Morigami stood looking at the prey, Itty Cora turned the prey over and said, 'I want my usual cut; the middle part of her right thigh.'

Arthur James made a mark on her thigh and made a note in his notepad. Itty Cora moved back and told Morigami, 'Now it is your turn.' When Morigami tried to turn the victim over, Arthur James eagerly helped her. She stroked the prey's ample buttocks. Then, like a seasoned customer, she pinched the prey in a couple of places. Then, as if satisfied, she slapped the prey on her bottom. Even in an unconscious state, the prey winced in pain. 'Being a singer I don't think she has sat down a lot. It's quite soft. I want this cut.'

Arthur made a mark and noted it down. Itty Cora winked knowingly at Morigami. She asked Arthur James to lay the prey flat once more. It was to make sure that there wasn't a tattoo of twin serpents beneath her navel. Satisfied, she left the room.

'Please come at five if you want to see the slaughter or come ready for the party at seven. You have to wear black. No guests are allowed. You can unleash all your perversions at the party. You can't refuse anyone. Don't hesitate to celebrate the basest instincts of your life. Please fill in the card with details of the brand of liquor of your choice.'

Arthur James himself filled in the card and the two of them returned to their apartment. As Itty Cora drove the car, Morigami sipped beer from a can.

'Cora, your club is wonderful. The prey looks like a succulent pig ready to be stripped.'

'It is not always so. It's just luck that we've got such a good prey this time.'

'Whose luck?'

'Definitely yours. My first taste was the liver of a man who had died in a car accident.'

'My mouth watered when I saw the prey. I wanted to bite her. I don't know where the revulsion I felt for human flesh has vanished.'

'It is like all other taboos. Once broken, it can never confine you again. We become different from other people once we join Cannibal's Club.'

'What has actually happened in the last couple of hours?'

'If you think deeply, nothing of great import has occurred, but on the other hand your life has changed irrevocably. It is like your life before and after having sex for the first time. Your life can be divided into two phases: before and after becoming a cannibal.'

'Somehow, I don't understand.'

'You are a cannibal now. That's all.'

Itty Cora bought her a pair of black leather shorts as a gift for her induction into her Cannibal's Club. Eager to see her in the new outfit, her asked her to try it on as soon as they got home. In a black leather jacket, micro shorts, and sheer stockings, she was almost naked.

'Great! You look more like a night club dancer than a college teacher. It seems as if you've shed fifteen years. The only problem is that your wounds are quite visible.'

'That's all right. Its half past three now. Let's go back to the club.'

'Do you want to see the slaughter?'

'Of course!'

They reached the club before five. Only ten of the thirty-one members had come for the slaughter. There was not a single woman among them. When Morigami came in, everyone stared at her. By the time they had introduced themselves, it was time for the killing. Arthur James and Agnes brought the dazed and dopey prey into the room.

As everyone waited with bated breath, Arthur James introduced her: 'Friends! Meet Sophie Alexander, the famous rap singer from Chicago. She will entertain us with her sexy voice tonight.'

In her semi-conscious state, hallucinating that she was on stage, she waved a hand at the guests. The music from one of her popular songs arose from the music system. Within seconds, a sharp axe had split her head in two. Blood spurted in all directions. Everyone looked on with pleasure at the prey writhing on her way to death. When the last movement of her body had stilled, everyone silently filed out of the room. Arthur and Agnes filled two crystal jars with blood. Then they stripped the skin off and cooked the parts that the guests had asked for.

The party began sharp at seven. All thirty-two members— eighteen men and fourteen women—assembled in the hall. Arthur introduced Morigami to everyone and made her take the oath of the club. Immediately afterwards, Itty Cora gave her a bowl of the prey's blood. She looked at everyone and smilingly raised the bowl to her lips. As the salty, warm blood slipped down her throat, she felt a fire spreading all over her body. Then, Itty Cora put the prey's right forefinger into her mouth after dipping it in salt and pepper. As she bit into it everyone surrounded her, loudly singing, 'A New Cannibal Is Born'.

The night was filled with music and dance. The members of the club ate their chosen cuts from the body of the prey, selected their mates, and danced with them. Men and women competed to touch and fondle Morigami, who was easily the most beautiful woman there. Morigami and Itty Cora reached their apartment tired out in the morning of 22 December, and slept for twenty-four hours, completely forgetting Arthur's advice.

On board the Air India Boeing 777 flight at 9.30 p.m. on 23 December, Morigami and Itty Cora flew to India from JFK airport. Most of the people on the flight were Indians settled in the US. Though it was a routine academic trip for Morigami, it was different for Itty Cora. It was a last attempt at regaining his lost prowess. His face shone with hope. When he laughed, joking with the pretty airhostess, Morigami pinched him.

'You are very happy. Is Rekha that beautiful?'

He compared Morigami to Rekha. If she looked as she did in video chats, Rekha was more attractive. She had beautiful eyes. But Morigami's figure was better. That could be because he knew Morigami's body quite well while he didn't know Rekha's at all. Without answering, he looked pleadingly at Morigami.

'I can't understand why I am starving though I have a rich dinner before me.'

'I can understand that, but I can't figure out what led to your condition.'

'I've no explanation. It happened, that's all. I never intended that girl in Fallujah to die. I just wanted to have sex with a girl who resisted me.'

'Is that sex or is it mere violence? What pleasure can that afford?'

'All pleasure is born of violence. Sport is the best example. What happens when Brazil and Germany play football? Chess? Tennis? Your only aim is to defeat your opponent. It becomes more intense in sports like boxing and bull fighting. All competition, whether in sports, business, or war, is a celebration of violence. We try to best our opponents' physical or mental abilities and manipulations.'

'But sex is different, isn't it? The participants celebrate the pleasure equally.'

'That is a misconception. Then life would become as drab as a football match where rival teams have decided that it will be a draw even before they enter the field. If violence were to be completely eliminated, human life would be very dull.'

'Are you saying that you are against peace?'

'Certainly. Peace is an inactive state.'

'Are you an anarchist?'

'I don't know. I am a cannibalist.'

'Well, now I'm also a cannibal like you.'

'But you are not a cannibalist. You still cherish a hope that revolutions will triumph. All cannibals need not be cannibalists.'

'Don't you have any hopes of the future?'

'Hope is the mental refuge of foolish revolutionaries like you.'

'Itty Cora, I don't understand you.'

'I can't understand myself; my views are quite often self-contradictory. I'm a US Marine who hero-worshipped Saddam Hussain, and who went to Iraq to rape a girl. It was not out of sympathy for Saddam or the conviction that the US policy on Iraq was wrong that I admired Saddam. It was just greed for violence.'

'Greed for violence?'

'Yes, an insatiable greed. Gluttony for conquests. A hunger to see blood and tears.'

Not knowing what to say, Morigami silently leaned back in her seat.

27
Pray, Read, Sacrifice

You who are and will be pure, you are just in your justice because men spilled the blood of the prophets and the pure, you gave them blood itself to drink. They deserve it.

— The Oracle

At 8'o clock, along with the D'Souzas we set out for Kunnamkulam in an Innova car that belonged to the UTC. Paulson, a handsome young man, escorted us. He was quite taciturn, and there was hardly any conversation. When we passed Kannipayyoor, he asked the driver to stop and handed us each a piece of black cloth.

'You have to blindfold yourselves. The way to the First House is a secret.'

'But we belong to the 18th Clan. Why should it be kept a secret from us?' I argued. But my effort was futile.

'I don't know. It's Pranjiettan who insisted that all of you should be blindfolded on this journey.' Though D'Souza wanted to say something, his wife stopped him. Paulson made sure that we had tied the blindfolds securely over our eyes, then asked the driver to start the car. Though I couldn't see anything I had some idea of where we were going, as I was very familiar with Kunnamkulam roads.

We were allowed to remove our blindfolds only when we reached the inner hall of the First House. The room in front of the nilavara, the underground cell, was crowded. Though no one welcomed us, we sat down on some empty chairs, amazed at the number of members the 18th Clan had in Kunnamkulam. In the light of the single oil lamp placed on four or five benches joined together to form a sort of platform, no one was recognizable. Fumes of frankincense and joss sticks and a frightened silence filled the room. On the decorated table there was a book covered in silk, which I guessed was the Gospel of the 18th Clan. Near the door of the cell was St. Andrew's cross in rosewood.

Within ten minutes of our arrival, a sixty-year old man wearing a long red garment embroidered with gold thread and a velvet cap on his head appeared, holding a two-foot metal rod in both hands. All the electric lights in the room were switched on. We too stood up with everyone else as a mark of respect. I recognized the person when Bindu whispered in my ears, 'Isn't that Pranjiettan?' The old man looked at the gathering and placed the rod on the table. It was the sign for everyone to sit down. I saw that Bindu had noticed the cross only as the electric lights were turned on. She turned to me and asked, 'Scripter, do you see the cross?' I remembered that a cross had recently been mounted in the Liberation Centre of the School. I had been told that it was upon the request of a client who did not wish his name to be known.

'Praised be Holy Corappappan in the skies above. The One who is and who will be, Corappappan with eyes like stars, he who protects us. Praised be the Gospel of Corappappan. Praised be the eighteen

maidens Corappappan sowed with the holy seed and praised be
you the descendants of the eighteen Satan's virgins.'

The audience raised their right hands and said thrice, 'Praised be
holy Corappappan who is and who will be.'

'We are conducting Corappappan's Christmas celebrations as
we do every year. But this year is special because the ritual of
Corakku kodukkal is being conducted after a lapse of seven years.
D'Souza, his wife, and his daughter Leena have come here for that
purpose. Their relatives and members of the 18th Clan, Pereira
and his wife from Australia, are also here. They are the ones who
came in just now and sat on the chairs in the front row. We had
to blindfold them because it is necessary to guard Corappappan's
secrets.'

Then Pranji took the metal rod, twirled it around, and threw it to
the audience. It fell on the lap of a girl sitting in the seventh row on
the left. She joyfully took the metal rod, went to Pranji, and stood
with her head bowed. He took the metal stick and moved it thrice
around her.

'Aren't you Kunhannama? Kattambil Elikutty's daughter? I
remember you were offered to Cora seventeen years ago. You have
been chosen for today's prayer.'

As Pranji closed his eyes and pointed the thumbs of both hands
inwards touching his chest, ready for prayer, everyone stood up and
started chanting. Kunnhannama started chanting Corappappan's
prayer in a mellifluous voice. Everyone sang in chorus.

He who is and will be the holy Corappappan.

May your blessings always shower us with gold, money
and happiness.

You are the Father, the Son, and the Holy Ghost. You are
our inspiration.

Our prophet and our teacher. You are our God and
priest. Show us the way to happiness and prosperity.

Show us the way to joy and celebration. Show us the way to success and profit.

He who is and will be the holy Corappappan.

Accept our prayers.

May your blessings always shower us with gold, money, and happiness.

We shall forever guard your secrets.

We shall make our offerings to Corappappan without fail.

When our daughters mature we shall give them to you the next Christmas night.

~

Oh, Corappappan! You who taught us that there is no heaven or hell.

No caste or creed.

That the church and the priest are false. May your name be praised.

You who taught us that the justice of trade is the true justice.

You who taught us that one who only tells the truth is a fool.

You who taught us that life is given to us to celebrate.

May your name be praised!

~

Oh you who flow from the sea to the sky in the form of a black tiger.

You who with fire burning from your starry eyes watch over us from the sky.

Free us from fear of sin.

~

Bless us with the art of writing, mathematics, and knowledge. You who taught us to weigh forty pounds with three pound measures and measure forty nazhis with three nazhi measures.

You who calculated the distance to and the weight of the stars.

~

When Kunnhannama ended the prayer, bowed to Pranji, and descended from the dais, everyone sat down. I felt that Leena D'Souza hadn't understood a word of the prayer. As this prayer was chanted daily in all families of the 18th Clan, she ought to have known it. Maybe she had been staying in a hostel for her education and was unfamiliar with it. She hadn't overcome her nervousness at being blindfolded. I couldn't catch what her mother whispered to her. Then, Pranji started speaking about Cora.

'Praised be Corappappan, our Saviour with starry eyes in the sky. The year past has been a good one for us of the 18th Clan owing to his kindness and blessings. Most importantly, one of us has been sworn in as a minister in the central government. Though Kuttan's father Kochouseph was a cabinet minister, he was not of our blood. He only wedded a woman of the 18th Clan. Kuttan's mother Thresyakutty was given to Cora in the cell here years ago. When the whole world is moving in the direction of Corappappan's teachings, it is not a small achievement to have a cabinet minister amongst us. Let us pray that Kuttan will be showered with Corappappan's blessings.

'Another important success we have had is the rise in our business fortunes. As the price of gold soared, so did our profits.

Other business ventures did well too. We own more than half of Kerala's liquor trade. This year, we doubled our profits over last year. Whether it is trade in rice, cloth, petrol, or movies, the 18th Clan leads Kerala. We are doing well abroad too.

'Who you think is responsible for all this? We cannot claim all credit. It's all Corappappan's doing. Hasn't the whole world admitted that Corappappan was right? Trade is the most coveted profession. The smart ones don't go far. They may get into the civil services. They may do their MBAs, and where do they go then? To America. The communists here used to despise America. Even their attitude has changed, and how can it not? Earlier, in the Hindu caste hierarchy the Vaishyas, the trading caste, came lower down the ladder than Brahmins and Kshatriyas. And now? The trader makes the laws. The law is for the merchant. Everything has been liberalized, liberated. Everyone is following us. All agree that it is not wrong to make money from business. This is no minor achievement. It is a milestone in human history. Earlier, there were groups of people who forced the 18th Clan to go underground. Now, there aren't many people like that. Even if there are, they have no followers.

'People are now smart. They have understood the belief that sinners will go to hell is false if you accept that heaven and hell are here on earth itself. So, celebrate life till you die.

'Still, you may ask why there are people flocking to temples and churches. They do so not to reach heaven or escape hell. They just do it because they don't want to miss any opportunity to profit. Everyone wants to make a profit. The end justifies the means. This is Corappappan's law. It is only now that everyone has understood it. Everyone abides by this philosophy now. Will any intelligent person be willing to live according to the philosophies of Christ or Gandhi or Marx?

'Have you understood what I'm saying? This is the age of Corappappan; hence, it is the age of the 18th Clan. There are many who are jealous of us. But they too are emulating us.

'But they believe in powers other than those of Corappappan. The Church is behind them. They are acting against us. They are always spying on us and trying to ferret out our secrets. They are eager to find out what we do with the Corappanam, the money we offer Cora. This has been going on for centuries. But their plans always come to naught. They have never been able to identify the members of the 18th Clan in their midst.

'Each one who has tried to discover our secrets has been punished. All of you are familiar with Porinju B.A.'s story. There are some people who have started probing afresh. Some of them even reached the First House. We haven't been able to track them down and punish them. This Christmas, my message to you is this: Never divulge our secrets. If anyone tries to trick you into betraying our secrets, don't hesitate to kill them.'

As Pranji stopped for a sip of water, Bindu pressed my hand and looked at me worriedly. The recording device was in her bag. We realized that if we were caught we wouldn't leave this place alive. The D'Souzas looked impatient as if this speech was of no relevance to them. Pranji continued.

'Many denominations of Christians, including the Catholics, do not like us. As Corappappan advised us, we never enter into arguments or fights with them. Though we know their secrets, we don't generally use them. But tell them that you will use those secrets as a last resort.

'Now, we move to the next stage of today's ritual—the reading. The reading that we usually have on the tenth Sunday is being done today specially as part of our Christmas rituals. The manuscript of the gospel written in Corappappan's own hands will be read by Narikkattil George's wife Susannah.'

While Susannah who was seated right behind us stood up, got up on the dais, and bowed before Pranji, her husband George sat proudly in the audience. Maybe it was a matter of pride for them to be selected to do the reading.

'Susannah, there is a special reason I chose you today. You, who entered the underground cell to atone for a sin committed unknowingly, are the last woman Corappappan has seen. You were reading the gospel day and night during those days. Now, let us begin.'

All the electric lights in the hall were turned off. Susannah straightened the wick of the oil lamp to make it burn brighter and stood respectfully near the holy book.

'Susannah, before you remove the silk covering of the gospel, take off your outer covering and submit yourself to Corappappan.'

I was happy. I had expected to see Leena naked, now I would get to enjoy the sight of Susannah's voluptuous body. The fair plump Susannah reminded me of Donna Lucrezia in Mario Vargas Llosa's *In Praise of the Stepmother*. Thinking of Jacob Jordan's nude painting included in the novel, I completely forgot Bindu. As everyone watched silently, Susannah took off her clothes.

When she was completely naked, she raised her hands upwards in prayer to Corappappan. As she was behind the table we could only see the upper part of her body.

'Now, go round the holy book thrice and pray on our behalf to Corappappan.' As she circumambulated the book, everyone had a clear view of her bare body. As she turned towards the cell and started praying with her back to us, she looked exactly like the woman in Jacob Jordan's painting. Bindu pinched me to catch my attention, which was entirely taken up by Susannah's voluptuous derriere.

'Serve Corappappan mutton and cumin seed liquor.'

As Susannah bent over to serve Corappappan the food and liquor arranged on a stool near the left side of the dais, she provided a delectable spectacle.

'Now, give yourself to the cross of St. Andrew.'

She stood against the cross spreading her legs as wide as she could. Pranji handcuffed her with leather cuffs to the cross and turned down the wick of the oil lamp. The hall was dark. Someone sat down behind Bindu's chair and whispered in her ear, 'You whore! Did you think I wouldn't recognize you?' I too heard this and immediately texted Rekha, 'Need urgent help ... start immediately.'

Our only desire now was to escape as quickly as we could. As we were thinking of a way of escape, the lights were turned on. Pranji freed Susannah and brought her to the dais. She was sweating profusely. She looked as if she were possessed. Without waiting for Pranji's instructions, Susannah took the holy book and started reading. Pranji got off the dais and disappeared. Everyone except the two of us listened respectfully.

We were really terrified.

'I am reading the Holy Book of Corappappan, who is and will be for all of you of the 18th Clan. Henceforth, the "I" is not me but Corappappan. The words are not mine but Corappappan's. What he has written ...'

She opened the palm leaf manuscript and started reading. 'You of the 18th Clan: I am your Corappappan. You have no church or priest other than me.

'My blood flows in the seventy-nine children I begot of eighteen women from eighteen countries, their children, and their grandchildren.'

Susannah's reading began this way, but after that differed from the version in Morigami's blog. Maybe the eighteen houses had eighteen different versions of the gospel, or perhaps Alok's translation wasn't accurate. As Susannah continued reading in a soft voice, someone called Bindu, 'Come, Pranjiettan is calling you. We have to get you ready for the ritual of offering to Cora.' As Bindu looked at me doubtfully, a muscular hand dragged her away. Sensing danger, I followed.

The hall ended in a small room. Pranji was seated on a chair, surrounded by three or four people. I recognized the minister's son at once. I guessed that the other man was George. Before I could hear what they were saying to Bindu, someone hit me on my head from behind, saying, 'What is your business here?' When I opened my eyes, I was tied to a stone pillar. A fire burnt brightly in front of me. Four men were propping up Bindu near the fire. Her head was lolling to one side. I realized that she had been brutally tortured and was unconscious. I felt pain in every inch of my body. Pranji, in the attire he was wearing was on the dais, Mariyamma, and a few others were near the fire. I believe we were in the underground cell or some such secret place.

Pranji placed the metal rod on Bindu's head and declared, 'Her punishment is death. She is the main link in the Kochi group that is trying to get hold of our secrets with the help of some foreigners. It's been thirty-six years since we offered a human sacrifice to Corappappan. It's our great fortune that we are able to make a human sacrifice on Christmas day. It is Corappappan's blessing that the prey has come in search of us.

'Holy Corappappan, who is and who will be. Accept this human sacrifice. Forgive us for not having made this sacrifice for thirty-six years. She is our enemy, an enemy who tried to discover Corappappan's secrets. Accept her and bless us.' Bindu's captors pushed her towards Pranji, and he pushed her into the fire. Maybe she was already dead, for she made no sound as the flames enveloped her. My heart ached for her.

As the flames greedily licked her still body, all of them praised Corappappan.

When the fire started dying, Pranji came to me and slapped me across my face. 'You bastard, how dare you try to trick us? You will follow this woman.'

George suddenly intervened. 'No, Pranjietta. This man is a well-known writer. He got into this because of the woman. If we kill him, we will be in trouble. Let us make him promise not to divulge our secrets. If he disobeys, we will sacrifice him too.'

I begged for my life. Luckily, they let me go, threatening to burn me alive if I betrayed their secrets. Pranji shouted, 'You shouldn't be seen in Kunnamkulam again.'

They took me in a car and pushed me out on Ponnani Beach.

28

Francis Itty Cora and Raphael's Death

*IIlle hic est Raffael tinuit quo sospite vinci, rerum magna parens
et moriento mori.*

(Here lies the famous Raphael by whom nature feared to
be conquered while he lived and when he was dying feared
herself to die.)
> —From the epitaph on Raphael's tombstone in the
> Pantheons.

MORIGAMI WOKE UP AS THE AIRCRAFT WAS FLYING OVER EUROPE
after crossing the Atlantic. Itty Cora was still fast asleep. Morigami
started reading the article Claude Andree, the French artist, had
written about the painter Raphael in the journal *Art and History*.
It was Claude Andree's article that first mentioned Itty Cora in

connection with western art and culture. Though Pal Erdos had told Morigami about Claude Andree's article, she was able to lay her hands on it only yesterday. After a long search she had managed finally to locate a copy of the September 1972 issue of *Art and History* with Yamini Mukherjee, Alok's artist friend.

Claude Andree was a Frenchman born in Algiers. *Art and History,* which was a quarterly journal, started publication in 1970 from Paris but only eight issues could be published before Claude Andree was killed after the September 1972 issue was published. It was suspected that the two controversial articles, 'Holy Mary or Hypatia, Who is the Real Pieta?' and 'Francis Itty Cora and the Death of Raphael' published in the September issue led to Claude Andree's murder.

On 21 May 1972, an Australian geologist Laszlo Toth tried to destroy Michelangelo's Pieta in St Peter's Basilica using a hammer. Laszlo Toth was screaming 'I am Jesus Christ' when he tried to destroy the statue. Though Laszlo Toth was arrested, he was declared insane and therefore was not punished but deported to Australia.

The Pieta was restored and a heavy guard arranged. But no further inquiries were made into the incident. Claude Andree in his article 'Holy Mary or Hypatia, Who is the Real Pieta?' alleged that many attempts had been made to destroy the Pieta, but the Catholic Church never consented to an investigation into such attempts because the Mary in the Pieta was not really Mary but Hypatia. With corroborative evidence he tried to establish that many in the Catholic community knew this and hence several attempts had been and were being made to destroy the Pieta. Citing the fact, Laszlo Toth had been left unpunished, Claude said that the attempt to destroy the Pieta was made with the Pope's knowledge. It was in the article, 'Francis Itty Cora and the Death of Raphael', which was a continuation of 'Holy Mary or Hypatia,' that Claude wrote about Francis Itty Cora.

Francis Itty Cora and the Death of Raphael

Claude Andree

As mentioned in my previous article 'Holy Mary or Hypatia, Who is the Real Pieta?', the secret Hypatian School in Florence was established by Itty Cora, an Indian merchant. It counted many artists and intellectuals like Michelangelo, Botticelli, and Raphael amongst its members. Giorgio Vasari who wrote the biographies of important artists during the Renaissance was a Hypatian himself and so he was compelled to suppress the association these artists had with the Hypatian School.

Francis Itty Cora who was quite influential in the Medici palace was a pepper merchant from India. Cora who gained vast knowledge of mathematics and astronomy from a secret Hypatian School in Florence withdrew from pepper trade and settled down in Florence when the Portuguese deprived him of his monopoly over the business. The secret Hypatian School in Florence was housed in the small palace, Palazzo Cora, that he built on the banks of the Arno in the beginning of the sixteenth century.

Years before Itty Cora settled down in Florence, Lorenzo Medici introduced Michelangelo to him as the artist and sculptor of the future. Itty Cora saw his sketches and paintings and immediately recognized the spark of genius and of homoerotic desire. Itty Cora put three gold coins in his hand and blessed him, 'You will become great but never holy' and pinched his cheeks. 'Michael, every stone has a beautiful sculpture within it. You hew away the rest and the sculpture will be visible.'

'The sculpture is not hidden in the stone, it is in my mind.'

'Is it? Then you should learn Hypatian philosophy. Once you traverse the distance from the stone to your mind, the rest is easy.'

'I don't want to study philosophy. I am willing to learn science.'

'Hypatian philosophy recognizes the natural stimulus of the mind and guides you to a celebration of life. It will free you from the twin fears of sin and hell. But most of what Hypatia said is against the Bible. The danger of attacking the beliefs propagated by the Catholic Church is inherent in the perusal of Hypatian philosophy.'

'I will study it before I decide whether or not to attack the faith'.

Michelangelo accepted Itty Cora's tutelage and studied Hypatian mathematics and astronomy. Without his realizing it, Hypatian philosophy started influencing him. Adoration for Hypatia took Michelangelo to a different mental plane. Hypatia's form took shape in his mind. Every woman he painted became Hypatia. The image of a cruelly murdered Hypatia covered in blood filled Michelangelo's mind. This image had a lasting impact on Angelo, so much so that he was never able to feel sexual desire for a woman. He spent the rest of his life a homosexual.

When he was creating the Pieta his mind was filled with thoughts of Hypatia. That is the reason why, as mentioned in my previous article, in the sculpture Mary sitting with the crucified Jesus in her lap is 6½ feet tall. It was said that it was Itty Cora's influence that caused Michelangelo to sculpt Mary as a young and beautiful woman as against the Christian beliefs of the time. The Mary in the Pieta who looks as young as Christ himself is actually Hypatia.

In 1492, before starting work on the Pieta, the twenty-two-year old Michelangelo discussed it with Itty Cora in detail. Itty Cora would go to the Vatican occasionally to advise Michelangelo till the Pieta was completed in 1499. The Catholic Church would never allow anyone in the Roman empire to sketch or sculpt Hypatia. So Itty Cora advised Hypatians like Michelangelo to use subterfuge to recreate Hypatia's image. It is when you realize the significance of his inscribing the finished Pieta with, MICHAL (N)GELUS BONAROTUS FLORENTIN (US) FACIENAC(T)

(Michelangelo Buonarroti, Florentine, made it), that you recognize the importance of this sculpture in Michelangelo's life. After the Pieta, Michelangelo changed completely. He gradually moved away from Itty Cora and the Hypatian School. Why he did so remains a mystery. Was he compelled to do so by the church or did he feel that his career prospects would be brighter if he were under the umbrella of protection the Catholic Church offered him or was it because of the antipathy the Hypatian School developed for Raphael?

It was no mean feat for Itty Cora to have a sculpture of Hypatia's installed within the hallowed precincts of the Catholic Church and that too a sculpture that established that after the crucifixion, Christ had at last rested on Hypatia's lap.

But his efforts to induce Raphael to draw Hypatia's picture for the Vatican Palace did not succeed. Raphael was a Hypatian even before he met Itty Cora. Raphael who was a student of the secret Hypatian School at Urbino came to Florence in the month of October in 1504 and met Itty Cora. Though he was only twenty-one at the time he had already received recognition as a painter. Itty Cora thought that he could easily manipulate the incredibly handsome and well-mannered (unlike Michelangelo) Raphael and decided to use the Persian beauty Jameela Zavera for the purpose. Itty Cora told Raphel who had confessed that he was a Hypatian when they met at the Uzi Gallery that he would show him a Hypatia in flesh and blood and brought him back to the Palazzo.

Palazzo Cora on the banks of Arno River was built in a peculiar style. No matter which part of the palace you faced it seemed like the front entrance. There was a tower in the centre used for stargazing. The Palazzo Cora at first glance resembled Hypatia's Geometrica.

Raphael, who saw the palace from a luxury boat as he was crossing the Arno with Itty Cora, was spellbound.

'Itty Cora, this resembles the Geometrica.'

'Leonardo first designed Palazzo Cora. Michael and Botticelli effected minor changes.'

'It's beautiful. Now tell me, where is your Hypatia?'

Before Raphael could complete the question, Jameela Zavera came out to greet them. Following Itty Cora's directions, Jameela dressed in a light pink chiton with a blue lotus in her hands walked between two black beauties from Timbuktu who were dressed in deep red and green. She kissed Raphael on both cheeks and led him in. He looked at Jameela carefully. She seemed as if she were Hypatia herself. Each limb was created in the divine ratio. An enticing smile played on her lips, green stars glittered in her eyes. He gathered her to him with his right arm and walked in.

After the formalities of a sumptuous dinner, as she led him to the bedroom, Jameela whispered in his ears, 'You look like a beautiful girl.' Raphael did not reply. But it was true; with his long hair and smooth chin, the smiling Raphael did look feminine. When they entered the bedroom he hugged her lightly. Very soon she realized that he was a strong and insatiable man. But she was surprised that he did not ask any questions about her. He commanded and she obeyed. At dawn as he covered her with the chiton and got up like a conquering emperor, she pulled him back, 'Raphael, don't you want to know anything about me?'

'No.'

'Not even my name?'

'No.'

'Why?'

'You are Hypatia to me.'

'No, I am Jameela Zavera.'

'You lie!'

'What are you saying?'

'You are Hypatia. Hypatia, who was crucified a thousand years ago.'

'Are you insane?'

Raphael held her close and looked deep into her eyes, 'Yes, I am mad. Mad about Hypatia, mad for lust, mad for art, for colours and for figures. In this infatuation, all unnecessary knowledge is insane. Even your name.'

He pushed her back on the bed and left. He visited Palazzo Cora without fail each time he came to Florence. He addressed Jameela only as Hypatia.

Once he stayed at Palazzo Cora for sixteen days at a stretch and painted 'Hypatia Teaching the Art of Lovemaking' on the wall of a bedroom. It is unnecessary to say that Jameela Zavera was his model. Just like 'La Fornarina', this nude painting was also destroyed when Palazzo Cora was attacked.

For a period of four years, from 1504 to 1508, Raphael visited Palazzo Cora frequently. After Jameela Zavera died on the night of 10 September 1508, owing to excessive bleeding caused by an accident during an orgy, Raphael never visited Palazzo Cora again. When Itty Cora invited him he asked, 'My Hypatia is dead. So why should I come to Palazzo Cora?'

But as he received several commissions to paint there, Raphael settled down in Florence and continued his friendship with Itty Cora. In 1508, Pope Julius II invited Raphael to the Vatican and asked him to paint on the walls of his private chambers as well as the library. These pictures as you know are now considered masterpieces. Among them 'The School of Athens' is considered the most important. That painting embodies all that was sacred in Greek art and philosophy. Itty Cora urged Raphael to use the opportunity to include Hypatia in this drawing and Raphael agreed.

But try as he might Raphael couldn't draw Hypatia when he was painting 'The School of Athens'. Itty Cora had directed Raphael to paint Hypatia between Plato and Aristotle. When Raphael ensnared in the memories of Jameela Zavera started to rave and rant, his disciple Guilo Romano informed Itty Cora of his condition.

When Itty Cora went to Raphael's workshop in the Vatican, he found Raphael completely intoxicated, singing, 'Where is Hypatia? I am her Min.' He had smeared his body with a multitude of colours. Itty Cora went back and brought Margherita Luti who had acted as hostess in the Palazzo Cora and sent her to Raphael, completely naked. Obeying Itty Cora's instructions, she nodded when Raphael turned his burning eyes on her and asked, 'Are you my Hypatia? What is the proof?'

'The entwined serpents beneath my navel.'

'And?'

'My knowledge about the sun, the moon, and the stars.'

'And?'

'My confidence that I can satisfy your sexual hunger.'

'Let's try then, if you are so confident.'

Raphael experienced Margherita's confidence in her sexual prowess. But though he drew Hypatia in the sketch of 'The School of Athens' Raphael couldn't complete the painting the way he wanted to. He blurted out the truth when the Cardinal who was supervising the paintings asked him who the female form between Aristotle and Plato was. The Cardinal commanded Raphael to remove Hypatia from the picture as she was against Christian beliefs. Raphael removed Hypatia's image but cleverly included it on the left side below between Pythagoras and Parmenides in the guise of Francesco Maria I Della Rovere. But Itty Cora's schemes did not succeed as they had with the Pieta.

What came out of all this was that Margherita Luti continued to be Raphael's muse throughout his life. Raphael only addressed her as Hypatia. He liked Margherita though he complained that the lotus buds on her breasts were smaller than those of Hypatia. It is Margherita Luti whom we see in the painting 'La Fornarina'. It is said that Margherita stayed in a room close by and Raphael had sexual intercourse with her in between bursts of artistic creativity. But that celebration of sexuality ended on a Good Friday on 6 April 1520. In his thirty-seventh year, he died one morning because of overindulgence in sex the previous night, in a manner similar to Itty Cora's death three years earlier. He was at the peak of creativity and fame then.

Raphael, according to his wishes, was buried in the Pantheon. At the funeral in which thousands of dignitaries participated, Michelangelo was supposed to have said, 'It is that damned Itty Cora who caused his death.' But I do not agree with Michelangelo. Raphael's untimely death was an inevitable conclusion of the life he led. It is pointless to blame Margherita Luita or Itty Cora.

29
Adupputty Padiyola

THIS IS THE PADIYOLA WRITTEN BY THE 18TH CLAN, THE DESCENDANTS of Corappappan in Adupatty mansion, in memory of our Corappappan with his *kallu and kacha,* stone and waist cloth, bearing us witness at the dawn of the third Tuesday of *Makaram* in the year 675. We promise never to reject Corappappan who from the sea vanished into the sky in the form of a black tiger after the Portuguese and the Zamorin and the King of Kochi, swayed by the Portuguese betrayed him. We hereby swear that for us there exists no God or priest other than Corappappan. We will never betray his secrets. We will give him his Corappanam, liquor, and women.

Signed by

Aadyaveedu Karanavar, Adupputty Ukru, Kuttipal Lona, Pranoor Tharu, Narikottil Pailo, Vattekkadan Anthony, Iyyal Kotha, Kallazi Cheru, Kattambole Ittoop, Marthamkodan Vareeth, Parela Kandan Koran.

(Translation from old Malayalam)

Even after reaching Kunnamkulam, Rashmi couldn't contact Scripter or Bindu and she turned left on to the Guruvayoor road trying to remember the way to Kunhippalu's house where Susannah had taken her. Rekha was still trying to get Bindu, Scripter, or Benny on the cellphone. All three phones were switched off. Rashmi stopped the car near Arthaat St Mary's Orthodox Church.

As it was Christmas Eve the church was crowded, 'Rekha, Shall we go inside and try our luck?'

'Yes, we might stumble on a lead.'

They locked the car and entered the church. The morning mass had just ended and people were streaming out of the church. As they looked around anxiously, hoping to spot a familiar face, Roopa Alexander, Rekha's student, came running to her.

'What brings you here, Ms Rekha?'

'Nothing special'

'This is my mummy, Mary Alexander. She teaches at a government school here. My father is a lawyer at the high court. Mummy, this is Ms Rekha, she teaches us history.'

'Hello.'

'Hello, this is my friend Rashmi. We are looking for information on the heritage and traditions of the Christians of Kerala for a research project.

'Is this your first visit to the Arthaat church?'

'Yes'

'All right then, we will show you around.'

Mary gave them a guided tour of the church and narrated all the stories connected to it. What she told them echoed Kunhippalu's stories. As they bowed before priest Yakob's tomb and turned, they saw the Arthaat *Padiyola* engraved on the granite wall. It was written in old Malayalam script with the translation by its side. Rekha who was familiar with the old script noticed some discrepancies in the translation.

Aarthaathi Padiyola

This year 981 in the month of Makaram on Sunday all the newly converted Syrians of Arthaat church hereby present before the Divanios Bava Metroploita this palm leaf manuscript written before the Bava. Some of us under the influence of foreigners have swayed in the direction of Roman belief. They had disputes with us and you were upset about it. So if Rome or Bava or Anioches or other newcomers from foreign lands come to us we will not accept or obey them.

We will abide by Marthoma belief and rules.

This is the padiyola written before the Divinios Bava Metropolita.

Signed by Kuriyithu Kathanar

Cheruvathoor Kunjathu 2. Panakkal Thaaru 3. Kuthuru Chummar 4. Koladi Uttoop 5. Kakkacheri Mathu 6. Chungathu Iyyavu. 7. Tholathu Pathu 8. Cheeran Pathu 9. Pulikkottil Tharu. 10. Kidangan Cherunni 11. Mandumbal Kunjaathu, 12. Thengungil Kuriyakku.

Rashmi captured the padiyola on her mobile camera.

'We belong to Kakkacheri Mathu's Family. During Tipu's assault Arthaat church was looted and destroyed. Shaktan Thampuran rebuilt the church. This padiyola was written then. The original one written on a copper tablet is preserved in the Oriental Manuscript Library of Kerala University.'

'But during Shakthan Thampuran's period modern Malayalam was in use, so why use the old style *vattezhuthu?*'

'Official documents were still written in vattezhuthu.'

'Have you seen the original?'

'No I haven't. Paliyathachan, minister of the Kochi King, was in possession of the padiyola. Aru's father and a couple of others went to Paliyath and had it read by someone who could read the script and later had it engraved here. Then the manuscript was handed over to the library. We have a photograph of it at home. Why don't you come over and have a look?'

'Where do you live?'

'Nearby, just beyond L.F. College.'

'My mummy's house is at Mammiyoor.'

Everyone laughed at Roopa's joke. We followed them in our car. As soon as she got in, Rekha tried Benny, Bindu, and Scripter to no avail. But Rekha received a call from Ikka in Mumbai. Hearing his voice she completely forgot Bindu and Scripter and fingering her navel barbell, she coyly murmured, 'Hello.' Ikka was actually Ignatius Kuriakkose, a Christian from Kanjirappilly. He had a business empire that ranged from shrimp export based in Kochi to casinos in Mauritius.

'I am in Kochi tomorrow. Are you free?'

'Oh! I'm sorry. The foreign client I mentioned earlier arrives in Kochi tomorrow from New York. He is booked from the 24th to the 30th.'

'Oh, you have spread your net far and wide.'

'You taught me fishing.'

'I taught you to fish in a pond, but you have started fishing in the sea.'

'To net sharks you have to venture out into the deep seas.'

'Be careful anyway.'

'Don't worry. All clients have to clear the Eliza test before they are allowed entry, but I'm really sorry about tomorrow.'

'No problem. We will celebrate New Year together. A trip to Singapore. Bring a friend along. A business partner of mine will also be there. So get ready to fly.'

'Thank you, Ikka.'

'I should be the one to thank you. Tell me, how are you?'

'I'm doing well.'

'Have you given up your teaching job and taken this up fulltime as a profession?'

'I am a professional, but I haven't given up my teaching job. I need a front and I play the role of an academic admirably.'

'Wish you all the best.'

'Ikka, I've a problem.'

'Tell me.'

Rekha explained everything in detail. Finally he responded. 'Don't worry. I'll take care of it. You return to Kochi.' He disconnected the phone. Rekha looked at Rashmi in relief. By this time the car was entering the portico of the house. Rekha told Rashmi, 'Don't worry ... He will do something.'

Roopa's house was a richly decorated mansion. After welcoming them in, Mary brought the photograph of the padiyola. As the padiyola was written on a copper leaf folded in two, the photograph clearly showed the split in the centre. Rashmi took a picture on her cell.

'This is only about two hundred years old. Does the church have older documents?'

'I haven't seen any. My husband says that Buchanan's text mentions quite a few.'

'Have you heard about Corappappan who renovated the church?'

Mary flushed but tried to hide the fact that she was disturbed. 'I've heard Koran's people talk about it when they come for *Velakali* at the church.'

'At the church, they have Velakali?'

'Yes, they do in Arthaat church. The Virgin Mother's birth is celebrated every year on the 7th and 8th of September. On the 8th afternoon after the church rituals and poor feeding, Koran's people come near the wall of the cemetery. A few people playing drums and cymbals accompany them. After the priest comes out and gives them permission to enter, they come to the front yard and begin their performance. They have the right to perform Velakali in the church. They are given a basketful of rice, curry, 7½ measures of coconut oil, and one rupee. After the priests give them their due, they go to the Kalari temple behind the church.'

'Can I meet Koran's people?'

'My driver Chandran lives there. His father Thupran is always to be found under the banyan tree near the temple. He will tell you all about Corappappan.'

Mary sent Chandran along with them. Sure enough, Thupran was sitting under the banyan tree near Thekkiti Kalari temple. Rekha put the bottle that she had asked Chandran to buy in his hands. Chandran said, 'They are from Kochi Palace. They need some information from you.'

Thupran tried with great difficulty to stand up, saying, 'How can I sit when you are standing.'

Rekha stopped him saying, 'No. We will sit here.'

Thupran sat down after they did. He might have been anywhere between ninety and hundred. His face was so wrinkled that his eyes were mere slits and his eyebrows and eyelashes had completely fallen off.

'What do you want to know Thamburatty?'

'When did the Velakali start?'

'I don't remember ... maybe a thousand years ago.'

'One thousand years?'

'Well ... Maybe five hundred'

'What is the basis of your calculation?'

'Chandra, when did Corappappan become a tiger and go to heaven?'

'I don't know.'

'The Velakali started the year after that.'

'The Nairs and Namboodiris were not powerful during Corappappan's time. Even inside the Arthaat church, Cora and Koran had equal status. Even their confessions were heard together. The Portuguese pigs hadn't yet come here and destroyed our land.

When Corappappan went to heaven as a black tiger the poison entered into everyone, even the worms. Cheralath Thamburan and the priest at Arthaat resumed their powerful status. Dark-skinned people were not allowed to enter temples and churches. But we were allowed to perform the *Vela* at church once a year.'

'Nobody has said that you mustn't enter the church.'

'No, but we don't want to enter the church. We have our Corappappan and his padiyola and that's enough for us.'

'Corappappan's padiyola?'

Thupran lowered his voice. 'It's a tablet, we call it Adupputty Padiyola. Something is written on it. We got it when Tipu burnt the church down. After we placed it in the temple we have only tasted success. Now we even have a magistrate amongst us.'

'Can you show it to us?'

'Yes, but you can't take it away. I will hold it and you can look at it.'

He brought the tablet and put it on his lap. As Rekha read out the fading letters on the leaf aloud, Rashmi noted it down. Then she took a picture on her mobile.

Adupputty Padiyola

This is the padiyola written by the 18th Clan, the descendants of Corappappan in Aduppatty mansion in memory of our Corappappan with his *kallum kachayum* bearing us witness at the dawn of the third Tuesday of Makaram in the year 675. We promise never to reject Corappappan who from the sea vanished into the sky in the form of a black tiger after the Portuguese and the Zamorin and King of Kochi, swayed by the Portuguese, betrayed him. We hereby swear that for us no higher God or priest exists. We will never betray Corappappan's secrets. We will give him his due—money, liquor, or women.

Signed by

Aadyaveedu Karanavar, Adupputty Ukru, Kuttipal Lona, Pranoor Tharu, Narikottil Pailo, Vattekkadan Anthony, Iyyala Kotha, Kallazi Cheru, Kattambole Ittoop, Marthamkodan Vareethu, Parcla Kandan Koran.

As he watched Rekha reading the tablet with ease, Thupran gazed at her in respect.

'It is not a small thing to know Corappappan's language. We couldn't read it. What will happen if you come to know of Corappappan's pathway as well?'

'What is Corappappan's pathway?'

Thupran turned the copper leaf over. Rekha saw an inscription that looked like a map of Kunnamkulam—a web of roads leading from the main crucifix at the junction.

'These are the routes of the paths under the Kunnamkulam market. You cannot understand these routes by just looking at the map. You have to travel on these paths.'

'Have you done it?'

'I have tried but didn't succeed. I was lucky to get out alive.'

'Why?'

'There are caves under Kunnamkulam market. The entrance is right behind this church. It is hidden under a big stone. If you remove the stone there is a small hole. A man can enter if he lies down flat. You have to fold your hands against your chest and crawl in. Girls like you can't do it. If you go a bit further the hole widens a bit allowing you to crawl on your elbows. A little further it widens again and you can go on all fours. A bit further and you can walk bent. Then we get on to Corappappan's road. It's a tunnel made of red stone. Two or three people can easily walk abreast there.'

'Did you get there?'

'No, when my waist was halfway in I couldn't breathe and I screamed, beating my legs till someone pulled me out. I have heard that Parembedath Uttoop managed to walk the entire length and that's the reason he was thrown out of the church.'

When Rekha realized Thupran was talking about the Uttoop whom Scripter had met earlier, they bid Chandran and Thupran farewell and made their way to Parambedath.

Uttoop welcomed them joyfully thinking he had customers. He took up the two crosses on the table, one made of ivory and the other sandalwood, placed them on his forehead and prayed for a while before opening his eyes and looking closely at the two women. Sensing that he was searching for a mark on the left side of her neck, Rekha started speaking. 'We are from National Geographic. We want to make a documentary on the underground tunnels in Kunnamkulam. Could you give us some information?'

As expected, Uttoop's face clouded over. He put down the crosses in displeasure.

'But who told you there are underground tunnels in Kunnamkulam?'

'We found a reference in the old records of the Geological Survey of India. It is documented that in 1936 Samuel Johnson, a geologist, was trapped in the Kunnamkulam underground tunnels and buried alive.'

'All right, why come to me about these tunnels even if they do exist?'

'We heard that you are the only person to have walked through these tunnels recently. Buchanan has written that only Kunnamkulam has catacombs like those in Paris. He has also mentioned that those who manage to enter this place are gifted with magical powers. If you promise to help us we plan to make a documentary. It will help you in more ways than one.'

Uttoop's face brightened.

'The underground tunnels of Kunnamkulam aren't like the catacombs in Paris. In Paris they are underground tunnels about two-hundred-and-sixty kilometers long. The catacomb is a small part of this tunnel where skulls and skeletons are heaped. It's a tourist attraction now. Anyone can buy a ticket and enter. The Kunnamkulam underground tunnels aren't like that. There are several secrets hidden behind them. All roads leading to them are shut now. The 18th Clan built them hundreds of years ago.'

'How did you get in?'

'It's a secret. The 18th Clan call this tunnel "Corappappan's Pathway". They will never talk about it to outsiders. It starts from Adupputty mansion and leads to Arthaat church and it was built during Corappappan's time. He constructed a similar tunnel to the First House in Cheralath. There are many such tunnels that the 18th Clan built. It is a confusing network of winding roads. Whichever direction you take, you will never return to where you started. The song of Cora says that if you sing his song as you walk, "Three right, left, right two left, right one left," you will reach Adupputty mansion from Arthaat church. The directions are said to be inscribed behind the copper leaf of Adupputty. No one knows where this copper leaf is now. Eight Christmases ago I tried to navigate the route following the directions in the song. I had only reached halfway when I came to a wide space. Five or six tunnels ended here. Water was dripping drop by drop there and a funeral pyre was burning in the middle. People were standing around it. As they screamed, "Catch him," and charged towards me, I fainted. When I opened my eyes I was in the ICU of Mission Hospital.'

'Don't you remember how you got out?'

'No, but they defrocked me four days later. There are other problems involved. I advise you not to get mixed up in this'

'Journalists can't afford to retreat in fear.'

'You will have to face the consequences. But don't come back to me.'

As Uttoop said this both of them said goodbye and left. 'Rekha, let's go back. How long can we wander aimlessly like this?'

'I wish I could contact Benny.'

As the car left Kunnamkulam and turned on to the Trichur road, Rekha's cell sang, 'Cut my life into pieces.' A strange landline number.

'It's me Benny. Scripter is in Lakeshore Hospital. He is still unconscious. Where are you?'

'In Kunnamkulam.'

'Don't stay there. It is dangerous. Come to Kochi quickly.'

'Bindu?'

'I'll tell you when you get here.'

As the cellphone was on loudspeaker mode, Rashmi had heard everything.

'Rekha, will you get upset if I say something?'

'Tell me'

'I fear Bindu has been murdered.'

'Yes. I think so too.'

'We can't even file a missing person's complaint because she disappeared under a false name.'

'What will we do now?'

'Do you believe in love?'

'No.'

'Then forget about her. Tomorrow Itty Cora will come. We will celebrate a week with him and then we will fly to Singapore with Ikka.'

'Supposing something like this happened to you or me?'

'The other will behave in the same way.'

'You are so heartless.'

'Yeah.'

She switched on the music. Papa Rocha's 'Cut my life' filled the car.

30

Itty Cora Shot dead

O bitter is the knowledge that one draws from the voyage.
The monotonous and tiny world, today, yesterday, tomorrow,
always, shows us our reflections. An oasis of horror in a desert
of boredom.

—*Le Voyage*, Charles Baudelaire

IT WAS WHEN THEY SHIFTED ME FROM THE ICU TO A PRIVATE ROOM AT around 1.30 in the afternoon that I heard the shocking news on CNN that an American tourist had been shot dead at Kochi airport. Benny anxiously kept switching channels. When he finally put down the remote, a local channel was showing a news bulletin in Malayalam.

'Xavier Fernanto Itty Cora, an American tourist, was shot dead by unknown assailants this morning at 4.30 am at Nedumbassery International Airport.

'The president and the prime minister expressed grief and said that they were shocked that an American tourist had been shot dead in India. The central home minister in Delhi said that all efforts would be made to track down the assailants and the FBI would be approached if necessary. Nedumbassery International Airport has been put on high alert.

'Xavier Itty Cora and his companion Hashimoto Morigami had come to Kochi from New York on vacation for two weeks. He was shot down as they were coming out of the airport after customs clearance. Itty Cora who was shot four times in his chest and stomach died on the spot. His friend Morigami who is a research scholar at Princeton University had a miraculous escape. The police are questioning two women, Rekha Thomas and Rashmi Chandran who were at the airport to receive them. Rekha Thomas is a lecturer in a private college in Kochi and Rashmi Chandran works in a bank.

'Now, we have a live report from Kochi International Airport.'

'Nandagopal, what is the position at the airport now?'

'The airport has been shut down after Xavier Itty Cora, a US citizen was shot dead here. The police have completely taken control of the airport and a search is on for the culprits who may be hiding inside the airport. The public including the media were forcibly removed from the airport.'

'Is there any new information about the assailants?'

'The assailants shot four rounds of bullets at Itty Cora who was coming out of the airport at 4:30 am this morning and escaped in a Toyota Qualis. The police are still questioning Hashimoto Morigami, Itty Cora's companion, and the two women Rekha Thomas and Rashmi Chandran, who had come to receive him at the airport. But sources say that the police have not got any information from them. Against the background of the attack on the Taj Hotel in Mumbai, the possibility of an international terrorist plot behind the murder cannot be ruled out.'

'Why did Rekha Thomas and Rashmi Chandran come to meet Itty Cora at the airport?'

'Hashimoto Morigami, a research scholar at Princeton University, has come to Kochi for an international seminar at Gandhiji University. Rekha Thomas told the police she is a lecturer in history and that she and her friend Rashmi Chandran had come to welcome Morigami, who is a guest of the University. The police are not entirely satisfied with this explanation. Over to you, Suresh.'

'Thank you, Nandagopal. We will come back to you. Chandni from the US consulate at Delhi is with us now. She will give us the official response of the Government of the United States. Chandini, what does the White House have to say about the murder?'

'The official response from the US government was released just a while ago. The government expressed deep sorrow that a US citizen was killed in India and has requested the Government of India to pay urgent attention to the safety of US citizens in India. They have promised all help in tracking down the assailants.'

'Do you have any further information about the victim, Xavier Itty Cora?'

'Xavier Itty Cora was a US soldier. It is not clear what he was doing after being discharged from the marines. He was in the Alpha Company of the Third Marines Battalion and was part of the Al-Fajr operation in Fallujah.'

Benny switched off the TV. 'What do we do now?'

'Nothing, whatever happens we have to face it. I expect a visit from the police soon.'

'Wonder what has happened to the girls!'

'Nothing worse than what happened to Bindu.'

By the evening the main suspects of Itty Cora's murder Mirsa Ali (21), Hussein Raj (24), Siyad (22), and Faizal (21) were arrested at Metur near Selam in Tamil Nadu by the Tamil Nadu Police. Mirza Ali belonged to Kashmir and the others were natives of

Ramanathapuram in Tamil Nadu. Close-ups of the e-mail sent by
the Lashkar-e-Taiba from an unknown place to the central ministry
and media, claiming complete responsibility for the murder were
shown on television channels. Lashkar-e-Taiba said that they had
been plotting for quite some time to kill Itty Cora who was a US
marine and had played an important role in the Al-Fajr operation
at Fallujah.

'Benny, see how beautifully they have twisted the story.'

'Supposing it's true?'

'Are you mad? They have capitalized on the new trend of blaming
Muslims for all acts of violence. People eagerly buy the explanation
and inquiries are diverted. I clearly heard Pranji say, "There is a guy
who claims to be a descendant of Corappappan. Finish him the
minute he lands in Kochi."'

The news channels kept repeating the news that the US
government had congratulated the Indian government on arresting
the criminals within just fourteen hours and FBI agents had started
for India to investigate whether any international terrorist groups
were involved in the crime. In the discussion aired on TV, Major
Reynolds and Lieutenant Shepp spoke at length of Itty Cora's
commendable efforts in destroying the north bridge across the
Euphrates and thereby isolating Fallujah and capturing Talen Park
during Operation Al Fajr. The political leaders, members of the
investigation team, and experts in terrorist attacks who participated
in the talk shows on Malayalam channels, followed the Fallujah
line. No one mentioned the 18th Clan.

The next day also Itty Cora figured large in the visual and print
media. Even the papers, which usually do not come out the day
after Christmas, cancelled the holiday and printed special editions.
A Malayalam paper published an interview with Morigami.

In the interview, Morigami stated that her research centred on
the contributions of a fifteenth century Malayali pepper merchant,

Francis Itty Cora, towards the development of mathematics. He believed in Hypatian philosophy. Itty Cora who had eighteen wives and seventy-nine children in different parts of the world entrusted his children, grandchildren, nieces, and nephews with propagating Hypation philosophy. Unfortunately with the passage of time they moved away from Hypatian philosophy and became extremely superstitious, selfish, and cruel. They later became the 18th Clan, which is a secret sect. The activities of the 18th Clan, who resort to devious methods to secure huge gains in business and trade, are shrouded in mystery. Morigami said that she suspected the 18th Clan had killed Xavier Itty Cora.

Morigami's revelations changed the course of the investigation. But as the 'real' criminals had been arrested, the police visited Rekha and Rashmi to question them. Morigami, a guest of Gandhiji University, was kept under police surveillance. All editions of the papers on 27 December carried shocking reports about 'The School' and the 18th Clan. It was said that the police who had come to question Rekha and Rashmi at the flat were shocked to see the Body Lab and the Liberation Centre. The national daily that carried pictures of the movable cot and the St Andrews cross in the Liberation Centre on the back page carried a centrespread of a bikini-clad Rekha relaxing on a beach with the caption 'The 21st Century Malayali Beauty'. It was a picture mounted on the wall of the Body Lab in honour of Itty Cora's visit. The front page was full of the history of the 18th Clan and their cruel and mysterious ways. Some papers had even printed excerpts from K. Porinju B.A.'s *Nakshatra Cora*. But all the papers gave prominent place to Rekha's bikini-clad picture. The channels celebrated the mysterious 18th Clan and the sex racket involving the elite in Kochi. The winter session of parliament was on. The MPs from Kerala holding aloft the papers that carried pictures of Rekha in a G-string bikini, demanded a detailed inquiry into the murder of Itty Cora. They alleged the case had underworld and sex angles apart from the terrorist angle. But the central home minister who answered the questions took the stand that these theories were deliberately being floated to divert the investigation. He said that everyone knew who controlled the paper that had published Morigami's interview and that their motives were questionable. The culprits had already been arrested and all that remained was to investigate whether international terrorist groups were also involved. He gave a written statement to the Lok Sabha regarding the case, adding that the Indian investigation team would work with the American Federal Agency.

It was under these circumstances that Morigami spoke at the seminar on the History of Mathematics in the School of Social Sciences, Gandhiji University on 28 December. The media, which usually ignore such seminars went live with Morigami's talk.

Dear students, teachers and friends,

When the eminent historian and vice chancellor of Gandhiji University, my friend Dr Gurukkal, invited me for this talk I agreed to speak about Francis Itty Cora, the pepper merchant who was born in Kerala in the fifteenth century and his contributions to mathematics and astronomy. You all know that unfortunately I am not in a suitable frame of mind to talk on the subject. I've made arrangements to circulate among you the paper I was to have presented here. We will discuss your questions before I go back to the US. Now I wish to talk about something that has no real connection with my area of research.

In academies, similar to the misconception that mathematics and history are two disciplines or areas of knowledge that share no common ground, there exists the belief that mathematics and literature represent unrelated areas of knowledge. Though it is not easy to explain the connection between them, it is undeniable. Because of the relationship between life and literature I've often wondered whether what we call an accident or a coincidence isn't a mathematical order, for example, the shooting of my friend Itty Cora at Kochi International Airport. When four bullets penetrated Itty Cora's body, I was only few centimeters away but escaped unhurt. Not only that, a bullet merely grazed Rekha, who had come forward to welcome him with a bouquet. All the bullets struck target. Is the murderer's expertise in shooting all the explanation? I don't know how practical it is to construct a mathematical model based on such coincidences.

I feel that my being selected for the BSM at Budapest, meeting Pal Erdos there who told me about Itty Cora, and meeting Grothendieck were all coincidences. If the first incident had not happened, the second, third, and fourth wouldn't have occurred. Thus, if I hadn't been chosen for BSM, I wouldn't have been witness to Itty Cora's murder. The same goes for Itty Cora. If he hadn't gone to Fallujah during the Iraq war, he wouldn't have gone to Peru to meet Katrina nor would he have met me, come to Kerala with me, and been killed.

Whether you believe in religion or not, you may feel that what I'm saying is absurd. If you are a believer you will say that Itty Cora would have been killed on Christmas morning at Kochi Airport irrespective of whether he had met Morigami or not. If you are not, you will mock me saying that any accident can be linked to another and that the connection is not based on logic. But my friend the Spanish writer Roberto Boleno told me fifteen days before he died on 15 July 2003 that both these perspectives are quite absurd. He gave the example of the suicide of the famous Japanese writer, Yukiyo Mishimi. Boleno argued that the reason Mishimi had committed hara-kiri on the evening of 25 November 1970 could have been an event that occurred on the evening of 15 August 1957—the meeting of present Japanese Empress Michiko and present Emperor Akito. Michiko, a pretty literature student at Sacred Heart University

in Tokyo, was a fan of Mishimi's. The young prince Akito met
Michiko at the tennis court and was attracted to her beauty. The
entire country bowed before his decision to marry Michiko in spite
of her being a commoner. But when Michiko left for the palace as
crown princess, Yukiyo Mishimi was devastated. Boleno said that if
Akito hadn't met Michiko, Yukiyo Mishimi's life might have taken
a different direction. I didn't think much of the idea. I felt that
Mishimi's politics and philosophy as revealed in his work pointed
to hara-kiri as the inevitable end. Boleno laughingly replied, 'It was
because Mishimi was not able to marry Michiko that his politics and
philosophy became what they were. I am not speaking of marriage
as a social institution, but about the sex within this institution. Sex
has a tremendous impact on the formation of one's political and
philosophical attitudes. If he could have lived with the gorgeous and
intelligent Michiko, Mishimi's attitude would have been different.
That is why I say thoughts of religion and thoughts of logic are
absurd.'

There is another reason why I spoke about Boleno's opinion of
Mishimi today. The hot topic of discussion in today's media is Rekha
Thomas's school and her g-string photo. Everyone says that she has
shamed your society and your country. I was shocked when I heard
that the communists, feminists, and revolutionaries who speak of
freedom are one with the religious fanatics and reactionaries on this
issue. It is absurd. I saw the photo in today's newspaper, a marvelous
photograph of a beautiful woman. Instead of congratulating her
on her beauty, she is dragged away for questioning. You should be
ashamed of yourselves. I think your attitude towards beauty and
sexuality is absurd. But for your society such absurdities are the
reality.

It was when I read Boleno's novel *2666* that I realized that
illogical absurdities are closer to reality than logical deductions. The
hundred-page *2666* was published in 2004 after Boleno's death.

Now an English translation has also been published. Boleno chose Baudelaire's line, 'An oasis of horror in a desert of boredom' from his poem 'Le Voyage' as an epigraph to *2666*—a novel that can be called a saga of violence in twentieth century Latin American society. The stark reality of Latin American life is exposed in *2666*. Itty Cora's death reminds us that it is the same all over the world.

In an interview I gave to the papers two days ago I had spoken of the 18th Clan—the descendants of Itty Cora. The descendants of Itty Cora, who used his knowledge of mathematics and astronomy received at the Hypatian School to attack superstition, are spread all over the world. In Kunnamkulam in Kerala, Estraap in Peru, Tarlabasi in Istanbul, Jardin near Paris, there are members of the 18th Clan. Unfortunately they are steeped in superstition now. Itty Cora who was once known as *Nakshatra Cora* is now Corappappan to the people of Kunnamkulam: an icon of superstitions and miracles. It is alleged that activities of the 18th Clan who have become extremely wealthy through their businesses are mysterious. I strongly suspect they are behind Xavier Itty Cora's murder. But your internal minister is trying to divert the inquiry by claiming to have the culprits under arrest. Who are the real culprits? Why did they kill Itty Cora? These questions remain unanswered. It shows the powerful influence of the 18th Clan.

As the TV channels showed Morigami being arrested in the middle of her speech, my calling bell started to peal insistently: *'Ccdlaron Racha cama ricy auccaurac Yahuamly hichas Cancuja.'*

Glossary

achappam	a fried sweet snack
adavu	a stance
appan	father
appapan	grandfather
apuka	father
arakacha	cloth worn around the waist
athazhapuja, ushapuja and uchapuja	night, morning and afternoon rituals respectively
attar	perfume
chanthu	red paste used to adorn the forehead of women
chenda	drum
cheriathampuran	younger nobleman

Cherumas	landless labourers who were considered to be of backward caste
Chingam	month in the Malayalam calendar that falls in August, considered to be auspicious for marriages
Cora kutty	Cora's child
Corakku kodukkal	offering to Cora
Corakuthu	Cora's punch
Corapaattu	Cora's song
Corapapappan	Grandfather Cora
Corapootu	Cora's grip
Corappanam	Cora's money
Corappera	Cora's house
Doric chiton	a Greek dress consisting of a rectangular sheet folded in two and pinned up; a very simple outfit
guru	spiritual teacher
himation	a formal Greek dress
Inti	Sun God of the Incas
kaachi	length of cloth Namboodiris wore
kalam	decorated ground
kallu and kacha	stone and the sacred cloth
karanavar	patriarch of a family
kasavu mundu	ecru silk cloth
kettilamma	matriarch
kohl	eyeliner
kotha	woman
kovilakam	home of an aristocrat
Kumara Sambhavam	A work by Kalidasa. The title meaning the conception of Kumara

madrassa	a place where Muslim children learn their lessons in religion
Mals	slightly derogatory abbreviation for Malayalis
mapla	Non-Hindus. Usually referring to Muslims and Christians.
molu	a term of endearment for a girl
moosaris	blacksmiths
muhoortham	auspicious time
mulakacha	cloth worn around the breast
Nair	the warrior class
Nakshatra Cora	Star Cora
nakshatra	star
Narasimham	an avatar of Vishnu, half man half lion
Nasrani	a Keralite Christian
Njaatuvela	a day suitable for transplanting paddy seedlings
Onathallu	a ritual connected with the harvest festival Onam where people engage in physical fights
Pachacamac	Earth Goddess of the Incas
padakuruppu	commander of warriors
palakka	a traditional necklace used by upper-class Hindus in Kerala
Pallivetta and Aarattu	the beginning and culmination of temple festivals
Panickers	professional astrologers
Panickers, Nairs, and Warriers	high-born Hindus

parotta	a fried pancake made of flour
Parayas and Malayars	tribals
pudava	a cloth signifying marriage
thamboolam	betel leaves
puja	religious rituals
rantha	veranda
sloka	verse
Somayaagi	master of ceremonies
sora	gossip
Thachans	carpenters
Thakshak	the mythical king of serpents
thamburan	nobleman
thamburatty	female of the noble class
Thiruvathira	a festival celebrated by the women of Kerala in worship of Lord Siva
Thulam	the Malayalam month which falls sometime in September
Vaastu	the Kerala belief system regarding the location of buildings
yagna	holy sacrifice
Zamorin	The royal ruler of Kozhikode

About the Author and Translator

TD Ramakrishnan is a novelist whose craft and themes have kept pace with the technological and aesthetic predilections of the times. He puts new communication technologies and the changing contours of cyber space to their fullest use. At the same time, he has the dexterity to navigate to the past and adjust with the present. He is the author of four bestselling Malayalam novels: *Alpha, Francis Itty Cora, Sugandhi Enna Andal Devanayaki* and *Mama Africa*. He is a recipient of several awards, including the Kerala Sahitya Akademi Award and the prestigious Vayalar Award. The English translation of *Sugandhi Enna Andal Devanayaki* titled *Sugandhi Alias Andal Devanayaki* was longlisted for the DSC South Asian Literature Prize 2019. TD Ramakrishnan is also a translator and screenwriter. He won the E.K. Divakaran Potti Award for Best Translator in 2007 for introducing numerous Tamil literary works to Keralites. He has written the script and dialogues of *Olu*, the inaugural movie at the Indian Panorama, International Film Festival of India, Goa, 2018.

Priya K. Nair teaches English at St. Teresa's College, Ernakulam. She has previously translated *Alpha* and *Sugandhi Enna Andal Devanayaki*.

HarperCollins *Publishers* India

At HarperCollins India, we believe in telling the best stories and finding the widest readership for our books in every format possible. We started publishing in 1992; a great deal has changed since then, but what has remained constant is the passion with which our authors write their books, the love with which readers receive them, and the sheer joy and excitement that we as publishers feel in being a part of the publishing process.

Over the years, we've had the pleasure of publishing some of the finest writing from the subcontinent and around the world, including several award-winning titles and some of the biggest bestsellers in India's publishing history. But nothing has meant more to us than the fact that millions of people have read the books we published, and that somewhere, a book of ours might have made a difference.

As we look to the future, we go back to that one word— a word which has been a driving force for us all these years.

Read.

Harper
Collins

HARPER
FICTION

HARPER
NON-FICTION

HARPER
BUSINESS

HarperCollins
Children's Books

HARPER
DESIGN

Harper
Sport

HARPER
PERENNIAL

HARPER
VANTAGE

हार्पर
हिन्दी